REDEMPTION

A JOE BURGESS MYSTERY

To the fascinating Mary —

REDEMPTION

All Best

Kate Flora

KATE FLORA

FIVE STAR
A part of Gale, Cengage Learning

GALE
CENGAGE Learning®

Detroit • New York • San Francisco • New Haven, Conn • Waterville, Maine • London

GALE
CENGAGE Learning·

Copyright © 2012 by Kate Flora.
Five Star Publishing, a part of Gale, Cengage Learning.

Set in 11 pt. Plantin.

LIBRARY OF CONGRESS CATALOGING-IN-PUBLICATION DATA

Flora, Kate, 1949–
   Redemption : a Joe Burgess mystery / Kate Flora. — 1st ed.
     p. cm.
   ISBN-13: 978-1-59415-379-2 (hardcover)
   ISBN-10: 1-59415-379-5 (hardcover)
   1. Police—Maine—Portland—Fiction. I. Title.
PS3556.L5838R43 2012
813'.54—dc23   2011036307

First Edition. First Printing: February 2012.
Published in 2012 in conjunction with Tekno Books and Ed Gorman.

Printed in the United States of America
1 2 3 4 5 6 7 16 15 14 13 12

To my husband, Ken

ACKNOWLEDGMENTS

Thanks, as always, go to my mentors: In the Portland, Maine, police department, Deputy Chief (Ret.) Joseph K. Loughlin, Detective/Sergeant Tommy Joyce, Sergeant Danny Young, and Sergeant Bruce Coffin, and from the Maine State Police, Sergeant Matthew Stewart and Detective Scott Harakles. To the Waltham, Massachusetts, police department, for letting me take their Citizen's Police Academy. To Concord, Massachusetts, retired police chief, Len Wetherbee. And to Detective Sergeant Brian Cummings of the Miramichi, New Brunswick, police, who is constantly trying to expand my knowledge of interview and interrogation procedures. A great teacher even when I'm a very slow student.

Special help on this book came from Paul Rollins, Rollins Scuba Associates, South Portland, Maine.

I could never do this without my readers: Brad Lovette, Nancy McJennett, Jack Nevison, Diane Englund, and Brian Cummings, who catch my errors, firm up my characters, make wise suggestions, and generally keep me and Joe Burgess on the straight and narrow.

CHAPTER ONE

The two boys on the curb shot out into the street so abruptly Burgess had to stand on the brakes to avoid hitting them. It was seven A.M. Saturday. Columbus Day weekend. The weather was perfect. The city was quiet. And even as he rocked to a stop, shoved the truck into park, and rolled down the window, he knew from the wild look on the taller boy's face and the single gasped word, "body," that his day, and probably his weekend, was lost.

In the rearview, he watched Nina and Neddy cease their happy chatter about school and the upcoming picnic and go quiet, their bright heads still, their faces wary. *Body* was a word they knew too well.

It was no prank. The taller of the two, a gangly kid with a lamb's pelt of curly dark hair, freckles standing out against his pale, drained skin, was wide-eyed with alarm. "Excuse me, sir," he gasped, his fingers tightening around the window frame to steady himself, "There's a . . . Do you have a cell phone? We need to call the police. There's a body in the water."

"I am the police," Burgess said. "I'll park and you can show me."

He pulled to the curb and turned to the kids in the back seat. "Stay in the car. I'll just be a minute." He'd hoped they hadn't heard, but Neddy's coxcomb of red hair was pressed up tight against his sister, his eyes squeezed shut, and Nina wore the stricken look he kept hoping time would erase.

Cursing quietly, he followed the boys out onto the wharf, wishing he could have just made a phone call passing this to someone else. But he was a cop, a homicide detective here in Portland, Maine, and the boy had said *body*. A few minutes earlier or later, the boys would have stopped another car and he could have gone on with his day. He might have made it out of cell phone range before word went up the food chain and came back down to him, making it someone else's problem.

Neddy and Nina didn't need this. They'd already been through more trauma than a combat vet. This was what they got, Burgess feared, for hanging around with him. He tried to keep his personal and professional lives separate, but trouble had a way of rising up and smacking him in the face. This was a perfect example.

His girlfriend, Chris, wanted to adopt these two foster kids, rescue them from the crap that life that thrown at them. After what they'd seen and had done to them, it was no simple task. Endearing as they were, Nina and Neddy were damaged. First, from having witnessed their father killing their mother. Later by being the targets of a disturbed and violent pedophile. He wasn't sure he was on board for another thing in his life that was this demanding. His day job—hell, his day, night, weekend, whole life job—was demanding enough.

The boys, moving with herky-jerky eagerness, led him out the wharf to a spot where two fish poles and some gear were propped against a railing, and pointed down into the water. "Down there," the tall boy said. "Do you see? Floating on bottom, there in the seaweed?"

"Is it really a body?" the smaller boy asked. He was blond, pink-cheeked and blocky, and tended to stay behind the other boy.

Burgess followed the boy's pointing finger, peering down through foam and flotsam into the choppy green water. Lot of times, you looked into the water, you couldn't be sure what you saw, but this one was pretty clear. A man's body—at least, it looked like a man—face-down, fully dressed, and shifting with the currents down there on the murky bottom.

In the moment his eyes confirmed that this *was* a body, a series of tasks vested. He needed to pay attention to what he was seeing here. He needed to get information about these boys, and to be sure they were okay, given what they'd seen. He needed to put the series of calls in motion that would bring divers and cops and evidence techs and the ME down to the waterfront. He needed to reassure Neddy and Nina until he could get Chris down here to pick them up. All this meant that his day's plans were canceled—no more holiday and no picnic— and that he and Chris would fight.

Burgess's day was fucked. At least he was still breathing. He pulled out his phone and called dispatch.

The boys—the taller one was Reese Pullman, the shorter Teddy Robideau—told him they'd come down to the waterfront for some early morning fishing. For the last hour, they'd fished on the other side of the wharf. When they'd moved over here to see if they'd have better luck, they'd spotted the body. Lucky for the dead guy, and Portland PD, these kids had consciences. They didn't try to snag him with their hooks or ignore their discovery in favor of their planned recreation. They'd raced right out to Commercial Street and flagged him down.

Burgess got their names and contact information, then said, "Your families know you're down here?"

Reese looked at his watch. "Yeah, and now we've only got thirty minutes before we have to go do family stuff."

"I'm sorry," Burgess said. "You're not going to be able to fish here anymore today. We're going to have to close the wharf while we get this body out of the water. But thanks for stopping me. You're good citizens, you know."

The shorter boy grinned shyly and shuffled his feet. "Maybe you oughta tell that to my mom. She thinks I'm just a big loser."

"I can do that," Burgess said. "You want me to send a letter?"

Teddy's eyes lit. "Jeez, would that be on official police paper and everything?" Burgess nodded. "Wow. That would be so cool. Can Reese get one, too?"

"You bet." Burgess watched the boys gather up their gear. "Either of you guys see anyone around when you came down to fish? People on the wharf or the waterfront, someone in a car?" A long shot, but he might as well ask.

Reese shrugged. "Nope. There were some trucks and stuff. You know. Making deliveries. You see anything, Teddy?" The shorter boy considered, then shook his head.

"One more thing." Burgess made his voice very serious. "I don't want either of you talking to the press—the TV or newspapers, okay? I know it sounds cool, being a celebrity but . . . do either of you watch TV? Watch those cop shows?" The boys nodded. "Well, that stuff about keeping the details away from the public—that's true. What you saw this morning is important. We don't want people knowing about it. Just your parents. Nobody else. Okay?"

He waited for their solemn nods, then gave business cards to each boy. "Hold on to these," he said. "If anyone pesters you to talk, you call me, okay?" Another pair of solemn nods. He walked them back to the street, then pulled out his phone and called Chris.

Instead of "hello," she said, "Where the heck are you?"

"Down on the waterfront. We've got a floater in the harbor."

All she said for the longest time was "No," but she got paragraphs into that one word. Then, finally, "Did the kids see?"

"No. A couple boys who were fishing flagged us down. I

walked out on the wharf with them, saw the body in the water."

"I guess that's a shred of good news," she said. "They certainly don't need any more bodies. But what does this mean for us . . . for today? Can't you hand it off to someone else?" Before he could speak, she answered her own question. "It means Detective Sergeant Joe Burgess is going to be working today after all. It means . . . oh, never mind, we both know what it means. I'll take them myself."

"Chris, you know . . ."

"What your life is like? Yes, dammit, I do. I'll come get them."

She slammed down the phone and he went back to the car to explain to two kids who'd already had way too much death in their lives that he couldn't spend the day with them because there had been another death.

After Neddy's whispered, "Are we still going to have the picnic?" and his reassurance that they were, they took it well, if polite silence and pale, fixed faces below their bright red hair could be interpreted as "well." It left him wanting to go kick something, but that wouldn't have helped a damned thing.

"Chris is coming down. She'll pick you up, okay?" he said. "You wait in the car until she does." He hated to leave them, but there were things to do.

Burgess's call had put the series of other calls in motion that would mobilize the Portland police dive team and the police boat, call out detectives, patrol, and another police boat to fend off the curiosity seekers, and a call to the medical examiner's office up in Augusta to send an ME to the scene. The discovery of a body also called Portland Detective Stan Perry away from *his* weekend plans and down to the waterfront to deal with an unattended death.

Burgess's phone rang. His boss, Lieutenant Vince Melia. "What've we got, Joe?"

"Don't know yet, Vince. Body in the harbor. On the bottom,

not a floater, which maybe means fresh, maybe means weighted. Fully clothed, as far as I can tell. Looks male, but we won't know 'til we get it up. Patrol's roping off the wharf. Dive boat's on the way and Stan and Wink are coming over. ME's office is sending Dr. Lee."

"Keep me up on it."

"Sure thing, Vince. Gonna be a while, though."

"Don't I know it. Nice day. You'll probably get a crowd."

"Already got one. I've got marine patrol sending out a boat to keep the gawkers away. I'll let you know if I need another."

"You got enough patrol?"

"I hope so."

"Need anything else?"

"Disposition transplant?"

"Your body would reject it." And Melia was gone.

Burgess *was* cranky—something Chris said was getting too common. He loved being a detective, the way his mind started ticking when he heard about a body or rolled up on a crime scene, wondering, planning, anticipating what he might find. He loved getting justice for victims. He relished that essential confrontation between himself and the bad guys—the conflict he *had* to win. Not that there was ever a good time for a body, but today's timing couldn't have been worse. Things had been tense between him and Chris lately. Even the most understanding partner gets sick of a detective's hours, the distraction, the broken dates.

Today's outing was to have been a step toward mending the breach. Instead, as so often happened, his personal life would have to be postponed. A body took precedence over everything. Depending on what the divers found down there, it could be hours, days, even weeks before life got back to normal. If there was any such thing as normal for a homicide detective.

A few minutes later, some young patrol officers, including

Remy Aucoin, arrived to help control the scene. As Aucoin and another officer started stringing up crime scene tape to keep people off the wharf, a gray Taurus jerked to a stop, and Stan Perry got out. Perry snatched a windbreaker from the back seat, jammed a Portland PD ball cap on his shaved head, and pushed his way through the gathering crowd, growling at people who didn't move fast enough. Burgess, being an able detective, surmised that his colleague wasn't in a good mood either.

"Sheesh, Joe," Perry said. "I was in bed when Melia called."

"Lucky you."

"I wasn't alone," Perry said, "which is the good news. Bad news is that I'd promised her breakfast at Becky's. And now look."

Burgess studied the young detective's bloodshot eyes and puffy face. "Doesn't look like you got much sleep." Stan could take it. Soon he'd be clear-eyed and perky. One of the advantages of a youth Burgess had long ago left behind. These days, wear and tear, and regret dragged behind him like an invisible tail. Chris had been nudging him out of it, but lately, she'd become as much a part of the problem as the solution. She said he avoided responsibility and connection. He thought he had enough responsibility, more of which would vest when the boat brought the body ashore, and he'd been working on connection.

"Not much sleep but man did I get laid." Perry's grin widened. "Whew! This one is a wildcat." Burgess rolled his eyes. Stan's exploits were legend in the detectives' bay.

They stood at the edge of an old granite wharf that reeked of lobster bait, as the two divers, seal-like in their sleek black suits, and the personnel on the boat struggled to load the basket holding the bagged body. Beside them, Assistant Medical Examiner Andrew Lee bounced restlessly in his spiked beige golf shoes. The body was not small, the clothes heavy with water, and the Stokes basket kept slipping as they tried to raise it up.

Pleasure boats circled like sharks, carrying morbid gawkers the cops called blood maggots, kept back by a patrolling police boat that periodically barked arrest threats through a bullhorn to those who came too close. Too bad they couldn't just string a half-mile of crime scene tape out there. They had strung it up on land to create a secure area where they could unload and examine the body. A noisy crowd had gathered behind it, the noise augmented by news vans and news crews and the loud thwack of a helicopter overhead. Two gulls squabbled over a donut some wiseass had tossed.

The scene had all the hallmarks of a carnival and none of the gravity it deserved. He was glad that SOP for water recovery was to bag the body underwater so the gawkers who'd brought binoculars didn't get to violate the victim's privacy any more than they already had.

The warm and windy October day was so beautiful it hurt. The sky and the dancing sea were a deep, sapphire blue, the trees in the city rising up behind them in the full glory of a Maine fall. Fishing boats tied to the dock creaked and groaned and the rigging on berthed sailboats clanged. Farther out, the water was dotted with white canvas as sailors squeezed in one last day before their boats got hauled and shrink-wrapped.

Despite the fishy smells permeating the old wharf, the air seemed nutritious and refreshing. It was a day made for hikes and picnics, for apple picking and seeking the perfect Halloween pumpkin. For breathing in the crisp fall air and being glad to be alive. For law enforcement, it would be a long, slow day for death.

The general public's view of crime scene investigation was formed by television, where entire crimes were discovered, processed, and solved in an hour. The public, general or otherwise, didn't know squat. In the real world, after good observation skills, deep curiosity, the ability to spot a lie, and a healthy skepticism, a detective's most important characteristics were tenacity and patience. Half the job was patiently watching and waiting, like they were doing now. Once the body came ashore, their job would begin. But hours of work by public safety personnel had already gone in.

The general public, going about their business on this lovely Saturday, probably never gave a thought to how many people's days had been disrupted by this event. The dive team—at least three divers, two to retrieve the body and a safety diver on the boat, as well as a supervisor—had to be called out with all of their assembled gear. A police boat and crew—in this case, two police boats and their crews—had to be deployed to carry the dive team, retrieve the body, and keep the public from mucking things up. Detectives and crime scene techs had been called in, ready to go when the body arrived on shore. Because it was protocol to treat a body like this as a potential homicide, someone from the ME's office had to be there to do a preliminary exam.

Nor did the salacious crowd have any idea what was actually taking place under the surface of the choppy sea. A while ago, he'd heard someone complain, "The fuck's takin' so long? I wanna see this before I gotta go to my grandma's for dinna. Cops are just doin' it for the overtime. That's what they all do." Like they enjoyed standing around for hours enduring public scrutiny and the pressure on bad backs and knees. Like they didn't want to be enjoying this beautiful weekend day just like any other citizen.

There was nothing simple or quick about retrieving a body in the water. They didn't just swim down and stuff it in a bag. It took a series of dives and a set of carefully choreographed steps. First, the divers would make a preliminary location and verification dive to determine whether they were, in fact, dealing with a body. Divers had been called out for dead dogs and deer bones, dead sharks and bundles of clothes that people had reported as bodies. On those initial dives, the team would carry slates and pencils and, if the presence of a body was confirmed, take notes on what they found, including information about the state and position of the body.

Conditions permitting, a second dive would be made with underwater cameras to record the scene. On subsequent dives, divers would bag the hands, head, and feet to preserve any evidence that might remain, including foam in the nose or anything in the corpse's mouth or under the nails. Only after these evidence-preserving dives would they go down with the body bag and the Stokes basket, bag the body, and put it in the basket for retrieval. As Burgess knew from friends who'd done it, getting a decomposed body into a bag, or doing it under murky conditions, could be a real bitch. Some dive teams practiced doing it with blacked out masks to prepare for the difficult reality they sometimes faced.

A gruff voice pulled his attention away from the operation out on the water. A grizzled man in a shabby army jacket, the hood of a gray sweatshirt pulled close around his face, waved a dirty hand. "Joe . . . I needa talk to ya." The people standing around him had moved away, leaving a small clearing where he pressed against the tape. Some ostentatiously held their noses.

Burgess walked back to the tape. The man was short and his bent posture made him shorter. He smelled of poor hygiene, tobacco, and unwashed clothes. He coughed into his hands as Burgess leaned down. "What's up, Benjy?"

"Oh, hey, Joe. It's—"

"Excuse me." A woman with a peremptory voice tapped him on the shoulder. Turning, Burgess found a well-dressed blond woman with two children, maybe eight and ten. Something about her seemed familiar. He erased a dozen years and three dozen pounds, and came up with a name. Shelli something. He'd dated her briefly. She didn't seem to remember him.

"Are you with the police?" she asked. He nodded. "Well, look, officer, my kids are having a real hard time seeing from here. Couldn't we just slip under the tape and go a little farther out on the wharf so we can see what's going on?"

"Joe?" Benjy said. "I only need the minute."

The woman glared at Benjy, her sculpted brows lifting, carefully drawn mouth pursing with disapproval. "Get away from us, mister. You're disgusting," she said.

With a hurt look, Benjy ducked his head and turned away. Burgess put a hand on his arm. "Wait."

He turned to the woman. "There's no call for that. Benjy here does the best he can." He watched the self-satisfied face register surprise. "You want to know what's really disgusting, Shelli? People like you bringing their kids to gape at tragedy like it's some kind of entertainment. Some poor soul has lost his life. Why would you want your children to see that?"

The woman's face went red. She took a step back, slapping a hand with bright red nails against her chest. "My God," she said. "My God. I can't believe the police are allowed to talk to me like that. I should report you."

"If you want to report that a police detective refused to allow you to cross a police line and interfere with an investigation so your young children could get a closer look at a crime scene, ma'am, you feel free."

She grabbed her childrens' hands and dragged them away, her shoulders stiff with outrage. He turned back to Benjy.

The old man's rheumy pale eyes stared out from a chapped and wrinkled face as he rubbed a couple day's white stubble. "Sorry to trouble you, Joe. It's only that Maura's worried about Reggie. He didn't come see her last night."

Reggie was one of the street people Burgess tried to keep an eye on. Home was a shabby room in a cheap rooming house on the back side of the hill. And Maura was a delusional on again/off again alkie who, when she didn't take her meds, was as likely to see people who weren't there as notice those who were. Still, she and Reggie had been a couple for the last decade. It was probably nothing. Reggie was back in detox or in the tank drying out or had gone to see his brother. Reggie's cycles were like the seasons. Spring he vowed to reform. Summer he did pickup work and got healthy. Went up north to his brother's farm to work or worked in the city parks. In the fall, without work to structure his life, he'd fall apart, drinking through winter until he ended up in the hospital, jail, or a program. Then he'd dry out and start the cycle again.

"You see her, tell her I'm checking around, Benjy, okay? Tell her I'll come see her if I learn anything. She called his brother?"

"I dunno." Benjy ducked his head. "I'll tell her, Joe. I will. She's real worried is all. Hope you can find him."

The phone buzzed. The supervisor on the boat. They had the body loaded and were coming in. At the end of the wharf, a slanted ramp led down to a waterside dock. The fishing boat that docked there had been moved to make a space for the police boat.

He ducked under the tape and walked back to Stan and Dr. Lee. "They're coming in."

Lee checked his watch and nodded. "I've got a two o'clock tee time. Should make it in plenty of time."

"I can't see you as a golfer," Burgess said, his eyes on the boat heading toward them. On the anonymous black bagged shape. "What's the attraction?"

Lee shrugged. "Gets me out of the morgue? I can take out my frustrations on a little white ball, which beats fighting with my wife. You should try it, Joe. You might lighten up."

"Not sure the brass wants homicide light," Burgess said. "It's kind of a dark calling."

Lee raised one eyebrow. "And that makes me what? The merry medical examiner?"

"With a slice and a dice and a hey nonny nonny," Burgess said. "Has a certain ring to it."

"And we can just imagine how the defense attorneys would use that."

"Fuckin' bloodsuckers," Perry said. He'd just had a case come to trial against Portland's meanest and most effective defense attorney. After a day on the stand, he'd come back to 109 snarling. "Feels like he's pulled out my guts and put them through a shredder and the prosecutor couldn't do a damned thing." They all went through it. Put heart and soul on the line, then watch your work get pissed away by the injustice system. No wonder cops were cynical.

Together, they walked to the end of the dock to meet the boat, Wink Devlin, the head evidence tech, trailing behind them with his gear. Dani Letorneau was there with a camera, looking cute as a bug and distinctly uncoplike in soccer shorts and shin guards. She shrugged off Burgess's scrutiny. "Came straight from the field when Wink called. Captain Cote doesn't like it, he can drive down here and bring me some clothes."

They stood somberly while the Stokes was unloaded and the divers gave their preliminary reports. Then Dr. Lee reached for the zipper.

"We bagged him face-up, not face-down the way he was floating. Otherwise, he's just like we found him. Not fetal," Rick Chaplin, one of the divers, said, "and he wasn't wearing shoes. You need us anymore? We'd like to get back down. Do the evidence search while the water's clear. Way the wind's coming up, it's gonna get a lot murkier."

"Later's fine," Burgess said. "Here or at 109." Police

headquarters was at 109 Middle Street, about a quarter-mile away.

Chaplin waved his thanks, and he and the other diver stepped back into the boat. While the detectives were processing the body, they'd do an evidence search of the area within one hundred feet of where the body was found. A balloon floating on the surface marked the spot where they'd start.

Burgess turned back to the body. The bagged head and hands seemed alien. The wet clothes gave the body the dark, slick look of a marine creature, the only scent the briny tang of the sea, suggesting the body was fairly fresh. Decomp started fast and even coming out of cold water, the smell was unmistakable.

"Let's get a look at him. See what we've got," Lee said. Carefully, he peeled the bag off the head and handed it to Wink to preserve, then leaned in to examine the body.

Peering over Lee's shoulder, Burgess stared down at the wet, white face. Lee pushed back the long tangled hair that obscured the features, and Burgess found himself staring down into a face he'd known most of his life. Reginald Woodford Libby. Reggie the Can Man.

He closed his eyes against his sudden, unwanted tears, then rose to his feet and moved away. This was where Reggie had been heading since they were both nineteen years old in the jungles of Southeast Asia. Burgess had been hauling Reggie out of the pit, sticking on bandaids, and setting him back on the path for decades. It had been Sisyphean work, and he had done it gladly. There but for the grace of God and all. It hurt like hell that it had come to this.

CHAPTER TWO

Long before the boys fishing off the wharf this morning had spotted him, Reggie the Can Man had been lost. Reggie was—had been—an alcoholic, mentally ill Vietnam vet who'd supplemented his disability by collecting cans and bottles and returning them to the redemption center. He'd lived on the streets or in shabby rooming houses for decades. Reggie and his shopping cart were a familiar sight on the streets of Portland, and he'd been called Reggie the Can Man so long most people had forgotten his last name. Not Burgess. He'd known Reggie in high school, where Reginald Woodford Libby had been popular, handsome, and a star athlete.

After high school, both unsure what they wanted to do with their lives, and with Uncle Sam offering an inflexible option, they'd gone to Nam together. A year of his life Burgess kept in a lockbox in his brain. Burgess had come back okay, scarred but okay, become a cop and found his calling. Reggie had come back seeming okay, fallen into a black hole, and bounced between fine and seriously disturbed ever since.

Still cradling Reggie's head between his gloved hands, Dr. Lee looked up from his careful examination. Seeing Reggie's head cradled, and the peaceful stillness of death, even if the hands were gloved and impersonal, pinged something in Burgess, starting a train of wishes that there had been more touches and caring while Reggie was alive.

"You know this man, Joe?" Lee asked.

Burgess stomped on his feelings and went back to kneel beside the body, trying not to look directly at the hard-worn face. If he let it start, a dozen Reggies from other times and places would cram into his mind. He was here to do a job. The rest could wait. Cops didn't wear their hearts on their sleeves. The public and the press were always looking for ways to fault cops. Exposed hearts made easy targets.

"Yeah, I knew him," he said. "Name's Reginald Libby."

No surprise that he'd know a victim here in Portland. A lot of policing went into dealing with the vulnerable, lost, and damaged. Cops knew their cities and the people in them. Even now, years since he was a street cop, the city remained a map of stories. He couldn't go a block without recognizing someone. In some parts of town, half the houses he passed had history. Take a civilian on a ride-along, and if a cop were inclined, he could tell stories nonstop, reading the buildings like a guidebook of crime and bad luck.

Lee nodded and went back to examining the body. "No obvious signs of trauma," he said. "I don't want to undress him out here. Too much risk of losing something if this is suspicious. I'll know better when I get him on the table. Could be this fellow just fell in and with all these clothes, he couldn't save himself. Was he a drinker, Joe?"

Burgess nodded. "Vietnam vet." It felt like breakfast was going to come up, and he hadn't eaten breakfast. He pulled out his notebook and started taking notes. Document everything. That was the rule. A year or two down the road, a case could turn on the smallest thing. That was why they took the time now. The black shadow of a gull passed over them like a bad omen. Burgess shook it off. Saw that Dani was trying to take pictures and moved back. When she was done, Wink checked the security of the bags on the hands and feet, did a quick search for a wallet or other ID, and came up empty.

Lee zipped up the bag. "I can do this tomorrow morning," he said, consulting his BlackBerry. "Nine work for you?"

Burgess looked at Stan and Wink. They nodded. "Nine works for us." Nine meant eight or earlier, and the ME's office in Augusta was an hour away. Saturday and Sunday now both gone. Chris wasn't going to be happy, though they'd both known it would be like this since Burgess had uttered the word "floater."

"If you're done with me," Lee said, tapping a golf shoe, his spikes clanging on the old wood, "I'll be off."

"Body's yours 'til you release," Burgess said. "He ready to go?"

Lee nodded, turning to go, then swiveled back. "Don't be too hard on yourself. Sometimes, whatever you do, you can't save people."

Burgess stared after him, surprised. Dr. Lee was a good ME, smart, observant, fast. On the stand, he was great. Many a defense attorney had made the mistake of assuming that Asian and *from away*—without six generations of Maine in his pedigree—meant ill-informed and mediocre, the best a poor state could do, when Lee was anything but. If he could fault the man anywhere, it was in the area of compassion. The first ME he'd worked with had had such a reverence for the dead; Lee treated them like bodies. They'd clashed over this on his last big case, a conflict that had given him more insight into the man. But Lee had never been so personal, and it was disconcerting. Burgess wore his cop's face in public—and public included Dr. Lee. He was uncomfortable that he'd let his guard down.

Chris would have laughed at him, she of the lancet observations, following her laugh with one of her incisive comments. Here it would have been something like what was wrong with caring about someone he had a thirty-year history with? Nothing, of course. In her world—Chris was a nurse—being a caring person was a good thing. Fine in his, too. You just kept it to yourself. Other cops thought you were too emotionally involved, they wouldn't trust your theories and observations, and often with good reason. Get too emotional and sometimes you couldn't trust yourself. You'd see what you wanted instead of what was there; get locked into your assumptions instead of keeping an open mind, violating that basic principle of investigation—don't let your assumptions get ahead of the facts.

Burgess shook himself. He hated it when he wallowed. He was out here to do a job. "Stan," he said, "I'm going to talk to some people, see what they know about when Reggie was last seen. You and Wink stay here, be ready to debrief the divers when they come in. Take care of anything they find down there. Be sure you get written reports. Body position, animal feeding, water depth and visibility, temperature. Make sure they got water and soil samples. Chaplin's good. He'll think of all that. Get a tide chart for the file. Put the word out to patrol, we want to know when anyone last saw him. Anything significant, you call me."

Stan nodded. "Sure thing, Boss."

"I'm not your . . ." Stan was grinning.

As soon as he stepped over the yellow tape he was mobbed by the media. All those fuzzy mikes and made-up talking heads coming at him in a group squawk, everyone vying for his attention and talking at once. Charlene Farrell smiling like he was her own special sweetheart, cooing "Joe," in her breathy little-girl voice. He held up a hand. "Come on, guys and gals, you know the drill. Any statement about this case will come from Lieutenant Melia or Captain Cote. I'm just a poor cop trying to do his job. Appreciate it if you'd let me through."

Even at that, he had to push his way back to the Explorer, first through the press and then through the crowd, screening out the idle chatter, the comments, the noise, as he planned where he'd go first. As he passed an idle group of laughing, beer-swilling young men—well into it, by the sound and smell, though it was barely past noon—he heard one tell a newcomer, "Yeah, I heard it was an old wino fell in. No big loss."

"Shit, no, man," the other replied. "You see anything?"

"Nothin' but a body bag."

His rage boiled up. He tried to choke it off. Cops heard this all day long. It was supposed to bounce like water off a duck's back. As he turned to look, the speaker tossed an empty off the wharf into the water and grabbed another from a cooler.

Burgess dropped a hand on the guy's shoulder. "What's your name, son?"

The shoulder twisted away. "What's it to you?" The flabby young face swiveled toward him, all arrogance and attitude.

Burgess showed his badge. "It's littering, an open-container violation, and refusing to cooperate with an officer," he said. "For starters. You want to see where else you can take this?"

He thought the kid would wet himself as the flab flushed crimson. The guy's buddies moved away. "Oh, shit, officer, I'm sorry. I just . . . you know . . . guess I wasn't thinking."

"You got that right," Burgess agreed. "Now why don't you take yourself and your pals somewhere else. Maybe think about the fact that someone's dead and it's really not that funny."

Big-mouth and his buddies fell all over themselves getting out of there, leaving their cooler behind. Burgess flipped the lid and saw about two dozen beers left, so he drained it and took it to the car. Just doing his civic duty, keeping the waterfront clean, but you never knew when a cooler full of beer might come in handy. Then he hefted himself into the driver's seat and headed for the back side of the hill. Practicing his self-control. He kept this up, he might as well go stand in the park and give speeches about civics. That wouldn't do Reggie's memory any more good than a bunch of loudmouthed louts or a mother with misplaced family values.

He'd already sent patrol to sit on Reggie's room. The way word traveled in this city, if he hadn't, by the time he got there, Reggie's possessions might have been subject to a little equitable distribution. It was a logical street mentality. If Reggie was dead, he didn't need his stuff. Living the way he did—hand to mouth and in a shitty place—there were probably no caring relatives who'd be coming around. And though they'd been a longtime couple, Reggie and Maura didn't live together. Mostly 'cuz he came and went, while she'd been in the same place for years.

He turned off Cumberland onto a side street, pulled up in front of a peeling gray three-decker with a mangy yard and saggy front porch. Two men sat on the porch enjoying the sunshine, passing a paper bag back and forth.

"Hey, Joe," one of them said, "nice day, huh?" The toothpick-thin man grinned, showing a scattering of tobacco-stained teeth. "You come to see Reggie? He ain't home. Wasn't home yesterday, neither. Maura's in a state."

Burgess sat down on the steps. "Benjy told me. When's the last time you saw him, Jim?"

The man squinted up his eyes, considering. "Dunno. Today's what? Saturday? I saw him on Thursday, I think. I was up early. Thursday my daughter comes by, brings me my clean laundry, takes away the dirty stuff. I tell ya. I was shit for a dad when she was a kid, but she's nice as can be to me. Bakes me stuff. Does my laundry. Sometimes she even brings the kids by, let's 'em say hi."

He fumbled through his pockets, extracted some photos from a tattered wallet, and offered them to Burgess. "That's my Diane. Ain't she just the prettiest thing?"

The woman in the photo was heavy, with bleached blond hair tending toward orange. The kids were both pudgy and sullen.

The lighting made them all look slightly green. It was a bad studio photo that Burgess wouldn't have paid two cents for, but it said family, and holding on to any kind of family when you were a drunk was something. Besides, it was nice out here in the sun. He wasn't eager to face Reggie's room.

He handed it back. "She's got a real sweet face, Jim. How old are the kids?"

"Dakota's eight and Shawna's six." Jim returned the pictures to his wallet with great care. "Yeah, woulda been around eight, eight-thirty, I'm thinkin'. That's when she woulda been drivin' the kids to school. She was carryin' the basket of laundry up the steps, I was holdin' the door, and Reggie came out past me and got into that van."

"What van?"

Jim looked at the other man. "You see him, Chub?" Chub hunched his shoulders and looked longingly at the bag that held the bottle. "Well, I think it was a van," Jim said. "Unless it was a truck. I dunno. I guess I wasn't paying much attention. Diane was saying she'd brought me cinnamon rolls, like her mom used to make. Which were always my favorite."

He ducked his head and grinned again. "Woulda stayed married to her mom just for them rolls, only she threw me out for the drinkin'." His eyes were suddenly clear and sad. "She's a good woman. Didn't deserve the likes of me."

He crumpled the bag tighter around the bottle. "And hell, I wasn't even so bad back then. Kept down a job and everything. Even after she threw me out, she never tried to turn the kids against me, see. That takes character. I dunno, the situation was reversed, I'd of done so good."

He was about to take a drink when he remembered who Burgess was. "Reggie's got him a job."

Burgess nodded. "What kind of job?"

"Workin' in some factory. Cleanin' 'n stuff. Part-time. Paid under the table, ya know." Another duck of the head. Another recognition that maybe he shouldn't be telling this to a cop. But then he grinned. "You don't care none about that, do ya, Joe? You're his friend so probably you're just glad Reggie's workin', huh?"

Burgess wasn't ready to tell this man Reggie was dead. "I'm always glad when Reggie's working. It keeps him straight. You know who he was working for?" Jim shook his head. "Where he was working?"

Another shake. Maybe there would be something in Reggie's room that would say. "So, you saw him Thursday early, huh? And not since then? Hear about anyone seeing him?"

Jim squinted up his eyes again. "Something happen to Reggie?"

"What makes you ask?"

"Coupla things. You got a cop sitting upstairs in Reggie's room. And that when Reggie's workin', he's real regular, and he ain't been regular."

"You'd make a good detective, Jim."

The man laughed and slapped his thigh and took a drink from the bottle. "Little late for that. I shoulda thought of it sooner." He passed the bottle to the other man, Chub, and tilted his face toward the sun. "It's a hell of a nice day. Sure hope it keeps on like this. Winter's a bitch."

"You got that right. Look, you hear anything about Reggie, you let me know, okay. Be glad to know if it was a truck or van, too, Jim, in case you remember."

He gave Jim his card and went inside, up the dark creaking stairway that smelled of age and urine and old cooking. Reggie's room was on the second floor. Burgess knocked and pushed open the door. The young patrol officer who sat on a rickety chair reading a paperback thriller seemed very glad to see him.

"Anyone been by?" Burgess asked.

"Those two old guys downstairs. They seemed real affronted when I told them they couldn't touch anything. The guy across the hall." The officer checked his notes. "A Kevin Dugan. He had a key, though, that's how I got in. Said he was just stopping in to check on Reggie, that he and Reggie did that for each other. He said Reggie hadn't been feeling too good lately. Oh . . . and . . . uh . . ."

The officer, whose name tag said Robeck, put the book down. "And a woman came by, looking for him." He pulled out his notebook. "Maura O'Brien. You want her address?"

"Thanks, I know it," Burgess said. "I'll take the info on the guy across the hall, though. What did Maura have to say?"

"Well, she wasn't exactly articulate. She was kind of hard to understand, sir. She said something about dark spirits and bad signs. Said she'd seen dark clouds around Reggie lately. Then she said she thought he was probably dead."

"You ask her why she thought that?"

"I tried, sir." Robeck shuffled his black shoes on the floor. "She said she and Reggie, they usually had sex on Fridays. That was their day. And she'd gotten herself all fixed up and then Reggie didn't show." The young cop's expression said he found that unlikely.

"Every Friday for at least ten years," Burgess said, "unless Reggie's out of town or one of 'em's drying out or in the hospital. Put in enough time, Robeck, you'll learn. People aren't always what you think they are, and neither are you."

"It's just . . ." The young officer looked uncomfortable. "That . . . you know, sir . . . she didn't look like the type to have an active sex life."

Ah, youth, they always assume they've got a corner on the market. Like sex, particularly inappropriate sex, wasn't the driver behind crimes and misbehavior at all ages.

"Geriatrics have sex lives, Robeck. People with Alzheimer's

have sex lives. We've got people bed-hopping in assisted living and nursing homes. Maura and Reggie were a longtime couple. You spend enough time on the street, you'll learn your people. Like those two old guys downstairs? For one thing, they're not old. Jim's about my age, which"—Burgess raised an eyebrow— "contrary to the stories you may have heard about me being in the department since the dinosaurs died out, isn't that old. Chub's a few years younger. Jim was an accountant, had a nice house, nice family. He got injured in a car accident, ended up with chronic pain, started treating it with alcohol. Eventually the bottle swallowed him. There must be some value in him. His ex-wife manages his disability money; daughter bakes for him and does his laundry. He's got pictures of his grandkids in his wallet."

He looked around the room. Not much to see, but in his way, Reggie had made it personal: his special hat on a hook on the back of the door, a photo of a much younger Maura beside the bed. "I'm going to search the room now. Be a big help if you could track down the landlord, tell him we're going to change the lock on this door, seal the room until we know what we're dealing with. Then find me a locksmith, sit on the place 'til he can get here."

"Sure thing, sir." Robeck was eager to leave. "I'll get the information from those guys downstairs. Make the calls from my car, sir, if that's okay. Unless you need me here?"

That was just fine with Burgess. He liked to work alone. He especially wanted to be alone here in Reggie's room, where he could have his own internal conversation with his lost friend, touch Reggie's things without worry about displaying emotion. "I'll call you back when I need you," he said. If there was anything to collect, he wanted to do it before another set of eyes, but he didn't need or want those eyes during his initial search.

Robeck thumped away and Burgess sat down in the chair he'd vacated, slowly running his eyes around the room, not looking for anything particular, just taking it in. There wasn't much to see. A bed with a scarred bed stand holding a few books and a lamp. A small kitchen unit with sink, apartment-sized stove, and under-the-counter refrigerator. Cabinets above for a few dishes and food. A table and two chairs. An easy chair facing a small TV sitting on the dresser. It was all dull and brownish and tired except the thick comforter on the bed, a clean brown and blue stripe.

Burgess had bought him that at the Salvation Army, after Reggie complained about always being cold. The comforter, a couple L.L.Bean fleeces, a pair of brown corduroy pants, and some warm socks. So little he could do. Sit and listen and provide a few creature comforts. If they'd had a strong, clean soul, an orderly mind, or a jar of happiness, he would gladly have bought those as well.

After a bit, having absorbed all the room had to tell him, he slipped on some gloves and began to explore. He started with the bedside table. Matches, a few hard candies, some appointment cards for doctors and social service workers, a number of the appointments recent. No money, not even change. No pay stubs or correspondence. Then he did the dresser drawers. He found a small stash of cash in the pocket of the good corduroy pants. An envelope with some letters from Reggie's brother, Clay, and Reggie's mother. Another fat envelope with papers about his disability. A single black envelope with Reggie's name on it in silver ink, a return address in Falmouth, a name Burgess didn't recognize.

Going through the clothes in the closet took all of five minutes. Not much hanging there except an outdated brown suit, two clean shirts, a ragged flannel bathrobe, and a couple heavy flannel work shirts. Nothing in the pockets. One pair of dusty slippers, some worn athletic shoes, and some work boots. Flip-flops for the communal shower. On the inside of the closet door, an oversized fluffy blue towel. On a hook above, a toiletries kit. On the shelf above the clothes was a cardboard box, tied with string, and a cheap suitcase.

Burgess didn't bother with the box—he knew what lived in there—Reggie's demons. He pulled down the suitcase, set it on the bed, and opened it. Inside were several more of the black envelopes with the silver writing. He picked one up and pulled out the single sheet of paper. There was no greeting and no signature, just a message centered on the page, in elegant handwriting:

You may refuse to admit it, but that doesn't change what you did or how it ruined my life. I will hold you in the black part of my heart always. I will call down curses upon your head and I will wish you ills and demons and destruction every waking moment of my life until someone finally, blessedly, brings me the happy news of your death.

What the heck was this? He thought he knew all about Reggie, but Reggie had never mentioned anyone called Star Goodall or getting these letters. Burgess put it back in the envelope, returned it to the suitcase, and continued to search. This, he knew, was coming back to 109 with him. He finished the room, checking under the mattress, in the bedding, and under the carpet. Inside one of the books he found an envelope with Reggie's name scrawled on it being used as a bookmark, but there was no return address. There was nothing in the refrigerator. No clues, no ice, no food. Ditto the cupboards, which were bare as Old Mother Hubbard's.

It was just so goddamned depressing. A whole life that fit in one miserable suitcase.

Unable to be in the room any longer, he went downstairs to

get Robeck instead of calling. Jim and Chub were still passing the bottle back and forth in an amiable way.

"Hey, Joe," Jim said. "Chub's got somethin' to tell you."

Chub mumbled something indecipherable, swiped the back of his hand across his nose, and took another drink.

Burgess leaned down. "What was that, Chub?"

Chub sniffed. "Truck," he said. "What Reggie left in. Weren't no van, it were a truck."

CHAPTER THREE

His phone rang while he and Robeck were collecting items from Reggie's room, Burgess putting them into evidence bags, Robeck making the list. He pulled the phone to his ear. "Burgess."

"Joe, it's Stan. Maura O'Brien's over here at 109 and she wants to know if that's Reggie we pulled out of the harbor this morning. I've got her waiting in an interview room and I haven't said anything. What do you want me to do?"

"Get her a cup of coffee and some food and tell her I'm coming to see her. And Stan?"

"Yeah?"

"Get her something sweet, a pastry or something. Maura's got a serious sweet tooth."

"You bet, Boss. Oh, and just so you'll know. She's way out of it. Took me half an hour to pull that much from her."

Maura was on his list of people to see, but this didn't sound promising. Maura at her best was challenging. Right now, neither of them were at their best. He clicked his phone shut and looked around. They were just about finished. He added Maura's picture to the box. Watched Robeck add it to the list.

"I'll be going then," he said. "Wanna give me a hand getting this down to the car?" He jerked his chin at the suitcase and held out his hand for the list. Robeck grabbed the suitcase, he picked up the box they'd filled and Reggie's box of demons, sealed tight with layers of tape and wrapped repeatedly with twine, and they headed downstairs.

"What's up with the landlord and the locksmith?" It sounded like the title of a song, something Irish and jiggy. Lots of noise and fiddles. Not unlike his life.

"Landlord thought we were asking permission. Tried to get another week's rent for letting us change the lock. I thanked him for his cooperation, told him it was already in process, and I'd see that he got a key as soon as the police were finished with the premises. When he squawked, I asked did he want us to keep a police seal on the door for the next month or so, or was he gonna let us do our job?"

"Well done," Burgess said. This kid had potential. Learning to be in control and stand up to people was part of the job. Don't let 'em push you around, yet be polite enough so they're not banging on the door over at city hall, not calling up some captain to whine. Sometimes it was a hard balance to strike. He'd had a couple once, ran a convenience store, who failed to mention a surveillance tape showing the suspects in an attempted rape because they were holding out for a reward. There were plenty of good people, too, like the kids this morning, but there were a lot of jerks out there. Part of a cop's job was learning to manage the jerks.

He stowed the stuff in his car, left Robeck to wait for the locksmith, and headed back to 109, dreading what lay ahead. Doing notifications—notes, they called them—was a basic part of police work. Like doctors and ministers, cops were society's carriers of bad news. The importance of this job was stressed throughout their training. In the early stages, before the victim's advocate got involved, the detective was the essential liaison between the department and the family. Oftentimes, too, family members were potential suspects, making it a real tightrope walk.

Today, his dread was of another kind. No question Maura

counted as family. She was one of the few who had truly cared about Reggie, probably the one, after his brother, Clay, who would be most hurt and grieved by his death. She hadn't seen Reggie—as that bitch down by the waterfront had—as society's detritus, a disposable human being. He'd been her lover and companion. Both of them might have been categorized as losers; both might have drained a whole lot more from society than they contributed, but they had never given up trying to fumble through their fog and pain to live good lives.

But while Maura probably had valuable information, he couldn't be sure anything he said would be received or any of his questions answered. Talking to Maura wasn't easy. Her thought processes and conversations weren't linear. When she took her medicine, Maura could organize her life and hold down a job. But like many of the mentally ill, she hated the tamped-down, fuzzy way medicine made her feel. As soon as she'd been doing better for a while, she'd decide she was fine without it. Then she'd lose her job, start wandering the streets, and Portland PD would be scooping her up and taking her home, or to Preble Street, or the ER. There was a daughter, a prosperous realtor in town, who paid the rent so Maura would always have a place to stay, but she'd made it clear she didn't want to hear about her mother's troubles.

He parked in the garage and took the box of evidence and the suitcase to evidence control, leaving Reggie's demons in the car. No sense in sending things up to Wink in the lab until they knew what they dealing with. If Reggie had just gotten tipsy and fallen in the harbor—not an unlikely scenario since it was the season for Reggie's annual descent into the bottle—he could just give all this to Reggie's brother and move on.

That was what he wanted to have happened, he supposed, if Reggie was going to be dead, which he indisputably was. A quiet death and a quiet funeral, so they could all move on to mourning. But SOP and his instinct said otherwise. Cops learned to trust their instincts, so until Dr. Lee confirmed that there was nothing suspicious, he was treating it as a potential homicide.

Maura was in a bad way, the worst he'd seen her in years. She sat in Interview 1, rocking and mumbling. Along with her usual gypsy layers of bright sweaters, coats, and skirts, she wore fluffy pink bedroom slippers and neon green socks. Her long hair was matted and uncombed. Her slash of hot pink lipstick didn't follow the contours of her mouth. She'd drawn eyebrows half an inch above her own. When he sat down, she looked at him without recognition.

"Hey, mister," she said, "you got any more of those pastries?"

"Maura." He moved in closer so she had to focus on him. "It's Joe Burgess. Joe Burgess. Reggie's friend. You remember me?"

She looked around the featureless room, then back at him, still without recognition, keeping up a steady rocking on her chair. "Reggie's missing. I've been looking for him since Thursday." She hesitated. "I think it was Thursday. We had a . . ." She twisted a long strand of hair around her finger, wound it tight, and let it go. Something girls did, but few grown women. "Missing. We had a date." She smiled brightly, like a child amused by something. "Friday we always have a date."

She studied him curiously, squinting as if that would let her see him clearly, and lowered her voice. "On Friday, you know, we have sex."

"So you didn't see him Friday for your date. Do you remember when you did see him?"

"Sex," she repeated, rubbing her hands along her thighs from knee to hip, hip to knee, and rocking. It made him dizzy to watch. "On Friday we have sex." Her face got sad. Even carrying too much weight and with her thick auburn hair going gray, it was possible to see the vibrantly attractive woman she had once been. "I miss Reggie."

"Maura, when did you last see Reggie?"

"Last?" She tipped her head to the side, like a bird studying something. Then tipped it the other way, considering. "Maybe Tuesday? We had . . . dinner? At the church. Good dinner, too. Chicken and pie."

Maybe someone there had noticed Reggie. Talked with him. "Which church, Maura? Do you remember which church?"

"I think it was white." Her humming was a low vibration, like a speaker might make when the wire is loose. No matter, he could find out which church served dinner to the homeless on Tuesday. If it really was Tuesday.

"Do you know where you are right now?" he asked.

She studied the room. "Not hospital," she said.

"No. Not hospital. You're at the police department. You came here to ask about Reggie. Do you remember? You came to ask us if something had happened to Reggie." He gave that a minute to register. "What made you think something might have happened to him?"

"He didn't come on Friday. I got dressed. I fixed . . ." She considered as she rocked. "Food. Dinner. I fixed Reggie's favorite." She searched for the word, then said, with a trill of delight, "Meatloaf." She leaned forward and whispered, "My Reggie loves meatloaf."

"So you made meatloaf on Friday and Reggie didn't come. That's sad. You must have been disappointed."

Her head bobbed. "Maura was very sad. Do you think he didn't come because of the meatloaf?" When Burgess didn't respond, she said, "Because Reggie was sick. His stomach was hurting him. Maybe I did wrong. Maybe meatloaf was bad for Reggie."

She folded her hands over her own stomach and rocked. "Sometimes Reggie hurt so much he cried. He went to see the doctor but he wouldn't tell me what the doctor said." She shook her head. "He had a friend who hurt like that and he died. Reggie was afraid he'd die, too."

"Reggie wouldn't tell you what the doctor said?" Instead of answering, Maura started humming a tune vaguely recognizable as a hymn.

Was any of this useful? Was she suggesting that Reggie might have gone into the sea to end some terrible pain? Burgess didn't know. What he did know was that talking about stomachs made him think of his own, how empty it was. He needed coffee and food. It was afternoon. He'd missed breakfast, his plans to eat with Nina and Neddy derailed, spent hours at the harbor, gone from there to Reggie's place.

Another piece of the cop's reality. The public thought that cops spent their lives eating free donuts and drinking free coffee, when sometimes that donut and coffee were the only break—and food—in an eighteen-hour day, a few minutes spent regrouping between one grueling service call and another. They usually weren't free, either. Little came free these days. You took free stuff, people expected breaks you couldn't give them.

He pushed back his chair. "I'm going to get some coffee. You want some, Maura?"

"Hot chocolate," she said. "Hot hot hot hot chocolate." She switched her hum to The Beatles. "Oh yes. Maura would love hot chocolate. And something sweet. Danish, maybe?" She looked a little anxious, clutching at her sweater. "You'll bring it to me? I can wait right here?"

He patted her shoulder. "Sure, Maura, sure. I'll bring it to you. You wait right here." She was afraid that it was just a ploy to get her out of the building. Move her along to another place where she'd become someone else's problem. Street people got used to being moved along.

He pushed back and left the room. Across the detective's bay, he saw Stan talking to Rick Chaplin, and walked over. Chaplin was an incredibly fit-looking man, built like a runner. He still had a summer tan and his longish hair was streaked with blond. He smiled when Burgess approached and held out a hand. "Sergeant. Tough business this morning."

"You got that right. Find anything down there?"

"Brought in a couple things," Chaplin said. "A towel. A shoe. A cinderblock. All near to where the body was." He shrugged. "Ya never know. Figured I collect 'em, let you clever detectives decide if they're important." He grinned at Burgess, "And yes, I did get your soil and water samples." For all his nonchalant posing and surfer dude looks, Chaplin was a careful and thorough cop.

"Thanks, Rick," Burgess said. "Better to be safe." A towel, a shoe, and a cinderblock. Very interesting. "Just one shoe?"

"Just one. Brand new, too. We looked but we didn't find another. Body had no shoes."

Not a bad idea to search the waterfront, see if the other shoe was there. "Already on it, Joe," Perry said. "Got a couple people down there looking around, checking the trash. Tide goes down again, we'll do the shore, too, if there's enough light."

"I'm going for a sandwich." He stopped on his way out of the building and called Robeck, hoping he was still at Reggie's. Got a brisk, "Robeck."

"It's Burgess. You still at Reggie's?"

"Just leaving, sir."

"Before you go, can you check the shoes in the closet, see what size Reggie wore?"

"I'm on it, sir."

Burgess snapped his phone shut and lumbered off, an aging carnivore in search of food. Following the detective's rule, eat when you can, he got a substantial cheesesteak sub and a large coffee for himself, hot chocolate and two pastries for Maura. He might think, as any judgmental person would, that she'd be better off eating something healthy, but it was what she wanted. Sugar and chocolate were comforting, and given the news he was about to deliver, she would need all the comfort she could get.

He gulped the sandwich at his desk, then carried her food and his coffee back into the conference room. She seemed not to have moved in the time he'd been gone. Just sat there on her chair rocking and humming. "Hey, Maura," he said. "I'm back. Brought your hot chocolate."

Her vague eyes fixed on him. "You look familiar," she said.

"You know me, Maura. Joe Burgess. Reggie's friend."

She tapped a finger against her temple. "The cop?" He nodded. "Oh. I came to see you," she said.

"Well, I'm right here," he said, unwrapping the pastries and setting them in front of her. "What can I do for you?"

"Reggie," she said, leaning close. "He's gone. I came to ask if you'd seen him."

Burgess shook his head. "When's the last time you saw him?"

"Tuesday. We had dinner. Chicken. It was good." She grabbed the first pastry and stuffed half of it into her mouth.

"You haven't seen him since?"

"I always see him on Fridays. On Fridays we—"

"Have sex," Burgess finished. "But Reggie didn't show up?"

Now her hands were running up and down her thighs again and he could see that this would be an endless loop in which he'd never get any answers. Burgess tried another tack. "Jim says Reggie had a job. Do you know where he was working?"

"Cleaning job," she said. "He liked having a job. He bought me a present." She set down her pastry, pulled up the battered tote she used as a purse, and dug through it. Eventually she drew out a rectangular white box, the shiny cardboard smudged with fingerprints.

"Open it," she urged, offering it to him. Inside was a nice pair of fleece-lined deerskin gloves. "For the winter, he said. To keep me warm. You know . . ." She lowered her voice to a conspiratorial whisper. "Reggie was making money. Lots of money." She nodded solemnly, her eyes wide. "You know those people he lived with. They'd take anything. So he had it hid. Hid real good."

She kissed the box and returned it to her bag. Then she looked at Burgess, tears in her eyes. "Reggie was a good man, Joe. He didn't deserve how she treated him. Those awful letters."

For a minute, at least, she knew him. "Who is she?" Burgess asked. "The one who wrote those letters?"

"Oh, she's evil," Maura said, "A crazy woman." She laughed. "Even crazier than me. And mean. Not like Reggie's brother. It was all lies, anyway. Reggie wasn't that kind. He would never of done what she said. Reggie was a good man."

The humming grew louder as she began fiddling with her layers, fumbling with the material as she began a ritual of tightening and buttoning. Her eyes had gone vague. "I have to go now. I have to go see the police. I have to find Joe Burgess and ask him if Reggie is dead. If Reggie's gone in the harbor and he's dead."

She stared through Burgess with faraway eyes. "The police took a body out of the harbor this morning. I have to go ask them is it Reggie. You see Joe Burgess, you tell him something is wrong. Reggie didn't come on Friday."

"Maura," he said, "You've found me. Him. I am Joe Burgess."

"You are?" She studied him curiously, a bird eyeing a shiny object. "Burgess the cop?"

She shook her head as if clearing away the fog. As recognition came back into her vague eyes, he decided he'd better tell her about Reggie before she disappeared again.

"I'm sorry to have to tell you this, Maura, but Reggie is dead. That was Reggie we took out of the harbor this morning. That's why I need to know—"

Her scream was sudden and explosive. She jumped out of her chair, clapped her hands over her ears, tipped her face toward the ceiling and howled—a pure, instinctive, animal expression of the grief he'd been feeling since Dr. Lee lifted the matted hair and revealed Reggie's face. He wanted to let go. Join her. Let another voice rise in anger and sorrow. But this was the goddamned police department. He worked here. And cops were all about control.

He wrapped his arms around the screaming woman and pulled her tight against him. "It's okay, Maura," he whispered into the matted hair, the scent of unwashed body and unwashed clothes filling his nose. He held her, patting her back and rocking as she screamed, letting her get it out, until, just as he was sure his hearing was destroyed, she fell completely silent, like an alarm had been turned off.

The screams changed to sobs that wrenched her body like spasms. Finally, quiet, she lifted her head from his shoulder, her eyes clear again and sadder than any eyes he'd ever seen. In a church whisper, she said, "He's gone, Joe? He's really gone?" Burgess nodded.

He watched the knowledge go home. An immense shudder rocked her body. He braced himself for another bout of screaming, but she surprised him. "I'm so sorry," she said, patting his shoulder. "I know you loved him, too. So you'll find out who did it, won't you."

CHAPTER FOUR

He arranged for patrol to give Maura a ride home. Once he'd seen her into the car, he called her daughter. Even on a beautiful autumn Saturday and getting the call at home, Sheila O'Brien Lawson answered like a professional, a crisp "This is Sheila Lawson." He supposed the weekends were when realtors did much of their business, but it spoke of a world where people never relaxed. He wondered if she'd sound the same at six A.M. on a Sunday.

"Ms. Lawson, this is Detective Sergeant Joe Burgess, Portland police—"

"If this is about my mother," she cut in, "I don't want to hear it."

"Ms. Lawson, I'm calling to let you know that your mother's longtime companion, Reginald Libby, was found dead this morning. She's taking the news very hard."

"I don't know how many times I have to say this . . ." Crisp had become icy. "I do not want to be informed about my mother's situation. I don't care what happens to her. I tell you people that again and again. What do I have to do to make you hear it?"

You people. As if cops and social workers and ER personnel belonged to some different, and annoying, social class. Like it or not, she was her mother's next of kin, the responsible person on all kinds of legal and medical papers. Burgess expected Ms. Lawson would be getting a call from the ER sometime in the next twenty-four hours that, as her mother's guardian, she couldn't blow off. For the moment, though, he'd respect her wishes.

It was hard to have a relative in Maura's situation. It did tax compassion. But there was something in him—probably that which had driven him to become a cop and stay a cop—maybe some echoes of the Baltimore catechism, that always kept him hoping for redemption. In the mother and the daughter. "Sorry to have bothered you, ma'am," he said, resisting the impulse to urge her to have a nice day.

He cruised by Stan's desk to see if there was anything new. Found the young detective staring at two shoes sitting on a plastic trash bag. The one from Reggie's closet was old and worn, the other, still oozing salt water, a fancy Reebok, fresh from the box. "Same size. Eleven," Perry said. "I don't get it, Joe. Why buy new shoes if you're going to jump in the water?"

"We don't know that he jumped. You got a witness says he jumped? Got a note saying goodbye, cruel world, or are you tuned in to some psychic hotline?"

"Okay. So why take off your shoes if you're going to fall in the water?"

"Maybe he took them off because they weren't broken in and hurt his feet. Maybe they fell off when he fell in," Burgess said. "Maybe he was running from something. We got any reports of people harassing the homeless lately?"

"You mean, more often than every day?" Perry said. "Waterfront's right next to the Old Port. Kids in the Old Port, they're getting drunk and bothering people all the time. Homeless or la-di-da homeowner from Cape Elizabeth, Falmouth, or the West End. We got equal opportunity drunken assholes."

"Not exactly social progress," Burgess said. "I meant maybe a sharp young detective shows up at roll call, asks did anyone see or hear anything and can they keep their ears open."

Perry looked around the empty detectives' bay. "You see any sharp young detectives around here?" He yawned. "I am so freakin' tired I could put my head down on these goddamned shoes and sleep."

They studied the shoes. The old, worn-out running shoe and the clean white new one. Both shoes were untied. "It could have fallen off," Perry said, "but then where's the other one? Was he wearing socks?"

"I didn't see, did you? Feet were bagged and we left them on 'til tomorrow at the ME's."

"We both going?" Perry asked, stretching. He dropped his arms like they were too heavy. "Man, you think I'm young, Joe. I'm thinking I'm getting too old for this—screwing all night then bringing a fresh, alert mind to a crime scene. How do you and Terry do it, anyway?"

"Practice," Burgess said. "Besides, we're too old to screw all night. That's for kids like you." He stood up. "I need my beauty sleep."

"Hate to tell you, Joe, but you could sleep as long as Rip Van Winkle and it wouldn't make a difference. So. Tomorrow? Augusta? Crap of dawn?"

"Yeah, and bring an alert mind with you. I don't want to have to start giving you a bedtime."

"Oh, I was in bed nice and early."

"Spare me," Burgess said.

He took his camera down to the waterfront and snapped some pictures of the balloon still marking the spot where Reggie's body had been, some more of the wharf and the street. Then he swung by his house to get Reggie's brother's number and address. Clayton Libby lived fifty miles from Portland, too far to drive unless a phone call confirmed that he was home. While he was there, Burgess changed his shirt. Maura had left most of her lipstick and eyebrows on him as well as her tears.

The house was eerily quiet. A clock ticking. The annoying drip in the shower that he'd already fixed twice. Sunlight coming through the windows illuminated Chris's touches—shiny floors, fresh paint, two colorful posters, and some green plants. She'd left his crime scene photographs, the ones he went back and took after the scene was processed, when it was empty, a visual reminder of the questions he had to answer, the spaces he needed to fill in. His memoir, reframed and rehung in groups. The centerpiece was where Kristin Marks had been found. Smoky purple shadows across the trash heap.

Under his photographs she'd put an antique bookcase full of books, topped each week with fresh flowers. His mother's bookcase, which Chris had found in the garage and refinished; his mother's vase, which Chris had found in the back of a cupboard. Behind the sink in the spotless kitchen, his mother's African violets, the only plants he'd ever failed to kill, were thriving under Chris's expert care. It looked like a home, not the spare quarters of a depressed detective. He wondered if that was about to end.

He found Clay's number, then sat on the couch a while, phone in hand, watching dust motes float in streaks of slanting sunlight. Nothing new about this. He'd been calling people with bad news—calling and showing up on their doorsteps—for decades, but the phone seemed too heavy to lift to his ear. His fingers too stiff to dial. He should have handed this off to Stan. Couldn't have, though. He owed it to Reggie and Clay to do this himself. Finally he forced his fingers to move.

Clay was breathless when he answered. "Sorry, I was out in the yard."

"Clay, it's Joe Burgess."

There was silence. Calls from Burgess meant trouble. Then Clay's cautious voice, the predictable response from someone conditioned by decades of such calls. "What is it this time?"

"I'd like to come and talk to you, Clay, if you're going to be home this afternoon."

"I'm home. Got four cords of wood to split and stack. What's up?" When Burgess didn't answer, he said, "Come on, Joe. It's a nice day for a drive, but you wouldn't be coming all the way out here if something hadn't happened. Is Reggie okay?"

No sense in playing games. Clay had answered the phone a hundred times over the years expecting this news. And they had enough of a relationship so Burgess owed Clay the truth. Clay beat him to it. "You don't have to beat around the bush, Joe. We both know what Reggie's life was like. You wouldn't want to come out here if it wasn't serious. We've done this over the phone a dozen times, easy, probably more. Putting together a plan to stick more patches on Reggie's life. It's been a lot of years. So you must be calling to tell me it's . . ."

Reggie's brother grabbed a shuddering breath. ". . . the end this time."

Burgess pictured Clay's callused fingers gripping the phone, the chiseled face so much like Reggie's staring into space in the comfortable farmhouse kitchen. The striking greenish eyes that on Clay had looked smart and compelling and on Reggie had been closer to a madman's stare. However weary he'd grown of picking his little brother out of the mud, Clayton Libby had loved Reggie. Like Burgess, he'd never stopped hoping Reggie's life would turn around.

Finally, Clay asked the hard question, "Accident or suicide?"

Burgess wasn't raising the third possibility. Not until he knew something. "We don't know yet. Divers took his body out of the harbor a couple hours ago. Because it was an unattended death, the medical examiner has scheduled an autopsy for tomorrow. I'm sorry," he repeated. "I wish I were bringing you better news." He wanted to get off this goddamned phone before one of them lost it.

"I don't want to sound coldhearted, Joe," Clay said, "but there hasn't been any good news about Reggie in a long time." There was a pause. "Hell, I guess I *was* hoping for some good news. Reggie was in great shape when he left here in September. He had a job, something that sounded steady, and he was feeling pretty up about that. He did call, said he wasn't feeling too well, and was gonna see the doctor, but I figured that wasn't bad news—he really was seeing the doctor and trying to take care of himself. And he wasn't drinking."

There was a pause, a muffled sob. "That was a step in the right direction." There was a crash, sounding like a chair had fallen over. A muffled, "Oh fuck!" Then Clay said, "Listen. Joe. I don't think you better come out here today. The two of us, we start looking at each other and talkin' about Reggie, we'll bawl our eyes out."

He had that right. It would start before Burgess got out of the car. Christ, just seeing Clay's face, looking like a healthy, unhaunted Reggie and the hurt would tear right through him.

Clay was talking again. "Guess I just need a little time to process this by myself. You wanna come tomorrow, come tomorrow. Tonight, I'm gonna sit here and get shitfaced and think about that goddamned war that stole Reggie's life. Mary's off visiting her sister. Got no one around to fuss over me. Know what I mean?"

Another chair fell, and a crash that Burgess imagined was the chair getting kicked into the wall. Good thing Mary wasn't home. "Okay, Joe?" Clay said. "That okay with you?"

Burgess felt the pain start, like someone had stuck a buck knife into his stomach and was twisting it. Probably a good thing Chris was gone, too. "Gonna go kick some chairs myself, Clay. You take it easy. I'll call you tomorrow, let you know what I learn, see if you're ready for company."

"You take care, Joe. Get shitfaced, too, if that copshop'll let you. Lift one for Reggie. Hell, lift two. Three. Four." The phone went dead.

CHAPTER FIVE

The Sunday of Columbus Day weekend Burgess rolled out of bed early, leaving Chris asleep. Another beautiful day he got to admire through his windshield as he drove north to Augusta. An hour alone in the car while he tried to get a grip on the chaos in his personal life and clear his mind for the job ahead, trying to ignore the fact that this morning in the autopsy room, personal and professional would collide.

Thirty years ago, he'd dragged Reggie out of a rice field, screaming and bleeding from shrapnel wounds. Today, laid out on the table, Reggie's physical scars would be visible; the scars on his soul would not. Jesus. Fuck! He pounded the steering wheel.

His job was to deal, to function, moving calmly through a universe of suffering and bad deeds, trying to make the world right. He did it the way all cops did—by keeping the bad stuff at arm's length, boxing it up in process and order, putting distance between himself and emotion. You couldn't do it any other way and survive the job. The bad stuff just kept coming, year in, year out, while he waded through an endless sewer pipe, trying to carry the good people on his shoulder like St. Christopher.

Not that he'd ever felt saintly. Now, with things going to hell with Chris, he felt even less so. He should have heeded that voice in his head that said alone was the only way to go. He'd just been so damned tired of being alone, and Chris lit him up.

She made him feel alive and hopeful, like it was possible to have a life and do the job. Like some hungry old bear, he had wandered out of hibernation and there she was. She'd put some balance in his life. Now it seemed like she was bent on undoing all that.

Sure, there had been strains before. Sometimes she got frustrated with the way his job controlled his life, with the calls and the hours, the danger and the canceled plans. But it seemed like they were working through that, that she'd accepted the nature of his job and been okay with it. Until this week.

Four days ago, over a pleasant dinner and recap of their days, she suddenly set down her fork, and said, "Joe, there's something we need to talk about. I know it'll be kind of a shock for you. It will seem too early in our relationship." She'd smiled her knowing smile. "Changing you is like turning a supertanker, Joe. So you're going to think I'm pushing too hard or wanting too much too soon. But I've been thinking about this for a while, and I don't think I can wait much longer . . ." She'd tilted her head back and forth, mocking herself the way she did. "You're going to think I'm out of my mind."

He set down his fork, too, his stomach tightening. She looked so serious. Older and more tired, too, as though coming to this decision had aged her. He was usually pretty good at anticipating, but he had no idea what was coming.

She picked up her fork again, pushed some shreds of chicken like a mop through the gravy on her plate, and set the fork down again without eating. "Joe, I want to adopt Neddy and Nina. I'm afraid if I wait, they'll have been placed . . . or at least, Neddy will. I can't imagine many families will be eager to take Nina . . . and he'll have gotten settled someplace. Nina needs stability." A pause, a deep breath. "And she needs to be with Neddy."

Not "We should adopt Neddy and Nina," he noticed. She

had said "I." She also hadn't asked for his opinion, probably because she already knew what he'd say. She'd gone on, ignoring his stunned silence, mentioning the attic as a third bedroom. How much fun she and Nina would have making the guest room into a girl's room. How much the children needed a stable and permanent family and her mother would be able to help. He had let her talk on without interrupting because he couldn't think of a single positive thing to say.

It had been a huge challenge for him to allow one person into his life after spending so much of it as a solitary creature. She knew that. He was learning to make the adjustments that went with their living arrangement—curbing his temper, learning to be patient, explaining his comings and goings instead of simply doing whatever he thought needed doing. He tried not to be impatient when she questioned the demands of his job, when she asked where he was going or when to expect him home.

He was learning to share his bed and his dark dreams; figuring out how much he could tell her about the ugliness that papered the inside of his head. He was coming to understand why so many cop marriages failed. How hard it was to balance the instinct to protect and the necessary practice of boxing up feelings with the need for sharing and intimacy. Hard to change habits decades in the making. He felt their situation was hopeful, yet still fragile and precarious.

And now this. He certainly wasn't ready to bring more players into the mix. Doubted he ever would be. Chris should have known this, yet she acted like it was no big deal. Despite her facility for discussion and building their relationship, in spite of the many times she'd pushed him to talk when he felt black and silent, when he tried to explain why he thought it was a bad idea, she refused to discuss it, not even the fact that Neddy and Nina, having seen so much violence and death in their short years, were incredibly needy children who would tax the most stable of parents. Something he most assuredly was not.

He pulled his attention back to the road as a huge sheet of cardboard, planing like a waveboard across the lane in front of him, suddenly reared up. There were cars on either side and no place to go. He had no choice but to hit it, the force sweeping it up over the hood and plastering it against the windshield. For a heart-stopping moment, he was driving blind at sixty-five. Then it let go, flying off over the roof to resume its dance of death behind him.

He pushed Chris and everything else that didn't have to do with today's case into a locker, slammed it shut, and turned the key. The last thing he needed was complications in his life that kept him from doing his job.

He'd already had the button-pushing call from the brass, in the form of Captain Paul Cote. Cote had called Burgess at home to complain about all the manpower and overtime hours being wasted on some unfortunate wino who'd fallen into the harbor. Though he should have known that Burgess and the deceased were friends, Cote hadn't spent a word on sympathy or regret before launching into a lecture about budgets and the department's limited resources.

There were many on the force, Burgess included, who believed that Cote had been built in a robotics factory somewhere and that the techie who programmed him had forgotten to install the part of the program that mimicked humanity. He'd counted to ten, deleted the expletives, and said, "It's all SOP for an unattended death, sir. We wait until tomorrow and then the ME tells us it's suspicious, we've lost the first twenty-four, along with potential evidence and witnesses."

Cote had harrumphed and muttered something about locksmiths and too many divers. "The diving thing is safety, sir." Burgess, choking on the "sir," reminded himself that he saluted the rank not the man. "Securing the residence just good practice." No use mentioning that without Robeck's quick thinking, Reggie's room would have been quickly stripped of anything useful. Cote had no concept of life on the streets. He probably thought Reggie'd used the money from returning those cans to put steaks on the barbie. Buy a better grade of beer.

He forced himself to listen as Cote continued. "Well, I'm laying odds you're going up to Augusta tomorrow to find you've got a wino that fell in the harbor. Just exactly what it looks like. Nothing suspicious. We don't need two detectives for that." So Stan Perry got to sleep in this morning, getting rested after his night of unbridled lust, while Burgess faced near-death out here on the highway at the hands of a vagrant piece of cardboard.

Burgess had not said to Cote what he would have said to any of his detectives—don't let your assumptions get ahead of the facts. Cote had no use for facts, at least not of the case-solving kind. It was as though, as he moved up the ranks, his mind was swept clean of everything he'd learned in his previous job. He loved data of all sorts, though. Numbers, especially good numbers—good solve rates, low overtime, coming in under budget—made him smile. The badge numbers, the cops who did the work, solved the crimes, earned the overtime, were mere annoyances.

Reggie was out of the body bag and lying on the table. Now Wink was pulling the bags off Reggie's feet. Clean, pale feet that looked especially naked because the rest of the body was so heavily dressed. There were no socks. Next, Wink pulled the bags off Reggie's hands, carefully examining them. The thumb of the right hand was slightly swollen and there were scrapes across the knuckles. Wink looked at Burgess. "Do the fingernails?"

"I would," Burgess said.

When Wink was done, they started undressing the body. First the heavy olive drab jacket with "Coates" over the pocket. The one that said "Libby" had long since disintegrated. Reggie had been wearing army jackets for thirty years. When one wore out, he picked up another at the Goodwill. Underneath, there was a quilted vest over a brown "Life is good" hooded sweatshirt, a gray waffle-weave thermal shirt, and a gray Gap tee shirt. A thick brown belt held up too-large khaki cargo pants.

As he bent to undo the belt, Burgess spotted a scraped patch on the leather and leaned in for a closer look. The belt was worn. It might just be a place where Reggie had fastened something to his belt and it had worn away the finish, but the wear in that spot was significantly greater than anywhere else on the belt, as though something had been tied to the belt heavy enough to rub the brown surface down to raw leather and wear a groove in the top of the belt.

"Take a look at this, Wink," he said.

Wink studied the belt, and reached for his camera. He photographed the belt in place, then undid the buckle and loosened the belt so he could twist it to study the back side. Clinging to the rougher inside leather were some whitish threads. "Dollars to donuts these match the rope on that cinderblock Chaplin brought up," he said.

Burgess watched Wink collect the threads with tweezers. "What do you think it means?"

"You're the detective," Wink said, "but if they match, it could be this gentleman wanted to be sure he'd stay down once he went into the water."

"Or someone else wanted him to stay down."

"Or someone else did," Wink agreed. "But right there on the waterfront's a pretty dumb place to dump a body."

In cold water, a properly weighted body in an obscure location might not have surfaced for weeks. By the time it did, most indices which could have told them about the death might have been corrupted or eradicated. Did that mean Reggie had done this because he only cared about staying down long enough to keep from changing his mind? Or had some stupid or impatient criminal dumped him in the first convenient place, not thinking about how easily the body might be spotted?

"Here's something." Wink, who was putting the sodden jacket into a bag, held out his hand. In the palm was a business card. Nicholas Goodall. Sculptor.

"Something to look into," Burgess said, "assuming we're looking into any of this."

In the same pocket, Wink found a black envelope. Too wet to open or try to read, but it looked like the ones in Reggie's suitcase. Burgess remembered Maura's ramblings about an evil woman. The threatening letter he'd read. The return address had been Goodall.

There were no more surprises. Some things in Reggie's pockets, mostly paper, which would have to be spread out and dried, along with the clothes, back at the lab in Portland. Unless Cote's fallible instincts were right and the matter would be ended by this morning's autopsy. Then he'd be giving Reggie's things to Clay.

Dr. Lee flew in just as his assistant, Albert, and Wink had finished removing Reggie's clothes. Lee was capped, gowned, and ready to roll. He strode up to the table and stood looking down at Reggie, his eyes scanning the pale skin. Burgess watched the unreadable dark eyes moving over the body and wondered what Lee was seeing. When Lee was ready, he nodded, the body was turned, and he gave Reggie's back the same slow, careful scrutiny.

It was cold in the room, temperature cold, and the tile walls and floor and all the stainless steel and sharp instruments gave it a cold, hard edge as well. Burgess had the absurd impulse to cover his friend to keep the chill away and protect him from prying eyes. Instead, he forced himself closer to the table to watch what Lee was doing.

Lee was the expert, but Burgess had been studying victims for clues since the ME was riding his trike on the sidewalk. Now he thought that Reggie's body was trying to tell him something, and he looked at Lee to see if the ME was seeing it, too. Lee looked up from his scrutiny, met his eyes, and nodded, pointing to a strange circular bruise on Reggie's back and a pattern of bruises at the base of his neck.

"If that's pre-mortem," Lee said, "this bruise pattern suggests someone put a knee in this man's back, put their hands on the back of his neck, and forced his head under water. Just conjecture at this point. We'll see what else he's got to tell us. Wink, you want to get your pictures?"

After Wink had photographed the bruises, Lee took tissue samples of the bruised areas. Burgess watched the ME carefully examine the rest of Reggie's skin, touching it lightly, turning the limbs, examining the fingers and noting the bruised thumb and scraped knuckles. Then they turned Reggie back over. It struck him then that despite the sense of bulk provided by his clothes, Reggie was terribly thin. "He used to be a big guy," Burgess said. "My size."

They all looked at the bruising on Reggie's stomach, mottled patches of purple that could have been from a fist or from being jammed against a hard object. Again, Wink took pictures and Lee took tissue samples. Then Lee nodded. "If you gentlemen are ready?"

Wink backed away as the ME examined Reggie's mouth and nose, dictated some findings, and picked up his scalpel. As the knife sliced through the pale skin, Burgess felt a pain so sharp he might have been the one being cut. He closed his eyes, momentarily dizzy.

He felt a hand on his shoulder, vaguely heard a barked command, as he was pressed down into a chair and ordered to lower his head. Even as the floor swam before his eyes, he cursed himself for letting an autopsy get to him. As pathetic as a rookie.

He raised his head, humiliated, and met Lee's eyes. "I'm sorry," he said. "I don't know what . . ."

"You should have sent someone else," Lee said. "I wouldn't do an autopsy on a friend. You shouldn't watch one."

"If he was killed," Burgess countered, "I need to know that."

Lee held his ground. "Some other cop couldn't tell you? You're the only one on the planet who can handle this?"

"It's not that," Burgess said, feeling like an idiot. "I didn't realize . . ."

"Well, I've got to do this now." The ME, being both Asian and a doctor, had a completely inscrutable face. "Got two kids waiting to go apple picking. What do you want to do? Stick it out or go sit in the hall? We haven't got time to wait for a replacement."

Burgess had never heard Lee mention a family before. Usually the doc was impatient to go play golf. He pushed up off his chair. "I'll stick." He understood Lee was making him mad so he'd get past his emotions. And it was working. His face felt hot and his hands had clenched into fists. He worked on his breathing, decades of training whispering in his brain—if you can breathe, you can think, you can respond. He forced his fists to uncurl.

"Okay. I'm fine," he said. "Let's do this."

Watching Lee ply his knives and saws on Reggie, watching that poor lost man reduced to meat and bone and organs weighed and sampled was one of the hardest things he'd ever done. He'd found autopsies on kids grueling. Seethed with anger as he stood through the autopsy of a fourteen-year-old raped and eviscerated by her stepfather. Soul sick at the autopsy of little Kristin Marks. This one just hurt.

He tried to hold himself in the room, an observant, dispassionate cop, but tripped by Reggie's puckered scars, the open flesh, and the coppery tang of blood, his traitor mind sneaked back to Nam. Back to their days and their nights, the long talks in the dark, the endless hours spent waiting, necks prickling and sweat running, for the bullet, the bomb, the mortar shell to come whizzing out of nowhere and end it all. Even in the icy room, the meaty body smell brought back the remembered scents of wounds and death, the weird rotten-vegetable smell of the air, the crazy dope-filled haze.

Memory carried him back to a day in a rice paddy. The green rice so tall you couldn't see anything. To the sudden explosion of gunfire, mortar shells, a chaos of voices yelling warnings and commands. He'd lost Reggie somewhere and was all alone in that green sea, hunkered down and still amid the bursts of gunfire until suddenly Reggie was screaming. "Joe, Jesus, Joe, help me!"

He'd floundered through the muck, heavy-footed, found Reggie writhing on the ground, wet, slick with mud and blood, screaming. Burgess had hauled him up and pulled Reggie off the field, trying not to panic at the gushing hot wetness of Reggie's blood, his awareness of how exposed they were. Trying to offer comfort as Reggie clung to him, pleading, "Please, Joe, don't let me die. Joe, don't let me die."

He'd dragged Reggie back to some cover while they called in a chopper to take the wounded away. Finally, a blood-soaked medic giving Reggie a shot. His friend's screams dying away.

Christ, they weren't ready to die; they were barely nineteen. Once Reggie was loaded and the chopper lifted off, he'd gotten down on his knees in a frigging rice paddy, deafened by the whomp overhead, and prayed that Reggie would make it. He'd been pulling for Reggie to make it ever since. Until he'd given up on the church, he'd spent plenty of hours on his knees, praying for Reggie. Now he faced the indisputable evidence that Reggie *hadn't* made it.

"Going to sample some of this water in the lungs," Lee was saying. "And some from his sinus cavities." He dictated some notes on the frothy fluid in the airways and lungs, the congested lungs, and fluid in the paranasal sinuses and went to work on the organs, carefully drawing blood from the heart.

As Lee recorded a steady stream of comments about his findings, he cast the occasional assessing look at Burgess. When he pulled out the liver and weighed it, he paused.

"He hadn't gone in the water, this would have killed him. Soon. Certainly accounts for the emaciation." He looked at Burgess. "I think I should see his medical history." Burgess made a note. Lee made some comments as he sliced and sectioned the liver for further study. "You said he was a drinker?" Burgess nodded. "Could just be that, but I'm going to take a closer look. I've seen a lot of cirrhotic livers. Something different about this one. Funny necrosis."

So it went. Burgess hanging by a thread, Wink watchful, and Lee coolly professional until he'd carefully replaced the removed and sectioned organs. Then he nodded at Albert, and stripped off his gloves.

"You've definitely got a death by drowning, Joe," he said. "Beyond that, I've got some things to look into. Take a look at the lungs and that liver. The water in his lungs and his stomach. Toxicology. Analyze the heart blood. Get that bruised tissue under the microscope. If you're looking for something to tell your bosses . . ."

He arched one dark brow, as though he knew which boss was waiting to write off the guy on the table. The Maine law enforcement community was small. Burgess's history with Cote, and everyone's frustration with the man, were well known. "You can say that the initial autopsy results were inconclusive but that there are a sufficient number of oddities suggesting it wasn't a natural death, that the case warrants further study."

There was a trace of a smile on the thin mouth. "Enough to keep you working?"

"It's enough," Burgess said. "Thanks, doc."

Again, that trace of a smile hovered. "You want my unofficial opinion, Joe?"

This was unusual. Dr. Lee rarely theorized about anything. "I do."

"I won't go on record until I have some testing to corroborate this, but I believe those bruises will prove to be pre-mortem." Lee paused, unable to resist a bit of drama. "There's no laryngeal spasm to suggest he went into cold water. There isn't lividity in his face and head. The initial report says he wasn't found in a fetal or semifetal position. I've got that hair I found in his lungs. And some of the changes in the lung tissue suggest that when we test the water from his lungs, his sinuses and his stomach, we'll find this was a freshwater drowning."

CHAPTER SIX

On his way to see Reggie's brother, Burgess checked in with Melia, alerting his lieutenant that the autopsy was inconclusive and they were still dealing with a suspicious death. Then he left a message for Captain Cote. Cote insisted on getting regular reports, even on weekends when he wasn't there to receive them. He often paid no attention when he was. Despite his inattention, Cote had a habit of holding press conferences and blurting out details they wanted kept under wraps. Burgess had found the best way to keep information confidential was to bury it in the middle of reports.

Here Burgess wanted it up front. When he was flipped to voicemail, he said, "It's Burgess. About the Reginald Libby case. The autopsy was inconclusive. ME thinks we're looking at a suspicious death, pending test results." Then he pushed Cote and associated aggravations out of his head.

He headed west from Augusta toward Belgrade, a part of the state dotted with beautiful lakes, some nice farming country, and a lot of evidence that whatever economic boom might have raised the rest of the country, rural Maine was still pretty heavily into making do. That evidence included the number of aged cars and trucks by the roadside with "For Sale" signs. Dooryards littered with the junk of perpetual yard sales. Foundations banked with hay and attic windows lined with plastic in preparation for winter. Vehicles on blocks with people working on them, and enough worn, peeling, and blistered paint on dwellings to suggest a mass exodus of house painters to more lucrative climes.

There hadn't been a frost yet and the gardens he passed bloomed with fall flowers, explosions of color against the still green grass. Gardens his mother would have loved, that woman who could coax Eden out of the meager yard of a cheap three-decker. The summer had been dry and hot but fall rains had revived wilted gardens and sustained a late crop. Farm stands still offered baskets of ripe tomatoes alongside apples, raspberries, pears, melons, potatoes, pumpkins, and squash. Big signs announced homemade pies and cider. Occasionally, a capped truck along the roadside advertised "Whoopie Pies."

Nina and Neddy, great lovers of whoopie pies, always clamored to stop, and Chris was happy to join them. Burgess didn't have a sweet tooth; he had a meat tooth. Not the best thing for preserving heart health when he was overweight and under-exercised. He was less overweight than when he'd met Chris, and better exercised. But salads, however healthy, couldn't sustain him through missed meals. When he was on the road or coming off a ten-hour crime scene, he never longed for mixed lettuce or a handful of baby carrots.

Today, though he was an appetite-driven man, he had no appetite. He longed for anesthesia—the kind that came in a bottle and had ruined Reggie's life. The kind that had destroyed his own father and caused his mother so much pain. He knew better. He rarely drank during a work day, even when that day became night became day again, and a quick shot offered tempting relief. The exception was those times he'd drink with someone to get information. If sitting down with a bottle was going to lower someone's guard and loosen their tongue, he might do it.

Willpower only negated the action, though, not the urge. Sometimes, when the urge was strong, he could almost taste bourbon's sweet heat and bite, feel the way a thin slick of it would coat his mood like an antacid, spreading out along his nerves, soothing as silk. Like now, when his weekend, his mood, his relationship—hell, his whole life was so fucked up.

The general public might not know it, but this, too, was a big part of the cop's reality. Asked to live with these crazy hours, horrific sights, screwed up family life, and never exhibit any emotion. Cops were expected to have self-control. Right now, a corrosive mix of anger at Cote's dismissive "nothing but an old wino," the pain of seeing Reggie carved up, and the ugly possibility that someone had taken Reggie's life was eroding his self-control, filling him with seeping black rage.

He jerked the wheel suddenly, pulling off onto a side road and bumping to a stop in an abandoned gravel pit. He slammed the Explorer into park, grabbed two big orange traffic cones from the back, duct-taped two of Cote's glossy black and white official photographs to the cones, and set them up against a high gravel embankment. Then he backed off and emptied a clip into the first one, stenciling a perfect cross on his boss's face. Probably as close as that asshole would ever come to religion.

He wondered if anything in Cote's miserable, paper-pushing life had ever sent him into a church to pray. Whether Cote had ever asked for anything for someone else. Maybe a heartworm cure for his dog? Cote was very attached to something allegedly canine that resembled a fluffy rat. CID had had a photo of him kissing said canine up on the wall until Melia made them take it down.

He shoved another clip in the gun, backed up farther, and shot again. Only half done, he walked back to the truck, reloaded the clip, and finished the job. There wasn't much left of Cote's face under the peace sign, but Burgess felt better. He threw the massacred cones into the back, shredded Cote into confetti and let the breeze take him. Then he drove to Clay's.

It was going to be like two guys rubbing themselves with sandpaper, but he had to go. He owed Clay the decency of a face-to-face about Reggie's end. He tried to do for people what he'd like done for him, to show respect for the dead and for the living. He also needed to learn what Clay knew about Reggie's recent activities, health, and job. Clay hadn't said much on the phone, but a lot of times, people weren't aware of what they knew. On the phone, he'd had to let Clay go have his grief. Face-to-face, he could take his time. Watch and listen and follow up. He'd told Chris not to expect him for dinner.

Traveling the long dirt driveway to Clay's farm made his bones ache. Not only because potholes from the recent rains made it a jarring ride. This road, lined with tired split-rail fences and fading roses, reminded him of all the times he'd brought Reggie here. Sometimes in good shape, talkative and optimistic, ready for his summer of work on the farm. Other times just out of the bin, or so strung out on drugs and booze his pores reeked of alcohol and he was alternately nodding off or incoherent. Between them, he and Clay had patched Reggie together countless times, always hoping this would be the time it would finally take, the wounds would heal, Reggie would stay on his feet. It was like bailing an emotional sea. But when you care for someone, when you're bound to them like he and Clay were to Reggie, you always let hope triumph over experience.

A dog, some smart, sturdy, middle-sized country dog mix, met him at the road and trailed him up the drive to the house. It positioned itself between the truck and Clay as Burgess parked and got out, giving a few warning barks so Burgess knew what was what.

Clay sat on the front steps, staring out at nothing. He stood when Burgess climbed out of the truck, a heftier, grayer, slightly stooped version of Reggie. He had his hands in his pockets, his head just slightly tilted to one side, like he was listening for something. He quieted the dog with a murmur. When Burgess got closer, he saw Clay's eyes were red.

"So what happened to my brother?" he began without a greeting. "Was it an accident or did he finally decide he'd had enough?"

Procedure was to not answer the question. Say what you need to say, don't share anything more than you have to. Just deliver your news, ask your questions, and get the hell out. A good cop absorbed the training and learned how to make judgments about it—reading situations and deciding when to follow procedure, when to be more open. "ME isn't certain yet. He's got more tests to do. But his tentative opinion . . . ?"

Reggie's brother leaned forward, his lips slightly parted, holding his breath the way people did when they anticipated bad news.

"He thinks it's a suspicious death."

Clay gasped, half to get some air and half in shock. "Suspicious? You mean someone did this deliberately? Like murder?" Burgess nodded. "Oh, no. No!" Clay shook his head vigorously. "It doesn't make any sense. Why would anyone want to hurt Reggie?"

"I'm hoping you can help me figure that out."

Clay swung his arms wide, Reggie's eyes staring from his brother's face, a reddened muddle of incredulity. "I don't see how I can help with that, Joe. You know he wasn't the confiding type, but I wouldn't have thought Reggie had enemies. You'd better come inside. I'm feeling like I need a drink. Pour you one, too, if that's okay. Mary's still away, and drinking by myself last night? Shoot, Joe, you know, by about half past twelve, I wasn't sure I was me or I was Reggie."

Burgess nodded, knowing it was only because Chris and the kids had been there that he hadn't done the same. As it was, he'd been awake half the night, thinking about Reggie. His eyes were probably as red as Clay's. "A drink would be good."

Inside the homey old kitchen, Clay sagged heavily into a chair while Burgess found glasses and grabbed the bourbon bottle off the counter. Next to the bottle was a framed photograph of three children: Clay, Reggie, and a little girl. Burgess brought it to the table, poured them each a drink, and settled into his own chair. To get the conversation going, he asked, "Who's the girl?"

"Our cousin Cindy. Dad's brother's daughter. She pretty much grew up with us through junior high, when they moved away. She's around here somewhere but I don't see her anymore. She's gotten real weird. Into herbs and tarot. Calls herself Star now."

Star was the name on the black envelopes. "Star Goodall?" Burgess asked.

"That's it. She's somewhere down near Portland. But Reggie probably didn't have anything to do with her. Like I said, she went all weird, back, maybe ten, twelve years ago, got this notion in her head that Reggie'd molested her. Went to one of them shrinks that helps people with their memories? Shrink convinced her that me and Reggie'd done something. You know the type, ones who'd say anything to get some poor fool to pay 'em some money."

Clay shook his head. "Like we would, right—our own cousin, more like a sister the way we were raised? There's some that are like that, trailer trash maybe, but not us Libbys. But logic had no effect on Cindy. She come after me screaming and hollering and saying how I should go to the shrink with her and help her work this through. I figured since we were kids together and she was family that I'd go down there, see if I could set her straight. Only there was no fixing it."

Clay tipped up his glass and drained it. "Shrink was just as looney as she was. Whatever I said, they'd twist it up into something sick and wrong. Then she starts talking about how because I done this I owed her . . . well, they weren't listening to me anyway, so I just got up and walked out. Cindy . . . Star, as she now is . . . she sent me some letters." He looked at Burgess, as if asking could the detective believe this. "Black envelopes. Black writing paper. After the first one, we didn't even read 'em. Mary threw them away; said we didn't need that nonsense."

He refilled their glasses. "She's real sensible, my Mary. Awful torn up about Reggie. She wanted to know should she come right home. I told her maybe she should give me some time."

"So you don't know if she was in touch with Reggie. Star, I mean?"

"Nope. But if she was doing this to get some money for herself, there'd be no sense in bothering Reggie, would there?"

But she had been bothering Reggie. Burgess wondered why. Figured he'd have to pay a call on Ms. Star Goodall, who had conveniently left her address on the envelopes. "Doesn't Reggie still have some land up here?"

"Nice piece of waterfront," Clay said. "It's about eighty acres on a lake. Mostly farm land. There's an old farmhouse, not much of a place. Land's leased to a young couple doing organic farming." After a silence, Clay said, "Land's all in trust, so Reggie can't sell it. So his creditors can't get it. As if Reggie had creditors. Reggie didn't have jack shit. He ever did get himself anything, he'd give it away."

He had that right. Reggie had been kind of a damaged saint, walking the streets with his grocery cart, taking cans and bottles for the redemption center for a little money, then using that money trying to look after people worse off than himself. He'd get abused, robbed or beaten for his troubles. Then something would stir up those demons, he'd fall in some black hole, have to be pieced back together again.

The country going into Iraq had really done it. One night Burgess had found him sitting in his room, surrounded by news-paper photos of soldiers in Iraq. Reggie had grabbed a handful and held them out. "Look at this, Joe. These kids are us. God-damned president is doing it all over again, government fucking over another generation of kids. You watch. They'll come back damaged and the VA will shrug and put 'em on some god-damned waiting list for two, three years. When they do see someone, doc'll just shove 'em a fistful of pills and send 'em home. No one to listen or help with the shit inside their heads."

Reggie had that right. Bunch of old neocons and a dry drunk president with daddy issues who didn't even want the public to see the boys and girls coming home maimed or in boxes. Let the broken ones fester in rat- and roach-infested hospitals or drowned them in paperwork. But it didn't help Reggie to say he agreed. He'd gotten Reggie to promise to throw the pictures out and go talk to someone at the VA. And for a while, Reggie seemed better.

Clay was still explaining about the land. "It's in a trust . . . goes to the boy when Reggie dies . . . the rotten little prick. Joey, I mean. As if those two had ever given Reggie the time of day. They treated him like scum."

Clay looked away, silent for a long time. "I haven't called mama yet. She's awful frail for this kind of news. I can't say what it might do to her. She's still praying every day for a miracle. I didn't call Joey, either. He's still living at home with Claire."

He slapped his palms onto his thighs. "I gotta tell ya, Joe. I'm not one to shirk my duty. But calling Claire and Joey . . . the two of 'em so goddamned bitter, done Reggie so much harm . . . I'm just not up to it. Can't bring myself to go through that first burst of anger just so's I can tell her something she doesn't care about anyway."

Clay's shoulders had a dejected slump. He was a simple man who believed in doing the right thing. Couldn't understand people who spent a lifetime bearing grudges.

"Never mind explaining to them about the land. It don't even belong to him yet," Clay said, "and that boy's already had surveyors up, thinking about how it could be developed. I wouldn't have known, only the couple that's leasing it—they're four years into a ten-year lease, no sense in putting in the work to make it into a decent organic farm unless they've got some security, see—they called up to see why someone was on the property surveying. So I drive over and there's Joey and this surveyor and Joey's all excited, telling me he's got a buyer wants to put in a bunch of houses."

Clay's slumped shoulders rose and fell. "He wouldn't even listen when I told him it was under lease for farming. He said that didn't matter and wasn't binding on him. We had words, not that anything I said seemed to penetrate. Joey just shrugged me off, said his mother would take care of it. So you can see why I'm not keen on talking with them." Clay emptied his glass. "I swear that little bastard couldn't wait for Reggie to die and Claire ain't no better. She was on the phone that very afternoon, wanting copies of the documents."

He poured a slow stream of bourbon into his glass, shaking his head. "I just listened and hung up. I can't see where she's got any rights. Joey's an adult. Based on his birthday anyways."

Burgess knew dealings with Reggie's ex-wife had always baffled Clay. A few years after their return from Nam, Claire Fontaine, smart, young, and pretty, working on a masters degree in social work, had married Reggie as her personal social work project. When her charm and textbook platitudes failed to cure Reggie of night terrors, his inability to sleep or concentrate, and all the rest of the web of sorrow so many vets carried, she'd left in a huff, taking their young son with her. She'd never relinquished a drop of the bitterness she hadn't legitimately earned. Had raised the boy to despise his father.

"It's not like she didn't know who he was when she married him," Clay said. "Reggie was in a bad way when he got back, as you well know. She was just a prissy little do-gooder thought she'd reform him and turn him into a perfect house pet. Then she finds out she can't and it's like it's all Reggie's fault. I used to think, maybe, he got himself the right woman, it might make a difference. But probably, like so many things with Reggie, that was just another pipe dream. Maura might be crazy as a bedbug, but bless her soul, she loved Reggie as best as she could."

"Does the land automatically go to Joey if Reggie's dead? It's a sure thing?"

"When he's thirty-five. Dunno about before that. Lawyer who did the trust would know if Reggie's death changes things, but I don't think so. I'm trustee. I make sure the rent gets collected and the taxes get paid, keep a tenant there so the land's cared for and people aren't dumping used cars and their trash out there. That's what trustee means to me. It's all legal gobbledygook anyway."

"Know the lawyer's name?"

"I'll give you the damned thing. You can make a copy and send it back." He scratched his head. "Actually, this is a copy. Original's at the bank. I figured it was safer that way."

It was getting dark in the kitchen, the slant of the light getting steeper, days in October as short as days in March. Neither of them moved to put on a light, though. It seemed right to sit in growing darkness. Clay splashed more bourbon into Burgess's glass, then lifted his. "Here's hoping he's finally at peace."

"At peace." Burgess clinked and drank. "I'll tell Claire and Joey if you want."

"I want."

They sat silent. A clock ticked. Something in the cellar whirred. A gust of passing wind stirred some chimes. "Reggie made those," Clay said. "So good with his hands, if only he could have stuck to something."

"I've got a set, too," Burgess said. "Listening to them in the wind last night, I kept wondering if Reggie was trying to tell me something."

"That noise there?" Clay wore a gentle, faraway look. "That was him complaining that we're drinking without him." Then, as the sound of the chimes faded, he said. "You seriously don't think this was an accident?"

Burgess shrugged. "I was ready to let it go. Get on with missing him and hoping he's in a better place, but the ME has doubts. Some things that don't look right. So I've got to treat this like an investigation until I'm told otherwise." No sense mentioning he'd already been told otherwise by Cote.

Clay lifted his glass, holding it so the light coming through the window gave the liquid a golden glow. "So what do you do now?"

"Talk to people who knew him. Get a handle on his life."

"*He* never could."

They listened to the clock tick, so much left unsaid. Burgess had spent uncountable hours, probably years of his life, on uncomfortable kitchen chairs, slowly gleaning the bits and pieces that let him put stories together. "What do you know about Reggie's job?" he asked.

"Not much. Some guy hired him to clean up at his business. Reggie never said what kind of business. Something to do with manufacturing. Reggie did the usual—swept the floors, cleaned the offices and the bathrooms. Cleaned materials and got 'em ready for the next day's work. Sometimes he cleaned the machines. Coupla times he said he even fixed some of the machines, got right inside and replaced parts and stuff. He liked that."

"How did he get to and from work?"

"Someone would pick him up. Sometimes someone would drive him back or he'd call a taxi to get home."

"You know if he worked days or nights?"

"Afternoons and evenings, I think. Not sure, though. I dunno if it was regular."

"I didn't find any pay stubs in Reggie's room."

"You wouldn't. It was all under the table. Reggie's not supposed to be working anyway, with the disability. Only he'd rather work, when he could. Reggie didn't like just sitting around. That's why he did the cans. It wasn't just the money. It got him out and around. Kept the city clean. Poor crazy bastard. He could have been such a fine man."

Clay made a tent with his hands, tapped the fingers lightly together, then left them tented on the table in front of him. A gesture Burgess had seen him make before, but today, with his eyes closed and his head bowed, Reggie's brother looked like he was praying. Burgess realized he didn't know if Clay was a religious man.

Without opening his eyes, Clay said, "So you looked through his room. Did you find the money?"

"About a hundred bucks in a pants pocket."

Clay's eyes opened. He dropped his hands into fists and leaned toward Burgess. "Should have been a lot more than that. Reggie was getting at least four hundred a week for that cleaning job. He wasn't drinking and his expenses are small. He's been working, let's see." He looked at a calendar on the wall. "Maybe four, five weeks. He should have had over a thousand bucks."

"Maybe he's got it in a bank somewhere. I can check."

"You do that, Joe," Clay said, a hard edge in his voice.

"Because if he doesn't have it in a bank—and Reggie wasn't much for banks—then someone's taken it." He swung his eyes to Burgess's face. Despite the redness, they were sharp. A piercing light greenish-blue with very dark rims around the irises. Reggie's had been just the same. Shark eyes, someone in Nam had called them. Reggie had liked that. Reggie had been a gentle man but those eyes had made him look dangerous. Now, looking into Clay's eyes, Burgess saw there was a lot of anger behind the sadness. He hadn't read it clearly enough, a few minutes ago, when Clay had been talking about Reggie's ex-family. When he'd been thinking like a friend instead of a cop.

"You don't think someone would kill Reggie for a lousy thousand bucks, do you?" Clay asked.

Burgess wished he could say no, but in his experience, people killed for many reasons the ordinary citizen would find astonishing. He countered the question with one of his own.

"Who was Reggie close to? Who might have known he was working or that he had some money?"

"Any of those guys Reggie hung out with, they'd know because Reggie wasn't hanging around with them. People who lived in that dump. Or Maura. She'd never mean Reggie any harm, but there's no telling what she'd say or who she'd say it to. She knew he had a stash, she might blab about that. Lady's not the sharpest tool in the shed."

"The guy across the hall evidently had a key to Reggie's room." Burgess got out his notebook, flipped through until he found the name. "Kevin Dugan? You know him?" Clay shook his head. "Reggie ever mention him?"

"Not that I recall."

"Maura and this guy, Dugan, both said that Reggie hadn't been feeling well. He'd been seeing a doctor. He say anything about that?"

Clay tented his hands again and studied them. "He called

once, a week, ten days ago, said his stomach hurt something awful. I told him to go the ER. Call an ambulance. It wasn't anything to fool around with. All the drugs he's been given over the years, along with all that drink, who knows what shape his insides are in." He shook his head angrily. "Were in."

"Did he go to the ER?"

"Said he did. Said they were doing some tests. Gave him something for the pain. That was the last I heard. Reggie wasn't the chattiest guy. He'd call if he needed me. He always could. He knew that. When you said he'd gone in the ocean, I don't know. I guess I figured he'd just had enough. Then I started with all the things I maybe ought to have done, wondering could I have kept this from happening. If I should have gone down there, never mind how many times I done that before." He shrugged wearily. "Fall's a busy time. I didn't go."

The tent came apart, Clay's hands swooping up and slamming down hard on the table. "FUCK! Joe, I can't stand this. All the times we've thought he was done, tried to get our hearts and minds ready for it, and he's bounced back. Finally it's really looking like he's getting better, and wham! He's gone."

He folded his arms on the table and put his head down, his shoulders heaving convulsively. He didn't make a sound.

Burgess might have had more questions, but he'd asked enough. He made mental notes about the pills and the money that he hadn't found in Reggie's room. It was time to go. He patted Clay's shoulder. "I'm going to take off," he said. "I'll call you about arrangements. You can call me. Anytime. You know that, right?"

Clay mumbled something from the cradle of his arms.

"Mary coming back tomorrow?"

Clay nodded.

"Okay. I'll call Claire and Joey, then."

Clay lifted a tear-streaked face, blotched red where it had

pressed against his arms. "You tell them this, too, Joe, okay. You tell them I don't want to hear one goddamned word about land or money until Reggie is decently in the ground. I think maybe the Veteran's Cemetery, don't you? It's nice out there. They do a good service."

Burgess nodded, too choked to talk. Then he walked to the door and let himself out. Clay's sobs hurt so much they were like a knife in his own gut. The dog nudged his leg for attention and he stopped in the deepening dusk to pet it. He made it to the car before sorrow got him, too. He put his forehead on the wheel and let it come.

CHAPTER SEVEN

He should have gone home. Chris would be waiting to comfort him, but he wasn't ready to accept comfort. He felt solitary and uncivil. He needed some time alone to process the last thirty-six hours. The only person he would have felt comfortable with was his fellow detective and close friend, Terry Kyle. Kyle was a great sounding board and familiar with his dark side. Burgess could have bounced some ideas off him, gotten a second "detective's gut" reacting to the case, but Kyle was out of town with his girlfriend, Michelle.

For the last six years Kyle's vindictive ex-wife, Wanda, had put him through hell, culminating in her threat to move his beloved daughters to Texas. Kyle had been endlessly patient with her, but given the choice between being decent and honorable and losing his girls, or fighting back, Kyle had hired a lawyer. He'd shown the court all of Wanda's erratic, vindictive behavior, produced her notes, her threatening messages taped by dispatch and on his answering machine. He'd shown how often Wanda arbitrarily canceled visitation after he'd moved heaven and earth to free the time, and how devastating it had been to the girls. It had been brutal and ugly, but he'd won custody. Now in a new relationship with a loving woman, Kyle deserved a weekend without a phone call from Burgess about a possible homicide.

By the time he got back to Portland, it was after seven. Dark and with a bite in the air that held the taste of things to come.

The grays and browns of November. The false gaiety of December. The endless stretch from January through March of dirty snow and slippery brick sidewalks, dry, pinched faces and shoulders hunched against the cold. If he lived in the now, he would have enjoyed yesterday and today, two perfect, if fleeting, fall days.

It was an odd expression—living in the now. Detectives rarely lived in the now. Most often, they lived in the "then," reconstructing the events of the crimes they investigated, first the day and time of the crime, then going backward through time to the events leading up to the crime, the last time the victim was seen, who might have had a reason to want to harm him, etcetera, then moving ahead to the events coming after. It was like following a rock thrown into a still pond. First you looked back to figure out who threw it and why, then followed the rings of ripples, trying to see who was affected and how, probing for the lies in statements like emotional dentists searching for decay.

The station was quiet at this time of night on a holiday weekend, just the way he liked it. He parked in the cement bunker that was their lot and went upstairs. There was something soothing about the quiet hum of electronics, the occasional ring of a phone, maybe one or two solitary detectives talking in low voices on their phones or writing reports. All the paper clutter of a detective's life without the human commotion.

He looked up an address and phone number for Claire Fontaine Libby, unsurprised to find she was still in the stately home her parents had bought to provide a proper place for their daughter to raise their grandson. Claire had gotten Reggie when he was still hopeful. Damaged but hopeful and believing that what he should do next was get as normal as possible. Normal was go to college, get married, have a family. Reggie had tried so hard to do normal, but it was hard to do college when he couldn't sleep, when being around "normal" people made him nervous, when he was having explosions of anger and bouts of deep despair he couldn't understand or control.

In the midst of Reggie's struggle, Claire had announced she was pregnant. Reggie knew he wasn't ready and they'd agreed to wait before they had children. But Claire was an indulged only child who'd always done what she wanted when she wanted, and she was no different with this. So while Reggie was struggling to get his demons under control and learn to be a good husband, he found himself also a father.

Reggie had been genuinely awestruck by Joey's arrival, and for a while it seemed like he finally had achieved normal. Claire had not been pleased when her husband wanted to name their son after a beat cop with a high school education, nor had she wanted Burgess to be godfather, but she'd gone along. The pressures of school, marriage, and parenthood, though, had proved to be too much for Reggie. Within the year, he'd been involuntarily committed twice. Claire got him a shrink, heavy-duty drugs, and finally, a private hospital placement. But when he hadn't proved an easy fix, she'd dusted her hands together like someone wiping off crumbs, shoved him out the door, and locked it behind him.

She had never remarried. Too hurt by her failure with Reggie, she said. Too grasping and controlling was what Burgess thought. When her smile revealed fangs, men more attuned than Reggie had recognized her for the bloodsucker she was and backed away. Even the pale white skin and long dark hair had fit Claire's vampire image. The only thing that didn't was that she could move about in the daytime.

He could understand her disappointment. Living with a vet who had PTSD was hard. What he couldn't forgive was her lack of understanding or sympathy or patience. Her lasting and vindictive anger at Reggie because he couldn't fix himself and her cruelty in barring Reggie from contact with his son. Burgess would admit he was prejudiced. Being thrown out of his house by a wife he'd loved, losing wife, home, and child all at once without the possibility of reconciliation, and then being barred from their lives completely had put Reggie on a terrible downward slide. He'd never fully recovered. Burgess knew Reggie had been difficult to live with. He still blamed Claire.

He closed his eyes and tipped his head back against the chair. Man. There was nothing this case wasn't going to dredge up. He'd probably start having the horror dreams and attention issues himself. Dr. Lee was right. He should just give this case to Stan and Terry. It was messy to try to work with something that involved a friend. But he wasn't sure that Lee was being truthful, saying he wouldn't work on a friend. He thought Lee was equally certain and controlling. Lee would do the autopsy on a case he cared about because of his certainty he'd do it best. Burgess didn't think he was arrogant—though there were those who'd disagree—but he believed he was competent and that a personal connection with a case meant he'd work harder to find the truth. There was something to be said for detachment, though. Professional distance was a lot less painful.

He went back into the computer to check on Joey. Reggie's son's only known address was still with Claire. His godson. Black-haired, shark-eyed, tall and handsome Joey. In the early years, he'd tried to do the job Reggie had given him. Trying to be there for Joey as Reggie couldn't be; taking Joey on weekend afternoons, throwing a football in the park, bringing the boy to see his mother. Claire had resisted until she'd managed to turn the child against him, too.

Cops are persistent and patient. They're used to taking abuse. It had taken him a long while to admit it was hopeless. For years after that, he'd kept track from a distance as Joey went through school, following his father onto the football field. He and Reggie had gone to the games, felt the pleasure and pride as Joey reprised some of their moments of glory.

He'd also watched Joey's slide into abusing drugs and alcohol during college. Bailed him out once or twice for small things—what the general public might call minor corruption, but what cops, and everybody else, did for each other. But there was something rotten in Joey. For all her holier-than-thou posing as the noble victim and her harsh condemnation of Reggie, Claire turned out to be the one without soul or conscience. She raised their son to be just like her—utterly selfish and indifferent to the hurt he caused. His godson was a narcissistic monster. Burgess might be willing to intervene to protect Joey when the situation involved a small drug offense or a minor accident; he hadn't been willing to do the same when Joey abused his girlfriends.

After the second time police were called to Joey's apartment to protect a battered and hysterical young woman and the second restraining order, after the second or third "You gotta help me, Uncle Joe" phone call, Burgess had sat Joey down and had a talk. He explained that Joey was right on the edge. Another incident and he was going to jail. Joey responded with the defensive whine of all cowardly batterers. Not his fault, they'd asked for it, driven him to it. They were all lying, manipulative bitches.

Based on his experience with his own mother, Joey might have been right, but that didn't make it universal, and Burgess had said so. Joey clung to his excuses. Women just used him and abused him. If he occasionally struck out in frustration, who could blame him?

Finally, pissed off, Burgess had growled, "Just don't try it in my town again," and left.

Sadly, Joey had taken the advice literally. He'd gotten an

apartment thirty miles away and put his next girlfriend in the hospital. That one sent him to jail. A slap on the wrist, like too many young offenders got, but it earned him a record and jail time. It was the last one Burgess heard about. What he didn't know was whether Joey had changed his ways or just gotten smarter about picking his victims. Whether he lived at home so Claire could keep an eye on her wayward darling.

Reggie had blamed himself. Burgess believed that at a certain point, whatever the family circumstances, a person had to take responsibility for his own life and stop blaming others. But he also knew too well how much harm a toxic family could do. Something the public didn't always understand was that toxic families weren't confined to the poor side of town. It wasn't just welfare moms, alkie dads, and trailer trash who fucked up their kids. Toxic families could drive Mercedes and their kids could go to Waynflete or Exeter or St. Paul's. The socially prominent were as good, if not better, at destroying their children or raising a new generation of predators.

And now Joey had been out surveying the land that would someday be his.

Burgess printed out some relevant bits of Joey's information and put them in the file. Not even a confirmed homicide yet and the binder was already fat with reports. Time to do the chore he'd promised Clay he'd handle. He picked up the phone and called Claire. She answered on the second ring, stabbing an anxious, slightly breathless, "Claire Libby," into his ear.

"It's Sergeant Burgess," he said, "Portland police." She knew damned well who he was. He could have just said "Joe," but he wanted to keep this formal.

"What's happened? Is Joey okay?" she asked.

"Any reason he shouldn't be?" When she didn't respond, he moved into the purpose of his call. "I'm calling about Reggie."

"I'm not interested in hearing anything about Reggie, Joe.

You know that perfectly well."

Even under these circumstances, Burgess was fascinated by her anachronistic use of "perfectly well." Claire might have been her own mother, from whom she had undoubtedly learned that locution. "Then it's your good fortune that this is just about the last time, Claire."

Shifting to his formal "deliver the bad news to the family" voice, he said, "I'm sorry to inform you that your ex-husband, and Joey's father, Reginald Libby, is dead by drowning. His body was taken from the harbor yesterday morning. The department will notify you when the medical examiner releases the body, so funeral arrangements can be made. Please accept my sincere condolences." He barely got those last words out. Such calm, serious, dignified words, when what he felt was closer to a screaming agony that Reggie was dead, and deep disgust at having to use them to deliver news to someone as indifferent as Claire.

She surprised him with silence. He'd expected a brusque brush-off and a click. Instead, she said nothing, though he could hear breathing so he knew she was still there. "I don't understand," she said finally. "You're telling me Reggie's dead? And the medical examiner is involved?"

"Yes, Claire, I am." She had been so sure his call was about Joey that she hadn't listened to his words, which made him wonder what Joey was up to these days.

Another long silence. He tried to imagine what she was doing. Pacing the room? Pouring herself a drink? Raising her fists in silent celebration? Certainly not any acknowledgment of his own loss. He'd expected the usual Claire Libby brush-off, a quick "Thank you and goodbye." This hesitation was puzzling.

After a while he heard the clink of ice in a glass, the audible slosh of liquid. "Oh dear," she said. "Oh dear." He heard the glass lift, the clink and the swallow. Imagined her standing in her elegant living room. Dark wood. Soft colors. The cut crystal glass. "How did he die, Joe?"

"It appears to be a drowning, Claire. We found him floating in the harbor."

"What about Joey?" she said. "Does Joey know? Have you told him yet?"

"The only number I have for him is this one, Claire. So no, I haven't told him yet. I'd like to, though. It seems like it should come from me. Can you give me his cell number?"

"No," she said. Too loud. Too anxious. Delivering a clear message—she didn't want him anywhere near Joey—that much, she was too rattled to censor. Another clink, rattle, sip. "No, don't bother," she said, sounding more like herself. "Don't. I'll tell him when he comes back . . . uh . . . when he comes in tonight. I'll tell him."

"When do you expect him?" Burgess pushed her a little. "I could come by then. I know they weren't close, but it's still sad news."

"I don't know when he'll be home. Late," she said.

"Have him call me when he gets in. It doesn't matter if it's late. I'd like to talk with him," Burgess said, and gave his number. He could tell by the swish and tinkle of ice and the audible swallow that she wasn't writing it down.

He was about to ask her to read the number back when she pulled in a breath. "Just tell me . . ." Burgess waited. His job was predicting people's behavior, and he knew this woman, but he couldn't tell whether he was going to get "Did he suffer?" or "Does this mean Joey will get the land?" In the end, she only said, "Never mind. Thanks for the call," like he was some functionary, not Reggie's friend, and put down the phone.

Moving along, he did a search on Star Goodall. She might be just your run-of-the-mill whack job, all bluster and bombast, but he'd be negligent if he didn't take those letters seriously.

From the paper trail, it seemed that if Ms. Goodall was a witch, as Clay said she claimed to be, she was no smiling Glinda of the sparkling dress. She was more like the wicked witch, though in a low-key way. Her record was dotted with the signs of a chronic complainer, a bad neighbor, and a terrible driver. He printed out her information, put her number and address in his notebook, snapped it shut and stowed it in his pocket. He raised his arms, and stretched. He'd skipped breakfast and lunch, and now dinner, and he was finally beginning to feel hungry.

He checked his watch. After eight. It was a long shot, but he picked up the phone and dialed his home number. Chris answered on the first ring. A single word. "Joe."

"I know it's late," he said, "but it's a Saturday night and you're answering the phone, so maybe you're free. I'm thinking of steak and red wine. Have you eaten?"

"Just sitting here by the phone, buffing my nails and hoping someone would call."

"I'm lousy at relationships," he said. "Told you that from the start. But I would very much like the pleasure of your company."

"Come get me," she said. "That will give me time to get all gussied up."

All gussied up. That was the kind of thing she said. He drove home through a city with the deserted look it got on weekends when a lot of people went out of town. No one around but a handful of tourists, a pod of the prosperous heading toward one the best restaurants, and the bad guys. He'd spotted three potential troublemakers before he was out of downtown, pleased to see a patrol car already watching one of them. You did that on patrol. Drive around, giving the "watch yourself" nod or the "I see you," wave to the bad guys. Let 'em know you were there.

He took the time to change into a clean shirt and tie. His green shirt. Her favorite. His new jacket. He checked the mirror. My, but he was a fashion plate. It was the scar that did it, he figured. That and the salt and pepper hair made him look devilish.

Chris came out of the spare room, where she'd been checking herself in the full-length mirror. She was wearing heels. A dash of lipstick. Something blue, discreetly low-cut, and clingy. All it took was something blue for her to be gussied up. Blue made her cobalt eyes vibrantly alive, brought out the honey in her long hair. Heels did what they always did for well-built women, made her chest stand out and her legs look like a million bucks.

"You look so good." He shook his head in appreciation. "Guess I lucked out tonight."

Her smile started small, then took over her whole face. "I thought maybe we were done for." A knockout punch to his heart. She opened her arms.

His throat tightened as he stepped forward to meet her. Knee deep in damage and death, when sorrow had its claws deep into him and he was feeling hard-edged and mean, she had a way of sneaking past all that and touching him.

CHAPTER EIGHT

"We still going out?" she asked, a warm, vibrant voice in the darkness. "Because now I'm hungrier than ever."

He turned on the light and propped himself up on his elbow. She looked so lovely cocooned in the blue sheet, honey hair tangled, eyes heavy-lidded. She wore a "cat that just ate the canary" smile and Burgess didn't mind being the canary. Given time, if this case or two needy kids didn't send him into a cut-and-run tailspin, this relationship might have a chance.

It wouldn't take a detective, studying the trail of clothes leading from the bedroom door, to understand what had happened here. The bedside clock said nine.

"You're still hungry?" he said, putting a hand on the sheet where it covered her breast.

She slapped his hand away. "Not that kind of hungry, Joe Burgess. Steak and red wine hungry. Isn't that what I was promised? Why I got all gussied up?"

"I like you better like this," he said.

"Well, I am not going to a restaurant dressed like this. And anyway, that's a new dress lying there on the floor and I've been dying for a chance to wear it." She jabbed him with her elbow. "So get up and get dressed, before all the restaurants close and we have to settle for takeout burgers."

"You got a chance to wear it. It looked great on you. Look what it made me do."

"Jerk." She shoved back the sheet and reached down to the

floor for some underpants. They were blue, too, with a wide band of lace.

He folded his arms under his head and watched her dress. Blue bra. Blue slip. Blue dress. She picked up one stiletto-heeled shoe and brandished it at him. "You'd better get cracking, mister, because I am armed and dangerous."

Reluctantly, he shoved back the covers. He should shower, wash off the sex, their sweat, her perfume. It would be the civilized thing to do. But it was late, that would make them later, and anyway, he liked wearing it. It was good and where Reggie's death was taking him was not good at all. Better to hang on to the good as long as he could. Any minute, the phone could ring and he'd get hauled out into the night to deal with someone's bad news.

He pulled his clothes back on, shirt still crisp, wrinkle-resistant pants doing their job. Tied his shoes. Checked his pocket for a wallet. Badge. Gun. Cuffs. Radio. Cell phone. The radio, cuffs, and gun could stay in the truck, but they were his version of the American Express card. He didn't leave home without them. The one time he did would be when he got a call that there was an emergency he needed to roll up on NOW. And he'd have to tell dispatch, "Sorry, I gotta stop at home and get my stuff." Every time he let down made it that much harder to hold the younger guys to a standard. So his gear came along. Even on a date with a lovely woman, he went prepared for the worst.

At nine-thirty on a Sunday night, the steak place was almost deserted. The hostess seated them almost grudgingly, despite the sign on the door that said they were serving for another hour. The wait-staff behaved better. Almost immediately, a smiling young woman was there, asking if they wanted a drink. Chris grinned and ordered a girly pink Cosmo, what she called "a martini with a tutu." He got a Manhattan with more of the bourbon he'd been craving all day. Where Clay's had been medicinal, this was for pleasure.

They ordered steak. Medium. Retro wedges of iceberg lettuce with blue cheese dressing and baked potatoes. Yes to butter and sour cream. Enough cholesterol to cause cardiac arrest. Chris didn't mention his weight, or exercise, or healthy eating. When the waitress brought a basket of bread, they fell on it like wolves, Chris no more restrained than he. It was one of the things he liked about her. If she was hungry, she ate. If something was on her mind, she said so. If there was something she needed, she asked for it. After a lifetime of liars and crazies and cheaters, of posers and bad guys and whores, this frank and honest woman was a continuing source of wonder. And if lately she'd been a little difficult, it was nothing to how he could be when he got his teeth into a case.

When their steaks were only some discarded bits and pools of pink juice on their plates, he set down his fork and knife. "About the kids," he said, "Chris. I know you care about them. I just don't think . . ."

At the same moment, she leaned toward him. "The autopsy this morning . . . Joe . . . was it awful?"

"I don't . . ." he began.

"Let's not . . ." she said. She put a finger to her lips. "Not now, Joe. That's so complicated. Right now, we're having such a good time. We're lucky to get a time like this in the middle of a case. I'd just like to enjoy it. Think about the good time we just had, and are having, and leave it at that. Would you mind very much?"

He wouldn't mind at all. He was just trying to be a good sport. Didn't women always complain that the problem with guys was they wouldn't talk? There he went. Doing what he hated people to do. Treating Chris like a generic. Putting her in the everywoman box. He put a hand over hers where it rested on the table. "This is nice."

"They have good cheesecake," she said.

"Only if you promise that tomorrow you won't say I'm too big for my britches."

Her smile was like a sunrise. First, a hint, then it grew until it spread like a glow over her face. He realized she hadn't been smiling much lately. Neither of them had. It was just a fact of life. They each got so busy with work and the everyday of their lives that they didn't pay attention to each other. Like a couple old farts.

"We could share," she said.

As they were each eyeing the last bite, he felt his phone vibrate in his pocket. It could wait, he thought. If it was a real emergency, they'd call again.

"I hope Terry and Michelle are having a good time," she said, stabbing the last bite. "It's not easy being involved with a cop. If your generic civilian guy is good at not talking about things, you cops have raised it to a fine art. As solid and opaque as a wall."

"Hey," he said. "I thought we weren't going to talk about the bad stuff tonight."

"It just slipped out." She looked away.

His phone vibrated again. Had to check it. Stan's number. "Excuse me. I should take this." He cupped his hand over the phone. "Burgess."

Stan's voice, shaky and desperate, exploded in his ear. "Jesus, Joe, it's hit the fan. You've gotta help me."

"Hold on." Burgess looked at Chris. "Stan's in trouble. I'll take it outside." He tossed his credit card on the table and hurried out into the parking lot. "Okay. I can talk. What's up?"

"Long story," Stan said. "Short version is that wild woman I told you about's accusing me of breaking and entering and attempted rape and I got two Westbrook cops here with plans to haul my ass to jail."

"Where are you now?"

"Outside her house. Sitting in a patrol car."

Burgess fumbled out his notebook and opened it on the hood of the car. The air had a distinct chill now and the hood was damp. He clicked his pen. "What's her name and address?" Stan gave them in a shaky voice. "You alone or are they sitting on you?"

"Alone. Jesus, Joe. This is so fucked up. She invites me over, then pulls this. Can you come?"

"I'm out to dinner with Chris. I'll take her home and head on over. Can you stall them for a while?"

"Hey," Stan said, "they're pretty good guys. Just doing what they gotta do."

"Gimme the short version."

"Her husband, goddammit! Fuckin' gorilla came at me with fists like hams." Stan's voice was strangled and incoherent.

So Stan's wild woman was married. Stan had that kind of luck, especially when he was thinking with the one-eyed guy. Burgess cut him off, "Control it, Stan. Take a breath. Get your head straight and try again, okay. You don't sound like a cop, you sound like an idiot."

There was a long pause, then Stan said, "Thanks, Dad. I forgot."

"Quit screwing around, and give me the story."

"Okay. This girl. Lorraine Barton, the one I was with on Friday night, she calls me up, okay? Says we had such a great time the other night, can I come over, let's do it again. I'm no fool, at least, that's what I was thinking then, so I say sure. She says maybe she'll be in the shower, so if she doesn't answer the door, I should just let myself in. When I get over there, I knock, and she doesn't answer. I try the door. It's locked. She's said let myself in, so I figure she's just forgotten. Her apartment's on the first floor, so I go around back. The slider's unlocked."

Stan grabbed a breath. "Easy, Stan. Easy," he said. Stan was a sharp detective, but it was hard for anyone, finding himself on the other side of the table. This was one time when Stan's impulsive nature wouldn't serve him well. Better rein him in before he did something stupid. "Remember, you got cops there wondering did you do what she said. Their job is to take her at her word until they have reason to think otherwise. So be sure of what you're saying, okay. Don't shoot from the hip. Be sure. Be slow. Be careful. I know you want to explain it all to them, make them see how it was all a misunderstanding, right?"

"Right." Stan's breathing was still ragged.

"Don't do it." Burgess said. "Okay, give me the rest." He was already thinking who he knew in Westbrook PD that he could call. Had come up with a name.

"I hear the shower running, like she said, so I go into the bathroom, tell her it's me, so she won't be scared. She pulls back the curtain. Man, she's wet and naked and smiling and she is so hot." Stan's words tumbled over each other in his haste. "I'm working on my belt when the goddamned apartment door opens and some guy yells, 'Lorraine, honey? You here?' Suddenly she's screaming, 'In here, Wes. In the bathroom. There's a man in here.' This big gorilla charges into the bathroom and takes a swing at me. I hit back and the next fuckin' thing I know, she's calling 9-1-1, telling fuckin' dispatch I've broken into her apartment and attacked her."

This was bad. "Stan, tell Westbrook patrol to take you down to the PD, put you in the conference room. That's all you say, Stanley, understand. Don't try to explain or talk your way out of this. Just wait 'til I get there. You got that? I'll call Timmy Collins, give him a heads up."

Stan didn't say anything.

"I'm on my way, Stan. Okay?"

"But Joe, I think maybe, if I can just explain this—"

Burgess cut him off. "Have you got that, Stanley?"

The words went home. "Yes, Sergeant. I got that. Sir."

"Good. Hang on to it. One more thing. The guy who came through the door. You know who he is?"

"I do now. Her effing husband. Wesley Barton."

"You *knew* she was married?"

"She said she was divorced. She wasn't wearing a ring."

"And you met her where?"

"Bar in the Old Port."

"Alone or with friends?"

"Alone."

"Okay. Sit tight. I'm on my way."

He made a quick call to Sergeant Tim Collins, out in Westbrook, who said he was on it, then he called Lieutenant Melia. Stan would be mad that he did, but if they couldn't fix this and Stan got arrested, Melia would be beyond pissed if he was left out of the loop. He was a good lieutenant who backed his men when he could. But he was also seriously by-the-book. If they handled this right, Melia might be okay with it. Put egg on Melia's face or Cote on his ass, and young Stanley would be back on patrol and Burgess short a good detective.

Melia went from sleepy "Hello" to staccato questions in less than two seconds. A CID lieutenant got used to being interrupted. "Keep me up on this, Joe," he said, and was gone. Back to grab some sleep before the next interruption.

Returning to the table, he told Chris, "Stan's in trouble. I've got to go bail him out."

"Woman trouble?" she said.

"What else? Woman trouble that's just gotten him arrested."

"I guess I shouldn't say he deserves it, because I don't know. But Stan's an idiot about women."

"Thinks with his . . . uh . . ." Burgess found himself embarrassed.

96

"Pecker," she suggested. "Dick. Cock. Prick. Johnson. I'm not a virgin, Joe. I'm a nurse. There isn't much I haven't heard."

He signed the check and helped her into her coat. She slipped an arm through his. "I like it that you try to protect me. That there's still a lot of old-fashioned gentleman about you." She rested her head on his shoulder. "Our timing might have been a little off, but now I'm seeing that it was a good thing we went to bed first and then went out to dinner. Think how disappointed I'd be if I was counting on a romantic encounter when we got home?"

"Sorry about this," he said. "I was kind of hoping for *another* romantic encounter when we got home. But I need Stan at work, not in jail. And it doesn't look good for the department."

"Meaning a load of manure from Captain Cote?"

"Exactly."

He opened the car door and watched her do that cool thing women in dresses did, where they sat, then lifted their legs and swiveled. Chris told him she'd learned it from her mother. It was supposed to let you get into a car gracefully without show-ing your slip. Until he'd noticed her putting on the blue one tonight, he hadn't thought women wore slips anymore. Cops dealt with populations more likely to be confused about wear-ing clothes at all than on choosing proper and elegant undergar-ments. But it was graceful, something about that moment when Chris's feet in their sexy shoes sat together on the pavement, and then her legs lifted and rose, and her skirt slipped up just a tad, giving a quick peek at her thighs, and he closed her into his car. How could such a minor thing be both erotic and familiar and domestic?

He shook his head, then walked around and started the engine. She put a hand on his thigh, warm through the cloth. They'd driven halfway home in silence before she said, "Maybe you can wake me when you get home."

CHAPTER NINE

Burgess stopped to talk with Sergeant Collins before going to see Stan. Collins, albino pale with rusty hair and rusty freckles, grinned and shook his head. "Your boy fell right into the honey trap, Joe."

Burgess dropped into a chair. "That's how it sounds. Bring me up on it, Timmy."

Collins shook his head. "Sorry to get you messed up in this. Perry had panicked and called you before we could get him out of there and tell him the straight story. Then I couldn't get him to shut up and keep his head down. He kept telling me he was a cop. Like once wasn't enough. Like we don't try and look after each other. My guys had already called, given me the heads up. I was on my way out there when you called. I figured we'd let him cool off a little before we cut him loose. Seems like the kid could use a lesson in judgment."

A little harsh, but Collins was probably right. Stan's good judgment about bad guys, strong interview skills, and great cop's instincts for things that didn't seem right were noticeably absent in his personal life. Funny, too, how he and Collins could think of Stan, now in his thirties, as a kid. It showed how old they were getting. Collins didn't seem to age, though. He'd looked pretty much the same for a decade. He just got a little more dried out, wrinkling like a forgotten apple in a fruit bowl. He'd kept his sense of humor, which was important. It was too easy to get sour on the job.

"So you know the lady?"

"Oh, man," Collins laughed. "That is no lady. She's a hot little piece of trouble. She and her husband Wes have a kinky sex thing going where they stimulate their appetites by bringing other people into the mix. Wes is a long-distance truck driver. When he's on the road, he nails whatever he can while Lorraine goes out and picks up other guys. She brings them home, they have sex, and she videotapes the whole thing. When he gets back from a trip, Wes tells her what he's done, then she and Wes watch the tape. That gets them all worked up and they go at it like raccoons in heat, hitting and thumping, screaming and smashing things. Leave a recorder under the window when Wes is home, you could get the soundtrack for a porn flick."

Collins shook his head, his expression half wonder, half disgust. "We can usually tell when Wes is home by the number of complaints from the neighbors. They don't give a shit who sees them, either. Once she ran out buck naked into the parking lot and he fucked her up against a parked car while three little kids on tricycles watched. That didn't go down too well with the neighborhood, though the lady who reported it took the time to tell me Wes had a ding dong came near to his knees."

Collins rolled his eyes. "Next time they started up outside, the old guy next door turned his hose on 'em."

"Stan likes them hot," Burgess said, "but maybe, getting burned a little, he'll be more careful next time. You get the video?"

"We weren't going to leave that behind, not with a cop involved," Collins said. "Perry's been watching it in the interview room. Last I checked, he was looking a little sick. I guess what happened tonight was Wes told Lorraine he was back tomorrow, and neglected to update her when things changed."

Collins flipped a photo out of a file. The husband was huge, six-foot-five easy, and built like a refrigerator with tattoos. "He may not think so, but Perry's lucky Lorraine called 9-1-1 and we had a guy in the neighborhood. Otherwise, you'd be over at the ER watching your boy get put back together, unless it was the morgue."

He put the photo away, flipped out another. The woman was wearing a tank top cut just a whisper above her nipples, cleavage like a mail slot, and cut-offs that left no doubt she'd had a Brazilian. She had full, dark, country singer hair and half a pot of gloss on puffy, collagened lips. It looked like Tammy Faye had donated the eyelashes.

"Seems like Wes doesn't mind what she does when he's away, but he goes ape shit if he finds someone with her when he gets home. He's put one or two guys in the hospital. She was probably just making trouble with that call, but she might have been trying to save your boy's life. He's a scrapper but he's pretty beat up."

He shook his head. "Whatever happened to the good family man? Seems like too many cops getting into trouble these days." Collins pushed back his chair, stood, and handed Burgess some keys. "I had the guys drop his car at his house, figured you'd want to drive him home, maybe give him a piece of your mind."

"I'll do that." Burgess stood, too. "Thanks for the help, Timmy. Young Stan is a work in progress. He's a good cop. Turning out to be a really good detective, he's pulled a couple rabbits out of hats. But when it comes to women . . . ?" He shrugged. "I'm thinking of putting a clothespin on it. At least make him tie a string around it, maybe remind him to take it easy the next time he thinks it's a good idea to whip it out. You know the old joke about the erection so big it drains all the blood from the brain?" Collins nodded. "That's Stan."

They walked down the hall, stopping outside a door labeled "Interview 1." Burgess looked through the glass. Sitting in the interview room, his shirt torn, his lip swollen, blood in his nose, and one eye black, Stan looked more like an Old Port brawler than one of Portland's finest. He was staring, slump-shouldered, at a blank TV screen.

Collins opened the door. "All right, Detective. On your feet. Your ride is here."

Stan stood, grimacing, looked past Collins, and met Burgess's eye. He turned like he was considering running away, but the room only had one door. Hauling himself together, he straightened his shoulders, tried to fix his clothes, then gave up and shambled toward Burgess, unsteady and pathetic. Maybe this was what had driven Burgess to choose life as a solitary man. The risks of passion seemed too great.

He put a hand on Stan's arm. "Say thank you to Sergeant Collins, Stan."

Stan straightened up and put out a hand. "Thank you, Sergeant. I really appreciate this. Appreciate it even more if that tape could disappear."

"What tape?" Collins said.

Stan's battered face wore a lopsided smile as he followed Burgess out to the car.

When they were rolling, Burgess asked, "You need a doctor?"

"No way."

"You don't want to be a hero," Burgess said. "I need you working this week, not home in bed moaning."

"You ever known me to stay home in bed moaning?" Perry snapped. "I ever let you down, Joe?"

"Tonight."

"Fuck!" Perry's fist slammed against the dash. He winced as blood oozed out along his torn knuckles. "You tell Vince?"

"You know I did. Timmy Collins hadn't stepped up for you, can you imagine how pissed he'd be if one of his police was in jail for banging some married woman and getting in a fight with her hubbie, and he was the last to hear?"

Catching Perry's sulky look, Burgess said, "Like it or not, the food chain is what it is, and we have to live with that. You want to keep your private life private, keep it clean."

"Shit, Joe. You don't think I meant for this to happen?"

"What I think is that you're an adrenaline junkie like the rest of us. You keep it tuned up by being a bad boy and walking on the edge, only this time, you slipped." Burgess stopped at a red light. "Look, we're all human . . ." The phone in his pocket buzzed. He'd forgotten to take it off vibrate. He pulled it out. "Burgess."

"You've definitely got a homicide," Dr. Lee said.

"It's after midnight on a Sunday," Burgess said. "I thought you had a wife and a family." The light turned green. He went through it, turned into a convenience store lot, shoved the truck into park. This was the news he'd been hoping he wouldn't get.

"You're answering your phone and it doesn't sound like I woke you," Lee countered. "Someone at the lab had some free time, and I was curious, so I asked her to run some tests. Went by and looked at some things myself."

"I appreciate it," Burgess said, which he did and didn't. Like he'd told Cote, they had to treat this like a suspicious death. But like he'd told Clay, what he wanted was to close this and get on with grieving. "So what have we got?"

"That bruising was pre-mortem. And the water in his lungs? It had soap scum and it was chlorinated. Your buddy drowned in a bathtub."

When Burgess didn't respond, Lee said, "I know you were hoping for an accident. Maybe you want to think hard about whether you should work this case."

Now Burgess found his voice. "Would you?"

"What do you think, Joe?"

Lee had spent too long around cops. He'd gotten in the habit of countering a question with a question. Or maybe that was how MEs were, too. "You would hang on to it," he told Lee. "Because you wouldn't trust anyone else."

"You might be right," Lee said, a tinge of amusement in his voice, like he enjoyed a nocturnal game of verbal ping-pong. "You might be wrong. We're not all as tenacious as you. I'll fax you my report in the morning. We've still got toxicology to do. Slides to look at. More stuff to come. But you've definitely got a suspicious death here, and I'd say it's more than likely a homicide. An accidental drowning where someone panicked and dumped the body in the ocean doesn't explain those bruises. Or why he was fully dressed except for shoes."

Burgess heard Lee draw a breath and then the ME sent the little plastic ball ponging back across the table. "Over to you, Joe. Good night and good luck."

"Thanks. I guess." Burgess figured tomorrow was soon enough to tell Vince about this. Not a bad thing to let the lieutenant get some sleep. Some nights he got little to none. Some nights none of them slept. He pulled back out onto the empty street.

"What was that about?" Stan said.

"Reginald Libby. ME says it looks like a homicide. He drowned in a bathtub."

"Fuck that," Stan said. "A bathtub?"

"That's what the water in his lungs says. And he's got bruises on his back and the base of his neck, like someone put a knee in the middle of his back and held him under."

"That's ugly, Joe. But why? Reggie was just a harmless street guy. Someone wanted to kill him, there are a lot simpler ways than that."

"Unless they wanted to make it look like an accident. If it was supposed to look like Reggie got intoxicated and accidentally toppled into the harbor. He was a disposable human being. Why expect the ME to take a hard look?"

"Still doesn't make sense," Stan protested. "Why kill Reggie?"

"Hey, you're the detective."

"Thought I was the screwup."

"Reggie's brother said he'd been working. Had some money stashed in his room. A thousand or more. I didn't find it when I searched and we didn't find it with the body, unless it's in the lining of his coat or something. I'll see what Wink's come up with. He was waiting for the clothes to dry."

"Money's always a motive. But for who?" Stan shifted on his seat and groaned. "Man, I am hurting. Are we working tomorrow?"

"It is tomorrow. Past tomorrow." He pulled up in front of Stan's building, a pleasant-looking, well-maintained three-unit house on a quiet street, and stopped. It didn't look like the right place for a guy like Stan. He ought to have been in a sleek singles complex with a workout room and a pool. Stan had moved in during a brief bout of domesticity and been too busy or unmotivated to leave when his girlfriend did.

Stan stayed slumped in his seat, so inert Burgess thought he'd fallen asleep. He put his hand on Stan's shoulder and rocked him gently. Stan snorted and came awake, full alert and fists up until he recognized Burgess. "Where are we?"

"In front of your house. Time for you to put your jammies on and get some beauty sleep."

Stan ran an absent hand over his face, his fingers exploring the tender mouth, blood-crusted nose. Swollen eye. His hand dropped to his lap. "Vince is gonna be pissed."

"It happens." Burgess shrugged. "Everybody makes mistakes."

"Not like this, they don't."

"Don't flatter yourself," Burgess said. "Everybody screws up. If they're lucky, the good-luck fairy, or another cop, or pure chance, bails them out. If they're unlucky, they may end up fighting to save their job. That puts you among the lucky ones. Try to remember that, okay. Maybe think twice next time, use what you know about judging people to make choices in your personal life, not just your professional one. And pay it back by cutting someone else a break some day when they need it."

"I'll bet you never screwed up like this."

"You'll never know. Now get out of my car. I need to get some sleep, too."

"You working tomorrow . . . today?"

"I'm working. Go upstairs. Take four Advil and a hot shower and see if you can convert yourself into something that looks professional. I don't want you dragging around 109 looking like a cat's plaything. Call me when you get up and I'll fill you in. We can sit down with Wink, go over the file, work out some strategies."

"Wink have a home or does he just hang under the counter like a bat?"

Burgess had forgotten that today, Monday, was a holiday. The politically incorrect celebration of the arrival of Europeans on the North American continent. The "discovery" of America. The weatherman was promising mild temperatures. Another perfect day for leaf-peeping and family outings. A day when Wink, who actually did have a wife, though he rarely mentioned her, should be home, relaxing. When Chris's face, so happy earlier this evening, would be sad as he dressed and left. It didn't always help that he'd met her during a homicide investigation. She knew what he did and how dedicated he was. That didn't keep her from being human.

The bay would be quiet. Everyone taking the day off who could. It would be an excellent day for sitting down with his notes, and Reggie's clothes, and the stuff he'd taken from Reggie's room, and seeing what it all had to tell him. A good day for trying harder to tie down Reggie's last day.

It was clear that he would have to open the box of demons in case Reggie had put something in there. Opening that box was best done in daylight. Sitting at his desk at this time of night, the demons could get him, too. He wanted to keep their past as much in the past as possible, not open himself up to memories. Sometimes just a whiff of rotting vegetation or a car backfiring across town was enough. With the crippling suddenness of a stroke, he'd be lost to these times and fully back in those. He did not want to go there. But the box was waiting.

He took the box into the conference room, snapped on the too-bright lights, and spread out the contents. Several of those black letters from Star Goodall. Paperwork about his disability and his many hospitalizations. Letters. Photographs of Reggie and Claire in happier times, and pictures of Joey at every stage. At the bottom—demons. Dozens of photographs of the horrors they'd seen, the wallpaper inside Reggie's head since he was nineteen. Grotesque, God-awful scenes of death. And at the bottom of that stack, The Boy.

The Boy was a little one-legged Vietnamese boy they'd found standing in an abandoned village, leaning on his crutch, waiting patiently for someone to return. No one was going to be coming back. The VC had killed them all. Reggie had given the boy some water and then some food, and for the rest of the afternoon, the boy had stuck to him like glue. When they left the village a day later, The Boy had come along, hopping along like a little cricket with his crutch and his one sandaled foot.

Nobody knew what to do with him, so they'd let him tag along. Back at camp, he'd stuck by Reggie's side and slept beside him at night. It had gone on like that, the brass making plans to find someplace to send the child, the realities of war interfering, until The Boy had become almost a part of the landscape. A week passed, then two. The Boy would wait for them when they were on patrol, his bright little face by the perimeter for their return, his high voice trilling, "Reggie," as they marched in.

Until they were gone two days. Then The Boy couldn't wait. When he saw them coming, he dodged past the sentry and took a shortcut across the field to meet them. For security, the camp was ringed with mines. One way in, one way out. Even as Reggie and the rest of them were screaming, "Boy! No! No!" the little crutch came down on a mine. In Reggie's box of demons, he had photographs of The Boy's head, hand, leg, and the remnants of the crutch. The hand and leg looked like dirty red rags.

CHAPTER TEN

Going home, he detoured past Reggie's place. It was a habit he'd had for years. A way of checking up on Reggie, making sure he was okay. When he wasn't tangled up with his demons, Reggie had been a good sounding board, and straight or not, had helped remind Burgess why he'd chosen the path he'd taken. The habits of decades die hard.

Despite the ungodly hour and the night's chill, Jim sat on the steps, huddled in a worn quilt, smoking. He didn't seem surprised when Burgess got out of the truck. Just patted the step beside him and offered the bottle.

"No, thanks," Burgess said, settling down beside him. "I'm working."

It was tempting. Something about the quiet darkness and sitting here so close to the last place he'd been with Reggie, but he'd already gotten one buzz on out at Clay Libby's farm and another at dinner with Chris. He didn't think his system was up to any more. Better to just get home and grab some sleep. He'd be heading home soon. This was a stop, not a visit.

"I miss him, you know?" Jim said. "He's only gone what, two, three days, and it seems like forever. Reggie was just always there for people. He'd got a kind word or some advice. Sometimes, nights like this when I couldn't sleep, he'd just sit out here with me. Not saying anything much. Just here and that was enough."

Jim stared up at the sky, where some clouds were scudding

across a sickle moon. "You know how people think of us, Joe. Dirty winos. Useless street people. Like we're not as human as them." The quilt rose and fell with his shrug. "Reggie could make me feel like I still mattered. I'd be down and he'd say, 'Jim, you still got family.' Which, I've gotta be grateful, I do."

There was a rustle as he sipped from the bag. The younger guys didn't bother to hide their bottles, but for the older guys, like Jim, it was a nod toward propriety. "You know, some of the guys have been wondering is there going to be a service or something. Whether his family's going to do that for him. We'd like to pay our respects."

"When I know, you'll know," Burgess said. He'd know, since it looked like it would to be up to him and Clay to make it happen. He let some time pass, then said, "The guy across the hall from Reggie, what's his name, Kevin? Tell me about him."

"Oh, Kev's okay."

"Okay's not very helpful, is it, Jim? And it's pretty lukewarm."

Burgess debated whether to give Jim some version of the truth. Whether Jim could keep it to himself. Decided it was okay either way. It might not be such a bad thing if the story got around, if people on the street started wondering about Reggie. Sometimes the invisible people, the disposable ones whom the better situated tried to ignore or really didn't see, noticed a lot.

"I'm starting to think what happened to Reggie might not be an accident." He let that percolate, then repeated his question. "So, this guy Kevin. Who is he?"

"I don't know. He hasn't been around very long," Jim said. "Comes from down Massachusetts somewhere. I don't know much about him. He kinda keeps to himself, except he and Reggie were sorta friends. I think they worked together."

"Oh, yeah. Reggie's work. You remembered anything about that? Where he was working? Who he was working for?"

"Nope. Sorry, Joe. Reggie was kind of secretive about that." His arm moved and the bag rustled. "He never said why. I thought maybe he didn't want the rest of us going after his job."

"Secretive? Like how?"

"Like I asked him coupla times where he was working, thinking maybe there might be something for me, and he just changed the subject. Same thing when I asked was he getting paid decent. Or how he got that job. Because, you know, I wouldn't mind having a job. Make a little money, buy Diane and the grandkids something nice for Christmas. Be a good thing after all they do for me."

"But Reggie wouldn't tell you?" That didn't sound like Reggie. He'd always been so willing to share. But if he'd been working under the table, and from what Clay said about him being paid in cash, it sounded that way, maybe the employer didn't want it to get around and Reggie was just respecting that. Reggie was always respectful of other people's boundaries. Probably because the world his illness forced him to inhabit was so disrespectful of his.

"How long has Kevin been living here?"

Jim looked up at the sky again, considering. "Couple months. I think. Maybe not so long. I get a little vague about time. I think he moved in around the time Reggie came back from his brother's place, because it was on a day that Diane took me along when she took the kids school shopping." He scratched his head. "Funny how I tell time by those kids, huh? But I dunno. It might have been when she was taking 'em Halloween shopping."

"About Reggie's job. Chub said you saw a truck picking him up?" Jim nodded. "You notice any writing on it? Maybe a logo or something?"

"Not that I recall. Just a big gray truck. Double cab. Maybe a couple guys in it. Driver and one other. I dunno. Diane might remember something. She's real observant. My mind . . ." Jim tapped a finger against his head. "It sure isn't like it used to be. I used to be real good with numbers, Joe. You'd never believe it now, but I was."

Burgess had been down this road before. Once Jim got going on his lost life, he'd stay on the subject for hours. It was sad, and people needed listening to, but Burgess had done his share of listening to this story. It was late. If he couldn't get information, he should sleep.

"You notice anything about the driver? Was it always the same man?"

"Sorry, Joe. Like I said. My brain . . ." Jim sounded mournful. Burgess didn't know if it was from missing Reggie or from missing the keen mind he'd once possessed. He'd never been sure whether alcoholics whose minds were affected, those guys who told the same stories over and over, were aware of what they did and couldn't control it or they simply didn't recognize the endless loop of repetition.

"But you think it was a truck with a guy driving. And it picked him up regularly?" Jim nodded. "You see Reggie going to work on Friday?"

"I know I saw him Thursday. I'm not so sure about Friday. Diane might know. I think she was here on Friday to bring me some groceries. She does that. Diane's real good to me. She brought things to Reggie sometimes. She felt sorry because his own kid wasn't nice to him."

"How did she know his son wasn't nice?"

"Oh, she saw him here, once or twice. My Diane, she's got a kind heart. She thought he was real nasty," Jim said, "which he was. Boy treated Reggie like a dog."

So Joey had visited more than once. He definitely had to find Joey and have a talk, however much Claire wanted to keep them apart. Burgess got Diane's full name, her number, and her address. "You said Kevin worked with Reggie?"

"That's what I think." Jim tilted the bottle, lowered it, and studied the sky again. "Maybe you oughta ask Chub. He remembers stuff. Or Kev. Except, I forgot. He's gone. Moved out right after you were here. Soon as that cop was sitting on Reggie's room left, Kev came down with a suitcase and a coupla boxes, some things stuffed in a pillowcase. He waits here for awhile and then a guy comes and picks him up."

"You talk to him?" Burgess asked. "Ask where he was going?"

"I guess I said hey and asked was he moving out. He said yeah. When I asked where he was going, he didn't say. He just stood there, looking down the street, like he was wondering where was his ride. But he never was much for talking. Sometimes he'd answer back if you asked, but you didn't say anything, he wouldn't." Jim's shoulders humped under the quilt. "He didn't think much of us."

"You out here when he was picked up?" Jim made an affirmative noise. "You see who it was? Anyone you recognized? Was it the same truck?"

He realized he was asking too many questions. Jim might seem coherent, but his thoughts tended to go in circles. He had trouble focusing on more than one question at a time. Burgess tried a single question. "You see who picked him up?"

Jim tapped his skull again, like he was gently prodding a thought into place. "I didn't see the guy. He never got out, but the car looked like that fancy one Reggie's kid drives. You know. That red one?"

Damn. He'd checked Joey's records and looked for a phone number, but he hadn't done a registry search. He took out his notebook and wrote that down. Check on vehicles owned by Joey and Claire. His brain was getting as bad as Jim's, and he didn't even have the excuse of alcohol. But that was okay. A detective's notebook was all important. He might get hit by a garbage truck on his way home tonight, but as long as he didn't bleed through the pages, someone else could pick it up, know where he'd been and who he'd talked to, and go right on with the case.

"So Joey's been coming around?" he said.

"Joey. That's Reggie's kid?"

"Yeah. Joey. Big handsome dark-haired kid?"

"He's been here a few times," Jim said. "Once, when Reggie was just back from Clay's place, he came. The kid, I mean. I was thinking it was so nice 'cuz I knew that Reggie and him hadn't been close. Only I guess it didn't go so well. They went up to Reggie's room and I could hear him hollering at Reggie. I couldn't get much of it 'cuz I was sitting out here and they were working on the street up there to the corner. Making a hell of a racket."

Jim gave him a coy look and Burgess realized that whatever Jim knew, it was going to get doled out slowly so Burgess would stay and talk. Even a cop for company was better than nothing when it was late and the bottle was empty, when one of the few people who'd listen to you was gone and you couldn't sleep.

"Tell me what you did hear."

"He said 'Why can't you just let me have it now when it's gonna be mine anyway one of these days?' Then Reggie said something but it was so soft I couldn't hear it, but whatever it was, it made the kid some mad. He said something about 'what Claire wants,' then came slamming down the stairs, got into that car, and peeled out. Didn't look around or anything, just pulled out and took off. Chub was crossing the street and he had to jump out of the way. You ask him, he'll tell you. Chub gets knocked on his ass and that kid flips him the bird, doesn't even slow to see if he's okay. Might be Reggie's kid, but it doesn't seem like there's much of Reggie in him."

"Joey was driving a red car, like the one that picked up Kev yesterday?"

"Yeah. Can't say for sure that it's the same one, though." Jim tapped his skull. "You know, I used to be so good at remembering things. And I was real good with numbers. I ever tell you that?"

"You did, Jim," Burgess said. He was tired. Without the benefit of a cushion of alcohol like Jim had, the wooden step was getting uncomfortable. "You said you thought they worked together. When Reggie went to work, did Kev go, too?"

Jim cleared his throat. "Now that's odd, you know?" he said. "I thought they worked together, but Kev never went in the same time as Reggie. Same truck would come pick him up, Reggie, I mean, but it came later. Not every day, either. So maybe whoever they worked for had two places, Kev worked at one and Reggie at the other."

The quilt shifted as he lifted his shoulders, lowered them again, and tilted up the bottle. Then he made a disgusted sound, shook the bottle, and set it down hard on the step. "I miss him, Joe. You know? It's only been what? Two, three days, and already, it seems like so long. Gonna be an awful long winter without Reggie. He was always good for a chat. Maybe had used some of that bottle money for a pint. Or we'd sit in his room and watch his TV. Play cards. He was easy to get on with, Reggie was. And generous. Not like some. That guy, Kev, now. He was okay to have in the house 'cuz he was quiet and all, and we like to keep this a quiet place. But he never shared nothing. He had a bottle, he drank it all himself. He got a pizza or something, he'd go in his room and close the door."

Jim held up the bottle. "This one, now. He left this behind in his room, still half full. That kinda surprised me, him wasting any liquor. But maybe he was in such a hurry he forgot. He didn't take all his stuff." He tipped the bottle again, snorted in disgust when nothing came out, and set it on the step beside his foot. "Maybe he's coming back. If he is, he'll be disappointed." He looked at Burgess. "You don't have a bottle on you, do you, Joe?"

"I don't think that would go down well with my bosses, Jim, me driving around with a bottle in the truck."

"Probly not." Jim stood and stretched. "Guess I'll call it a night." He clumped up the steps and went inside.

Burgess had a couple of questions about the place. About Kev's room. Figured he'd go inside and take a look. If he saw anything of interest, he could always come back with a warrant. He picked up the bottle, which might well have Kevin's fingerprints on it—people, in his experience, didn't always use their real names—and put it in the Explorer. Then he went quietly inside and up the stairs to where the door of Reggie's room was closed and locked and marked with a police seal.

Kevin's room stood open.

Someone had packed in a hurry. Drawers were pulled out and hangers jumbled on the closet floor. Some paperbacks and magazines, some mostly empty toiletries, and some extremely worn clothes had been left. An old pair of athletic shoes. None of the clothes had anything in their pockets. There was a little tired takeout in the fridge. If any food had been left in the cupboards, it was gone now. There was a blanket but no sheets, pillows but no pillow cases. Nothing under the mattress, taped to the bottom of the dresser drawers or the back of the dresser.

Burgess pulled on gloves and looked through the wastebasket. It was a wasteland indeed. Nothing to suggest an active human life. No mail. Nothing with an address label. No store receipts to provide a date and time. No handwriting or personal notes. A brown paper bag. Two empty red plastic cups which might have meant drinks on two separate occasions or a visitor. Burgess put them in the empty paper bag. The only interesting thing was a confetti of shredded envelope with a piece of a logo in the corner, interesting only because the occupant had taken the time to shred it. He slipped the piece with the logo into his pocket.

He closed the door behind him, and went down the hall to the bathroom. It was small and not too clean and held only a soap-smudged sink with a spotted mirror, a shower, and a toilet. No bathtub. He climbed the creaking staircase to confirm there was no tub on the third floor. Nor was there one on the first. Wherever Reggie had died, it wasn't here.

It was later than late. Time to go home. He went back down the creaky hall and down the steps to the street. Driving home through the quiet city, he felt like an alien visiting from another planet. A dark planet whose inhabitants knew secrets the residents of this planet only imagined as they read novels or chose violence as entertainment when they flicked on their TVs.

Drive down a street at night, you didn't see whether a place needed painting or someone had a nice garden or a new car. You thought about the body hanging in the basement, found by a kid sent down to bring up the laundry. Or the battered grandmother beaten with a baseball bat, alive only because neighbors had smelled the smoke from a burning pan on the stove. Seen close up and personal, with all the smells and bodily fluids, the ugly truths and uglier lies and the painful aftermath for those involved, it wasn't really that entertaining.

He showered quickly and dropped into bed. The clock said three A.M. He'd either get enough sleep to function well tomorrow, or he'd be the lucky recipient of a cheery wake-up from Paul Cote at some outrageously early hour in the morning. Cote had an astonishing knack for calling bright and early on days when Burgess had gone to bed late. So astonishing he'd once or twice driven around the neighborhood before parking at home, just to assure himself that Cote wasn't out there watching.

Just as he was drifting off, Chris snuggled up close. "Don't worry," she whispered. "If he calls, I'm answering. I'll say you're out training for a marathon and I don't expect you back for at least two hours."

He fell asleep with a smile, half-hoping that Cote would call and get that message.

CHAPTER ELEVEN

Chris waited impatiently by the door, tapping her foot, while he made a quick call to bring his lieutenant up to speed. Let him know Stan wasn't in jail and what the ME thought about Reggie's death.

Gina Melia answered the phone with a short, breathless, "Melia." Behind her, high-pitched voices sounded like a playground full of kids engaged in high-volume mayhem. "The twins' birthday," she explained. "It's a madhouse. Feel free to come over and help with crowd control. Vince says he'd rather run a SWAT team than cope with this. Hold on."

She hollered for Vince, then came back on. "Either he's been taken captive or he can't hear me. I'll have him call you back. You home or at 109?"

"Home," he said, "but I'm heading over to 109. He can call my cell when he gets free."

"I was sorry to hear about your friend," she said. "We always hope, don't we."

His throat tightened. "Thanks, Gina."

He hated the automatic grief response that came when people blindsided him with sympathy. Hated it in himself; he understood it in others. And he was grateful for her gesture. She was the perfect cop's wife. Supportive and understanding about the job. Mature enough to know her husband's neglect was not about her, able to put her foot down when she or the twins needed something from Vince and he was too busy to notice.

"There's no rush."

"Good, because even if you were calling with an emergency, I'd tell you to stuff it. One day a year I think I'm entitled to do that, and today's the day."

"No problem. You guys enjoy the birthday."

"While you go to work. I'm not going to ask what Chris thinks about that."

"We going?" Chris said. He nodded, stuck his phone on his belt, and followed her out. His own nod toward civility. They were taking a walk before he went to 109 and ruined the last day of their three-day weekend. A brisk walk around Back Cove and then breakfast.

"I'm having one of those Bismark things," she said. "Jelly filling, sugary dough." She grinned with the zest of a kid, bouncing lightly in her tennis shoes. "Man, I try hard to avoid treats, but sometimes I just feel like indulging."

"Indulge away," he said. "I don't know how I'd like it if you were skinny."

He got her sunrise smile again. She acted like no man had ever liked her as she was before. He wished he didn't believe it, but guys got stuck on super model and movie images of women built like Barbie dolls. He recalled an old joke. One guy telling another about his new girlfriend. "Yeah," the guy said, "she's got a twenty-three-inch waist and a forty-eight-inch chest."

"Wow," the other guy said, "what does she do?"

"Well, with a little help, she can sit up."

The path was crowded with people power-walking, strolling, biking, jogging. Skaters whipped in and out, quick as dragonflies. Toddlers left trails of cereal and crackers for the gulls wheeling overhead. Babies crowed with glee and waved their chubby fists. Dads threw softballs and Frisbees and footballs and kicked soccer balls, while moms wiped mouths and noses and tears and dished out snacks and drinks. It was as though in all those quiet homes last night, Portland's citizens had been resting up for today, then emerged en masse to grab one last good day before the cold moved in.

He and Chris were strollers, holding hands and enjoying the feel of the sun. "Vitamin D," Chris said, turning her face-up. "Twenty minutes a day is all we need."

He tried for a smile. Inside, he churned with anxiety. It was a fact of life—his life—that the first days after a murder were all important. Memories faded, evidence got lost, bad guys had time to cover things up. He didn't know how much time they'd lost before Reggie's body was discovered—probably no more than twelve hours, according to the ME—but now it was two days later and instead of being at his desk, consolidating what he knew and picking the best next paths to follow, he was strolling in the sunshine, acting like he believed Cote's assessment that Reggie's life didn't require a significant response.

His phone rang. Melia. "Vince," he said, "how's the party?"

"Birthday parties are hell," Melia said. "Only good thing I can say about this is that at least, with twins, we only have to do it once a year. What's up?"

"ME says Reggie Libby drowned in a bathtub."

"And when did you learn this?" Melia was an information junkie. Part of his job. The buck stopped at his desk. He briefed the brass; took press conferences when Cote didn't snatch the limelight. He was a good lieutenant, willing to cut his guys slack when they needed it, but lately he'd been edgy, the result of Cote's new push to up their solve rates. Melia was wondering if they were leaving him out of some loop.

"Lee called after midnight. I figured I didn't need to wake you."

"Thanks, I guess," Melia said. "So where are we on this?"

"Pretty much at square one. Lot of leads. Nothing solid."

"You and Stan have a strategy? You called Terry back in?"

Burgess looked around at the crowd of happy people, at Chris, staring at him in shock. "Stan's coming in. I've got a short list of people to see. Once we've sat with it, I'll update you."

"I'm coming in," Vince said.

"Finish the party," Burgess said. "There's nothing that won't wait." Nothing that wouldn't wait because they had nothing. A friend gets killed and Joe Burgess goes rain skipping. He had the sudden urge to hit something. What he ought to hit was himself.

A panting, obese woman with a supersized muffin-top pouring out of too-tight jeans knocked into him so hard he almost dropped the phone. "Hey!" Chris snapped, giving her a dirty look.

The woman squeaked a belated "Sorry" and waddled off.

"You feeling all right, Joe?" Melia asked. "You recently suffered a blow to the head or something?"

"Just trying to be balanced, Vince. Trying to act civilized."

"Comes to homicide, I don't want you civilized." He paused. "I do not want some bleeding-heart reporter saying we ignored this case because the victim wasn't important. See you in an hour."

Burgess decided not to share Cote's assessment.

"Dammit, Joe," Chris exploded as he put the phone away, "why didn't you tell me? You think I want you out here pretending to be having a good time when your mind is totally focused on Reggie? You've known since last night it was no accident? You never thought I'd want to know? Who the hell do you think I am? A possessive little birdbrain who doesn't respect what you do?"

He spread his arms helplessly. "I was just trying not to spoil your whole weekend."

She dragged him off the path and wrapped her arms around

him. "And I love you for it, okay? But when you're with me, I like you *with* me, not ticking off lists in your head." She dropped her arms. "You go work. I'm going to take a long walk, long enough to earn that Bismark, and then I'm going to enjoy every gooey bite of it. Call me later and let me know if you'll be home for dinner."

She patted her chest. "Grown-up." When he didn't move, she said, "I'll be okay, Joe. I came prepared." She pulled an iPod out of her waist pouch and held it up. "Loaded with walking music." As though she'd known their walk would be interrupted. "Go on. Go." She gave him a shove toward the path and strode away.

He went without arguing, skipping his lecture on the risks to women—especially attractive women like her—of going around plugged into some machine that made them oblivious to their surroundings. Like she'd said, she was a grown-up. She didn't need to hear this from him. For all he knew, she had pepper spray and a stun gun in that pouch. She tended to be wonderfully well-prepared.

He called Stan to come in, and went to work, heading not to his desk but to the crime lab, where he left the bags with the bottle and the two plastic cups from Kevin Dugan's trash on the counter and went into the room where Reggie's clothes were drying. The letter from Star Goodall might be dry enough to read. Maybe Reggie had left them some other clues.

He slipped on gloves and started going through the pockets. He found a torn piece of a label listing the ingredients in some chemical product, though without the name of the product. He found a card for a doctor's appointment on the coming Tuesday. He found a scrap of paper with the smudged words ". . . day morning" written in pencil along with a couple of phone numbers. He copied the doctor's name and appointment time, and the phone numbers into his notebook, then returned everything to the pockets. Wink would collect all of this and record it in the evidence log. Reggie's wallet, where he, like Jim, had kept family pictures, was missing. So were his keys and his glasses.

It all left him with more questions than answers. He went back out into the lab. On the counter, Wink had set the cinder-block the divers had taken from the harbor. The rope with its frayed end was still attached. Beside it, in a plastic envelope, were the fragments of fiber they'd found clinging to Reggie's belt. He switched on a brighter light and bent to look at them. Hard to tell without a microscope, but to his eyes, they looked remarkably similar.

Star Goodall's letter was pinned up to dry. He unpinned it and carried it into better light. It was briefer than the one he'd already read, a single paragraph in that striking silver ink:

Alright, Reggie. I am out of patience. You owe me, you and Clay.

I have waited long enough for you to repay me for the harm you did.

I know you've got land and I know the value of that land. When I see you on Friday we can discuss this further. You know what I mean. You know what I want.

Star

Interesting. First he'd heard from a couple sources that Joey was after the land; now it seemed this woman who called herself Star Goodall was interested, too. And she'd met with Reggie on Friday. This past Friday? It meant he needed to talk with Ms. Goodall. Sooner, rather than later, and he needed to read the trust documents Clay had given him. Probably a good idea to learn the name of the surveyor Joey had had out to look at the property, and learn how valuable it really was. Any piece of lakefront property in Maine had value. A large piece with development potential, if that's what this was, could be worth a lot. Was it enough to kill for?

Wink Devlin came in as he was pinning the letter back up. "Thought it was a holiday," Burgess said.

"Not when Lieutenant Melia calls and says we've got a homicide," Devlin said. "And Mrs. Wink thinks some overtime would be nice to pay for a cruise this winter. What have we got?"

"Reggie drowned in a bathtub," Burgess said. "ME says fresh water with chlorine and soap scum."

"And when did we get this exciting information from the ME's office? I didn't think the state crime lab worked on Sundays."

"Lee called last night . . . or early this morning. Guess he was curious and they had someone free, so they ran some tests."

"Lot of MEs would have missed that. Or not bothered to look," Devlin said. "His attitude sometimes needs readjustment but Lee's good. You got somewhere you'd like me to start?"

Burgess considered. "Fingerprints?" he said. "I've got a bottle and some cups here I'm wondering about. Then I'd like to know if those fibers from his belt match the rope on that cinderblock." He stopped. "Where would you start?"

"Those places are as good as any," Devlin said, pulling on some gloves. "You go on upstairs and start detecting. I'll let you know when I have something."

Burgess trudged back to the bay and made copies of a photo he had of Reggie. He found Stan at his desk, going through the file, Stan's face looking like he'd had a close encounter with a two-by-four. "Not much here to go on, is there, Joe? You got a plan?"

"I do. You ready?"

Stan opened his notebook open. "Ready."

"Okay. Right now, we don't even know when Reggie was last

seen alive, and by whom. Jim Fletcher, who lives in the same place as Reggie, thinks it was Thursday, but it might have been Friday. Says his daughter Diane might have noticed Reggie on the Friday. So we need to talk to Diane and see what she knows. Another guy who lives there, Chub Wallis, saw Reggie get into a truck on Thursday—a truck that regularly picks him up for work. We need to know any details that Chub can give about Reggie's job or that truck. Someone needs to talk to the rest of the residents, see if anyone else knows anything." He gave Stan the address, the contact information for Jim's daughter.

"While we're trying to tie down the last time Reggie was seen, it would be a good idea to go to roll call this afternoon, bring them up on this, and see if anyone noticed anything on Friday night, early Saturday morning. A truck, van, or car parked on the waterfront, anything out of the ordinary." Burgess checked his notes. "Coast guard can help us figure out if the body traveled, but first I want to see what Wink learns about that rope and cinderblock. If Reggie was weighted, his body probably didn't travel. But why leave it in such a public place?"

"Not so public," Perry said, "to someone unfamiliar with the waterfront. In the middle of the night, the area around that wharf looks pretty deserted. Or he could have been dumped from a boat. Body was ten, eleven feet down, barely visible at low tide? High tide and the water murky, it might have seemed fine. I'll check NOAA and see what the weather and moonlight were on Friday night."

He ducked his head. "Afraid I wasn't paying much attention to the weather."

"Good thought. Get on to marine patrol, harbor master, the coast guard, see who might have been out Friday night or early Saturday and if they noticed anything."

Stan looked at his notes. "Lotta ground to cover and we've already lost two freakin' days. You calling Terry in?"

"Let's see what Vince says."

Studying Stan's battered face, he wondered if he should send him out, or keep him driving a desk a day or two. Stan was young and the young healed fast. But it didn't make the department look good, sending out a detective who looked like he'd been in a street brawl. He knew he was being influenced by the circumstances. They'd all gone out hurting, cut, stitched, bandaged and bruised, because they were determined not to let the bad guys win. But those wounds were righteous.

But hell, it wasn't like he had a closet full of spare detectives, and Stan was good on the street. He could go from tough to tender in a second, depending on what he needed and who he was dealing with. And he was still close to the street, good at finding people who might have seen something useful.

Even if he could use Stan, he needed Terry. Too much time lost, too many bases to cover. Ask any cop in the city if Sergeant Burgess gave a damn about anyone's personal life and you'd get a cynical laugh or an eye roll. Burgess's reputation as a hard-ass was well earned. At least Terry'd had most of the weekend. He picked up the phone and dialed, thumbing through his notebook as he waited for an answer.

"Kyle, Investigations," a voice said. But it wasn't on his phone. He looked up. Terry Kyle, whippet thin, cold-eyed, and faintly smiling, bent over his desk like a stork. "I thought you'd never call," Kyle said. "That you didn't love me anymore."

"Just trying not to spoil your weekend," Burgess said.

"Yeah, right," Kyle said. "You had a personality transplant while I was away?"

"Let's take this into the conference room."

"Old Burgess is going soft," Kyle told Perry as they followed. "You ever know him to think about someone else's personal life before?"

"He thinks way too much about mine."

"Someone's got to," Burgess said. "You get yourself killed, I've got to start training some bright youngster all over again. I've ordered you a chastity belt. We're giving the key to Vince."

"As long as it's not Cote," Perry said.

"Why? Because he'd have to check twice a day to be sure you were keeping things clean and neat?" Kyle asked. "Vince coming in?"

"On his way."

"This thing is weird," Perry said, as they spread out around the table. "Domestic violence we know. Drugs. Sex. Money. This one, it's all whys. Why would someone want to hurt Reggie? Why drown him? Why a bathtub? Like, what's up with the shoes? He's wearing all his clothes including his jacket but no shoes and socks? And why go to such elaborate lengths? Someone's taking a lot of chances, moving a body around like that."

"Strange cases. That's why they need us," Burgess said. "We don't even know where it happened. There are no bathtubs where Reggie lived."

Melia came in, impeccable as always—blue shirt, striped tie, jacket over his arm. There was a swelling bruise along his cheekbone. "Disputed call in a game of pickup soccer," he said.

He studied Stan's face, shook his head without comment, hung his jacket over the chair, and sat. "Where are we, Joe?"

Burgess summarized the ME's findings and what they knew. "We're still waiting on more tests, but Lee says assume homicide. We don't know what day he was last seen. Lee says he wasn't in the water long, so the body was likely dumped late Friday night or very early Saturday. Beyond that, we've got a string of question marks. Reggie had a job, but no one knows where he worked or who he worked for. His brother, Clay, says Reggie was getting paid cash and probably had over a thousand dollars saved, but we didn't find much cash in his room. He'd been to the hospital and gotten pain pills, but those weren't there either."

"What about a bank?" Kyle interrupted.

"It's something to check, but Clay said Reggie would likely have kept it in his room. There was guy across the hall Reggie was friendly with. He had a key to Reggie's room." Burgess checked his notes. "Name of Kevin Dugan. Seems Dugan moved out right after the cop who was sitting on Reggie's room left. Someone's got to get on to the landlord and see if there's any information on him. References, forwarding address, anything we can use to find him."

"I'll take that," Kyle said. "Maybe me and Stan can go over there together, do the house. Then do Preble and the street."

It sounded like a plan. "Wink's working on some things might have Dugan's prints on them, in case that's not his real name, so ask the landlord did he see any ID." Burgess gave him the landlord's information.

"Reggie's got a son, Joey, who lives here in town with his mother, Claire, Reggie's ex. Got a prior for DV, bunch of ROs. I want to know everything we can learn about Joey. Is he working, his schedule, who he hangs out with. Is he really living at home. His PO might know."

Stan raised his hand. "I'll take him."

"There's more. Guys in Reggie's building say Joey was there visiting a few times and he and Reggie were arguing about some land Reggie owned. Reggie's brother, Clay, says Joey was out at the land recently with a surveyor, talking about development. Land's in trust, leased for farming for several years. Clay gave me a copy of the trust, so I'll take a look at that. And I'll call Clay and see when it was that Joey was out there and if Clay knows who the surveyor was. I'm curious what the surveyor was told, since Joey doesn't own the land."

Burgess looked at his notes. "I'm having a hard time getting information about Reggie's job. So, when you go by the Preble Center, see if anyone there knows where he was working. Ask when he was last seen. Same with the folks at the redemption center. Reggie was in there all the time, and Reggie liked to talk. He might have told someone something."

"We've got it, Joe," Kyle said. "Do the house. Do the street and Preble. The redemption center. Kevin Dugan. And Joey."

"About Joey," Burgess said. "You guys do the background, but if you find him or hear where he is, call me." They knew the relationship. "Couple more things. Reggie was getting letters from a cousin of his, woman who claimed Reggie had abused her when she was young. Clay says it's all bullshit, but the letters were threatening, and she was looking for something from Reggie. Sounds like circling sharks." He rolled his eyes. "So I've got to check her out." He gave them copies of Reggie's picture.

He looked at his watch. Almost half the day gone. "What do you say we meet at the end of the day for an update, unless something breaks sooner? Six? Seven?"

"Eight," Kyle said. "I promised I'd have dinner with the girls. It won't take long, but thanks to freakin' Wanda, I've still got the damned court looking over my shoulder. Gotta prove I can be a dad to my own kids." His clenched lips cut off the rest. They were cops on a case, not dads complaining.

There was a group murmur of agreement. Perry was halfway to the door when Melia stopped him with a peremptory, "Perry."

When he'd stopped, Melia said, "You sure you're feeling up to this?"

Perry flushed red. "I'm good to go, sir."

Melia sighed and pushed back his chair. "Watch out for two-by-fours, okay?" He gave it a beat, then added, "And things that seem too good to be true." He slung his jacket over his shoulder and headed for the elevator. Limping a little from the onslaught of nine-year-olds and finally beginning to show his age. Younger than Burgess. Still a few years shy of the big five O, but the buck stopped at his desk. Like Indiana Jones says, it's not the years, it's the mileage.

Things were in motion. However great his sense of urgency, micromanaging was stupid and inefficient. He couldn't do it all himself; had to trust that his guys were good. They'd bring him stuff, make progress. Burgess grabbed his keys and went to see a lady about a letter.

CHAPTER TWELVE

Star Goodall's house was set back from the road in a grove of trees so dense she might have lived in the middle of a forest. The dark brown house was small, a modern one-story prefab with lots of large windows. A deck along the front wrapped around to the side. Beyond the house, the driveway led to a substantial brown barn. A large sculpture beside the stone path to the door looked like a wrecked car tipped on its rear bumper crossed with dinosaur bones. An older model black minivan was parked in the yard. The license plate read WIKA.

He hadn't called ahead. Hadn't even done his usual "is she home?" phone call. He wanted a purely spontaneous interview, and since Reggie's name hadn't been in the paper yet, her reactions to the news of Reggie's death would be illuminating.

When he rang the bell, a dog started barking. Surprising, since there were no signs of digging or tracks to suggest a dog, until he recognized it as one of those artificial recordings people got to deter strangers. When no one came to the door, he rang again and the invisible dog barked in response. From the tone of her notes to Reggie and what Clay had said, she sounded like the type who would feel no obligation to answer the door if she didn't want to. Not a problem for him. Burgess was the type who would persist until someone either felt like it or ran out of patience and opened the door to order him away.

After the third press of the button and the third flurry of mechanical barking, a woman opened the door. She had Libby eyes, but that was the only resemblance. Unlike Reggie and Clay, who were tall and big-boned, their cousin Cindy was small-boned and petite. Her dark waist-length hair, caught back with sparkly black barrettes, was streaked with gray. She wore a loose black tunic over baggy black pants. A heavily embroidered purple scarf reminiscent of priest's vestments hung around her neck.

She blocked the door, arms crossed, and glared up at him. "I do not wish to be disturbed," she said. "Please go away and stop bothering me."

Burgess flashed his badge. "Detective Sergeant Burgess, Portland police. I have some questions about Reginald Libby."

"I don't know any Reginald Libby."

Even good liars usually have some giveaway mannerisms. Eye movement. Word choice. Facial twitches or clenching hands. Star Goodall's body was veritable symphony of deception.

"You grew up with him," Burgess said, stepping into the room and forcing her back. "And you've been sending him these." He held up one of the black envelopes.

The room behind her was truly bizarre. On a basic platform of simple contemporary furniture and rugs, she had added layers of what he supposed she considered appropriate witch décor. There were paintings of owls and bats and spiders. Half a dozen hanging dream-catchers. Bundles of drying herbs hung from hooks along the beams above the windows. Flat surfaces were covered with crystals and tarot cards, arrangements of twisted sticks, and crystal balls on stands.

"I don't know any Reginald Libby," she repeated. "You must have the wrong person."

He took a step closer and pointed to the return address. "This is your name, right? Star Goodall? And this is your address? And the letter was sent to Reginald Libby. You saying someone else wrote these letters?" When she didn't respond, he said, "Why would you use this address on an envelope if you didn't want to be found?"

Her hands came up in front of her, clasping under her breasts like the paws of a small mouse. They tightened into a knot as she stared at the envelope, her face changing as she considered and rejected responses. Behind her, spread out on the tiled island that separated the kitchen from the open living-dining area, were several sheets of black paper. A cup of metallic silver pens. A basket of black envelopes. Maybe a whole raft of people were the recipients of her ugly missives.

She glanced to his right and his left, assessing her chances of escape. He was big and between her and the door and he'd had lots of practice blocking people bent on escape. Finally, she lowered her hands. "What do you want, exactly, Sergeant Burgess?"

"May we sit?" he said.

She turned slowly, examining her couches as though checking for contraband or explosives. Perhaps she was. He'd formed no impression of her yet except defensive, uncooperative, and a liar. He'd already known from her letters she was strange. Underestimating a person's dangerousness was risky. Maybe she did dabble in explosives.

Abruptly, she turned and led the way to a couch. "You sit here," she said.

She planted herself across from him, ostentatiously arranged some cards and crystals on the table, then nodded. "Okay."

"In your series of letters to Mr. Libby, you have repeatedly threatened him with physical harm, Ms. Goodall. Can you tell me why?"

"He raped me," she said. "He was fifteen and I was eleven. I couldn't help myself. Reggie and Clay took advantage of that." She said it without passion, almost with indifference, as though describing something that had happened to someone else, and she watched him for its effect. He'd interviewed hundreds of sexual assault victims, many of them distanced by trauma or pain. Her delivery didn't ring true.

"Clayton Libby says that never happened. So does Reggie."

"Well, they would, wouldn't they? It's in their interest to, isn't it, Sergeant. And those boys always stuck together."

"Both of them attacked you?" She nodded. "And what was done about it?"

"I don't know," she said. "I repressed those memories for years. It wasn't until I lost my husband and started seeing a therapist that it came back to me."

She touched a crystal, moved two of the cards. "I might have told my parents. We did move shortly after that. I would ask them but unfortunately . . ." Her slender fingers shifted the Death card, "by the time I recognized what had been done to me, they were both gone."

"Did you report any of this to the police?"

"I expect you know the answer to that, Sergeant. You probably wouldn't come out here without having done your homework. Quite frankly, knowing how much publicity can stem from such a complaint, and how the complainant is generally pilloried, I preferred to keep it within the family. Clay and Reggie got all the family land, you know, and I've been attempting to persuade them to do the right thing. To share it with me as a sign of their repentance."

Burgess unfolded another letter, one in which she told Reggie that if he didn't do as she wished, he would die a horrible death. He held it out so she could read it. "This is one of your attempts at persuasion?"

She glanced at it dismissively. "Oh, who knows? I must have been in an agitated mood that day. Reggie knew I didn't mean it."

"How would he know that?"

"Because the next time I saw him, I told him so."

"You saw Reggie?"

"He was my cousin. So of course he was in touch after I lost Nick."

She studied him with her amazing eyes. "I'm sorry, Sergeant. I'm forgetting all my manners. I usually have something around this time. Would you like some coffee? Some tea?"

He hadn't had his coffee with Chris, or at the office, and could use some. "Coffee would be good." Making coffee would also give her time to arrange the next phase of her story. Despite the reports he'd read about her difficulties with her neighbors, there was nothing spontaneous about this woman. If she'd called the police or filed complaints with the town, they'd been studied acts. Only the speeding tickets seemed unscripted.

He followed her into the kitchen, watching while she chose a canister and started making the coffee. "I'm sorry to hear about your husband," he said, irritated with himself for not having learned this. But he'd only searched law enforcement records. He hadn't checked the newspaper archives. "Was it recent?"

"Four years ago," she said. "Almost five. You've probably heard of him . . . Nicholas Goodall? Quite a well-known sculptor. Nick was a little manic, as many artists are. After too much red wine, he went roaring out of the sauna one night in late October, plunged into the river back there in the woods behind his studio, and the sudden cold stopped his heart."

Her busy hands never hesitated as she assembled her equipment, measured, and brought out cups. "I dragged him out on the bank—not an easy task, as Nick was a large man—and gave him CPR. Then I ran inside and called 9-1-1. But I don't think I ever had a chance. He was lost at the hospital. I couldn't accept that for a very long time. My therapist has been helping me to understand that everything that happens is not my fault."

She poured hot water into the small French press, then more

into a teapot. "I'm not a coffee drinker," she said. "That will be just a few minutes. Do you take cream or sugar?"

"Black is fine."

"It's been a fascinating process of discovery, learning that I'm not always responsible." She shrugged. "I do try to take responsibility where it's warranted. It seems that others aren't as far down that road. Clay and Reggie, for example. When I spoke with Clay about what had happened, he acted like I'd lost my senses. Even after he came to one of my sessions, he wouldn't accept—"

She spotted something out the window, falling silent as she walked toward the glass and peered out, twisting her head to get a better view. "Vultures," she said finally, stepping back. "Amazing birds. There must be something dead back there in the woods."

There was a cold fascination in the way she said it. If he hadn't been there, she probably would have gone out looking for whatever it was. He wondered what she would have done then. Waited until the birds had picked it clean and collected the bones? At the end of the room, a shadowbox on the wall held what looked like bones mounted on black velvet.

She returned to the kitchen and finished making his coffee, pouring a cup for him and tea for herself. She pushed his across the counter toward him and remained standing on the kitchen side of the island. "Reggie didn't ask you to come and see me." It wasn't a question. She was sure. "So why are you here?"

"How long have you been sending Reggie those letters?"

Her shoulders shifted under the gauzy fabric. "A few years."

"How did he react?"

"Reggie? He never said much about them. When I would see him, he'd always be worrying about how I was. How I was adjusting to Nick being gone. Whether I was lonely, doing okay financially. You know how Reggie was."

How Reggie *was*. "When did you last see him?"

She tapped her jaw with a finger. Her nail was painted black with some elaborate white design on it. "What's today? Monday? So I saw him on Friday. He wasn't working that day, so we met for coffee. Someplace down by the waterfront where we could sit outside. The kind of dingy place where you wouldn't have wanted to sit inside, but outside was okay. It was almost his birthday. I had a present for him."

"New shoes?"

"That's right."

"What time?"

"Around eleven, maybe."

"You remember the name of the place?"

"I don't," she said. "Why? What does any of this have to do with my letters to Reggie?"

"I don't know yet. What did you and Reggie talk about?"

His coffee smelled delicious and tasted awful. After the first few sips, he gave up. Maybe her water was bad. Maybe she was trying to poison him.

"About his job," she said. "About the land. He said Joey had been pressuring him to convey it, and wouldn't believe him when he said it was in trust and he didn't have control."

"You said you were also pressuring Reggie about the land. So, did you believe him?"

"What an interesting question." She had picked up a deck of tarot cards and was idly shuffling through it. "At the time, I really didn't think about how it applied to me. Later, I wished I'd asked more questions. It just didn't seem like Reggie to be that organized, though. To have been able to take the steps to set up a trust, even if he was afraid of Joey. You know how he was always talking about planning for the future and how he never followed through."

"I don't get it," Burgess said. "You're writing him these ugly, threatening letters and you believe he's responsible for causing you serious harm, and yet you get together for coffee, you give him presents, and you chat?"

"The letters are part of my therapy," she said. "Reggie was okay with that."

She'd done it again. Referred to Reggie in the past tense. Suddenly, she thrust the deck toward him. "Here," she said. "Shuffle these and I'll do a reading for you." Reggie's eyes, right down to the demented gleam, flashed at him from her stranger's face.

"Thanks," he said, "but right now I'm not very interested in my long-term future, and in the short term, it's pretty clear."

"Is it?" she said. "Are you sure?" She brushed the deck over the back of his hands and started laying out cards.

"Pretty sure. I'm sorry to have to tell you this, Ms. Goodall," he said, "but your cousin Reggie is dead."

His words didn't interrupt the pattern of her deal. "I know," she said. "He died on Friday night. I saw it in the crystals. He went in the water, like Nick." Then she corrected herself. "No. Not like Nick. Because Nick was an accident. Reggie wasn't ready to go, was he? It's so sad."

She looked down at the cards on the table. "I see some interesting developments for you involving a child?" She studied the cards. "Or children? A close friend in trouble. A major life change for you."

He focused on something she'd said—that Nick was an accident. "Reggie's death wasn't an accident?" She shook her head, then looked down at the cards again, frowning. "What about finding Reggie's killer?"

She touched a card, still frowning. "That," she said, "is a little less clear."

A sudden, tearing pain in his stomach almost took his breath away. He looked over at her. She smiled a knowing smile. "Your immediate future," she said. She pointed toward a doorway in the corner. "The bathroom is just there."

As he rose, fists pressed against the pain, she said, "I told you I was not in the mood for company. Not even company as charming as yours."

When he came out of the bathroom, feeling like he'd been scoured from top to bottom with a rough file, Star Goodall and her car were gone.

CHAPTER THIRTEEN

The sun was low by the time he headed back toward Portland, blasting his eyes with its slanting light. It was a lovely light, bringing out deep blue shadows and a palate of golds and plums across the salt marshes that made him long for his camera. Someday he would have the time to stop and memorialize all these things he saw. Someday his contact with the world would not be through car windows, office windows, and the windows of victims, witnesses and suspects. He'd spend time outside just to be there, not hurrying to a crime scene or kneeling beside a body.

October had always been his favorite month, but lately it seemed like the years were rushing by too fast and the shortening days brought a sense of melancholy. Another year almost done when it didn't feel like he'd begun to live it yet. Maybe it was just the cumulative effect of spending so many of his years living out the motto Stan Perry sometimes wore on his t-shirt: HOMICIDE: OUR DAY BEGINS WHEN YOUR DAY ENDS.

An ugly motto but a lot of his life *was* ugly. You didn't muck around in the dirty things people did to each other and come up smiling. You got dirty. You got tainted. Talking to bad guys and witnesses who lied and misled and generally screwed around even when it didn't cost them anything, just 'cuz you were cops, you got jaded and cynical. And today, it seemed, you got your guts reamed by the whacked-out relatives of the deceased.

He was still trying to assess what he'd learned from his visit with Star Goodall, other than the information—rather shaky, given how often she changed her stories and how openly she admitted her lies and manipulations—that she'd seen Reggie on Friday because he hadn't gone to work that day, that she was the source of the new shoes, and that she had already known he was dead. He wasn't sure of much else about her, either. Whether those letters to Reggie were threats, as they appeared, or therapy, as she claimed. And whether her interest in the land meant she might be willing to do Reggie harm to get her hands on some of it.

The coffee she'd served was clear evidence a willingness to hurt others. He wondered what he was going to do about it. He'd brought along the contents of that cup, as well as a scoop of the grounds, and another scoop from the can, for Wink to test. She might have thought it was a perfectly appropriate way to express her displeasure with his visit, but Burgess's rule was that you didn't touch a cop and walk away from it.

Before he left, he'd walked back to the barn, wanting to be sure she hadn't just driven her car down there and hidden it. He'd also wanted to take a look at the barn itself. He'd already established that her bathroom had a nice, roomy tub. Kneeling on the hard slate floor, he'd become quite intimate with the room. He wondered if the barn had been her husband's studio, and if so, whether it might also have a bathroom.

The door was locked, but peering through the windows, he could see one huge, open space still occupied by several sculptures as large as the one beside her front walk, along with winches and chains and tanks and torches. Along one side, a row of low doors led into what might have been storage areas. At the rear, another door led into the space beyond, but when he tried see what was there, he found the windows blocked with thick black cloth.

He stopped at the house across from the end of her driveway, showed his badge, and asked the elderly man who answered if he could ask some questions about Ms. Goodall. The man had grimaced, craned his neck toward the driveway, and then refused to comment. All he would say was, "I don't know if she's a real witch or not, but folks who cross her find themselves havin' all sorta trouble. I just guess I'd rather be safe than sorry, unless you're telling me I've got no choice but to talk with you."

"No, sir," Burgess told him. "You always have that choice."

He'd tried another neighbor, gotten a sharp, "I wish the police had paid some attention when that bitch poisoned my dog, but they didn't, and beyond that, I got nothing to say to no cop," and one who just grinned and said, "I hope you didn't let her make you coffee." He wished he'd talked to this last guy before ringing the woman's doorbell. He gave up and headed back to Portland.

He was hungry and badly needed some unadulterated coffee, but his violated gut wasn't up for anything stronger than ginger ale. In an ironic way, Goodall's vicious ministrations had helped him achieve a kind of symmetry. He felt both spiritually and physically hollow. He stopped at a 7-Eleven, grabbed two sodas and a package of crackers, and headed back to 109.

There were no messages from Terry or Stan yet, so he opened the first soda, drank half, and called Clay Libby. It was Mary who answered.

"Joe Burgess, Mary. I was looking for Clay."

"He's chopping wood, Joe," she said. "It's a kind of therapy for him. I can interrupt him if it's urgent."

Urgent was two days ago, if they'd only known what they had. Urgent was following up hot leads, going hard during that initial phase. Urgent was not this maze of murky confusion. This was more like trying to read the iridescent patterns on a can of oil.

"It's not urgent, Mary. Clay mentioned that Joey had a surveyor out recently looking at Reggie's land. I wondered if he knew the surveyor's name. He can call me when he comes in."

"I can tell you that, Joe," she said. "He's a local. That's why Clay recognized him. Joey was sitting in the car, so all Clay saw was Rob Johnson out there with his equipment. He stopped to tell Rob that he was on private land and the family had no intention of selling. That was when Joey got out of the car. He told Clay it was okay. He'd hired the surveyor. Poor Clay . . . he's tried so hard to be a good uncle, but goodness has no effect on those people."

Mary's sigh was like a light wind. Burgess pictured her there in her warm, old-fashioned kitchen, the light fading as it had for him and Clay yesterday afternoon, shadows piling up in the corners. She would be cooking dinner. Mary was such a traditional woman. She would sympathize with her husband's grief by cooking his favorite dinner and letting him know she was available to listen.

Once, years ago, driving around the city looking for a witness, he'd found Reggie sitting on a doorstep, weeping. It would have been around three A.M., the saddest time of the night. Reggie's shopping cart, piled high with returnables, was beside him. He'd parked the car and gone to sit with Reggie and share the coffee he'd just bought. It turned out Reggie was crying because Clay and Mary had had a bad fight and Mary had moved out.

"Mary's the difference between Clay and me," Reggie had said. "Claire hates who I am and always wants to change me; used to, anyway. Now she just wants me dead and gone—while Mary likes who Clay is. She grounds him." Reggie had always held that image of Mary, always been respectful of her. He'd been relieved when she and Clay reconciled.

"You want his address and his number?" she asked. Burgess

143

heard the rustling of pages, probably of the phone book, then a sniff and a muffled sob. "Clay says somebody did this to Reggie. That it was no accident. Is that true?"

"We're awaiting further results from the medical examiner, but it looks that way."

She pulled in a trembling breath. "Here's that information for you." She read off the surveyor's name, address, and phone number. "You're going to find out who did this, aren't you, Joe? You're not going to let Reggie be disposed of like a piece of trash?"

"I'll do my best, Mary. You know I will."

"I do," she said. "It was foolish of me to even ask. Reggie couldn't have anyone better on his side. Look, Joe . . . if there's anything I can do. Anything at all that you need from me, promise that you'll call me, okay. I . . . it's . . . Clay thinks . . ." There was a long pause. "Clay thinks for sure that Joey had something to do with this. You've mostly seen the best side of him, Joe, with the two of you trying to help Reggie. But Clay's got quite a temper, and if nothing happens, he'll brood himself into thinking maybe he'll have to fix it himself."

He could almost feel her tension, the conflict between loyalty to her husband and fear that Clay might get himself in trouble. "Just let him know you're working on it, Joe. I guess that's what I'm asking. I don't want to have to stop him from getting in his truck and coming after Joey."

"Does he know where Joey lives?"

"Only that he was staying with Claire. That's all I've heard." Burgess was disappointed. He thought Joey had to have someplace else. He'd go crazy living any length of time with Claire. She wouldn't be easygoing about him bringing women home. Maybe Stan and Terry had learned something.

"Tell him I called, Mary, and what I called about. That I'll keep in touch. And Mary? I think Clay will be okay, but will you call me if you think he's coming after Joey?"

"So you can try and keep him out of trouble?" she asked. When he didn't immediately respond, she said, "Come on, Joe. I know you. That's what you do."

He thought what he did was come in after the trouble had happened and try to mop things up, but he liked Mary's vision of him. It was something positive on a day when his black cloud was wrapped so tightly around him. "So I can keep him out of trouble," he agreed.

"Okay," she said. "Okay. I will."

He gave her his numbers—cell, office, and home—disconnected, and called the surveyor's number. He got a brisk, professional "Rob Johnson," on the first ring. Assuming it was a recording, he was starting the leave a message when the voice repeated, "This is Rob Johnson."

A real human on a holiday Monday. "Detective Sergeant Burgess, Portland CID. I had some questions about a piece of property up in Belgrade you were surveying for Joseph Libby?"

"What kind of questions?" The voice was cautious.

"What he told you when he hired you. What his intentions were for the property."

"I doubt I'm at liberty to answer those questions about a client," Johnson said.

"Let's back up, then," Burgess said. "Were you aware that Mr. Libby was not the owner of that property?" He should be doing this face-to-face. So much information could be gleaned by watching expressions and body movement. Here he was limited to listening for clues in an unfamiliar voice. But if this proved fruitful, he could always make a follow-up visit.

"He said it belong to his father," the surveyor said carefully, "but would be his very soon. He had a buyer interested in developing it and wanted to check on the actual size of the piece, the amount of lake frontage. Put things in place to avoid delays down the road."

"Do you have a written contract detailing the work?" It was standard practice.

Another cautious silence and then, "I do."

"Can you tell me who signed that contract?"

"I'll have to look."

"You're in your office?"

"My home is my office."

"Then if you would, please," Burgess said. "I'll wait."

He heard a chair being shoved back, footsteps, the metallic opening and closing of a file drawer. Then the surveyor was back on the line. "Reginald Libby."

"What was the date that the contract was signed?" The date he was given was about four weeks earlier. Burgess made some notes, then asked, "As part of your work, do you check registry records to review the deeds to the property?"

"Of course I do. I have to," the surveyor said sharply.

Burgess didn't know whether the sharpness was because the surveyor felt his abilities were being questioned or whether he was anticipating the next question. "So you were aware, at the time that you went on the land to survey it, that the property in question was in a trust, and neither Reginald Libby nor Joseph Libby was a trustee?"

"What the fuck is this really about?" the surveyor exploded. "Are you trying to check up on my license? Is that what this is? Because that little fucker told me that it was okay with his father and okay with his uncle, who was the trustee, and I should just go ahead and do it. I'd already done part of the work. He said if I wanted to get paid, I'd damned well better finish."

"How did you stay in touch with Joseph Libby? You have phone numbers for him?"

"Just a cell," the surveyor said.

"May I have that number, please?" Burgess wrote it down.

"So you never had any contact with Clayton Libby?"

"Not until he showed up out there at the property and asked what I was doing."

"Were you paid for the work?"

"Yes, dammit, I was. I get the half of it up front. Have to, these days, the way people are. Some of them ask you to do a job and then you tell them that your preliminary survey shows they don't own the twenty acres they thought they did and suddenly you're eating your time and paperin' your walls with the bills. People from away are even worse."

"Who paid you?"

"The checks were written by a Star Goodall. Libby said she was his sister. I remember wondering about that, as she had a different address and wasn't mentioned in the trust, but I figured she was a married sister. Then he gave me a different address from hers to send the contract and the finished survey." He gave Burgess Claire's address.

Suddenly, this taciturn fellow was getting voluble. Maybe what Burgess had said about ownership had spooked him and he'd decided to be completely open, just in case there was some hanky-panky here. Some papers rustled, as though he was checking his notes, then the surveyor said, "Libby told me that wasn't where he lived, either. Guess I didn't think anything of it at the time, but the kid said I should send the survey plans there because he didn't have a regular mailing address. He said he was living on his boat."

"So you weren't surprised at one person hiring you, another writing the check, a third signing the contract, and a fourth being the record owner of the property?"

"Not really," the surveyor said. "Happens all the time, especially when people are thinking of buying a property and want to know can they do what they want if they get it."

Burgess thought it probably did. "I'd appreciate it if you

147

could send me a copy of your contract and a copy of that survey," he said. "If you've got any problem with that, I can have Clayton Libby okay it. Since he's the trustee, and all."

The surveyor sighed wearily. "That's okay, Sergeant. Just give me your address."

Burgess did that, adding, "I appreciate your help. Look forward to getting those papers."

"I can fax the contract, if that would help. Rest will have to wait for the mail tomorrow. I don't suppose you're going to tell me what this is all about?"

"Reginald Libby has been murdered," Burgess said. "Here's my fax number."

CHAPTER FOURTEEN

Off the phone, he made sure he had it all in his notes. The day and time of the conversation. The surveyor's name, address, and phone number. The details of the conversation. That poor, hesitant man had no idea how much information he'd divulged or how many new questions it had raised.

Burgess now had some follow-up questions for Star Goodall. Was it collusion, pressure from Joey, or simply her bitter whimsy that caused her to write that check? Knowing she'd been involved, somehow, in Joey's scheme, her wide-eyed statement that she hadn't thought Reggie was organized enough to set up a trust gave him a resonant pain in his gut.

The surveyor had also given him another place to look for Joey. He checked the Department of Inland Fisheries and Wildlife boat registry. Found nothing registered to Joseph Libby, Claire Libby, or Star Goodall. Just to cover the bases, he also checked Reggie, since Joey seemed to be using his father's name quite freely these days, and Clay. He drew a blank. But that didn't mean much. Joey could be staying on a friend's boat. Renting a boat. Or doing a little illegal crashing. There were plenty of boats in the harbor whose owners paid them little attention.

When the fax machine spat out the surveyor's contract, he wasn't surprised to find the signature bore little resemblance to Reggie's handwriting. It was one of Reggie's peculiarities that the large-boned former football player with his big, scarred hands had handwriting as delicate and precise as a Victorian lady's. His handwriting was more legible when he was wracked with the shakes than Burgess's on a day when he envisioned Sister Mary Peter standing over him with a ruler. What he didn't know was whether Joey had signed it, or his possible co-conspirator, Star Goodall. Or even mommie dearest.

He could answer part of the question right now. He unfolded one of the black letters, laid it on his desk next to the contract, and compared the writing. Looked like she was off the hook on forgery, at least. At home in his desk, he had a couple notes Joey had written to him over the years. None that were recent, but they'd be enough for a preliminary match. He also had a couple notes from Claire—her periodic injunctions to leave Joey alone—so he could check those, too.

He looked up the developer the surveyor had mentioned, whose interest in the property had spurred Joey's efforts, and wrote down his contact information. He was almost certain Clay had known nothing about any of this except what he'd learned from Joey that day; almost as sure that Reggie hadn't. Reggie usually confided things about Joey, both because of his concerns about his son and because Burgess was Joey's god-father, which, in Reggie's mind, had given him rights in the boy. Burgess had heard nothing about Joey's visits, either, though, so maybe Reggie had been embarrassed about them. Or maybe Reggie would have told him if Burgess hadn't been neglecting his old friend in favor of his new domestic life.

That was not somewhere he wanted to go. For all the years of his self-imposed emotional and physical celibacy—his "monkhood" as Stan and Terry would put it—he'd quietly yearned for a personal life. He'd just never seen how to fit it in. Now that he had one, he blew as hot and cold as a furnace on the fritz. Some days it struck him with wonder; others, he longed for the simplicity of the single life, the ability to be obsessed with his work without distractions. He thought he was better at that than at this crazy, awkward balance. He didn't understand how you went from the jazzed-up adrenaline high of the chase to the tender domesticity of the dinner table. He certainly didn't see how you'd add kids to the mix.

"Control it," Melia would say. "Box it up." It must work. Melia was a good cop and a good husband and father. Terry Kyle had failed at marriage but was great with his kids. Not without struggle and sacrifice, though. Burgess didn't think Terry was wired differently. Maybe he, himself, was just starting too late. A dog too old to learn new tricks.

Enough. He had a murder to solve and he was a murder police. He pulled out the trust document he'd gotten from Clay. All the legal gobbledygook was difficult to parse. It would have been nice to have a lawyer in his pocket—never mind that he thought most of the breed were flaming assholes—but he didn't, so he forced himself to reread the most relevant paragraphs. From what he could tell, the trust didn't automatically transfer the property on Reggie's death. Clay still retained the authority to decide whether to hold it, transfer it, sell it, or develop it for the benefit of the beneficiaries until Reggie's youngest child turned thirty-five. As Reggie had no wife or other children, the sole beneficiary was Joey.

Burgess picked up the phone and called Clay again. "Mary," he said when she answered, "I need to talk to Clay." When Clay was on the line, he said, "This may be something or this may be nothing, Clay, but I've got to say it. I followed up with that surveyor you mentioned. Seems Joey told him that he was going to come into the property very soon and had a developer who was interested in developing it. Joey ever talk to you about the land?"

"He did. I told him it was in trust."

"He ask for details?"

"Not from me. When we spoke, the boy was his usual charming self. Called me a liar and said I was just trying to keep him from getting what was rightfully his. I offered to show him the documents but he just slammed out, cursing. It's at the registry, though. He could have gone and looked it up. Him or his lovin' mama. Who, by the way, called and reamed me out for renting the place with a long-term lease."

"Do you understand this the way I do," Burgess said, "that you don't have to give it to Joey outright until he's thirty-five?"

"That's right." Clay's voice was slow and deliberate. And tired, like he'd chopped up a whole forest trying to put some distance between himself and his brother's death. "That was Reggie's idea. He kept hoping if he gave it enough time, Joey'd grow out of this young thug crap, become somebody decent."

"Right. Who becomes trustee if something happens to you?"

"Claire."

"You got the power to change that?"

"You bet I do."

"Do us both a favor, will you?" Burgess said. "Today, tomorrow, as soon as you can see the lawyer, name a different trustee. Put it in writing and be sure Joey and Claire know you've done it. Until then, forgive me for saying this, please watch your back."

"Already thought of that," Clay Libby said, something in his voice that was both iron and sorrow. "I'm keeping the truck in the barn at night. Got motion-activated lights around the outside and a loaded shotgun by the door."

Sweet Jesus. And this was his own nephew. "You didn't say anything," Burgess said.

"Hoping I was wrong and hedging my bets." His sigh said it all.

"I'm still hoping we're wrong," Burgess said. "I'm looking, but I can't find Joey."

"I'd guess he's pretty good at not being found if he doesn't want to be and there's no way Claire would help."

"You notice what Joey's driving these days?"

"Audi, I think. Red one. Convertible."

"You know anything about a developer named Charlie Hazen?"

"Hazen's a predatory, scum-sucking son-of-a-bitch. The kind who scares blind old ladies into selling their farms for pin money. Never met a lie he didn't like. Slick, though. Even when you know what the SOB is like, start talking to him and next thing you know, you're thinking he's really a great guy."

"Well, that's who Joey's been talking to," Burgess said. "I'll be in touch. Call me if there's anything I should know."

"Guess I should start planning a funeral," Clay said. "Since I haven't heard word one from the grieving son and ex-wife. Don't know why I thought they might step up, do you, Joe?"

"Wishful thinking? The absurd way we all keep hoping people will do the right thing?"

"I guess that's it." Clay Libby sighed again. "Funeral at the Veteran's Cemetery still sounds right, but I'm thinking Reggie wouldn't want to be stuck in a hole in the ground. You got any idea where we oughta sprinkle his ashes?"

Burgess did. A very good and absolutely outrageous idea. "I got one. What about you?"

"Mine wouldn't be legal."

"Neither would mine." Burgess wondered if they had the same idea.

"We'll talk," Clay said. "You take care, Joe."

"Yeah. You, too."

Burgess wrote a report about his interview with Star Goodall. Another about his conversation with Rob Johnson. He looked up Charles Hazen and got an address, a phone number, the make of his car, and his plate number. He had a feeling that

Hazen might be hard to locate if he thought cops were doing the locating. Rather like young Joey.

He drank the rest of the ginger ale, hungry but too queasy to do anything about it beyond the handful of crackers. He was restless. Eager to sit down with Stan and Terry and hear their news. He had time to kill before they were due in and no interest in spending it behind his desk.

It was Monday dinner time. An excellent time to pay a consolation visit to Claire and Joey. He called Chris to say he definitely wouldn't make it home, and humped his sorry self downstairs. The garage was cold and bleak, his steps echoing as he crunched across the cement. One empty cruiser running, its radio talking to no one. Beyond the cold overhead lights, the corners were as dark and empty as his spirit.

His city was quiet again tonight, people resting up after a busy weekend, getting ready to face another work week. The radio said rain for the next three days. Rain would bring down the leaves, changing the bright world to brown. Gray and rain suited his mood better than fall's glory, but he felt a flicker of regret for the fine weekend he'd missed.

He drove past a small knot of ragged men sitting on some church steps, another group clustered in a pocket park. Turning a corner, he spotted a tall man up ahead, wearing army green, pushing a shopping cart. He had the window down, Reggie's name on his lips, when it hit him. He'd never turn a corner and come upon Reggie again; never drive down a side street and see Reggie's big shoulders hulking along behind his trademark shopping cart. He, of all people, should know about life's transience, yet it felt like a blow.

Some instinct made him park around the corner instead of rolling up Claire's street and parking out front. Probably the same instinct that made him unsurprised when he saw Star Goodall's black van parked across the street, and a sporty red car in the driveway. A private wake or a cabal of the wicked? Claire probably didn't carry a stiletto in her girdle, but she'd go to great lengths to protect her son. Joey had no scruples, he knew, and neither did Star. Burgess decided it wasn't prudent to tackle this alone.

He dialed. Got an instant, "Stan Perry."

"You and Terry have any luck tracking down Joey Libby?"

"Fuck all. That kid is slippery as an eel."

"I think I've found him. I'm sitting outside Claire Libby's place." He gave the address. "Joey's car is here. This might be a good time to catch him, but I'd like someone watching my back. You free?"

"As a bird," Stan said. "I was just thinking about some dinner."

"Postpone it."

"Three minutes," Stan said.

"Block the driveway," Burgess said.

He put his phone away and studied the house. What he wanted to do was sneak up and peek in the windows but reality argued against it. Reality in the form of Captain Paul Cote, who operated with one standard for ordinary people and another for those who lived in a nice part of town like this. In Cote's book, folks who made nice political contributions and lived in nice houses had to be treated nicely, even if it meant not asking hard questions and not being pushy. It was all tread lightly and tug at your forelock. Here, Cote might couch it in terms of their obligations toward the grieving family. In reality, the nod was toward the family's pocketbook.

Then there was the practical reason for not sneaking up and peeking in the windows. He had spotted several exterior motion-sensor lights. Any approach to the house including a simple stroll up the front walk would be instantly illuminated. As soon as Stan's car came around the corner, he started walking toward the house. He was in the driveway, standing behind the red car, when Stan rolled to a stop and got out, closing his door silently and joining Burgess.

"How you want to play this, Joe?"

"I'll do the door. You stay here with the car in case Joey bolts."

"You think he will?"

"The way I see this? Claire stalls me on the steps and Joey makes a run for it. She's mother love writ large in a twisted sort of way. What I don't yet know is why he'll run." He shrugged. "I could be pleasantly surprised but I wouldn't put money on it."

"Cops haven't got money," Perry said.

"Well, I'm not betting my ass or my balls, either, and depending on who you talk to, my honor's kinda tattered."

"Know what you mean."

Burgess left him standing behind Joey's car, arms folded, looking battered and mean, and headed up the front walk. As expected, lights came on to greet him. Before he got his finger on the bell, a curtain twitched, so Claire knew he was there. She took her time coming to the door, though, and when she finally did open it, she stood blocking his way into the house. Impeccable in slim black pants, a black sweater, and simple pearls. Too formal for everyday. As though she'd been expecting a visitor, though not the one on her doorstep.

"This is not a good time, Joe," she said. "I have company."

"I won't bother you," he said. "I just need a few minutes with Joey."

"Joey's not . . ." She looked toward him, as though she could see through his bulk to the car in her driveway. "He's not here." She lifted her chin defiantly. "He left the car for the weekend. He's gone off with some friends."

"Weekend's over," he said. "You expecting him back soon?"

"Oh, Joe, you know young people." She tried for nonchalant,

a chummy note that was stiff as cardboard. "He'll probably be back in the middle of the night."

"But he is living here with you, Claire?" Burgess said.

Her answer sounded squeezed, as though lying to the cops came hard. "Yes. Yes, he's living here."

"I really do need to talk to him, Claire, sooner rather than later. I have some questions about his visits to his dad in the weeks before Reggie's death. His information is pretty important. We're trying to create a timeline."

"Joey hasn't been seeing Reggie. He's had no contact with his father for ages." She told this lie more smoothly.

"I've got at least four witnesses who disagree," he said. "Look, I don't want to interfere with your evening if you have guests. Maybe I could catch up with him tomorrow at work? Joey is working these days?"

The lines around her mouth tightened with displeasure. "Of course he's working." Her chin came up again and small spots of pink glowed in her cheeks.

"I'm glad to hear it," he said. "Just tell me where to find him and I'll be out of your hair."

She brushed at her perfect coif as though he were a bug that had gotten stuck there. "You know, Joe, he hasn't been working there very long. It might not be such a good idea for you to be showing up. Some people . . . some employers . . . aren't all that comfortable with cops coming around. It might reflect . . ." She studied her shiny shoes on the shiny floor, then back at him. "I don't understand why you need to talk to Joey, anyway. What is this about a timeline? Yes, Reggie's dead, and it's a sad thing that he never did get his life together, but why isn't that the end of it?"

"Because there are some things about Reggie's death that don't add up, Claire. We always take a closer look at suspicious circumstances."

"Oh, spare me." She rolled her eyes. "There's nothing suspicious about a habitual drunk having one too many, falling in the water, and drowning. The only strange thing about Reggie's death is that it didn't happen sooner." She stood straighter. Folded her arms more tightly across her chest.

"I wish it were that simple," he said. "And there's the funeral, Claire—"

From the driveway came a sharp, "Hey!" Then a squabble of voices. Stan's loud voice identifying himself as a police officer and asking for ID. There was a grunt and the sound of blows. A car door slammed, tires screeched. Perry was knocked aside as the red car shot backward across the lawn, around Stan's car, and out into the street, digging deep grooves in the nice green sod.

Claire emitted a shocked, "Oh, my God, Joey!" as she shoved past him and ran down the walk toward Stan Perry, who lurched up from the ground, raced for his car, and took off after Joey's retreating taillights.

CHAPTER FIFTEEN

She stamped back up the walk, her low-heeled patent shoes clattering loudly on the granite step, and stepped past Burgess into the house. He followed her in before she could shut the door. "Why did you lie to me, Claire?" he said. "Joey was home."

Her back went stiff. "I was trying to spare him," she said. "My son has had enough trouble with the police. And he's grieving about his father."

She lowered her head so he wouldn't see her eyeing the top drawer of the decorative little dresser here in her entry. What did she keep in there. A panic button? That wouldn't do her much good, calling the police because the police were questioning her about a murder. Pepper spray or cell phone? Same problem. She didn't seem the type to keep a handgun in the foyer.

"Spare him? Joey just bought himself a boatload of new trouble, Claire. He came within inches of seriously hurting a police officer." He didn't buy the crap about Joey's grief. She'd raised the boy to care about no one but himself. And when she'd told him that Joey hadn't been near Reggie, her tones had implied Joey had no use for his old man.

While she was gathering herself for an angry response, he said, "I see Star Goodall's van outside. Is she your company?"

"I don't know anyone named Star Goodall." She folded her arms across her chest and stared up at him. "And I would like you to leave now. You have no reason to be here and you're making me uncomfortable."

"Reggie's cousin Cindy?" he said. "Calls herself Star now. Married that sculptor, Nicholas Goodall. You're saying you don't know her?" When she didn't answer, he said, "Maybe she was here visiting with Joey and he forgot to introduce you? I know she and Joey are acquainted. They've got some real estate thing going." Her tight face looked like it might split.

He glanced back over his shoulder to see if the van was still there. It was. Star hadn't been as successful at sneaking out as Joey. Maybe she was lurking in the shrubbery, waiting for him to leave.

Claire's cool posture, the folded arms, the tapping foot, the stubborn raised chin, all made him want to walk right up until their bodies touched, march her backward into her own elegant living room until she plopped down on her creamy couch, and tell her what a destructive, heartless bitch she was. But that was a human impulse, not a cop's. A cop, when asked to leave a place he has no warrant to enter, has to leave unless he can exercise some wile to remain there.

"I need to talk to him, Claire," Burgess said. "He is living here?" She nodded. "He doesn't have another place?"

"He sometimes stays with a friend."

"Male friend or female friend?" She didn't answer. They both knew Joey's history. They also both knew that despite that, Joey's looks and bad boy attitude continued to attract women too easily. And what came next.

"Male or female?" he repeated. "What's the friend's name? And address?" She didn't respond. "Claire, I need to find him. Give me his cell phone number so I can call him, at least. If nothing else, there's the matter of Reggie's funeral."

"You can't seriously think we're responsible for that," she said.

"Well, the estate . . . Reggie's land. That's his only asset. And

Joey's his heir."

"It's in trust," she said quickly, then looked down at the floor, probably wishing she'd kept her mouth shut. She was usually so good at this cold indifference. Somewhere in the house a phone rang. Maybe Joey, calling to ask mommy what he should do.

"I have to get that," she said. "And you have to leave." She wheeled around and strode away, her heels clip-clopping across the polished marble like hooves on cobblestones.

He checked the living room and the dining room. Empty. So was the powder room. That was as much as he could do right now. As he passed, he pulled out the drawer she'd been staring at, and came very close to being surprised. She did have a gun in there. He added to his mental list to check and see if she had a permit. Not, given Maine's extremely bad-guy–friendly gun laws, that she needed one to keep a gun in her house. Disturbing, though, to know Joey, with his lack of impulse control and propensity for violence, had such easy access to a weapon. Convicted felons weren't supposed to be around guns.

He let himself out, quietly closing the door behind him. The black van was still there. He called patrol, asked them to put a unit on the house and let him know if the red car returned or the black van left. Told them to call him with a description of the van's driver, although he didn't expect anyone else would be driving a black van with WIKA on the plate, and to have someone follow it if a car was available when it left, but to keep someone sitting on the house.

Because Claire's outfit was too elegant for receiving Joey or even Star Goodall in her witches' gauze and ecclesiastical scarf, he asked for the plate numbers of any other vehicles visiting the house. Then he called Stan. "You okay?" he asked.

"I'm thinking this isn't my week," Perry said. "Whatever wasn't bruised before is now. I identify myself as a police officer, show my badge, and the little prick takes a swing at me. Then he jumps in the car, starts backing up, and I go ass over elbows trying to get out of his way."

"You still on him?"

"Lost him down in the Old Port when a pod of half-dressed, underage chickies lurched into my path. Normally, I'd be fine with that. Tonight I was so pissed I almost ran them down. Maybe it wasn't such a bad thing, though. Two of them were no more than sixteen and so drunk they were about to pass out. I called patrol and sent most of them down the station, one over to Maine Med. Lost that little shit in the process. I've got a BOLO out."

"As in be on the lookout for a red Audi convertible with a vanity plate that says STUD?"

Perry nodded.

"So what have we got?" Burgess said. "Assault on a police officer. Failing to stop for an officer. Driving to endanger. Speeding. Anything else?"

"I can come up with some things. We got any leads on where to look for him?"

"Not much. I'm working on it, though. Someone said he was living on a boat. We can talk about it when you and Terry come in."

"That's now," Perry said. "You back at 109?"

"Stopped for a chat with Joey's mother. I'm on my way now."

"I'm going to grab something to eat. You want anything?"

Burgess considered. He hadn't eaten all day. He ought to eat something just to keep his body and brain working; wasn't about to ask Stan to bring him chicken soup. "Golden Arches or Dunkin' Donuts?" he asked.

"DD."

"How about a whole wheat bagel, toasted. No butter. Cream cheese on the side?"

"This time of day, it'll be like munching cardboard."

"Cardboard's about all I'm up for. See you in a few."

"I'll bring something, case you change your mind."

He parked in the garage and went upstairs. Terry was pacing among the desks, lean and wired as a greyhound, looking neither rested nor happy. So much for his weekend away. He wheeled around when Burgess came in, checked his watch, and said, "Stan on his way?"

"He is. He was chasing Joey Libby through the Old Port when he ran into a bunch of inebriated teens and had to stop and sort that out. You get anything?"

"Lotta people feeling bad about Reggie, wanting to know when his funeral's gonna be. Lotta sympathy for Maura. Beyond that? Maybe my compassion's wearing thin, Joe, but me and Stan were out what, four, five hours, and we didn't find a working brain anywhere. I mean, all the years I lived with Wanda, trying to follow her train of thought, I oughta be good at this. Able to follow the thought as it bobs and weaves through the chaos."

He dropped into a chair, folding like a stork, inert except for one foot swinging like a metronome. "Maybe it's me. Today, my own thoughts kept getting in the way. I wanted to shake people, grab 'em up and say, 'Hey, somebody killed Reggie and I need information, not the same goddamned story all over again.' What's happening to me, Joe? I'm losing my compassion."

"Ah," Burgess said, "maybe it's not a good idea to pick your head up from the daily grind, get a taste of what life could be. Maybe we *can* only do this when this is all we do."

"I'm not ready to believe that," Kyle said, his sharp face suddenly lit by a smile. "I'm working on the opposite. I had such a good time this weekend."

Something about the smile, for Kyle smiling, except cynically, was rare, made Burgess feel more hopeful. "We'll break this thing," he said. He thought about the people they were trying to get information from. "We just have to listen well. Keep going back. Think scavenger hunt. Jigsaw puzzle. Stuff'll come in bits and pieces; our job is to put it together. But we'll get it."

"I hope you're right."

Stan came in, carrying a tray of coffees and two bags of food. "Special delivery," he said. "Saint Stanley, patron saint of drunken youth, is here."

He set down the food and held up a hand in benediction. "Bless you, my children. Bless all of you who bring order out of chaos and hope to the downtrodden." He had streaks of dirt down one side and his pants were torn. The shaved head, battered face, and demented grin made him look both jaunty and mean, someone you wouldn't mess with unless you were a little crazy yourself. Which, of course, was half the people they dealt with.

"Let's take this into the conference room," Burgess said, reaching for the phone. "I'll see if Wink's around."

He got a weary, "Devlin, Crime Lab."

"We're meeting," he said. "You want to join us?"

"Definitely a club of which I want to be a member," Devlin said. "My eyes are crossing here anyway. You got anything to eat?"

"I think Stan's brought you something."

"Joy and rapture," Devlin muttered. "I'll be right up."

They were a mangy-looking group. Devlin's eyes were red and weary. Stan wore the mottled purples and greens of healing bruises. A quick, unhappy mirror check had told Burgess his bout with Star Goodall's coffee had left him pale green. Only Kyle looked even vaguely healthy. Last summer, when they worked a case that had really beaten them into the ground, Burgess had nicknamed them "The Crips." Looked like the name still applied. The only person in the room who looked half-normal was Melia, and even he was bruised.

They hunched over their papers, waiting for Burgess to start, as Saint Stanley distributed food to the huddled masses—coffee, cups of soup, and lovely flatbread sandwiches for everyone, even Burgess, although he'd also brought the requested bagel.

They ate as Burgess began laying things out for them. He described his visit to Star Goodall, her relationship to Reggie, her interest in the property and the checks she'd signed for Joey. Of later finding her car parked at Claire Libby's and Claire's assertion that she knew no Star Goodall.

He detailed his call to the surveyor and what he'd learned: that there was a developer with an interest in the land; that Joey had stated the land would soon be his, even though under the trust he wouldn't get it outright until he was thirty-five. He showed them the contract from the surveyor, purportedly signed by Reggie.

"It's not Reggie's signature. But Clay's the trustee anyway, so he's the one with legal authority to sign, not Reggie, and, as I read the trust, Clay still has discretion about how and when the property is distributed. The land is leased to a farmer for the next several years, so there are a few obstacles in the path of Joey's 'get rich quick' scheme." He sighed. "I told Clay to watch his back on this one."

"I know he's your godson," Kyle said, "but he's a vicious little creep. Still, it's hard to believe he'd be involved in killing his own father."

"It is pretty cold-blooded," Stan agreed. "Forcing his head into a bathtub and holding him there until he drowned."

It was cold-blooded, and Burgess was still hoping they'd find another explanation for Joey's behavior, one that wouldn't force him to arrest the boy he'd known since Joey was born. He changed the subject. "We may have a break on the timeline, though. And an explanation of those new shoes." He told them about Star Goodall's statement that she had had coffee with Reggie on Friday and given him a new pair of shoes. "So, tomorrow morning we've got to canvass breakfast places down by the water and show them Reggie's picture. Be nice if we could track down one of her, as well. Maybe there was one when her husband died. Or of them at some function. He was a pretty well-known sculptor."

He shared the surveyor's information that Joey had said he was living on a boat. "There are no boats registered to Joey or to Claire, so this one is wide open, too. I think we start with a warrant to get Joey's phone records. He gave this as his cell phone number. And I want to see Star Goodall's phone records, too." He read the two numbers and Kyle wrote them down.

"Any boats registered to Cindy Goodall or Nicholas Goodall?" Kyle asked.

Burgess shrugged. "I didn't go that far. Let's check it out."

He told them about the handgun in Claire's foyer, because whoever finally found Joey would be a lot safer knowing he had access to a gun. "So, that's how I spent my day, making phone calls, visiting a witch, and getting poisoned."

He turned to Wink. "You got any ideas about that coffee?"

"Getting poisoned?" Kyle interrupted.

Burgess nodded. "Something in my coffee made me sick as a dog. Stan, I want you to go talk to her tomorrow, follow up on this surveyor stuff. She may not let you through the door, but if she does, do not eat or drink anything she offers." He gave Stan a copy of his report.

"I haven't gotten to the coffee yet," Wink said. "Still working on prints. But if that's your priority, I could shove some things aside. If I had to bet, instead of being a scientist, from your symptoms I'd say she put some purgative in the coffee. And if she's playing at being a witch, it might be mandrake root."

"Mandrake root?" Kyle said. "Wink, you can be downright

spooky sometimes."

"I don't get it," Perry complained. "What's mandrake root and why is it spooky?"

Kyle's eyes glittered. "According to legend, mandrake root would grow up where a hanged man ejaculated. And anyone trying to pull it up would die."

"That's bull," Perry said. "And anyway, there haven't been any hanged men in a long, long time. Unless Joe's friend Star Goodall has been stringing them up in her back forty."

"I wouldn't put it past her," Burgess said. "There were vultures circling."

Perry rolled his eyes. "How do you know this stuff, anyway?"

"We had it in a case once," Kyle said. "Some whack job who thought he was a wizard was giving it to his elderly mother to help her pass on. Neighbor called us, concerned about the mom's safety, and when we went in to check out mom, it was right out there on the counter. Weird lookin' stuff. Supposed to look like a little man."

Melia cleared his throat and checked his watch, and Burgess got back to business. "So what do you have, Wink?" he said. "Got anything for us yet?"

"No good news. I pulled some prints off those cups, ran 'em through the state and AFIS. State database picked up Joey right away. Other one's still spinning its wheels." He shrugged wearily. "This isn't CSI, you know. When the results come back, I'll let you know."

"Okay," Burgess said, "so we know . . . or can surmise . . . that Joey Libby was in Kevin Dugan's room, having a drink with him. Tomorrow . . ." He looked at his detectives, who waited patiently for some direction, and down at his notes, frustrated that they were so many hours into the case and had so little beyond this maze of suspicious connections. Kyle and Perry looked equally frustrated. They'd spent a lot of hours and gotten nothing.

"Terry, you check the boat registry and do those warrants for phone records. Talk to the landlord and see if he has anything on Kevin Dugan. Do a records check on Dugan, too. And see if you can get a photo of Star Goodall. Stan, you do the breakfast places down on Commercial Street and then pay a call on Ms. Goodall. I'm going to see Reggie's doctor, then see Charlie Hazen."

He got out his notebook and found the appointment card. "Doc's name is Lyndeman. Dana Lyndeman. Dr. Lee wants to see Reggie's medical records, so I guess we'll need some warrants for those, too, Terry."

"Right. And I'll get on to Joey's parole officer, see if he knows where Joey's working."

Burgess showed them the scrap of paper with part of a logo that he'd found in Kevin Dugan's wastebasket, explaining what it was. "It's the only thing in the room that wasn't completely impersonal, and he cared enough to shred it, so maybe it's significant. I'll make you copies."

He shoved back his chair. "Hold on," Melia said, circling the group with his eyes. "You guys got this covered or do you need some help on this?"

"We're good, Vince," Burgess said. "More bodies at this point will only confuse things." Another detective's rule—keep it small, tight, and lean. Get too many people in the mix and communication broke down, information got lost, things didn't get followed up.

Melia nodded and rose. "Keep me informed."

Burgess's phone rang. The cop sitting on Claire Libby's house, reporting that a man in a truck had just parked out front and gone in.

"I ran the plates, sir. They came back to a business. Charles Hazen Realty. Oh, and the black van hasn't moved."

CHAPTER SIXTEEN

Instead of going straight home, he swung by Claire's house again. Not because he could do anything there. She'd made it clear he wasn't welcome and he would have gotten a call if Joey had returned. He drove by because it might help him think.

This strange interweaving of characters didn't make much sense. Why would they get themselves involved in the killing of another human being to acquire some land that would come to Joey eventually anyway? What was the source of their urgency? Claire didn't need money; she looked after Joey, so he wasn't hurting; and Star Goodall seemed to be doing okay.

They couldn't be doing it *just* out of dislike for Reggie. None of them ever had to see Reggie unless they chose to. And a desire to finally be done with Reggie didn't explain surveyors and realtors, never mind the mysterious Kevin Dugan. Where did Charlie Hazen come in? Was he interested in the land because he was interested in Claire, or was he only there for the money? Was he aware of the steps someone had taken to accelerate Joey's inheritance? Was he visiting with Claire and Star Goodall solely for a jolly glass of wine or was he there to discuss what to do now that their staged "accident" wasn't being treated as accidental?

He gave himself a mental kick in the pants. All he had were suspicions, not witnesses or evidence. He didn't know that any of these people, however peculiar their current behavior, had anything to do with what had happened to Reggie. All he had, so far, was his cop's gut, and that told him there was too much damned coincidence. If it looks like a duck and quacks like a duck, it's usually a duck. Or a turkey. But while cops were often guided by hunches, and instinct, and their guts, what brought cases home was facts. Evidence. Credible witnesses. None of which he had.

The patrol car was still parked down the street, dark and quiet. Goodall's black van still sat at the curb. A big, black double-cab truck was in the driveway, HAZEN REALTY painted in gold on the doors. The house was brightly lit. He sat staring at it a while, wanting to walk over and peek in the windows. Wanting, with a childish meanness, to ring the bell just to annoy Claire and let her know he was watching. He didn't, though. Just stopped a minute to chat with the patrol officer, then rolled away.

Up on Cumberland, he spotted Benjy limping along, head down and coat wrapped tight against the night wind, the old man's characteristic step and drag unmistakable, even on a poorly lit street. He pulled up alongside and rolled down the window. "Hey, Benjy . . ."

The old man jumped, then shuffled back until he ran out of sidewalk and hit the wall. Crouched defensively, he stared with watery eyes until recognition bloomed in his weathered face. Then he smiled and ducked his head. "Sorry, Joe. I didn't recognize ya at first. Man's gotta be careful walking around at night, especially after what happened to Reggie."

Burgess was thinking that Benjy was unlikely to accidentally end up in the harbor when he was ten blocks away—there'd been no public announcement that police suspected it wasn't an accident—when the old man added, "Grabbed right off the street like that."

Grabbed off the street? What was Benjy talking about? It might be just a street rumor, spurred by what he'd told Jim, or something that Kyle or Perry had said, or even a fabrication of Benjy's confused mind. But Kyle and Perry had been out talking to the street for hours and come up empty, so he needed to know if there was something to this.

"Getting kinda chilly out there," he said. "I was going to get some coffee. You want to come along?"

Benjy edged closer. "I'd like that . . . if you're sure you wanna."

"I'm sure." Burgess apologized to his abused stomach for sending it more coffee acid as the man swung himself up onto the seat and shut the door, carrying in the scents of cold sea air, unwashed skin, and stale tobacco.

"Dunkin' Donuts okay? I don't much like that convenience store stuff," Burgess said.

"I could sure go for one of their blueberry muffins," Benjy said wistfully. "Been a while since I had me one of those."

"Let's hope they've got one, then."

Burgess swung into the nearly empty parking lot and shut off the engine. He followed Benjy inside, waiting impatiently while the man unzipped and unbuttoned and rearranged his layers and got ready to order. It took a while for Benjy to choose a muffin and decide what size coffee he wanted. Burgess knew it was all to prolong the time he was inside off the street, and warm, and with someone who didn't shun his company.

When the choice had been narrowed to two, he said, "Why not get both. It's a holiday weekend, right? People are supposed to enjoy themselves."

Benjy's head bobbed. "You're a good guy, Joe."

He let Benjy finish the first muffin before asking any questions. Luckily, the eating went faster than the ordering. Then, as the old man was carefully picking the last crumbs off the napkin, Burgess said, "What you said a few minutes ago, about Reggie being snatched off the street. What was that about?"

"You didn't hear?"

"Hear what?"

"About Reggie. I woulda thought, you bein' a cop, that you'd a knowed this already."

"Afraid not," Burgess said.

"That right?" Benjy seemed genuinely surprised. "What I heard was that he was just walking down the street, pushing his shopping cart, like always—"

The watery eyes locked on Burgess's face. "You know how he was always out with that cart, all hours, day and night." The grizzled head moved in a sad arc. "Poor Reggie didn't sleep so good. Did you know he even had a bike lock for his cart? Night-time, when he was gonna go in, he'd lug his cans and bottles upstairs, then lock the cart up to the light pole outside his place."

The door opened and shut, letting in a whoosh of cold as two delivery guys in heavy sweatshirts and watch caps came in. Benjy checked them out, saw no one he recognized, and shifted his eyes away. The larger one turned toward them, his face mean. "What you lookin' at?"

Benjy hunched his shoulders and started peeling the wrapper off his second muffin.

"Hey there, old fart," the man said, "I'm talking to you."

Benjy looked at Burgess and shrugged. "Lotta mean people around these days."

The friendly Hispanic woman behind the counter handed the man his coffee and his change and wished him a nice night, but he'd got his mind fixed on trouble. Instead of leaving, he sauntered toward them, the sway in his swaggering step suggesting he should have switched to coffee sooner. He had TONY in white script over his heart. He was maybe mid-thirties, with a gut that stretched the sweatshirt taut. He had a petulant mouth and small, ugly eyes.

"Old man," he said, "I betcha you never did a fucking thing in your life but live off us workin' guys."

The man he'd come in with hung back by the door.

Benjy tried to make himself smaller as Burgess pushed back his chair and stood. "Leave the man alone," he said.

"Yeah? And who the fuck are you?"

His buddy put a warning hand on his shoulder. "Jesus, come on, Tone. That's a cop," he said. "Let's just get out of here."

But Tony wasn't leaving without a final word. "You"—he said, jabbing his finger in the air at Burgess—"tell the old piss-pot to stop staring at people."

Burgess looked at the man who had his hand on Tony's shoulder. "Better take your pal out of here before he earns himself a ride downtown."

Tony glanced at Benjy and down at his coffee, his fingers scrabbling to get the top off. Like Benjy had said, there were a lot of mean people around. A guy had to be careful. As the lid came off and the man's hand started forward, Burgess countered with a hand under the cup, sending the coffee meant for the cowering Benjy all over the man's shirt and pants.

An enraged "Fuck!" brought all eyes in the room in their direction.

"Oops," Burgess said.

When the man still hesitated, he added, "Big penalties for assaulting the elderly. That what you want, Tony? To screw up your life because you couldn't control a bad mood?"

Tony stared stupidly, his half-pickled brain trying to process what had just happened.

"Go on. Get out," Burgess said. "I'm counting to three. One. Two." Burgess planted himself between the man and Benjy, his scarred face offering no compromise.

"Jesus, will you come on!" The other man grabbed the dripping, belligerent Tony and dragged him toward the door, just as the Hispanic woman came out from behind the counter, carrying a cup of coffee.

She held it out to Tony with a disarming smile. "Because your other one is spilled." He took it and she wrapped her hands around his, now holding the cup, and looked up at him, still smiling. It was a tender smile, the kind a mother wears when she tucks her children into bed. "I know, Tony, that you are upset about your wife. But I feel, in my heart, that it will be all right." Like a child, he took the cup, nodded his thanks, and let himself be dragged away.

Wishing he could have diffused the situation like that, Burgess shot her a smile. "Thanks, Magdalena." In his own misery, he was forgetting. Everyone has a story.

"He's not a nice man, Sergeant Burgess," she said, "but he's not usually as bad as this." Her shrug was philosophical. "He has the troubles at home."

Didn't they all. He sat back down. "So, Benjy. You were telling me about Reggie and his shopping cart?"

"Oh, yeah." Benjy shook his head. "He'd use that WD-40 on the wheels and steel wool on the rust, kep it nice and shiny. Ole Reggie took better care of that cart than some people do their cars." He leaned in close, like he was delivering confidential information. "They think we're all dirty, 'cuz we live on the street, but Reggie weren't like that. He was neat. Kept himself good when he wasn't having one of his spells."

"Tell me what you heard," Burgess reminded him, his vow of patience already being eroded by this meander down memory lane.

"Oh. Yeah. About Reggie gettin' grabbed. I heard he was just walkin' along, checking the trash for cans and stuff like he'd do, minding his own business, when this van pulls up and a guy gets out. He and Reggie start arguing, then another guy gets out, and the two of them haul Reggie into the truck and drive away."

Questions flooded his mind. Van or truck? What the men looked like. Burgess tried not to overwhelm Benjy by blurting them out all at once. "You didn't see this yourself?" Reggie shook his head. "Who'd you hear it from?"

Benjy kept his eyes down as he carefully removed the top of his second muffin, broke it into six pieces, and ate the first. "I dunno, Joe. I was somewhere, and people were talking. Maybe over to the park sharing a bottle? I heard it and it scared me, ya know. Life's hard enough on the street. There's always people think they can beat on us. Like that guy was just here? He coulda hurt me and no one would care. You learn to be careful, ya know. Stay away from the Old Port at night, especially on the weekend, things like that. Be real careful when you meet groups of young guys. Be extra careful when you pass them Africans. Heck, I know one woman, she got beat by a group of young girls."

The cops cared, but they couldn't be everywhere.

Benjy sighed and ate two more pieces of muffin. "I don't know what the world's comin' to. You gotta stay away from the crazies and the druggies when your check comes. Be real careful about who you hang with. There's always someone looking to make what you got theirs." He grinned as he ate the fourth piece of muffin. "This sure is good, Joe. I appreciate it."

He licked a finger and caught up some crumbs. "Me, I got direct deposit for my check. Some lady over to the Preble, she suggested that. Makes my money go a lot farther. Harder to spend if it ain't in my pocket and I gotta go to the bank to get it." The fifth piece disappeared as Benjy shook his head. "Sound like an ad for one a them banks, Joe, don't I?"

"You sure do," Burgess agreed, wondering if Reggie had had direct deposit. He'd found no bank stuff among Reggie's papers.

"So, you've got no idea who you heard it from?"

"Nope. I'll think on it, though. Sometimes, I go lookin' for information in my head and it ain't there. Then, later, I'm just walking along, mindin' my own business, and whammo, there it is, when it's no use anymore."

"I think that happens to all of us. Even if you can't remember who you were talking to, can you recall what they said happened to Reggie?"

"He was fightin' with them. Reggie didn't wanna get in that truck. Swung a fist at one of 'em. Hit him pretty hard, too. Reggie wasn't one to let people push him around. You know that, Joe. Wasn't never mean or violent, but he was no sissy. I've seen him stand up for Maura coupla times when guys were making fun of her. Reggie didn't take to people not being treated decent."

Benjy stopped talking as he ate the last piece of the muffin top, and drank some coffee. "I dunno what kind of truck it was. I used to know all my trucks and cars but there's so many more brands these days. Lotta foreign ones. This one was a double cab. Think it was American." He hunched his shoulders. "That's all I know. It maybe had a logo or somethin', but I'm not too clear on that."

"What day did this happen?"

Benjy looked surprised. "Friday, of course. Reggie wasn't workin' that day. He hadn't been feelin' too good, so he took him a day off. I thought you knew that."

He knew nothing. That's why he was here. Ordinary people had lives with schedules and habits and regular contacts with people. The forgotten people had some of those, too. Like Reggie's regular date with Maura. But there were a lot of blank spots, too. They lived meager lives without a lot of documentation. He couldn't use Reggie's social security number to look up his employer, for example, because he worked under the table. Couldn't trace phone records 'cuz Reggie had no phone.

The old man contemplated his empty napkin. Hefted his cup, but it was empty. "Sometimes he had Fridays off. That was day he and Maura . . ."

"I know," Burgess said. "Had sex. And that was why Maura was worried."

"How's Maura doing?" the old man asked. "I haven't seen her around."

"I haven't seen her, either," Burgess said. "Getting back to Reggie and that truck, did you hear where this happened?"

Again, the old man registered surprise, as though Burgess should know this. "Down by the waterfront. See, Reggie was down there having lunch with his cousin. That crazy one, ya know, thinks she's a witch. He used to spend time with her 'cuz he felt bad for her, on accounta losing her husband. She was real broke up about that, so Reggie, ya know, tried to look after her." Benjy giggled. "Kinda the blind leadin' the blind, you ask me, but Reggie done what he could."

"You know where on the waterfront?"

Benjy looked offended. "Sure I do. Not too far from where the bridge goes over to South Portland, that new bridge replaced the Million Dollar Bridge. We were walking along near there. It was a pretty nice day. The sun was out. Then all of a sudden, the truck pulls up and stops. Reggie, he stares at it and he gets this look, sorta half scared and half angry. Then he gives me a shove. 'Get on outa here, Ben,' he says. Well, I ain't fast, but I got. Went between two buildings and hid, but I could still see what was happening."

"So you were there."

Benjy slapped his palm on the counter. "Shoot, Joe. I didn't mean to tell you that."

"You see him forced into a truck, he ends up dead, and you don't want to talk about it?"

The old man's bent head shook from side to side. He wouldn't look up. He stuck out a hopeful finger, licked it, and stabbed at the napkin, searching for crumbs. Finally, he raised his eyes to Burgess's face. "I'm an old coward, is all," he said. "I just didn't wanna end up dead, too. And that's what the man said would happen if I opened my big mouth."

CHAPTER SEVENTEEN

Burgess slid off his stool. "Come on, Benjy, we're going for a ride."

The old man showed no signs of moving. "Right here's fine," he said. "I got a place not far away. You don't wanna drive me, I can walk there easy."

"What I don't want is any more bullshit, okay?" Burgess said. He felt old and heavy. Exhausted by the effort of holding a lifetime's images of Reggie at arm's length. Sick of being patient and understanding.

Benjy didn't move.

"Come on, Benjy. You were his friend. Something's happened to him and suddenly you want to play 'see no evil'? You're not a goddamned monkey and this is no game. Two days ago, when you're sidling up to me while we're taking a body out of the harbor because you've just got to tell me Maura's worried that Reggie is missing, you didn't say anything about seeing two guys beating on him and forcing him into a truck, did you? You're the fucking witness. How were we supposed to find this out? Read some goddamned tea leaves?"

People were staring again. He waited for a response but the old man wouldn't raise his eyes from the floor. "You're not stupid, Benjy. You had to know what you saw was important."

The old man cringed deeper into his coats, like a turtle retreating into its shell. When he spoke, his voice was muffled by heavy fabric. "Hey, come on, ya know what I said about my

179

brain. How it doesn't remember things when I need them and then remembers later. That's what happened, is all. I wasn't playing games with you. You're a cop, ya know? Why would I?"

Burgess knew a lot of reasons why people played games with cops and had little respect for most of them. With a lifelong friend discarded like human trash—dumped in the ocean the way everybody dumped everything in the ocean and assumed it was out of sight, out of mind—he had little sympathy with Benjy's "I'm afraid" ploy. Man was probably more at risk if the cops didn't know than if they did, because once they knew, there was less value in going after Benjy.

"You're playing games with me now, Benjy. With what you saw and what you'll tell. Now get your coats buttoned, because we're going over to 109 and you're giving a statement."

Benjy still didn't move. Exasperated, Burgess pulled him to his feet. "That's enough. Move it. Some of us would like to get some sleep before it's time to wake up again."

Benjy began his slow shuffle toward the door. As he passed the counter, Magdalena gave another of her wonderful smiles and held out a bag. "Here, Ben," she said. "Another muffin for the road."

Burgess looked back as he steered Benjy toward the door. "Thanks, Maggie," he said. "You're a good person."

That produced another smile. "You, too," she said. "Now you go along, Benjy, and help the sergeant out. No more fooling around. Or next time, there's no muffins for you." She shook a finger at him and Benjy ducked his head.

Burgess trailed him out the door and back to the truck, using his bulk to ensure that the man didn't bolt. He waited until Benjy had fastened his seatbelt, then drove back to 109.

He parked in the dusty garage. The icy cement chill, carried to his bones by tongues of sharp wind, hinted too clearly of the cold months ahead. Not what he wanted to think about tonight.

He was getting too old for four or five months of winter.

He put Benjy in an interview room with the muffin and went to set up the tape and check his messages. On his desk was a fat folder with a note clipped to it. Wink's writing. "Here's what came back on that second set of prints, presumptively your Kevin Dugan. This one's a real lulu. Name's Leonard Joseph-son. Got a sheet like a roll of toilet paper. His specialty is arson."

He picked up the file and scanned it quickly. The guy had a lot of aliases, including, no surprise, Kevin Dugan. And no scruples about burning buildings with people in them. Burgess shivered. Arsonists were scary people. There was something particularly cowardly and ugly about those who set fires. Murder was often a crime of passion or impulse or impaired judgment. Arsonists planned, and their victims, deliberate or collateral, died horribly, often with them sticking around to watch. Was it just coincidence that Dugan had moved in across the hall from Reggie or did he play a role in this?

There was a picture in the file, which he decided to show to Benjy. He also found a note from Kyle, with two pictures at-tached, which meant Kyle hadn't gone straight home, either. One was a PR shot of Charlie Hazen, the realtor who was interested in Reggie's property. Hazen looked prosperous and affable and very full of himself. The other was of Star Goodall, casting an adoring look up at a man he presumed was her late husband, Nick.

Taking the pictures with him, and adding one of Joey from his own file, he shoved back his chair and went to get Benjy's statement on tape. The muffin was gone, nothing left but a crumpled bag and crumbs on the table. Benjy was wrapped in his coats, only a shock of bristly gray hair showing, the gentle sound of snoring rising from the heap of clothing like some shapeless beast slumbered in the chair. Like they always say— the innocent sit nervously waiting to be interviewed; the guilty fall asleep. He shook the old man's shoulder. "Come on, Benjy, rise and shine. Time to go to work."

Benjy took some time to orient himself, shaking his head and fussing with his coats. Finally, he seemed to be ready. Burgess turned on the tape and identified both of them. Then he asked Benjy to go through the story he'd told at Dunkin' Donuts about Reggie's abduction. It was like getting a reluctant mule to plow. Benjy hemmed and hawed and fussed and forgot and did every damned thing he could to try Burgess's patience and avoid saying anything useful. After the better part of an hour, though Burgess dredged up enough patience to qualify for sainthood, he had a tape full of nothing and Benjy whining in the chair.

"What is your problem with giving us an official statement, when you have important information relevant to this investigation?"

Benjy studied his shoes. "I dunno. I guess I don't mind telling you, informal like, seeing as we know each other, but I don't want no official paper, saying that I told you all this."

"You're name's going to be on a paper anyway, Benjy, because I'm going to write up what you told me earlier and put it in the file. What's the difference?"

"I guess, 'cuz if you write it down, it ain't necessarily me that said it, ya know?"

He wanted way too badly to hit the old man and knock him right off his chair. Longed to commit worse elder abuse than he'd chided the guy about in the donut shop. Reggie was dead. Dead and most likely murdered and this man, who'd probably scrounged a thousand cigarettes and at least that many drinks from Reggie, who'd used Reggie repeatedly and for years, abusing his kindness the way pathetic losers did, lacked the guts or decency to come forward and help.

"You're a goddamned mooch, Benjy. Take whatever you can

get from anybody—me, Reggie, Maura—yet you won't lift a finger to help us find who killed him."

The old man hunched his shoulders and gathered his coats more tightly around him. "You don't unnerstand, Joe. I just don't wanna be next, is all."

"You're a lot less likely to be next if you talk to us than if you don't, Benjy."

"I gotta look after myself, Joe, ya know? I don't got a cop for a friend, like Reggie did." Idiot's reasoning. Look what having a cop for a friend had done for Reggie.

"You disgust me." He crossed the room and opened the door. "Get the hell out of here before I find some reason to lock you up."

"You ain't gonna drive me home?"

"You bet I'm not." He crossed back to where Benjy sat and scooped up his file. As he did, the pictures spilled out onto the table.

Instead of fastening his coats or getting up to leave, Benjy stared down at the pictures. Then, with a shaky finger, he pointed at one of them. "That's him, Joe. That's the guy from the truck. The one who was arguing with Reggie and then hit him."

Even though it had captured his angry words, Burgess was glad the tape was on. This was something. "The guy you're pointing at calls himself Kevin Dugan. He lived across from Reggie. You ever see him there?"

Benjy shook his head. "Nope. But I hadn't seen Reggie around much lately. Just on the weekends, when he was out with his cart. He kept pretty regular hours during the week because he was workin', ya know? Some of the guys were even complaining about it, 'cuz Reggie was always good for a drink or a smoke. You know how he was. If he had anything, he'd share."

Burgess pointed to the picture resting under Benjy's finger. "This guy, Kevin Dugan, is the one who got out and was arguing with Reggie, then hit him and dragged him into the truck?"

"Yeah. That's him. I'd a knowed that mean face anywhere." Benjy pointed at the man's face. "He's got this scar here under his eye." He tapped the picture with a finger. "This guy and the other one, it took the both of them to drag him into the truck."

"Is this the same guy who came after you and threatened you?"

"Nope." Benjy stabbed at another photograph with a trembling finger. "I think it were him." Burgess looked down to see where Benjy's shaky finger had landed, hoping, with an absurd, protective hope the boy didn't deserve, that he hadn't pointed to a picture of Joey. The gnarled finger was pointing to Star Goodall's husband.

He sank down into a chair, his head in his hands. He'd just wasted hours on a guy who wouldn't cooperate, who after enormous efforts at persuasion finally IDs one person they're looking at, then makes that ID look completely suspect by IDing a dead guy.

Fuck. He kneaded his forehead with his fingers, trying to push away the headache that was building. It wasn't working, so he gave up. "Come on, Benjy," he said, trying to keep his anger and frustration out of his voice. "Time to go home." As he opened the door to let Benjy out, he tried one final question. "You notice anybody else around who might have seen what happened to Reggie?"

Benjy thought long and hard about that one as they stood with the night wind blowing over them, carrying the tangy brine of the sea and the fainter smell of burned leaves. "There was a guy switching out them free papers . . . you know the ones that are in those boxes? There was a pregnant woman pushing a kid in a stroller. She left real fast when she saw what was happening. And there was one of them Africans. Somali. Sudanese. I can't tell them apart, myself. But you see him around a lot. Scary-looking fella with scars on his face?"

Benjy bobbed his head, as though he was having some secret internal conversation with himself. "He was sitting in a car parked in front of the building where I was watchin' from? He's so big, that guy, he coulda done something if he wanted. But he never does nothing for nobody, Joe. He's always just watching."

Another bob of his head as Benjy said, "When that big guy came and warned me off, he didn't even look around to see if anyone else was watchin', so I don't think he even saw the guy in the car. Guy sure saw him, though. I was watchin' those eyes, all white and wild in that dark face, and they followed him back to the truck and until they were out of sight. Then he started up his car and drove away."

"You notice what kind of car?"

"Old Mustang. Sixty-seven or eight. Baby blue. Cherry," Benjy said, limping off toward the garage. "You take care, Joe. I'll let ya know if I remember anything else."

Burgess went back upstairs to do a search on old Mustangs registered in the city.

CHAPTER EIGHTEEN

His eyes felt gritty as he stared at the screen. There were an awful lot of old Mustangs in the city. He sighed as he hit print and shoved the printout into his already bulging file. This could wait 'til morning. He didn't do anyone any good if he let himself get so bleary from lack of sleep he couldn't function. In the morning, he'd get Stan to track down the free paper delivery man. He headed for the door, leaving the detectives' bay to one lonely man in a corner speaking softly into a phone, and Detective June Barlow with her crazily uncombed hair, staring with tired red eyes at her terminal. Such an exciting life. No wonder everyone wanted to be a cop.

He was almost out the door when a thought sent him back. He'd taken it on faith, listening to Star Goodall's dramatic story of losing her husband, that her husband *was* dead. He'd believed her, but he hadn't checked, and that was careless. The rule of investigation was trust, then verify. He'd never forgive himself if he compromised Reggie's case because he hadn't bothered to check basic facts. He knew she was manipulative and dishonest.

He typed in "Nicholas Goodall" and scanned the results. No obituary. No dramatic front page stories of the artist's tragic death. No mention of any sort of the man's death. He checked death records. Nothing there, either.

"Fuck!" He pounded his fist on the desk. Then he went to the DMV and looked for driver's license information. Nicholas Goodall had a current license giving a Portland post office box as his address. He owned a three-year-old black Chevy Avalanche, also registered to the PO box. And he owned a 2002 Wellcraft 3200 Martinique Express Cruiser. There was no listing for a phone.

Now he had to wonder. Reggie had been consoling Star Goodall because she'd "lost" her husband. Lost him how? To a life away from her because of her craziness? Perhaps to someone he'd met at the hospital after a cardiac event? If they were estranged, though, Benjy's ID of Goodall as one of the men who'd taken Reggie didn't make much sense. But what had they learned about this case so far that did?

In the morning, he'd call Clay and find out what the story was, then hunt down Nicholas Goodall. He'd put Kyle on the task of visiting marinas and finding the boat Joey might be living on. Was it possible that it was Goodall's boat? Put Perry on the job of finding the Mustang and a potential witness to Reggie's abduction. Much crime investigation was pretty straightforward, but sometimes it opened into a series of mazes. This was going to be one of those.

This time, he got out of the building without a second thought. Got in the Explorer and headed for home. And found himself heading back down toward the waterfront instead. He parked by the wharf and grabbed his camera, snapping pictures of the empty wharf, the docks bobbing below, and then went back to the street and snapped pictures of the water and the wharf from there. Like the wall of photos at home. Pictures of emptiness.

The night was bright and the tide was low, the shore looking black and greasy in the faint, cold light. Something white wedged in the rocks caught his eye. It could be anything—a plastic bag, discarded coffee cup, paper plate. Or it might be Reggie's missing shoe. As he looked around for a way down, his phone rang.

"I'm going to bed," Chris said. "I'll leave the lights on for you."

A Taurus cruised down the street and came to quiet stop beside him. Stan Perry rolled down his window. "I tell you I asked patrol to keep an eye out for that shoe?" Burgess nodded. "Well, a guy out in Deering just called in. He pulled over in one of those industrial lots to write a report. Saw something in the grass and actually got out to see what it was. Sounds like it might be Reggie's other shoe. I'm on my way to check it out. You wanna come?"

Burgess looked up and down the empty street. "This isn't exactly on your way."

"I couldn't sleep. Still feeling like a jerk about that girl, I guess. I knew the tide would be low, thought I'd take another look around for that shoe. I was just turning off Franklin when I got the call." Perry grinned. "What? You think I was following you?"

"Let's check it out." Burgess started toward his car, then turned back. "Of course, Captain Cote would say that it doesn't take two detectives to investigate one shoe."

"Especially when the victim is just a crazy old wino. We got funny standards in this city, Joe. We got small-time merchants all over this city getting robbed at knifepoint and gunpoint by our new African neighbors and nobody hits the alarm button. Just wait 'til all that hits the Mall."

"Mall is in South Portland," Burgess said.

"Right," Perry said. "Not our problem."

"I'm glad something isn't," Burgess said. "I'll follow you." He started the engine, mimicked Stan's tight U-turn, and headed off through the empty streets. No one around but cops and robbers.

The patrol car was parked at the edge of an unused lot, the

crumbling asphalt growing up to weeds. Burgess grabbed his flashlight and he and Perry walked over. A middle-aged officer, face lined, body going soft in the middle, got out as they approached, holding a large flashlight.

"Evening, Steve," Burgess said. "Thanks for calling it in. What you got for us?"

The officer lifted his hat, pushed back sweaty hair, then resettled the hat. "Been one of those nights, Sarge. City looks quiet but the calls just keep coming. We've had a bunch of complaints from the businesses out this way about kids drinking in their lots, spray-painting the buildings, smashing windows and throwing trash around. I try to swing through here a couple times a shift."

He raised his light and pointed it into the dark lot, the yellow beam stabbing the night like Vader's light saber. "It's over here." The officer led them about twenty yards back into the lot, their feet kicking up the dusty herbal scents of fall vegetation, and illuminated the heel of a white running shoe. "Shoe's got those reflector strips on it that catch the light. That's how I spotted it."

Burgess clicked on his light and moved it slowly around, studying their surroundings. The lot was a big rectangle with patches of gray asphalt broken by knots of weeds and grass. It ran on for another ten or fifteen yards, ending in a row of scraggly trees. Where they were standing was close to one of the sides, delineated by bushes and trees and a sagging fence. Through gaps in the vegetation, he could see into the adjacent lot, where lights illuminated a brick building with closed doors opening off a small loading dock, and an empty parking lot.

He brought his focus back to the shoe, bending down to study it. He wouldn't know for sure until he could match it to the one the divers had found, but it looked like the mate. The one they had was a right shoe; this was left. This was the same brand and new. He couldn't read the size and didn't want to disturb it until it had been photographed in place. He straightened and looked around the dark lot, already running the possibilities. Why drop the shoe here when it would have been so much simpler, and safer, to wrap it up and throw it in the trash? Was that deliberate, part of some crazy cat-and-mouse game with a killer who would plant clues for them to find, or were they lucky enough to be dealing with stupid?

He didn't feel lucky.

There might be other things here, too, but this was no time to search, stumbling clumsily around this vast, dark lot, trying to do a thorough search with flashlights. This would now top his list for the morning, and until then, they needed to close off this lot and get someone to sit on it until it was light.

"Good work, Steve." He didn't mention the lingering scent of fresh urine that suggested the officer's real reason for stopping here and making this find. "I need you to sit on it until I can get somebody out here."

The officer smiled. His shift was almost over, which meant overtime.

Burgess was tying up patrol right and left tonight, wasn't he? He led the way back to the cars, trying, as much as possible, to follow the same route they'd taken coming in, already on the phone making arrangements to secure the lot until they could search in the morning. So much for sleep, but that was okay. Sleeping hadn't felt right since Lee had dropped the word Reggie's death was no accident. It was irrational, but that made the routines of ordinary life seem obscene.

Stan hadn't said a word. Now he said, "I'll drive the road, check out the businesses around here. Then go back to 109, see if any of them are on our radar screen. Warren Street's a good place to dump things on a holiday weekend, that's for sure. And probably a bunch of places out here got cinder blocks. What time you wanna do this tomorrow?"

Burgess checked his watch. It *was* tomorrow. Chris had been working on civilizing him, but given a choice, he defaulted to being nocturnal. He liked the peace and quiet of it. It was easier to be alone with his thoughts without all the daytime commotion. "Seven? Seven-thirty?"

Perry yawned. "I kinda like the sound of eight."

"All right. Go home and get some sleep. You can do the road tomorrow."

"Thanks, Dad. But I kind of want to drive around for a while, get a feel for the area at night. See what's dark. What stands out." Thinking like a detective. But there was something else in Perry's restlessness.

"Don't even think about it, Stan," he said.

"Think about what?"

But they both knew.

"That woman. Getting beat down by her husband. How that makes you feel. Makes you want to set it right. Get square. Let her know that she can't mess with you and get away with it. Don't do it. Stay away from her, from him, if he's out of jail. Box it up. Lock the box. Let it go."

"But she . . . but I . . ."

"But nothing, Stan. Stay away from it."

"Sure thing, Dad."

"That's an order, Detective." Burgess sighed and hoisted himself back into the truck, carrying the pleasant scent of crushed grasses in with him. He'd said it, whether Perry had heard it or not. That was the best he could do.

He pulled out onto the road and headed for home. He might not want sleep but he needed some. That, like so much else these days, made him cranky. He wanted to reach down inside himself, pull out a younger, more resilient Joe Burgess, and slip on that skin. Longed for the buoying excitement of the chase, the pleasing challenge of a case that was a puzzle and the satisfaction that came from solving it. Instead, he felt beleaguered. A grouchy old man who'd seen too much staring at a bunch of puzzle pieces that didn't make sense.

As Captain Cote was fond of reminding him, he had a bad attitude.

He humped himself home, hunched like an angry bear behind the wheel. Left his shoes by the door, took what another might have regarded as a relaxing shower, and climbed into bed.

Chris turned her back to him as he settled in, offering the curve of her body for him to settle against like a nesting spoon. As his heavy lids settled down over sore eyes, he caught the faint rose scent of her night cream. Just as he fell over the edge of sleep, he had a thought. Probably something important, but he was too far gone to pull himself back. He let the day go and tumbled down into dark.

Chapter Nineteen

He woke before six, torn from sleep by what sounded like a seagull convention outside his window. His idiot neighbor, the poetically named Celestine Beliveau-Smythe, more prosaically and appropriately known as "Les," who'd moved in a month ago and already established himself as an undesirable with everyone on the block, had put out the trash from his Columbus Day picnic two days early. The gulls thought Les had done it just for them. Before Burgess had even finished dragging his lids up over his still sore eyes, a murder of crows had joined the party, which now reminded him of long-ago weekends on Munjoy Hill.

Predictably, Les was sleeping through it.

Chris, who usually got up around seven, stirred, muttered an expletive followed by the word "Les," and pulled her pillow over her head.

By the time Burgess dressed and went next door to make sure his neighbor was awake to enjoy the commotion, a light rain had started. Just what they needed to make the morning's search that much more miserable. He stepped over the matted masses of paper plates and soggy napkins, the skittering paper cups and food-crusted plastic silverware, kicked aside an eviscerated watermelon, and went up the front walk, circling birds squawking complaints as he disturbed their picnic.

Les answered the door in what looked like a 1940s woman's bathrobe, probably his late mother's, a tatty faded rose chenille with shoulder pads. When Burgess explained the problem, he blinked like a surprised owl, wrapped his long bare toes around the threshold, and expressed dismay, followed by a profusion of apologies. Behind Burgess, the street was alive with the agitated flap of squabbling birds. A glossy crow the size of a piper cub cawed at him from the branches of a large tree.

"Hell of a mess out there, Les," Burgess said. "You'd better clean up before it gets any worse."

Beliveau-Smythe shoved up his sleeve, revealing a hairy wrist and a watch dial resembling the cockpit of a jet. He stared at the time, blinked, and reread the numbers. "It's not even six A.M., Joe," he said. "Don't you think—"

Burgess wasn't feeling neighborly, but he choked down angry words and forced an even tone. "What I think is that you've made a hell of a mess out here and those birds are waking up everyone on the block. The decent thing to do would be to clean up the mess pronto and stop disturbing your neighbors."

The man tried unsuccessfully to tuck errant strands of hair back into his graying ponytail, then shook his head, peering through his gold-rimmed glasses like Burgess was a particularly slow student. "Sheesh. Take it easy, man. I'll get to it. I just don't see why it's such a big, fricking emergency. I'll do it when I'm dressed and I've had my coffee. You don't expect me to go out there dressed like this, do you?" Bony fingers plucked at the robe.

Burgess didn't much care how his neighbor dressed. He just wanted the trash picked up. An especially loud shriek made Burgess turn just as a rising gull dropped what looked like a dirty diaper onto the hood of his car.

"You really can't see from here, can you?" he said. He grabbed the man's elbow and led him down the path to the street, Beliveau-Smythe's bare feet slapping lightly on the cement until one bare toe sank into a mush of paper plate crusted with what appeared to be potato salad.

Distaste turned the man's long face into a mask of prudish disapproval. "Oh, that's nasty," he said, scraping his toe on the grass.

"For all of us," Burgess said.

He left the man obsessively pawing the grass, plucked the dirty diaper off his car, and handed it to his neighbor. Distracted, the man took it, then recoiled. "What the hell!"

"It was on my car."

"Well, really, Joe, I don't think that justifies—"

Justifies? "Clean it up," Burgess said. "All of it. Or I'll see that patrol writes you tickets for littering. One for each god-damned piece of this shit."

He headed home, calling back over his shoulder one of those expressions he'd always hated. "Have a nice day." It was just so appropriate here.

Thus began another happy day in the city by the sea, a day that, once he was done being the trash police, caught him up in a swarm of "to-do" lists. No time for coffee or breakfast, not that he felt much like either after smelling the garbage. He had a search to organize, an outdoor search in the rain, then a zillion people to see. He caught Chris as she was heading sleepily for the shower and kissed her. "I told him to pick up the trash," he said.

"My hero," she said, batting her lashes. "I bet he was surprised."

Her hero headed out into the gray morning. The rain was falling harder now, and it had gotten colder overnight. At 109, he picked up Stan and Terry, Dani Letorneau, the evidence tech, and Sage Prentiss, their newest detective. Stan, turning his sleepless guilt into productivity, had made copies of the city maps showing the lots along that portion of Warren Avenue and annotated them with current business names. Burgess briefed them on finding the shoe and some basics on what they might be looking for, and they headed out. Perry rode with Dani in the crime scene van. Kyle and Prentiss rode with him.

For the next two hours, they searched the lot. It was an exercise in futility. In daylight, it was clear that the lot had become a dumping ground for people who didn't want to have to pay to dispose of large, unwanted household goods. The vegetation was crisscrossed with tire marks. At the back of the lot, dead sofas and chairs shared space with broken televisions, an old electric stove, a couple of refrigerators, stained mattresses and rusting bedsprings. Several chairs and a sofa had been pulled into a circle around a blackened area that marked the remains of a fire.

Last night in the dark, discarding a shoe here had seemed odd. In daylight, it joined such a mess of other trash that tossing it here seemed natural. Trash invites trash. They still had to look. The shoe might not be the only thing the killers had discarded. Someone needed to get on to the owner of this lot and get it cleaned up and chained off. Meanwhile, many more hours later, the investigation that was going nowhere nagged at him like an unscratchable itch.

Crisscrossing the lot, picking up his twentieth, fiftieth, hundredth piece of soggy paper, his nostrils were filled with the smells of crushed grass and weeds, mildew, and the sourness of rotting vegetation. Every season had its scent, and fall's crisp scents of fresh air and burning leaves were underlain by the odor of death and decay. Like his life. Spending this dismal, depressing morning looking for a needle in a haystack or, in this case, clues in a trash heap suited his mood perfectly. Between the unspeakable things people did to each other and the cases he couldn't fix, the iron that held him upright and hopeful was rusting. Depressing as Reggie's up-and-down life had been, as long as Reggie was there, he'd believed in the possibility of change. Reggie had been one of the Dumbo's feathers he clutched at to keep going.

When they'd admitted defeat and sent Dani and Sage back downtown, he and Kyle and Perry stripped off their gloves and got into his car. Their shoes and pant-legs were soaked.

"Look, can we get some breakfast?" Perry said. "I'm starved. And no fast food. I don't want greasy potatoes or prepackaged eggs that have been given CPR. I want real food."

"Diner?" Kyle said.

"Sounds like a plan." Perry tipped his head back and closed his eyes. "Wake me when we get there."

"Thought you were tireless," Burgess muttered.

"I'm sleeping," Perry said. "Leave me alone." Seconds later, there was a faint snore.

If they went to breakfast, Burgess would miss Reggie's appointment with his doctor, and doctors were notoriously difficult to interview because of their schedules. But it would be good for the three of them to sit down and review their game plan. He tugged out his notebook, handing it to Kyle. "Can you find the appointment card for Reggie's doc and give him a call, see if he can see me later today?"

In a second, Kyle was on the phone, starting polite, quickly switching to firm, then to unyielding. "Ma'am, I understand the doctor is busy. This is important. We're investigating a death here and we'd appreciate a little cooperation."

There was a pause, and Burgess could hear a woman's not-too-pleasant voice trying to put Kyle in his place. He'd heard it a zillion times. Doctor This and Doctor That were always such busy, important people. Doctors, lawyers, Indian chiefs, tinkers, tailors, soldiers, spies—everyone was busier and more important than a mere homicide investigator. People did so hate to be bothered by sordid stuff like crime.

Unfortunately for her, Kyle was already in his place. "Maybe

I wasn't clear," Kyle said. "We're investigating a suspected homicide. As in murder? Really appreciate it if you didn't impede the investigation by giving me a hard time. Sergeant Burgess won't need long, but he does need some of the doctor's time. Today."

Kyle sighed. Murmured. Listened. Stan Perry snored. The tires hissed through puddles and the wipers whined their metronomic whine. The detective's symphony ended as Burgess swung to the curb in front of the diner and stopped.

"Doc'll see you at eleven," Kyle said.

"IIow kind."

They shook Perry awake and went inside.

A perky waitress with improbable magenta braids was right there with coffee and back to deliver a fresh dish of tiny creamers before Stan Perry even had his eyes open. They ordered the protein-carb overload of food typical of hungry men. As soon as she was gone, they all got their notebooks open.

"Got a witness says he saw two men dragging Reggie into a truck somewhere down by the bridge to South Portland on Friday afternoon," Burgess said.

Kyle raised his eyebrows. "No kidding. Where's he been hiding?"

"It's Benjy."

"Oh. In a bottle," Kyle said. "Fuzzy recollection. Shit-scared to tell us anything. I feel sorry for him but the guy's a weasel."

"You got it. I think he figured on a lot of free food and coffee while he 'remembered.' Guy like that sees the world as a pocket to be picked. Best he would do, when pressed, was two men and a truck. He said when Reggie saw the truck, he told Benjy to run. Benjy says there was a scuffle." Burgess drained his coffee and looked hopefully around for the waitress. "When I brought him back to 109 to get a statement, he wouldn't talk for the tape. He did say that there were some other wits. Guy stocking a box with free papers. A woman with a stroller. African guy in a Mustang with scars on his face."

Perry hit the button first. "I've seen him around."

"Good. You can track him down, then. I've got a printout of old Mustangs on my desk." He looked at Stan. "Now that you're awake again. BOLO on Joey's car?"

"Of course. It's registered to his mother."

"We've got to talk to Joey. Terry, can you do the marinas today, see if anyone recognizes Joey's picture, knows if he's living on a boat? There is a boat registered to Star Goodall's husband, Nick—"

"Thought her husband was dead," Kyle said.

"So did I. She said she'd 'lost' her husband. Told me this dramatic story of the night his heart stopped. She said Reggie kept an eye on her because she'd lost her husband. So, Stanley, when you go see her, see if you can get some clarification on that story, okay? She may have lost him, but not to eternal life."

Perry looked up from his notes. "I got a pretty big to-do list here."

"That's so Terry and I can go rain skipping." He paused while his cup was refilled. "Benjy said one of the men who pulled Reggie into the truck looked like Nick Goodall."

Perry muttered an expletive just as the waitress delivered breakfast. There was no sound for a time but chewing. Then he said, "How would Benjy know what Nick Goodall looked like?"

"Ole Terry here got a picture of the Goodalls and put it in the file. It fell out with some others when I was interviewing Benjy. I thought he was gonna ID Joey, but he went for Goodall instead. I don't know that it means anything, though, the way his brain works." Burgess checked his watch. "Sorry, guys. Gotta go see a man about a liver." He threw down some bills.

"Joe," Kyle said calmly. "You're our ride."

He looked at their full plates and hungry faces. "Keep eating," he said. "I shouldn't be long. Be lucky if he gives me fifteen minutes."

Kyle smiled as he poured a lake of syrup on his pancakes. "We'll be right here."

"Yeah," Perry said. "Talking about you behind your back."

"Don't say anything good," Burgess said. "It would make my ears burn."

He took Deering up to Bramhall, stopped in front of an old brick home that was now doctors' offices, and climbed to the second floor, arriving at a generic waiting room where listless, unhealthy patients, mostly men, drooped in uncomfortable chairs. On the coffee table lay an untouched assortment of glossy *Men's Health* beside well-thumbed *Sports Illustrated.* At the counter, he gave his name in a quiet voice. The overweight receptionist, identified by her name tag as Glenda, shoved her glasses up her nose, looked at a screen, and then past him into the room. "Sullivan?" she bellowed.

An emaciated man pushed himself up and shuffled toward her. She mimicked a smile and pointed toward a door to her left. "Just go through there, Mr. Sullivan. The nurse is waiting."

Only then did she focus on Burgess. "Yes?" she said, as though he hadn't already spoken.

This had to be the woman Kyle had tangled with. Well, he'd tried to be respectful of the doctor's privacy and patient comfort, but if she wanted to be a jerk, she'd met her match. He pulled out his badge and waved it back and forth at eye level. "Detective Sergeant Burgess, Portland police," he said, loudly. "Here to see Dr. Lyndeman."

"Well." Red rose up her cheeks like Kool-Aid poured into an opaque glass. Her breath hissed out. "Well, all right," she huffed. "Hold on."

She picked up a phone, punched some buttons with stubby fingers, and said, "The cop's here." She replaced the phone with a clatter and pointed toward the door she'd sent Mr. Sullivan through. "Dr. Lyndeman will see you now."

Dr. Lyndeman was waiting just inside the door, dwarfed by the white lab coat she wore, a tiny, pale woman who looked about twelve, with efficient dark hair. She took his hand in a surprisingly firm grip. "Detective Burgess? Dana Lyndeman. If you'll just come this way."

He followed her into a cramped little office with light wood furniture and way too many files. On the wall above her chair hung a framed photograph of two small, bright-eyed girls. She saw him looking at it and smiled. "My daughters. Hilary and Ariana."

"Cute," he said.

"They take after their father." She leaned forward. "Glenda said you needed to speak with me about Mr. Libby. Something about a suspicious death?"

"He was found floating in the harbor on Saturday," Burgess said. "When Dr. Lee did the autopsy, he observed that Mr. Libby had a severely damaged liver." He stopped. Calling Reggie "Mr. Libby" felt too strange. "Dr. Lee said Reggie's liver condition would have killed him. Reggie was a drinker. I'm sure you know that . . ."

Burgess hesitated, not quite sure what he was asking. The status of Reggie's health? Details about his last days? He was looking for clues. For her observations. "I guess I'm here for your views on Reggie's medical condition." When she didn't respond, he said, "If you're worried about confidentiality issues, don't. We'll be collecting his medical records anyway. With a suspected homicide, the ME's going to need to see them. I'd just prefer not to lose a lot of time going through the subpoena process right now."

She nodded as she searched through the files on her desk and opened one. "Mr. Libby was a very sick man," she said.

"He came to the emergency room a few weeks ago in severe pain. We did some scans and a liver biopsy. The results showed severe cirrhosis and necrosis . . ." She followed that with a barrage of medical jargon he didn't understand, the long, complicated words and phrases tripping off her tongue with ease.

He had his notebook open, his pen poised, but there was nothing he could write down. Then she hesitated, looking up from the file and straight at him. "Yes, Mr. Libby admitted that he was a drinker . . . but we . . . I . . . suspected his condition was not entirely the result of alcohol. I, at least, suspected there might be some other exposure involved."

She shrugged. A woman of science, not entirely comfortable sharing speculations with someone who wasn't another doctor. With a cop. "It was a complicated scenario. There were a number of tests that needed to be done, some toxicology issues to be explored. Mr. Libby was not a cooperative patient. He was reluctant to take time off from work—"

Burgess was in over his head. Dr. Lee had also suggested that this damage might not have been the result of alcohol and was going to run some tests. "Let me get this straight," he interrupted. "You found Reggie had liver damage that was going to kill him, and you suspected that the source was not his drinking? Or not entirely his drinking?"

"That's the gist of it, Detective, although medicine is rarely that simple."

As though police work was? "Any idea what might have caused this damage?"

She shook her head. "It's a process of elimination, really. We come up with theories, and then we test them, eliminate things. New tests will suggest other possibilities. And then there's the information about the patient's lifestyle. That can be invaluable." She hesitated. "When they tell the truth." She picked up a freshly sharpened yellow pencil, tapped the lead against her notes, then set it down again.

"We . . . I . . . suspected that the source of the toxins damaging Mr. Libby's liver might have been wherever he was working. But . . ." She hesitated again. "You call him 'Reggie.' Did you know Mr. Libby?" She might look childlike, but her mind and observations were all grown up.

"We played football together in high school." His mind ran on with the list of what they'd done together. He had to jerk back.

She nodded and tapped her pencil again, deciding something. "Sometimes, being a doctor is a lot like being a detective. We gather what facts we can, put them together with our experience, and come up with theories about the case. With Mr. Libby, I thought it likely that he might be being exposed to something at his place of employment, but when I tried to get more information, he balked. He refused to tell me where he was working or to describe the nature of his work. I gathered—"

Someone knocked on the door and a nurse stuck her head in, "Excuse me, Dana . . . will you be much longer? Mr. Sullivan's getting restive." Her eyes rested briefly on Burgess, then she smiled. "What's the matter, Joe . . . don't recognize me in my working garb?"

Deb Palmer. A friend of Chris's. "Hey, Deb," he said.

"I was so sorry to hear about Reggie."

Dr. Lyndeman dug under the papers again and came up with a box of chocolates. "If I remember right, Mr. Sullivan's got a sweet tooth. Give him a few of these, tell him I apologize, and I'll be right along."

Reggie would have liked this woman. She was a straight shooter and she was compassionate. "Sorry to keep you," he said. "Mr. Sullivan did not look well. You gathered?"

"Many of my patients don't look well," she said. "Otherwise they wouldn't be seeing me. Okay. Two things. No. Three. That wherever he was working, it was irregular. Under the table or something. That his employers were emphatic about not having the arrangement known. Which, you'll agree, is odd. And that he was very proud of having a job and wanted to keep it."

Reggie in a nutshell. He so desperately wanted to work and be normal. And because he'd lived the humiliating life of the mentally ill and the street person, he'd learned to be deeply respectful of other's privacy. "When did you last see him?"

"A week ago Monday. He wasn't doing well."

"Can any of your tests show what he was exposed to?"

She shrugged. "I don't know. The lab might have that capacity. I don't know if they have the time."

She fiddled with the pencil again, her face serious. "Detective, can you find out where he was working? Because if it happened to him, and they fill his job, it could happen again."

He started to rise but she held up a finger, like a teacher holding a class back at the bell. "Hold on a minute . . ." She shuffled through the file, ran a finger down some paragraphs, and looked up at him, her face troubled. "Mr. Libby said he'd worked there last spring, filling in for someone, then left to go help his brother on the farm. He got the job back this fall because that someone got sick and couldn't do it anymore."

She shoved back her chair and stood, a quick, angry motion. "People the world regards as disposable, Detective. I see a lot of them in my practice. To me, all my patients have value."

She headed for the door, calling over her shoulder, "I hope you'll let me know what you find out."

He followed her out and hurried downstairs to the car, his brain clicking. Reggie gets a job, but he has to keep that job a big secret. He goes to work in a truck with a logo on the door, but no one seems to know what that logo is. Then he gets sick and then he gets dead. And he's not the first.

When he checked his watch, he'd had exactly the allotted

fifteen minutes. Just like a patient. The only difference was he hadn't departed with a prescription in hand. A dose of the latest thing the cute young pharmaceutical reps were pushing to cure whatever ailed him. He doubted that even the thoughtful and compassionate Dr. Lyndeman had something in her PDR to treat his current ailment—a severe lack of clues and reliable witnesses. Maybe the prescription for that would be like the time he'd tried Prozac. Just give it four to six weeks and maybe it might help. He couldn't wait four to six weeks. Burgess headed back to his cold breakfast.

Chapter Twenty

Back at his desk, Burgess stared at the pile of pink message slips and reports. Hazen's truck had left Claire Libby's at midnight. Goodall's black van hadn't moved. The red car never returned. While they were out in that wet lot spending hours and resources picking up a goddamned shoe, Lieutenant Melia would have been at roll call, handing out Joey's picture, pictures of Kevin Dugan aka Leonard Josephson, and info about the red Audi.

This case was like trying to put an octopus in a teacup. He picked up the phone to call Clay and got Mary again.

"Clay's not home, Joe," she said. "He's gone to see the lawyer." Burgess was both relieved and sad.

Before he could respond, she said, "He'll be a while, Joe. He's doing some errands, too. There was some commotion around the place last night. He's gone down to the Agway and to Lowe's. Getting fire extinguishers. More outside lights. Shotgun shells. Cement and some heavy posts. He's going to put a chain across the driveway. And he's going to stop by and see the tenants out there on Reggie's land."

He could hear a background clattering and the whoosh of water that sounded like she was doing the dishes. She'd be doing this with a phone clamped between her ear and her shoulder. Their household would not be equipped with a speaker phone or a hands-free headset nor was it a place where hands were ever idle. "This is just so sick, Joe. Everything about it is just sick and twisted. And so unfair. At a time when we should be mourning poor Reggie and planning for a decent funeral, Clay's seeing lawyers and worrying about watching his back."

There was the crash of breaking glass. Silence. The clink of glass on glass. Then she said, "Should we let the sheriff's patrol know so they can keep an eye on things?"

"I'll do it," he said. "And give me the names and address of those tenants, too." He wrote it all down. He'd do what he could but public safety coverage in rural areas was thin on the ground. "Does Clay carry a cell phone?"

"He doesn't hold with those kind of things, Joe. Says he doesn't want to live in a world where a person can't just be by himself now and then. He considered it, a while back, in case there was something . . . you know . . . an emergency with Reggie. But he's usually to home, or I am, so we decided not to bother." She sounded breathless and a little scared. "This is just all wrong, Joe. We shouldn't have to be doing this."

He respected her too much to offer comfort that wasn't comforting. "Tell me about the commotion."

"Around three A.M. Tucker, that's our dog, began barking like crazy. He likes being out at night until it gets too cold. Normally, he's a quiet dog. He'll bark to let us know someone's coming down the drive or get between us and strangers, let 'em know who's boss, but last night was different. He really let loose. Clay got up and went out. He said the motion lights were on and Tucker was standing in the yard, looking down the driveway like he was watching something. After a while, Clay heard a car start, then drive away."

The water ran again and something clanged into the dish drain. "Sorry about the commotion. Doing some canning today. I'm washing out the jars."

He pictured the kitchen. Warm yellow beadboard up to the chair rail and flowered paper above. A neat, clean, homey place cluttered with the stuff of a working farm at harvest time. Baskets of late tomatoes, let go as long as possible before the threat of a serious frost. Drying onions. Apples and squash. Full canning jars lining the shelves, empty ones filling the counters. Her big graniteware canner on the stove. Mary, slim and efficient in slacks and a freshly ironed blouse moving briskly through her kingdom, her curly hair pinned back with barrettes. The corner desk overflowing with bills and papers waiting to be filed during a quieter season.

Magazines always showed kitchens with granite counters and gleaming appliances; food, if it appeared at all, artfully arranged in fancy dishes. Farm kitchens weren't like that. They were work places, perpetually in the midst of processing and storing food. Seedlings in spring, produce in summer and fall. Stages in the journey from planting to the long winter. The long, cold winter. A phrase his mother always used, so imbedded that he never heard "winter" without adding "long" and "cold." Even in her city kitchen, the counters had been laden with produce and berries, the late summer and fall air scented with the vinegar and spices of pickles and the sugary warm fruit of jam.

"You know where we live, Joe. There's no call for anyone to be around here in the middle of the night. No legitimate reason, anyway."

Another jar clanged. "I'm concerned for the tenants. They're just a couple of sweet hippie kids who know about organic farming. I doubt they've even got a gun in the house. Not the gun ownin' type, if you know what I mean. Hardest working kids you've ever seen, but they're tree huggers. Probably wouldn't even shoot a woodchuck, and that's saying something. Blasphemy or not, Saint Francis would be tempted to shoot a woodchuck. After they got half a crop cleaned out in one night, Clay went over and shot a couple chucks, then got 'em a dog."

Mary sighed deeply. "Like we don't have enough on our

plates, worrying about ourselves. I'm trying to get the canning done and Clay's worn out hauling and splitting wood. Price of oil being what it is, we'll need that wood. Splitting wood is therapy for him, just now, but we're not so young anymore. He may come in with the mad worked out of him, but then he gets up aching. All we want is to get together a decent funeral for Reggie and then get on with our mournin' in peace and privacy."

He'd never known Mary to be this chatty. Normally, like Clay, she was taciturn.

"I guess you're used to it, but I still can't get my mind around it," she said. "That he's gone, I mean. That the phone isn't never going to ring again with someone saying there's an emergency down to Portland, can we come." A good woman, trying for normal, in a world suddenly grown threatening and uncertain.

Abruptly, she broke off. "Listen to me going on, when you've got work to do. Clay's gonna go over to the Baxter's, that's our tenants, and put up some lights for them, too. They're probably outside, getting the last of the harvest in, never mind that it's rainin', but if you want to try over there, I can give you that number."

He didn't want to make a big deal out of this, but Clay wasn't the type to jump at shadows. If Clay thought the situation called for caution, Burgess had to respect that. "I'll take that number, Mary. Thank you."

As he wrote it down, he realized Mary could probably answer his question as well as Clay. Might as well ask. It could take hours to track Clay down. "Nicholas Goodall," he said. "What's the story? The way Star talked, I thought he was dead."

"That's Cindy for sure. Always been the one for embroidering. She likes to make things dramatic. It's four years now and she still talks like he died on the riverbank despite her best efforts to save him. The truth's about as common as cheese. Nick had a heart attack and when he went to the hospital, he met a nurse who made him realize how difficult living with Cindy was. Not that he isn't pretty flamboyant, too. I guess that artists are."

She laughed. "Nick's version of normal is kind of what them artists like to have—what are they called? A muse? Somebody who supposedly inspires 'em? Only it's really someone who does the cooking and the cleaning and brings home the groceries and a paycheck and supplies freshly ironed shirts. He wasn't getting that from Cindy. She thought he oughta be ironing *her* shirts. He walked a fine line, though, trying to have that and not have Cindy stab him in the back or put poison in his food while he wasn't looking."

He knew way too much about Star Goodall and her poisons. His gut ached just thinking about it.

"Hold on a sec, would you?" He heard her set down the phone, and a door opened and shut. "Had to let Tucker out," she said. "Nick gave her the house, though he keeps the use of the barn for his studio. And he pretty much supports her, since I don't guess witches make a whole lot of money. I've always kind of wondered how his muse feels about that, since she works. He'd give a lot, I think, to be out from under his obligations to Cindy. Funny thing, isn't it, that he's a famous artist who doesn't make much money?"

"He's got a boat."

"Nice boat," she agreed. "He took it in exchange for a piece of sculpture he did. Then he found out how expensive boats could be. And how hard the darned thing was to sell. Smart, you know, but maybe not wise? Or practical."

"Sounds like you stay in touch with him."

"A little. We always liked him. He could be a bit grandiose, I guess, and kinda self-indulgent. He's been a real wimp about Cindy and makin' her let go, and I don't get that stuff he builds at all, but mostly he's just a regular guy trying to figure out how he ended up married to a nutcase. He tried to make it work with Cindy, I'll give him that. Sometimes, when things were bad, he'd call Clay for advice. Clay did his best. I guess we all did, even Reggie, but Cindy's like a snapping turtle. Once her mind closes on something, there's no budging her."

There was a sudden grunt, a crash, the sound of something heavy settling. He leaned forward, tensing, as though he could do anything from fifty miles away.

"Basket of shellbeans," she said. "Slipped off the table and knocked over a chair. Gotta get these things shelled and canned. I'm sick of seeing them sitting around my kitchen. Usually, Clay and I do them together. Sit and watch some TV and shell the beans. But he's too distracted to sit. Why are you asking about Nick?"

"Just trying to figure Star out, I guess. You got a number or an address for him?"

"Got both. Don't know if they're current. It's been a while." She paused. "You think she's mixed up in this?"

"Have to check every angle." Annoyed with himself for giving so much away, he wrote down the numbers. "One last thing, Mary. Do you know if Reggie was working last spring, before he came to you for the summer?"

"For a few weeks he was, I think," she said. "Covering for some other guy while he was out sick, maybe? He didn't say much about it."

"He never said where it was or anything? No check came for him, maybe?"

"Sorry, Joe. I don't remember him saying anything. Maybe he told Clay. Is it important?"

"Probably not. I'm just trying to figure out these last weeks and I'm having a hard time getting a good timeline."

"His last weeks," she said, a catch in her voice. "All I know is that he was keen to get back to Portland on account of that job. Otherwise he'd of stayed longer with us."

Better let her get on with shelling the beans. Fall on a farm. A lot to do before frost and winter. He had plenty to do, too. Like visit Charlie Hazen. He hadn't made an appointment. Hazen was likely to regard a police visit as inconvenient, and isolate himself behind a wall while extremely polite people declared that sadly, Mr. Hazen was unavailable. He had checked to see if Hazen was in.

He sat a moment beside Hazen's fancy truck, then fished in the glove compartment for his digital camera. He snapped the truck and a close-up of the logo, and tucked the camera in his pocket. Instinct born of decades on the job made him restart his car and park it behind Hazen's, like a man in a hurry who's just paused a moment to ask a quick question. Then he went inside.

The woman behind the reception desk must have had no mirrors at home. Her brassy Dolly Parton hair needed a touch-up, her chipped red nails needed repainting, and her billowing midriff needed a slenderizing undergarment or a billowing overgarment. Her breasts didn't need anything except covering. They oozed up out of her too-small black tank top like twin mounds of rising dough, flecked with freckles and moles, jiggling gently with every inhalation. A tank top in late October. The office wasn't that warm. Without makeup, she would have had a pleasant face. With it, she was zombie-movie scary. Behind her, the wall was lined with framed photos of Hazen, country-club dapper with a wide, white shark's grin.

She blinked brittle lashes at him and tapped a nail on the glass desktop. "Can I help you?"

He showed his badge. "Detective Sergeant Burgess to see Mr. Hazen."

"Oh." For about three beats, that was all. Then her hand

went to her chest, squashed the pillows, and drifted toward her phone. "I don't think he's . . . I mean he's . . . that is he said he . . ."

"Urgent police business," Burgess said.

She blinked a few more times, picked up the phone, and punched in some numbers, waiting tensely for a response. After what must have been the space of twenty rings, she cradled it, unsuccessfully suppressing her smirk. "Must be away from his desk."

Burgess was already moving. He jerked the door open just as Hazen backed away from his blocked truck, heading across the parking lot toward a muddy Jeep. Burgess went after him.

CHAPTER TWENTY-ONE

By the time Burgess reached him, Hazen had the key in the lock. Burgess blocked the door with his body and held out his badge. "Detective Sergeant Burgess, Portland police, Mr. Hazen. I need to ask you a few questions." This wasn't Simon Says. He didn't say "may I."

Hazen, pink with irritation under his tan, put his hands up in mock surrender, then produced his signature realtor's grin. Neon-bright teeth in a lined face were more jarring than attractive. "Okay, Chief," he said. "You got me."

If he were "Chief," he wouldn't have to put up with crap like this. Burgess produced an equally false smile and gestured toward the building. "Shall we go inside?"

"Here is fine."

"Then we'll use my office, so we don't have to stand in the rain." He herded a reluctant Hazen toward the passenger side and opened the door. He'd prefer better lighting and face-to-face but this would have to do. He'd hardly gotten his notebook open when his phone rang.

"Good thought about that boat," Kyle said. "Guy down here at the marina says Joey's been living on a boat the last six or eight weeks. Came tearing in last night, though, packed up his stuff and took off in one hell of a hurry. Didn't say where he was going." Kyle paused. "Actually, when the guy asked, 'cuz he's a nice, friendly sort who's done some favors for the kid, Joey told him to fuck off, suggested an anatomically impossible act, then left a strip of rubber as he departed."

Burgess didn't want Hazen to hear this. He said, "Excuse me," and got out of the car. "In the red Audi?"

"Yup."

"You'll want to search the boat," he said. "See if you can save us a little time, get the owner's permission. I got Nick Goodall's address and phone number from Mary Libby. You ready?"

Kyle was always ready. Burgess read off the information. "Got it," Kyle said. "You know if Claire Libby has another place? Summer place? Ski condo? Somewhere Joey might go to get out of town until things cool down?"

He tried to remember if Reggie or Joey had ever mentioned a place. Couldn't come up with anything. "Not that I remember, but it wouldn't surprise me."

"I'll see what I can find out," Kyle said, and was gone.

Something else Clay might know. Burgess would call him later.

He flipped to a blank page and got back in the car. Hazen wasn't waiting patiently. His feet danced on the floor and his fingers danced on his knees. "What's this about?" he demanded, before Burgess had even shut the door.

"Real estate. Reggie Libby's property." Agitation had heated up Hazen's aftershave or cologne or whatever the hell it was, filling the car with reeking man perfume that would linger long after Hazen was gone. It was better than vomit, he supposed. That also lingered. "You were out at the property a few weeks ago with Joey, having a survey done, weren't you?"

Hazen shrugged. "I'm a developer. Waterfront is hot and it's a big piece of land."

"How did you learn about the property?"

The realtor's feet shuffled on the carpet. His fingers danced until he willed them to be still. "I'm not sure," he said. "I don't know if it was from Claire or from Joey. It just came up casually in conversation that Joey had some land and—"

"That was how you understood it," Burgess interrupted. "That it was Joey's land?"

"Going to be Joey's," Hazen corrected. "That there was some land in trust for Joey."

"So you knew the land was in trust?" Hazen nodded. "Go on."

"Joey said he had no use for some piece of land out at the back ass of beyond . . . those are his words, Chief, not mine. He wasn't ever going to be a farmer and they didn't need another place on the water, so Claire . . . I'm pretty sure it was Claire's idea . . . reminded him that I was a developer and suggested maybe he should bring me out there to have a look."

When he didn't continue, Burgess said, "When did this conversation take place?"

Hazen shrugged. "I dunno. Eight weeks ago, maybe? Could be longer." A hand flutter suggested vagueness. "End of summer, early fall, we can be pretty busy."

"You went out with Joey to see the place?" Hazen nodded. "When was that?"

"A couple weeks later. Joey wasn't too clear about where the land was, that back ass of beyond remark was all the information he had, but Claire knew, so she came along. Pretty piece of land."

"Who suggested the surveyor?"

"I did. It was the natural next step. You need to know what you're dealing with. All these old deeds and surveys, so many times they're way off and there's actually less land than people think they own. Obviously, you can't even think about doing a development plan until you're sure of the lot size and configuration. I wasn't going to make an offer until I had a clear picture of what was there."

"Make an offer to whom?"

"Well, Joey, of course. Claire was very clear she didn't have any interest in the land."

"By interest, you mean legal interest?" Hazen nodded. "But the land was in trust."

"A formality," Hazen said dismissively. "As I understood it, the trust was just a dodge to keep owning property from affecting the father's disability payments. Joey said that wouldn't be a problem. His father would sign it over to him whenever he wanted."

"Who told you about the trust? Claire or Joey?"

Hazen hesitated, his hands doing a tap dance on his knees again. Then he said, "I'm not sure. I guess . . . I think . . . it was probably Claire. Joey was interested in money but he wasn't big on details."

"Any particular reason Joey was eager for money?"

Hazen shrugged. "Wanted to get a place of his own. Kid's kinda old to be living with his mother."

"You ever talk with Reggie? Confirm that what Joey said was true?"

Hazen looked right. Looked left. And lied. "That's right. When I talked with Reggie, he assured me that he was behind whatever Joey wanted to do."

"But Reggie wasn't the trustee, was he?"

Hazen's vigorous shrug threw off another blast of scent. Guy must buy the stuff by the gallon. "That's the uncle . . . Reggie's brother . . . he's the trustee. But he's supposed to do what Reggie wants . . . uh . . . wanted, right? So if Reggie had no problem, his brother shouldn't, either. That's how I understood it. That's why I was a little surprised when the surveyor's out there and the brother shows up all huffy, even after he's told it's okay with Reggie. But he's a farmer, you know. They're always reluctant to have anything to do with using land for development."

He frowned and looked at his watch. "I've got a lot to do, Chief, like to wrap things up. What's this all about, anyway?"

"Detective," Burgess said. "Or Sergeant. Either one's fine. You said you spoke with Reggie. When was that, Mr. Hazen? And where did the conversation take place?"

"How the hell should—" The hands tapped as Hazen slammed on his verbal brakes. "Pretty soon after that first conversation with Joey. I'd guess maybe seven or eight weeks ago."

So once Claire had mentioned the land, Hazen had moved fast. He'd have to confirm it, but Burgess didn't think Reggie was even back in Portland then. "And where?"

"Right here in my office," Hazen said. "Joey picked him up at that rooming house and brought him out here."

"Morning? Afternoon? When did you meet?"

"I don't remember."

Burgess flipped to a clean page. "Describe the conversation."

"I don't remember. He was an old guy. Kind of out of it. I don't remember that he said much. I told him that Joey had mentioned to me how he wanted to turn the land into cash and I asked Reggie if that was okay with him. He said the land was in trust and it wasn't up to—" Hazen tapped his knee and checked himself. "He said his brother was the trustee."

"And?"

"And nothing."

"You said Reggie seemed kind of out of it. Was he sober? Do you think he understood what you and Joey were talking about?" Hazen didn't answer. "Did he tell you that any decisions regarding the property had to be made by his brother?"

"Didn't I already say that? Look I asked and you didn't answer me. What is this about?"

"Did he appear to understand what you and Joey were talking about?"

The right answer, if he wanted to appear responsible, was a simple yes. But Hazen was annoyed. Like many wheeler-dealers, he wasn't used to being on the answering side. Words were *his* manipulating tool. "He didn't seem to understand a goddamned word I said. He just stared at the kid with these sad spaniel eyes and shook his head. Said I'd have to talk to his brother. And that went real fuckin' well. All I got from that SOB was that I was wasting my time. He said the land was under a long-term lease for farming. Like we need fuckin' organic vegetables more than people need places to live. Not that any of that matters any more. Now that the father's gone, it's Joey's land and he can make the calls."

"You're a realtor," Burgess said. "Does death of the grantor invalidate a lease made by the trustee?"

This time, he couldn't draw Hazen in. "You said you arranged for the surveyor. Did you pay the surveyor?"

Hazen's look said, "Do I look like a fool to you?" He said, "Joey said Claire would take care of it."

"Do you have a copy of the survey?"

"Goddamned slow-as-molasses country surveyor hasn't sent me one yet. What I get for trying to go local. He sent one to fuckin' Joey, who says he lost it somewhere on that goddamned boat, but not to me or to Claire, even though it was Claire's goddamned money that paid for it."

"Star Goodall didn't pay the surveyor?"

"With Claire's money. Miss Star Look-at-Me-I'm-a-Witch Goodall hardly has a pot to piss in. Just what Nick gives her."

This guy knew an awful lot about Joey and his family. "Did he send a plan to Star?"

"I don't know. Getting a straight answer from her is like trying to get one out of you."

"Just trying to understand the situation in the weeks leading up to Reggie's death."

"What does that have to do with real estate?"

"You all seem to be in a pretty big hurry, given that the property doesn't go to Joey until he's thirty-five."

Hazen's cheeks flamed. "Oh, fuck you, Chief. I don't know what kind of game you're playing, but I've got work to do." He did the knee tap for self-control again. When it didn't work, he grabbed the handle and opened the door. "Go ask fuckin' Joey what the trust says. He said on paper it was up to his uncle, but he knew how to work with his uncle, and lease or no lease, his uncle was going to give him the property real soon."

Hazen got out of the truck and slammed the door.

Burgess watched him stomp across the lot, then put the truck in gear and rolled away.

CHAPTER TWENTY-TWO

As he headed back into town, his phone rang. Kyle again. "Goodall says Joey's not his tenant anymore, and gave us permission to search the boat. You wanna join me?"

"There's nothing I'd like better. You at the marina?"

"I am."

"Be there in ten."

Ten was optimistic but with impatience driving his foot, he wasn't feeling too picky about speed limits. As long as he didn't run over a pedestrian, who was going to complain about a cop driving fast? The public wanted a quick response.

As he parked and followed Kyle's directions to Nick Goodall's slip, a man came out of a building. Burgess stopped and went to meet him. "Detective Burgess," he said, "here to take a look at Goodall's boat. You the guy who saw Joey Libby leave last night?"

The man's features were nearly hidden by a curly, sand-colored beard. He had the reddened cheeks and lined eyes of a man who's spent his time outside, and had a limp, apparently from some leg injury. "That's me. Bill Tolliver," he said, holding out a hand. "Let me know if there's any way I can help."

"I expect you can, Mr. Tolliver," Burgess said. "You going to be around for a while?"

Tolliver waved a scarred hand toward the building. "My office. My home. I'm pretty much always around, Detective. If I'm not out and around the boats, just knock on the door when you're ready." He shook his head. "That's a sorry kid. All kinds of people trying to help him and he just pisses all over 'em. I dunno what makes a kid turn out like that. Big, smart, good-looking guy, got everything going for him, and he's just as mean as a snake. 'Specially to girls. Women."

He shook his head again. "Even his own mother. Woman may not be very friendly, but she sure loves that kid. She comes down here to bring his goddamned laundry and the little bastard can't even be bothered to say thanks. But it's the cute little girl that bothered me."

He said it like Burgess should know what he meant. Burgess shook his head, so the man went on, "Plenty of girls on and off that boat. Joey's a real ass hound. But this girl, I saw only the once. Pretty young thing, fresh as a daisy and stars in her eyes."

He paused to make sure Burgess was paying attention. "You know. A nice girl. A real nice girl. Someone's daughter. I guess they're all that, but you know what I mean. Sweet and clean and innocent. Dressed decent and polite as you please. She comes tripping down here in her pretty yellow dress and those little white shoes, looking for Joey. I tell her where to find him, so she goes down to the boat, and a couple hours later, she's all bruised and her dress is torn and she's crying like her little heart is broke forever. I drove her home. She wouldn't let me take her to the ER, poor little darling. I spoke to him about that when I got back and he couldn't of cared less. 'Go fuck yourself' is his answer to everything."

Kyle was going to have to wait a few minutes. "When was this, Mr. Tolliver?"

"Week ago, maybe. Not long."

"You didn't call us."

"I offered. Tried to convince her that she needed to so's he wouldn't do it to some other girl, but she just kept shaking her head no, said it was all her fault anyways, and she was so upset and hurt already, and she'd begged me not to, so I let it go. Except for speaking to Joey."

"And he just blew you off?"

"Little prick said she was just a cock tease and had it coming. Like any girl ever deserves to get beat and have her clothes torn off. I told him anything like that happened again and never mind what the girl wanted, I was calling you guys. And I told him I was calling Nick Goodall. I didn't want him here in the marina anymore, doing like he was doing. He's got all the girls he wants with no hassle, so why's he gotta go and do something like that?"

He answered his own question. "Because he's gotta ruin something. Gotta spoil something good."

That sure sounded like Joey. "You know her name?"

"She didn't want me to know." Tolliver shook his head. "I can tell you where she lives, though." He gave very exact directions, no number but enough information to find it.

Burgess wrote it down. When he and Kyle were done here, he'd swing by there. For two reasons—first, because he was sickened that Joey was abusing women again, and he needed to know how far this had gone. Second, because it might have been this, not a desire to escape police questions about his father's death, that triggered Claire's stonewalling and Joey's flight.

"I'd like to get a written statement from you, if you're willing," he said.

"More than willing," Tolliver said. "I should of done it right then, only I was trying to protect her. I wasn't thinking about how he'd see it, thinking he'd got away with something. Not 'til after, when I talked to him."

"Did you call Goodall?"

"You bet I did. He's been pretty easy to deal with. Doesn't really want the boat anyway. He never uses it, but he knows he's got to keep it up if he's ever going to sell it. I keep an eye on it, tell him if things need doing. Only this time . . . I called him the next day, told him what had happened. He said he was too busy to talk, he'd get back to me. Which he never did. Then I got busy—fall's a busy time with the boats—so Joey was still here, until last night."

Tolliver shifted his eyes toward the boat. "Now what's he done?"

"Hit a cop."

"Guess I'm not surprised."

"We'll take care of Joey," Burgess said.

It was, as Mary Libby had said, a good-sized boat, the kind that sucks fuel like a thirsty elephant. It had a large cabin with a galley and spacious mid-cabin, and a big, comfortable berth. Plenty of room for a guy to crash. Although trash was really the operative word. Squalor. The fug of sweat, sex, and alcohol mixed with the sour stench of garbage. It looked like Joey'd only done dishes when he'd run out—the sink was filled with dirty cups and plates—and had never taken out his trash. Too freakin' lazy to carry it the thirty feet or so out to the Dumpster. There might be nothing here, but Joey sure hadn't stopped to clean up before doing his run.

Burgess was a little surprised Claire hadn't taken out the trash and cleaned up when she delivered Joey's laundry. Or sent her maid down to clean. Maybe Joey wouldn't let her.

"Welcome to Pigstye Acres," Kyle said. "Where the recently departed denizen seems to have lived entirely on pizza, canned pasta, and fast food takeout. It was a lot worse before I opened the door and the windows. Portholes. Whatever the hell they are. There sure isn't anything about this guy to like."

"You're gonna like him even less when you hear what Tolliver just told me."

"That's the security guy?"

Burgess told Kyle about the girl.

"You'd think he'd want to keep his nose clean, at least for a little while. How long has he been out?" Kyle said. His voice was level but there was an angry vibration in his thin frame.

"Six, eight months. I wonder what his PO has to say?"

"His PO," Kyle pointed out, "didn't even know where he was living. If you call this living. And couldn't tell me where he was working. Just that he had a job."

"Nick Goodall was cooperative?"

"Very. Anything we want. Happy to talk with us when it's convenient. I made an appointment for later," Kyle said. "Figured you'd want to be there, after what Benjy said."

"You got that right. Later, as in?"

"As in when we get done here." Kyle checked his notes. "Always available to help the police, he said. Sounded like a guilty conscience to me."

Burgess hoped that while they were here pawing through the garbage, Nick Goodall wasn't packing his things and heading out of town. But he was an adult. Established. Not the type who usually runs. "When we're done here," he agreed. He studied the messy room. "How you wanna do this?"

Kyle pointed at the banquette that made a "C" around the table. "I've pretty much done that side. Got some papers there on the table that might be of interest. Some roaches and a couple small green pills in an ashtray. I can finish in here while you do the sleeping area." Kyle's gray eyes flashed amusement. "Then we take the trash up on deck and go Dumpster diving."

"Spending time with you is always such fun, Terry."

"Isn't it. Just a merry old detective, me. It's all those years studying at your knee. And just think, if we hadn't made such savvy career moves, we could be working some dull nine-to-five. We could push paper. Push other cops around. Line up neatly sharpened pencils."

"Golly," Burgess said. "Imagine not having to grid-search a junk-filled parking lot in the rain, followed by a cheery chat with a realtor so slimy he could be entered in a greased pig contest, then hearing a sordid tale of innocence abused and now diving into some lowlife's trash. It makes me proud that I can do this for the poor, frightened public."

"And we both know how much they appreciate it. I lie in bed nights, filled with empathy and sympathy for all those worried citizens who're anxious and sorry over the death of a homeless guy."

"He wasn't homeless."

"They don't know that. The paper doesn't know that. Even the other homeless think he was homeless. Anyway, what does it matter? All the hours we spend doing this, John Q. Citizen doesn't give a tinker's damn." Kyle crossed the room and jerked open the refrigerator, sending the reek of spoiled food into the room.

"Yeah. Appreciation. It sure makes the job worth doing." Burgess said. "All those smiles, and waves, and being urged to 'have a good day.' But mostly it's all those donuts they leave out at reception."

Kyle peered over the refrigerator door. "They leave donuts at reception?"

"I've heard they do. Fat Wayne gets them. He's got a hell of a good donut detector."

Fat Wayne Bascomb, perhaps the city's most incompetent police, sat down in evidence control and ate all day, his career security protected by influential relatives who wanted him someplace where he couldn't do any harm and a police department that agreed. No one on the street wanted Fat Wayne watching their back. Burgess had been jonesing to beat on Fat Wayne since the man had messed with some evidence in an important case, and Fat Wayne knew it. Lately, the guy had done a good job of staying out of his way.

Burgess pulled on gloves and went to work. After the ninth used condom wrapper, he wondered about the type of girl Joey attracted. Even a woman out for a good time and a casual hookup must have some standards. Why sleep with a guy whose floor was littered with the relics of his prior sexual activity? Too lazy, horny, or drunk to care, he supposed.

Maybe the girl in the white shoes had been different. Maybe she'd come down here thinking Joey was a nice guy to spend some time with. God knew the kid could be charming when he wanted. Then she'd gotten here and seen what he was really like: a slacker who lived like a filthy pig. Maybe she'd said something and his ugliness had come out. Maybe she'd realized her mistake and said she was leaving when he'd had other plans.

In the corner of the berth, snagged in a tangle of blankets, he found the surveyor's drawings. For all his general indifference, Joey had been interested enough to take them out of the package, and when Burgess unrolled them, it was clear Joey had looked at them. Kid had even spilled food on them. Wouldn't Hazen love that? Burgess carried them out and put them on the table with the things Kyle had culled, then went back and finished the room. The rumpled sheets were dirty and semen stained, with a couple pairs of grimy boxers mixed in. Other than another saucer of roaches and small bag of marijuana, he found nothing else of interest.

He was ready to move on, but some instinct made him hesitate. He pulled the blankets and sheets off, tossed them in the corner, then flipped the mattress over. He found a cut in the cover toward the center, patched with a strip of duct tape. After changing his latex gloves for leather search gloves, he carefully loosened the tape and slipped his fingers in, feeling cautiously around until he hit something plastic and slippery. He pulled it out and held it up to the light. A couple hundred small green pills with an alligator logo he didn't recognize.

"Hey, Ter," he called. "Found something." He held the bag out. "Recognize these?"

"Might be Ecstasy," Kyle said. "Drug guys said they'd been seeing some green pills lately." He smiled. "That's enough for a warrant. And to revoke his probation."

"Now all we've gotta do is find him." Burgess looked around the small, messy cabin. "There might be more," he said. "We'd better get someone to sit on this boat until we can get a warrant and get the drug guys in. Better safe than sorry."

It might have been the detective's motto. No sense in working as hard as they did on a case and then losing everything when someone challenged their search. It created a constant tension between the need to work fast and move a case along, and taking the time to cross the t's and dot the i's to preserve things for the future.

"I'll see if Stan's back," Kyle said. "Be nice to move fast on this one before there's an unfortunate accident, like the boat sinking or a fire of mysterious origin." He returned to the main cabin and Burgess heard him on the phone.

A minute later, as Burgess returned the drugs to the mattress and restuck the duct tape, Kyle stuck his head in. "Stan's on it, and patrol is sending someone down. Ready for the real garbage?" He held a cluster of green bags. "I left some for you."

"I like that about you," Burgess said. "How you're always willing to share."

"Yeah. Misery loves company or something like that. Was this your dream, back in high school, when you were the hotshot football player? To one day be sorting through someone's trash in search of clues?"

"I don't remember having dreams back then," Burgess said. He'd worried about his mother, their precarious financial situation, his father's explosive violence, his sisters' safety. There hadn't been any space for thinking about a future. Life was about getting through the days.

What had he dreamed about? "Nookie, or actually, breasts," he said. "That's about all I thought about back then." He'd been a pig like all teenage boys are pigs. Overrun by hormones and baffled by his body. He'd marveled at what was happening to the young women around him. Puzzled at how it all worked. How big guys like him got together with women, when they seemed so small and breakable. But he'd never been anything like Joey. Joey seemed to think breaking them was part of his job.

"Until Sister Mary Peter whacked you with her ruler," Kyle said.

Burgess looked down at his hands. "You only have to say 'Mary Peter' and they tingle."

"I used to think she was about nine feet tall, you know?" Kyle said. "Saw her on the street a couple months ago and she's just a little bitty thing. She gave me the same old up and down, like she was lasering me for contraband, then said, 'Well, Terrence, I'm pleased to hear you've become such a success in the police department.' Other than for whacking, I didn't think she knew my name."

Kyle grinned, a thin-lipped twitch that came and went so fast you were never sure you'd seen it. "You can be sure my hands were tingling." Burgess followed with more trash as Kyle dropped his bags on the deck. "I think she's the only person who has ever called me Terrence."

It was a nasty job. The public has no idea how many such nasty jobs it asks its police to do. Year in, year out, cops are up to their elbows in society's messes. Sometimes literally. They don't complain. Occasionally, though, they might actually like that box of donuts, or homemade brownies, something to acknowledge the work they did. The smiles and waves they rarely got. After 9/11 they got them for a while, but when you wear the uniform, it's short attention span theater. People quickly resumed their sour "you've ruined my day" or "here come the po po" looks.

The rain had moved on. They had warming October sun on their backs as they worked, and noisy gulls dropping in to see if there was anything in Joey's trash for them. He wondered if Nick Goodall had visited the boat at all. It was an expensive item to leave in Joey's indifferent hands, at the mercy of so much carelessness. Maybe Claire was paying him rent?

Most of the trash was really garbage. Bags of sticky, smelly, stomach-turning stuff, some of which had begun to produce maggots. Burgess hated maggots. They made his skin crawl and his stomach heave. At a crime scene, at or around a body, they might be clues to timing and circumstances and were carefully collected. Here they were just ugly little wriggling white things that fed on carrion. He closed the bag, stomach flipping, and stepped away, gulping down some fresh salt air before opening another.

If his trash was any indication, Joey Libby had no life aside from eating, drinking, and sex. Some might say that was the ideal life, but most people were more connected to the world. They got mail. They got bills. They scribbled grocery lists and notes to themselves, wrote on the backs of envelopes, on bar napkins or coasters. They threw away charge slips that made it possible to track their movements, message slips with names and numbers that could be used for follow-up, discarded worn-out socks and clothes, prescription bottles, unwanted business cards. Maybe Joey left all that stuff at his mother's.

In the next bag he found a torn-up envelope with a piece of a logo that looked like the one he'd found in Kevin Dugan's wastebasket. A little deeper down, he found a napkin with a girl's name and number. He wrote them in his notebook and added the napkin to the pile to be saved. Kyle found one of Dr. Lyndeman's appointment cards with Reggie's name on it. There was a torn black envelope with some of Star Goodall's silver ink, and a crumpled, soggy sheet of black paper that would have to be flattened and dried before they had any chance of reading it.

That was the lot.

Like good citizens, they carried the trash to the dumpster, then returned to the boat to wash their hands. There were no paper towels and Joey's few towels were too filthy to use.

"Okay," Kyle said, running his hands down the sides of his pants to dry them. "What now, fearless leader?"

Burgess rolled his eyes. "We could take this back to 109, look it over, and log it in. We could have that chat with Nick Goodall. Or we could go see a girl about her date with a rat."

"Girl," Kyle said without hesitation. "Rat."

Chapter Twenty-Three

He drove, using Tolliver's directions, with Kyle following. The house was in a nice part of town and it was a nice house. A new house on a big lot with expensive landscaping and a sparkling white fence and healthy shrubs for privacy. There was a Lincoln SUV in the driveway. When he rang the bell, a real dog barked, and when a woman answered, the dog was right behind her.

Her "yes" was reserved and suspicious. People who lived in houses like this didn't get many Jehovah's Witnesses or hopeful peddlers on their doorsteps. They were wary of those who might be after their money or threatening their security and didn't like the sanctity of the home disturbed by uninvited visitors. Burgess was aware that his morning in the wet parking lot and getting up close and personal with Joey's garbage probably hadn't done much for his appearance, but at the best of times, he lacked sartorial splendor.

He showed his badge. "Detective Sergeant Joe Burgess, Portland police, ma'am, and this is Detective Kyle."

Surprise and concern flickered in her eyes. Otherwise, her face remained reserved and noncommittal. She was his age, he thought, though a lot less hard used and, even on an afternoon at home, was dressed with care and attention. Sage green slacks, a lighter green sweater, and a deeper green fleece vest. Green suede flats. Understated jewelry. Neat, short, ash-blond hair. Not a costume for cleaning the toilets or vacuuming rugs. Her hair and skin had the slightly dry look women got when they worked so hard to be thin they lacked basic nutrients. The taut and dusty look of so many Yankee matrons. She had the slightly overlong teeth, too. If you subscribed to the starving rat theory of survival, this woman and her kind would live forever, though always slightly crabby from hunger.

After she'd studied his badge and their faces, she said, "Lois Mercer," in a flat, careful voice. "What is this about?"

"We're looking for your daughter, ma'am. Amanda Mercer?" Burgess said. That was the name from the napkin.

Was that relief he was reading as the woman's head shifted slightly toward the dark house behind her? Then she folded her arms across her chest. "Mandy's not here."

"Ma'am, if you could tell us when—"

Footsteps thudded. A girl's voice called, "Come, Standish. Come. Time for a walk." The dog turned and trotted away. They all heard the sound of a leash snapping onto a collar and then the girl Tolliver had described appeared behind her mother. "Mom, I'm taking—" She stopped when she saw them on the step.

"Detective Burgess," he said, "and Detective Kyle, Ms. Mercer, Portland police. Could we have a few minutes of your time?"

Lois Mercer's already stiff body went rigid, her glare turned up to killer strength. She directed it at both of them before turning to her daughter. "Mandy, go back inside and let me deal with this. You don't have to talk to them."

The girl shrugged. "You're being rude, Mom. I can talk to them." Her lashes fell over her eyes and she lowered her head as a blush stole up her cheeks. She was exactly as Tolliver had described—bon-bon fresh and lovely. No makeup. No airs. No pushed-up breasts or swaths of naked skin. Just healthy and perfect in comfy old sweats and a giant gray sweatshirt, her thick hair pulled back in a bouncy ponytail.

"It's okay. I can talk to them," she said again, thrusting the leash at her mother. "You go. Go take Standish for his walk."

"I am not . . ." Lois Mercer's chin jutted angrily, her arms tight against her chest. "Not leaving you here alone with these . . . uh . . . these policemen." She stepped between them and her daughter.

"We'd be happy to walk along with you so you don't have to keep Standish waiting," Burgess said, "if that would be more convenient."

The girl's smile was grateful. "Okay," she said. She took the leash back from her mother. "Let's go, then."

"Mandy, I don't think . . . Please, dear, you don't have to talk with these . . . these men." When Mandy didn't respond, her mother said, "You're making a big mistake, Amanda."

To Burgess and Kyle, she said, "Mandy's only sixteen. Aren't I supposed to be . . ."

"Seventeen, Mom, remember?" The girl's spine stiffened in an unconscious imitation of her mother. She tugged on the leash. "Come on, Standish."

"I hope you'll keep your wits about you," her mother said. She turned and went inside, shutting the door rather too firmly behind her.

The mother's remark was some kind of shorthand, but shorthand for what? Burgess wondered.

They were an odd trio on the streets of that neighborhood, two detectives in shirts and ties, and the girl and her dog. He figured they probably looked like bodyguards, lacking only those little curly wires in their ears. Come a little too late, though. They should have been there while she visited Joey.

When they'd turned a corner and were out of the glare of her mother's eyes, she said, "So what's this about? You guys *are* cops, right?"

"We're trying to locate Joey Libby, in connection with an investigation, and we understand you know him?"

Her quick flip-flopped feet came to a rubber-squeaking halt. "This is about Joey?" Sensing tension, her real bodyguard, Standish, set himself between his mistress and the cops as her eyes searched their faces. "Why come to me?" Then, on the heels of that, "How did you find me?" And at last, her lips quivering, "Did that old man send you? The one down at the marina?"

That "old" man wasn't much older than he was, Burgess thought. And he'd taken on Joey Libby, who was a pretty big guy.

She jerked the elastic off her ponytail as she bent and patted the dog's head. "He must have sent you, otherwise you'd just go out to the factory, if you really wanted to find Joey. I mean, I'm the least likely person anyone would come to." Her voice was small and breathless. She shook her head, taffy-colored hair settling around her shoulders and veiling her face. Then she looked from one of them to the other, her eyes pleading. "What did Mr. Tolliver tell you? I begged him not to say anything." She looked stricken now, smaller and less confident.

"He didn't come to us, Mandy," Kyle said. "We went down to the boat, looking for Joey. In the course of our interview, you came up. Mr. Tolliver is a kind man. He was concerned about you, that's all. So are we. We're looking for Joey because we have some questions about his father's death. We came looking for you to see if you're okay."

"I'm fine," she said, looking down again. "It's nothing. I'm not . . ." One toe twisted. "He didn't . . . he tried but I wouldn't let him . . . I mean, I stopped him. That is, I got away. I tried to run, Joey grabbed me, I screamed, and there was Mr. Tolliver." Her voice dropped to nearly a whisper. "I just never thought. Oh!" The "oh" was sharp and sudden, and as she exhaled, she folded her arms over her stomach like she was in pain. "How could I be so stupid? I thought . . . I just thought he was a cute guy who liked me. I never . . ." Her hands pressed harder and the toe dug deeper. "It's my fault. All my fault. I'm just a dumb, trusting girl with bad judgment."

It sounded like a quote from someone older and judgmental. If he had to bet, Burgess would guess her mother, a general statement of how she regarded her daughter. The tension between them read like tension between a mother's determination to control and a daughter's need not to be controlled, not like a mother's protective caring. Had she known the nature of their visit, she was unlikely to have left them alone with her daughter.

But there were faint traces of bruises on the girl's face and a cut lip was still healing. She couldn't have missed those, yet she hadn't called the police. What was that about?

"It's not your fault," he said. "You're not the first nice girl to trust Joey and have that trust violated. He's a handsome guy who can be extremely charming. He's also been arrested several times for abusing his girlfriends. He's even served jail time for it."

She looked up at him through the curtain of hair. "He's done this before?"

This was how abusers got away with it. They picked on the vulnerable, the insecure, the loving, the innocent, then made them believe it was their fault. He felt a wave of shame, and guilt that he hadn't kept closer tabs on Joey. Not that it would have been easy with Claire the Dragon guarding the gate. He'd been guilty of that common policeman's sin—hoping the bad guys have changed. Now he needed to know what "this" was. What had happened to Mandy.

He looked at Kyle. Normally, he'd lead and Kyle would listen for the things he might miss. This time, he thought Kyle should lead. Mandy wasn't much older than Kyle's girls, and he sensed, from what she'd said, that she hadn't talked to anyone about this and probably needed to.

Kyle nodded and moved closer. "Yes, Mandy," Kyle said, "Joey's done this before. And he'll keep on doing it unless girls like you speak up. Believe me, we don't want to cause you any more pain. We don't like invading your privacy, but I think we need to know what happened."

Each time she spoke, she seemed to grow smaller. "Do I have to?" she said.

"No," Kyle said. "That's up to you. But if you can tell us, we may be able to keep it from happening to someone else."

The dog had gotten restless and they'd started walking again, a route that after a while brought them to a small park. Kyle pointed at a picnic table near an empty swing set. "We could sit here if you like. Just sit and talk about it." Kyle could be fierce, but now he wore his "father" face, the one he used with his own daughters, a smile that invited confidences and his gentlest voice. "We need to know what Joey did and what he said so we can keep other young women like you safe, Mandy. And you can stop any time you feel uncomfortable. Will you"—he swept a hand toward the bench, leaning down with something like a bow—"talk to us?"

"He said he'd hurt me if I told," she said. "He'd hurt me, he said, and hurt my . . . He said he'd hurt Standish, see, because I'd told him about my dog. And I really couldn't bear that." She put a protective hand on the dog's head.

The three of them settled down on the benches, Kyle on the same bench facing Mandy, Burgess on the other side, where he could watch her face. Kyle took out his notebook and clicked his pen. "How old are you, Mandy? Sixteen or seventeen?"

"Seventeen," she said. "Mom knows that. My birthday was Friday."

Burgess felt his hands curl in anger. He forced them to relax.

Kyle got her birth date, address, and phone number, then

said, "How did you meet Joey?"

"At work," she said, surprised, as if they should know this, and Burgess remembered her earlier remark that they could have just gone to the factory if they wanted to find Joey.

"And you work where?"

"In the office at my dad's business. Mercer Metals out on Warren Street. I worked there for the summer, and now I help out afternoons after school a couple days a week. Joey worked in sales. Works. He started back in the spring. I thought . . ." Her voice dropped and she stared down at her clasped hands, still holding the leash. "I thought he was cute. He'd stop at my desk sometimes and flirt a little. A couple times, he brought me a Coke or some chips. Nice stuff. You know. The kind of thing you hope a guy will do, instead of right off asking for a date."

"Did he ask for a date?" Kyle asked.

She shrugged. "Sorta. Kids don't really date much, you know. One Friday he offered me a ride home. I didn't have the car that day and my dad was supposed to drive me, but he forgot and went off somewhere—my dad does that a lot, actually—so Joey drove me home. He was real nice and polite, he even walked me to the door, which was so old-fashioned. My mom said she thought he was too old for me, so the next time I saw him, I asked how old he was. He said he was twenty."

Her fingers knotted tightly, her knuckles white. "Well, twenty's not so old," she said, "and he asked if I'd go out with him some time. So that next night, Saturday, I met him down in the Old Port, at some bar." She wouldn't meet their eyes when she said, "I forget the name. And Joey got the bartender to give us drinks. Real drinks, without asking for ID, which I thought was pretty cool, because I guess Joey knew the bartender from school or something. He asked for my number, which he didn't have 'cuz we saw each other at work, and I wrote it on a bar napkin. Then he drove me home . . . only . . ."

She shook her hair forward so they couldn't see her face. "He didn't take me home, he took me to this big empty parking lot, somewhere out near the office, and then he . . ." There was a long silence as she studied her fingers. Finally she sighed. "I told you I was stupid. He tried to do things to me, and tried to get me to do things to him, that I was no way ready for. I told him so and . . . and after a couple of tries, he stopped. He apologized, and took me home. And on Monday, he left flowers on my desk with a sweet little note. Later, he stopped by the desk and invited me to come see him at the boat some time, and gave me directions."

She pushed back her hair and raised her eyes to meet Kyle's. "I thought . . . I guess because of the apology and the flowers . . . I thought he knew he'd made a mistake that night in the parking lot. He'd thought I was one kind of girl and now he knew I was another. So on Tuesday, after school, after work, I put on a nice dress and got a girlfriend to drive me down to the marina. I had to ask that nice man, Mr. Tolliver, how to find the boat. I never thought—" She choked.

Kyle put a hand on her shoulder. "It's okay, Mandy," he said. "Take your time. Take all the time you need. We're in no hurry."

"I just never imagined it would be like that." Another choke, and a sob. She wiped her eyes with the back of her hand. Burgess gave her his handkerchief.

"Thanks." She sniffed and dabbed at her eyes. "You know . . . He was a guy who apologized and sent flowers. He looked good and dressed well and had nice manners, and well, I'm such a little idiot I thought, despite what happened in the car—" Her voice wavered to a stop. "I thought that meant he'd be nice."

She swallowed and went on so quietly they had to lean forward to hear. "And then, when I got on the boat, everything was just awful. It was filthy. He was disgusting. He kept trying to get me to drink, and he was drinking, and he kept pawing me and trying to get my clothes off, saying how I was going to be his fifth virgin, like he was keeping score or something. I fought him off a couple of times and then I'd had enough. I was mad. I told him what I thought of how he was behaving and that I was leaving. Only this time, instead of stopping, he went crazy. I was so scared." Tears swallowed her words. "He started hitting me and tearing my clothes. He tried to . . . he tried to . . ." They barely heard her say "rape me."

She looked at them, big, hurt eyes brimming with tears. "He would have, if that Mr. Tolliver hadn't pulled him off me, and hit him."

There were a million PC rules, safety rules, and just plain common-sense caution about touching an assault victim, a young girl, a witness. Kyle ignored them. He pulled the crying girl against his chest, holding her tightly until her sobs had finished, comforting her like you'd comfort any wounded child.

She'd just wiped her eyes and taken a breath, preparing to finish her story, when a passing patrol car, spotting them, stopped at the curb. A young officer got out and came toward them. He'd recognized neither Burgess nor Kyle. Probably figured them for a couple of perverts trying to pick up a young girl.

"Is everything okay here?" he asked loudly. "Miss, can you look at me, please, and tell me you're okay." The loud voice and sudden approach brought on another flood of tears and a glare from Kyle.

Quickly, Burgess was off the bench. He appreciated the officer's attention. They did make an odd group, and stopping to be sure everything was on the up and up was the right thing to do. But they had an interview to finish with a fragile subject. He didn't want it derailed. "Sergeant Burgess, CID," he said quickly. He grabbed the officer's arm and turned him around, explaining the situation as they walked back to the car.

When the patrol car had rolled away, Kyle said, "Sounds like Mr. Tolliver is a hero."

"He is," she agreed. "He's just the nicest man. Genuinely nice, I mean, not fake nice." She plucked at the sweatshirt. "This is his. He gave it to me to wear because . . ." She couldn't finish. "I wear it because it makes me feel safe."

They'd left Joey left lying on the floor, she said, and Tolliver had helped her off the boat and driven her home. "Were you okay? Did you see a doctor?" Burgess asked.

She shook her head. "I couldn't see a doctor without letting my parents know, could I? I guess I really didn't need one, though. Nothing happened."

Right. Nothing but a young girl beaten and terrorized, nearly raped, and left with her clothes, and her faith in herself, her judgment, and men, in tatters. Nothing but Joey confirmed in his belief that he was a victim of the duplicity of women. And what about the parents? A daughter comes home beaten and bruised with her clothes in shreds and they don't call the police?

"What about your parents?" Burgess asked. "Why didn't they call us?"

"Because they don't know," she said. "Dad was out, as usual. Something to do with his business, and Mom was at an appointment." Her shoulders rose in an apologetic shrug. "That was okay with me. I didn't want them to know. He would have started yelling at me and then she would have yelled at me and then they would have started yelling at each other." Another defeated shrug. "They never would have called you. Our family has to handle things ourselves. That's how it's done."

"They didn't notice you were hurting?" There were traces of yellowish purple bruising on her face. Kyle gently reached to push up her sleeve. She flinched, but allowed it. Her arms still bore the marks of Joey's fingers where he'd held her down.

"Maybe if I'd lost a leg," she said. "Or wrecked a car. They think I'm pathetic."

"We'd like to have you talk to our juvenile officer, Andrea Dwyer, and have her take some pictures and a statement. Would that be okay?" Kyle asked. "Andrea's really nice. She's a runner, like you."

"How did you know I'm a runner?" she asked.

"The way you walk," Kyle said, "like walking is always going to be too slow for you. My daughter's like that. She just started middle school this fall and she's gone out for track." He gave it a moment. "Will you talk to her?"

"Do my parents have to know?"

"That's up to you," Kyle said. It was kind of a lie. If Joey was charged and they had to go to court, her parents would know. Though it might not come to that.

Her muffled, "Okay," came through her curtain of hair. "Have her call me on my cell." Kyle nodded.

"Have you seen or heard from Joey since?" Burgess asked.

She studied the table. "I haven't been to work. I told them I had too much homework. He called twice but I didn't take the calls."

"So you've had no contact with him since the night he assaulted you?"

"I told you," she said, so humble Burgess wanted to shake the woman who'd raised her to be this passive, then go find Mandy a nice new spine, "nothing happened."

Kyle looked over at Burgess, one eyebrow raised. "Joey told you nothing happened, didn't he?"

She nodded.

"And he scared you into saying that."

Another nod.

Kyle's face tightened with anger. "Because he threatened you and Standish?"

A small, breathless "Yes." She gripped the leash so tightly her knuckles were white.

"When did you see him?"

Her face flamed red. "Last night."

Chapter Twenty-Four

"Thought we were supposed to be solving crimes, not collecting new ones," Kyle said, getting up to pace. "That poor girl. Reciting 'nothing happened' like a little robot. Bastard actually had her believing that everything that happened was her fault. For what? Trusting someone? Wanting a boyfriend? Needing someone to think she was pretty and special? Sounds like she doesn't get that from her family."

He slumped wearily back into his chair. "Just goes to show, as if we didn't already know, that money can't buy happiness." They were back in a conference room at 109, reviewing what they'd learned. Mandy's revelations hadn't been surprising, given what they knew about Joey Libby, but they were more depressing news in an already depressing case. To their list of crimes connected to this investigation, they'd now added assault and attempted sexual assault.

"We'll have to get a statement from Tolliver," Burgess said, picking up the phone, "and I'd like pictures of those bruises before they fade. I'll see if Dwyer's around."

"That miserable little piece of shit," Kyle said. "I almost hope I'm not around when you find him. Can you believe her parents didn't notice?"

"They noticed."

Andrea Dwyer answered. "It's Burgess," he said, "got a teen-age assault victim I need your help with."

"Always here for you, Joe," she said. "What's up?"

He filled her in on Amanda Mercer, gave her the address, home phone, and Mandy's cell number. "Like to get pictures of those bruises before they fade, and a solid written statement. She doesn't want her parents to know . . . so try her cell phone first. Maybe meet her somewhere away from the house?"

"She's bruised?" Dwyer said. "Then the parents know. This girl been in trouble before?"

"Farthest thing from it," Burgess said. "Unless she's got me and Kyle bamboozled, she's a real innocent."

Dwyer laughed. "If she can fool the two of you, there's not a prayer for me. Okay, I'm on it. You want this fast, right? I should try her now?"

"If you could. We don't want to give her time to decide she doesn't want the trouble." Dwyer was the perfect person to talk to Mandy. A strong, athletic woman with a deep well of compassion. They called her the "kiddie cop," but there was no derision in the term. Dwyer was damned good at what she did.

He put down the phone. "Mandy's mother thought we were there about something else," he said. "I wonder what? Seems we're going to have pay a visit to Mercer Metals." He shuffled through his notes. "Out on Warren Avenue, right? Where's Stan's chart?"

"I'll get it." Kyle shoved back his chair.

When the door opened again, it wasn't Kyle, but Perry, looking like he'd survived his visit to Star Goodall unscathed. He tossed a search warrant for Goodall's boat down in front of Burgess and dropped into a chair. "Yo, boss," he said, "that is one hell of a strange woman."

"That she is. She offer you coffee?"

"Too right she did. Said I'd just had some." Perry kicked back a chair and perched on it, edgy as a porcupine about to lift its quills. "I didn't get a heck of a lot. She did some weird things with cards. Said she must have grabbed the wrong jar when I asked about what she'd done to your coffee. Said she couldn't remember writing a check for Joey, but she might have done it as a favor. The boy was always after her for something, said his mother kept him on too short a leash. I gathered, though she didn't exactly say this, that the check was some advance for what Joey would get when the property was sold and Joey had promised to pay her back."

"She get that in writing?"

"Said she did, but when I asked to see the papers, she went all vague on me, started yammering about my aura. She hadn't been such an old skank, I would have thought it was a come on." He snorted. "You ever see a witch flash her tits before?"

Maybe there *were* some advantages to having become old and invisible. At least he'd been spared that. "She know why she was writing that check and to whom?"

"Whom?" Perry echoed. "Aren't we getting fancy." He flipped restlessly through his notes, not really looking at them. "There anything to eat around here?"

"Detectives don't eat, Stanley. They suck essential nutrients out of the air on their way to crime scenes or while interviewing witnesses. We're like those plants . . . what are they called? The ones that live on air?"

Kyle returned. "Bromiliads," he said, rolling out Stan's chart on the table. "Looky here . . . right close to that parking lot, we've got Mercer Metals."

"What the heck's Mercer Metals?" Perry said. "And by the way, I found that African guy. The one with the Mustang and the scars."

"Mercer Metals. Place where Joey Libby works," Burgess said. "Or worked. What about this guy in the Mustang? He see anything?"

"Oh, I've had a delightful afternoon talking with people who won't give a straight fucking answer to anything." Perry looked tired. It took energy and focus to deal with liars, and he hadn't slept. He stabbed a finger at Kyle. "Next time, I'm going with Joe and you can go to hell."

"I didn't go with Joe."

"Yes, you did."

"Did not."

"Did too."

They sounded like a couple of third-graders. Burgess looked at Perry's glum face and Kyle's slumped shoulders. "Pizza time, kids," he said.

"Can't," Kyle said. "Gotta get home and see my kids before the court them takes away and gives 'em back to the PMS Queen."

Burgess's phone rang. "Hey, handsome," Chris said. "I'm just taking a chicken out of the oven. I've got mashed potatoes and gravy and—"

"Got enough for two more?"

"That's my plan. Tell Terry that Michelle and the girls are here. And we've got apple pie. Homemade."

"We're on our way."

"Change of plan," he told the others, "Chris has roast chicken and apple pie. And Ter, Michelle and the girls are there. That be okay?"

"You don't deserve her, Joe," Perry said.

"Shut up, Stan," Kyle said. "Choices you make, you've got no standing to criticize anyone."

"You can shut the fuck up about that, Terry. It's not like you've never made a mistake. Which one of us married the fuckin' PMS Queen?"

"Yeah? Who fucks other people's wives and gets his head beat in?"

This was what happened when a case started grinding them down. What they really needed was a break in the case and some sleep, but a good meal would help. "The Mustang guy," Burgess interrupted, "he say anything useful?"

"Maybe if I spoke fuckin' Somali. Look, I've heard that ass-hole speak perfectly good English. I start asking questions and he acts like he's never heard a word of English in his life. I don't get it, you know, these people come over here because they want the good life, they want to live like Americans. So why the fuck won't they talk like Americans?"

"You're sure it was Somali?"

"Well, he fuckin' said it was."

"We can get a translator. Think you can find him again?"

"Did it once, didn't I? We any closer to finding that little bastard Joey?"

"Got more reasons we want him found," Kyle said. As they walked to the car, he filled Perry in on Amanda Mercer.

Burgess shook his head. He was starting to feel as cranky as Perry. Getting together and talking was invaluable, but what he wanted was time alone, driving around in the car or at his desk, trying to put the pieces together. What he *needed* to do was go to Mercer Metals. Find a translator. Talk to Nick Goodall. See if the lab had any toxicology results back. Find Joey. Find somebody who knew where Reggie had been working. He needed some kind of divine intervention to give him a clue and knew full well that the best kind of intervention had more to do with dogged persistence than divinity. Heaven helped those who helped themselves?

Captain Cote was in the hall by the elevator. "Burgess," he said, his plump white finger crooking in a slightly obscene "come hither" gesture, "got a minute?"

"I'm ten-seven, but I've always got a minute for you, Paul." He turned to the others. "You guys go ahead. I'll meet you there." He followed Cote downstairs.

Cote pursed his duck's-ass mouth and before the first word

emerged, Burgess knew what was coming. Amanda Mercer's mother. "Got a complaint from a citizen, Joe." Cote let it go a beat for dramatic effect, then, "A Mrs. Lois Mercer. She's very upset at the way you and Kyle pressured her into letting you interview her daughter. She doesn't think it was right for you to interview a fifteen-year-old without having her present."

"Started as a routine thing," Burgess said. "We were looking for a bad guy, thought the girl might know where we could find him. Girl's seventeen," he added, "not fifteen. Turns out guy we're looking for tried to rape her. She didn't want to talk about a physical and sexual assault by a convicted felon in front of her mother. We figured it was better to get the bad guy off the street than make a controlling mother happy." He sat up straighter so he loomed over the smaller man, and tented his own hands. "What's the problem?"

Cote sighed. They'd been around this barn so many times they'd worn a groove in the ground. "You have to tread lightly with these people, Joe."

"Unmarked cars," Burgess said. "No uniforms or lights or sirens. We didn't bang on the door or raise our voices, and we didn't leave the girl in tears." He shrugged. "I don't see how we could have been more discreet. It's not like we dragged anyone down here and shut them up in a small room. If the neighbors noticed anything, I'm sure they thought Kyle was a bible sales-man and I was his reformed convict assistant. Or we were both Mormons on a mission. Or spreading damp and tattered copies of *The Watchtower.*"

Before the duck's ass could spit out any more words, he added, "I hope you reassured her that Portland's finest would try not to darken her door again." He knew Cote had. The captain seemed to have decided his mission was to ensure that law enforcement was as difficult as possible for his officers.

"You still working on the Libby thing?"

"You mean the Reginald Libby homicide? Yes. We are."

"You don't need three detectives on it," Cote said.

"I'm the primary," Burgess said.

"I'm the captain. And I say you should reassign Perry to some of our other cases. City's going to hell and you're spending all these resources on some homeless guy."

Much as Burgess disliked the press, he wished to hell some bleeding heart reporter could have heard that remark. "Really? Today I was spending resources on a teenage assault victim. On a major drug stash down at the marina on a party boat. On two significant littering sites that have a strong negative impact on the quality of life in the city. On an assault on a police officer. Two assaults," he corrected himself, if he included Star Goodall. "Two police officers. On a suspected white-collar crime involving toxic chemicals." Leaning in closer, he said, "That sounds like wasted resources to you?" He shoved back his chair. "Was there anything else?"

"Discretion, Joe. Just use your discretion." Cote picked up one of his perfectly sharpened pencils from the line of them on his blotter. "You can go." As Burgess was going out the door, he added, "I assured Mrs. Mercer you wouldn't bother her daughter again."

Too right, Burgess thought. Dwyer would. Beating and a near rape were hardly enough to justify upsetting Mrs. Mercer. Why was she so keen to have him stay away?

He was leaving the garage when Burgess remembered something Hazen had said. Ignoring his hunger and the waiting chicken, he pulled out his notebook and thumbed through the pages. There it was. In describing Joey's decision to sell, Hazen had said, "They didn't need *another* piece of waterfront property." Another answer Clay Libby might have. One Claire certainly had but was unlikely to share. He made a note, put the book away, and headed home.

CHAPTER TWENTY-FIVE

Chris had made his favorite meal—roast chicken, stuffing, potatoes, gravy, peas and cranberry sauce—and she'd made a ton of everything not just because they had a crowd but because she knew he loved leftovers. Perry and Kyle were attacking their food like starving men, their moods visibly improving as they ate. Michelle sat quietly and smiled, something she did a lot lately, happy that Kyle was back on an even keel again after the hell he'd put all of them through in the summer.

Kyle's girls, growing up too fast as other people's children always did, were friendly, chatty, and polite. He caught Chris gazing at them with a longing that stabbed him. Just because he wasn't ready for a family didn't mean she wasn't, or that she should give up her desire to adopt Nina and Ned. He'd been alone before he met her; he could live alone again. Alone without all the warm, humanizing touches Chris brought to his place, and to his life. Order. Color. Pictures. Flowers. Food. Sex and sensibility.

As he gazed around the table at hungry people enjoying a delicious homemade meal, Burgess realized he was a lot like Reggie in his longing for normal. For decades he'd worked a job where there was no normal, or where normal was crazy hours, human violence, and a schedule that was never your own. He recognized the dichotomy—he feared normal because he worried that it might make him lose his edge. He longed for normal precisely because it took some of the edges off and

251

made him feel more balanced and human.

After a while, Kyle set down his fork. "So, what did Cote want?"

"He wants Stanley to stop wasting time on a worthless investigation and go work on some more important crime. And he wants us to stop bothering nice people like the Mercers, who get upset when there are cops on the doorstep."

"I'm not—" Perry began.

"We're not—" Kyle said. Perry glared and Kyle gestured that he could have the floor.

"That man lives with his head up his fu . . . freakin' ass," Perry said. "He needs to get out more. See what life on the street is really like instead of acting like Reggie's death and what we do doesn't matter. Like only important people matter. I'd like to—"

"Not at the table," Chris said, putting a hand on his arm. "There are children present."

He shook her hand off, then ducked his head apologetically. "Sorry, Chris," he said. "It's not you. It's just getting so fricking hard to be a cop in this city. Dealing with the public's hard enough and then that ass—"

"Stanley!"

Perry shut up, but everything about him said how much he wanted to speak. He rocked and wriggled on his chair, restless as a toddler. Kyle wasn't much better, nor was Burgess. Dinner was delicious and the company pleasant, but the interlude felt artificial, all three detectives poised like springs, ready to jump into action as soon as they were released. Elsewhere in the city, a drug team was searching Nick Goodall's boat. Nick Goodall waited to be interviewed. People with answers held them tightly to their chests and wouldn't share.

Chris started gathering up dishes, and Michelle rose to help. "Who wants pie? And ice cream?" she asked.

Everyone wanted pie and ice cream. Michelle and the girls finished clearing. As Chris started dishing out pie, Burgess wandered absently to check the top of the bookcase, where she always left his mail. The usual assortment of bills and police-related stuff, and a hand-addressed letter in a writing he didn't recognize. Curious, he tore it open.

He didn't recognize the return address, but the letter began, "Dear Joe," as though the sender knew him. He fast forwarded to the end and read the signature. Margaret Kimball. Maggie. He and Maggie had been an item for a few years, maybe fifteen years ago. They'd even lived together for a while. But Maggie, like other girlfriends, couldn't stand his dedication to his job, and he couldn't stand her constantly nagging at him to change. It had ended with surprising swiftness. He'd come home one afternoon to find her things gone. A note on the counter of the nearly bare kitchen said she couldn't take it anymore. She'd gone home. She'd asked him not to try and get in touch.

Home, he recalled, was somewhere in the Midwest. The return address on this envelope was Kansas. He went back to the beginning and started to read.

Dear Joe,

I hope you will forgive me for this letter, and for keeping this from you for so long. When I left, it was my firm intention never to be in touch with you again. I expunged you from my memory like you had never existed. I would have gone on that way forever and never bothered you with this, but recently I realized that my stubbornness is not always a virtue.

He stopped reading. He didn't have the stamina right now for a letter of regret or recrimination or a recitation, however important it might be to her, of the harm he'd done or what their relationship might have come to if he'd only been willing to commit. He started to stuff it back in the envelope, but realized it would haunt him until he finished, a distraction he didn't need. He unfolded it and read on.

You're probably expecting me to berate you about what might have been, but the truth is, I doubt that things would have been any different if I'd stayed. You were always so certain about who you were and what you needed to do. Certainty that made you an excellent cop and a bad boyfriend. That's not what this letter is about. I'm writing only because there is something I've kept from you all these years that you have a right to know.

He stopped again, a knot of anxiety forming in his gut. For a while, he just stood and breathed, holding the letter without finishing it, then forced himself to read on.

I left when I did, and as suddenly as I did, because I was pregnant. I knew you wouldn't pressure me to have an abortion and would have supported any decision I made, but I wanted to keep the baby and I didn't want you to marry me just because you felt you had to. That wasn't you and that wasn't me. Of course I wanted you to marry me, but I wanted it to be what we attorneys call "your free act and deed." I didn't want to spend the rest of my life with a man I loved who would always feel trapped, so I didn't tell you. I didn't give you a chance to have a say in the matter. I left and went on with my life without you.

My son . . . I should say "our son," Dylan Joseph Kimball, will be fifteen on his next birthday. And because of him, I have never completely left you behind. Take a look at the photograph. I didn't know you at that age, of course, but I'm betting he's the spitting image of you. Not only your looks, Joe, but your personality, so I guess there is something to that nature/nurture thing.

Burgess fished around in the envelope and came up with a

school photo of a dark-haired boy. He stared at it, seeing himself in the fierce dark eyes staring back, the stubborn chin, and narrow mouth.

Chris, passing with a plate of pie, glanced at his face, at the picture, and almost dropped the plate. "Joe?"

He didn't answer until she gripped his arm and leaned right into his face. "Joe," she said again, her low, insistent voice pulling him back into focus. "What's going on? Who is that boy?"

"I don't know yet." He felt as stunned and stupid as an accident victim. "I . . . it was . . . it was in the letter. Excuse me." He pulled away, turning his back on her stunned face, went into the bedroom and shut the door. The door muffled the sounds of confused questions and commotion as he sat on the bed and finished the letter.

I've had a husband for a while. Actually, for most of the time I've been out here. He's a good man, a superior court judge, and we've got two other children, a boy who's twelve and a girl who's nine. But Dylan knows he's not Stephen's child, and to tell the truth, they've never gotten along that well, though in fairness, both of them have tried. It's just chalk and cheese, or whatever the old expression is. Now that he's a teenager, it's getting worse. Dylan really wants to know who he is. Who you are. I told him that I would write to you and . . .

And now, Joe, I find myself at a loss for words. You might well smile. I never did seem to be, did I? There's no graceful way to do this, is there? I told Dylan I'd see if you were interested in meeting him . . . the first step, I think . . . toward the possibility that you might consider raising your son the rest of the way yourself.

There were smudges on the page that he did not want to think were tears. He knew they were. It felt so odd, so utterly surreal, to be sitting here in his room, on the bed he shared

255

with Chris, and fifteen years down the road, and having this all come at him like something out of a made-for-TV movie.

He . . . my . . . our son is a great kid. A credit, really, to both of us. Verbal and social like me, yet stoic and wise like you. He's a rock to his brother and sister. Yes, he plays football. And no, I did not raise him Catholic, though I know your mother—good soul that she is—would have liked that very much.

Writing this, I realize I don't know if your mother is still alive. For a long time, I kept in touch with people and they kept me up on the news, but not recently. That was always one of my regrets, that Dylan didn't get to know her.

Anyway, Dylan keeps asking if I've written, and I keep putting it off, but here it is. Think about this. Consider whether you'd at least like to meet him. I've tried not to raise any expectations on his part. He didn't know who you were—I mean your name, I always told him stories about you—until recently. He's been reading about you on-line. Kids these days are so much more sophisticated than we ever dreamed of being. And he says he wants to meet you.

So now, forgive the sports cliché, the ball is in your court. Let me know if you have questions.

I do apologize for springing this on you. I can imagine the fixed, shocked look you've probably got. Or is it anger? And soon, I know, you'll pull your cop's face down over it like a shutter, and go on with whatever it is you're doing. I'm sorry. I AM sorry for letting you go so long without knowing. That's what you'll be mad at me for. For letting you make fifteen year's worth of choices about life and relationships, not knowing the truth about yourself. The truth always mattered, didn't it, Joe.

I'm sorry. I'm sorry. I'm sorry. I'm so sorry. God, how you must hate me for doing this. You, who like to be in control, who likes your own life to be orderly and without surprises.

He's a nice surprise, Joe. Really. I'm glad I had him and the thought of him wanting to leave hurts terribly. So please, please think about this. About at least meeting him.

Love, still
Maggie

There was a postscript to the letter, in a different hand. A scrawly, masculine hand that looked affected by age or infirmity.

Sergeant Burgess: I found this on Maggie's desk yesterday. She didn't date it, so I don't know when she wrote or even whether she intended to mail it. But I must tell you that she was killed in an accident last week. Repeat drunk driver went through a red light and slammed into her van. I can't pretend to know if you'll care—but they say she didn't suffer.
I thought you should have this letter.

He grabbed a pillow and held it against his face and cried like he hadn't ever cried before except for little Kristin Marks, the murdered child for whom he'd never gotten justice. He didn't know if he was crying for himself, for Maggie, for Reggie, or for a boy he'd never met. He cried until he was hollow and aching and the pillow was sodden with tears and snot. Then he went and stood in the shower, shirt, tie, shoes and all, to hell with practicality, and turned his hot, sore face up to the shower-head, drowning all sound and thought and feeling in an icy blast of water.

CHAPTER TWENTY-SIX

He stayed until his trembling legs threatened collapse. When he came out, he saw from the mirror that his lips were blue. There was clean underwear on the closed toilet seat and his robe hanging on the back of the door. He hadn't heard Chris come in, but she was a competent nurse with a lot of experience moving around people without disturbing them, and in reading situations without having to be told. He wondered if she'd read the letter. He'd left it lying on the bed.

He was struggling to undo his tie and kick off his wet shoes when she opened the door, pinched little worry lines between her brows. "You want some help with that or do you want to be left alone?"

"Help," he said. "Please."

He felt monosyllabic. He felt a thousand years old, weary beyond speech, and as though all his joints had fused. Never had he been more in need of the Tin Man's oil can. The cold water had left him chilled to his core. Goose-fleshed skin shivered convulsively over his bones.

"Hold still," she said. Deftly, she undid his tie, unbuttoned his shirt, and stripped them off, her warmth reaching him like heat from a fire. She undid his belt and bent to untie his shoes. He couldn't remember ever being so helpless, though she might disagree. She'd nursed him through some tough times. "Lift your foot. Other foot. Good." She pulled a t-shirt over his head, leaving him to thread in his arms while she stripped off his soggy pants and underwear. Like a mom helping a clumsy child, she got him into dry underwear and into his robe.

"I read the letter," she said. "You must be so shocked."

"I've got no words."

"I sent everyone home," she said. "Though I wanted to give Stan a good spanking first. You'd better keep an eye on him—"

She broke off. "Listen to me babble. Terry wanted to stay, but he had Michelle and the girls. Had to put the girls to bed. That poor man lives in fear of the court these days. So afraid they'll return the girls to Wanda. He'll come back if you want."

He already knew that. He and Terry knew each other's secrets like a couple fifty years married. There was a kind of intimacy between cops, between partners, few other jobs produced. It came from spending so much time in the crazy grip of testosterone and adrenaline surges, from knowing the fear of the unexpected and the constant vigilance it demanded, from having lived days that went from the horrendous—a child half-killed by its parents—to the ridiculous—a tipsy matron calling the police because she's dissatisfied with her ice cream cone—in the space of hours. From understanding how they each had lockboxes in their heads where they stored the bad stuff. Together, they could circle up, unlock the boxes, and let the demons out to play for a while. Share them like forbidden pictures. It took some of the pressure off.

"Thanks." He shuffled into the bedroom, his steps geriatric and unsteady, dropped heavily onto the bed, and picked up the picture.

"You want me to stay?"

He shook his head. "I'm not . . . I don't . . ."

"I could make you some tea," she said. "Something warm might be good. Unless you'd prefer a drink?" She shook her head, her voice dropping into a lower, more intimate register.

The one that always reached him. "You want the drink, don't you."

He couldn't even muster a please, just a nod as he stared at the boy's face. Reread the letter. Betrayed. Betraying. The world's biggest jerk and biggest joke. Since his first sex at seventeen, he'd spent over three decades assiduously avoiding bringing a child into a world that was this fucked up, that constantly rolled over and showed him its filthy underbelly like a mangy dog wanting to be scratched. All that monkish abstention. All that caution and precaution. That grim and exhausting self-control. For almost half that time, it had been a lie. Life's big joke on him.

Chris came back with a glass of ice and the bottle. She set them on the bedside table and backed up a few steps, her hands on her hips. Just as lovely and decent as yesterday and now he could barely look at her. He looked at the bedside clock. After nine. Dark out and the rain was back, wind slapping it against the windows. Silently, she studied him, a skilled nurse assessing her patient. Then she crossed to the closet and pulled out a suitcase.

"Chris," he said, "please. You don't—"

She held up a hand like a traffic cop. "I do. I know you, Joe," she said. "I'd like to be wrong, but I think I can almost write the script for this one, and I don't want to stick around and watch." As she spoke, she moved quickly around the room, gathering clothes, underwear, and shoes and tucking them neatly into the case. When she was done, she snapped it shut and straightened, lifting it off the bed.

"Listen to me, Joe. However bad it gets, you are NOT your father. You can heap anything you want on your head, God knows you are a master at taking blame for the state of the world, but all you did was have sex with a woman you lived with and cared about, who then decided not to give you a chance to step up when that relationship caused a pregnancy. You can't know, now, how you would have reacted *then,* what you might have done."

He started to protest, but she waved him off. "She thought she knew, and maybe she was right. But she might have been wrong. Maybe she was a nice woman, but doing this to you . . . doing it like this? It's unconscionable. She always had a choice. She had fifteen years to set things right and she chose not to. She judged you and condemned you and gave you no say in the matter and now, the news arriving this way—with a husband's scrawled note—you've still got no say. What can you do? Tell this heartbroken family you won't see your son?"

She grabbed her suitcase and headed for the door. "I don't care if this makes me sound hateful. I wish I'd had a chance to punch her in the nose. And what the heck's wrong with the guy who's raised him, that he does this with a scrawled note at the bottom of a letter? He wants to keep his own kids and get rid of this other one? How adult and responsible is that? Oh, right. They've never gotten along. Like the guy took against some brave and protective little toddler and never got over it? Give me a break."

Halfway through the door, she paused. "I'm not leaving you, Joe. I'm just giving you some space so you can get as crazy as you need to. But if you break anything that I love, I'm going to punch *you* in the nose. Remember that. You know where to find me. I'll be at Mom's."

"You're too—"

"If you were going to say 'understanding,' don't," she interrupted. "I don't know if I'm understanding. This is hard for me, too. It just complicates the hell out of everything. I'm the one who wants kids."

She swiped at a tear that had escaped her brimming blue eyes. The knuckles on the hand that gripped her suitcase were white. "Call me. No. Don't call me. Not for twenty-four hours at least. If you need someone, call Terry."

And she left.

CHAPTER TWENTY-SEVEN

Even on a full stomach, the drink hit like a speeding train, knocking him back against the pillows and sending his brain reeling. He lay there, dizzy and slightly breathless, trying to summon the strength to sit up and pour another glass. It was the Burgess family way. The only viable and effective response to any major emotional stressor—and in his father's case, to the routines of daily life—was to pour a stiff one, wash it down with a stiffer one, then hold it down with a couple more.

Ugly as it was to take refuge in drink, and God knew he had a lifetime of experience showing that it was no refuge, sometimes nothing helped like putting that hot, sweet layer of good bourbon between himself and the intolerable aches and wounds of his nasty life. Even now, his head too heavy to lift off the pillow, he was drawn by the siren song, the longed-for taste on his tongue. He wanted with an addict's desperation to dull the rage and muffle his confusion.

Finally, he got enough control over his shaking hand to reach toward the bottle, but as his hand moved into the pool of light on the bedside table, the purple, shaking appendage he saw reaching for the bourbon was his father's hand, not his. His father had been weak, a man who'd let the responsibilities of husband and father turn him from an amiable and handsome fellow into a violent and loathsome drunk, his mother bearing the brunt of that anger to protect her children.

He'd always lived in fear of becoming his father. Seeing it

come this close stabbed in his gut like a knife. He stopped his hand six inches from the bottle, holding it there, its wobble and shake casting a wild black spider of shadow on the bottle, the glass, the nightstand, until his burning muscles gave up and it dropped heavily onto the bed beside him. He pulled it, icy and trembling, onto his chest, cradling it with his other hand as spasms wracked his body like a flu.

He was a cop. He'd been lied to and deceived for decades without letting those lies and deceptions drag him down to the level of the liars. Why should he let today be any different? Reggie was still dead. Reggie's murder still unsolved. A ton of work lay ahead. Burgess had a lifelong rule—when the personal and the professional collide, work wins. He played on the dead guy's team, and so far, he and his teammates, Kyle and Perry, hadn't laid a bat on the ball while the bad guys seemed to be stealing all the bases. They were fast becoming the strike-out kids. Falling into a self-centered snarl of despair wouldn't help even the score.

Pushing himself off the bed and turning his back on the bottle, Burgess lost the robe, pulled on corduroys and a warm wool sweater, and stuck his wallet and badge in his pockets. He went through the rituals of departure: Keys. Phone. Cuffs. Radio, pausing long enough to try and heave up the stabbing knife that was stuck in his gut. It wouldn't budge.

He headed down to the car. As he pulled out on the rainy street, he called Kyle. "It's Joe. Just so you won't worry about me if you call and no one answers, I'm going over to see Maura." He hesitated. "And Chris has left."

"I *was* worried." Kyle diplomatically didn't comment on Chris's absence. "Look, now that I've got you on the phone, you're not the only one I'm worried about. Didn't you think Stan was a little off tonight?"

"More than a little. He's been off ever since he got beat down by that hulking asshole." Stan had been edgy as hell tonight. The signs, if Burgess had been paying attention, of someone about to go off the rails. "You thinking what I'm thinking?"

" 'Fraid so."

"Call him, Ter. Tell him we're coming to see him and we want to find him there when we arrive. Tell him to stay put."

"If he's home."

"He goes off the reservation, we're in a world of shit. I had to call in a lot of chips to keep him out of trouble the last time. You'd think his ass would be burned enough—"

"Hurt pride," Kyle said. "He can't stand it that some woman jerked his chain like that."

"Boy's still thinking with his pecker." Kyle started to say something else and shut it off. Burgess's bad news also involved a wayward pecker, or at least, pecker trouble. "Not that we haven't all got troubles. Michelle's thinking about a baby."

"Don't they know what a fucked up—"

"Women are different," Kyle said. "We're thinking that no one without their head wedged could possibly want to bring a child into this shit storm we call life. They're thinking that children are about love and life and the future."

"Or the fucked-up past."

"I love my girls," Kyle said. From the background sounds, Burgess thought he was doing dishes. "Who knows? Maybe your kid will bring you pleasure. You ever think about that?"

"I'm Catholic, or I was. We don't think about pleasure, Ter, you know that. We think about the consequences of pleasure. Hell, pleasure didn't have so damned many consequences, cops and priests would be out of work."

"You shoulda *been* a priest," Kyle said.

"You're confusing us. You're the one shoulda been a priest." Kyle's lean, ascetic body and deep, suffering eyes were much more priestly than Burgess's bulk and glower. Or his temper.

And Kyle, for all his cynicism, was more genuinely religious. "Call him, then call me back."

His tires hissed through the wet streets, slithering occasionally on tight turns, the pavement coated with the leaves the increasingly wild rain was bringing down. It took him back to fall nights in his youth. A bunch of them would pile into someone's car and go out cruising. On a night like this, when wind and rain had brought the leaves down, skidding on slippery leaves had been a favorite activity. Slipping, sliding, cornering too fast, leaving rubber, coming way too close to going off the road. He'd had one crazy friend who liked to throw his mother's Buick, the one with Positraction, into reverse at forty, just to see what would happen.

Half the guys he'd hung with had had no sense of what a repair to the family car might cost. They just had a warped and wild sense of fun. They hadn't spent their childhoods afraid that something might break; weren't desperately aware that a mechanic's bill might mean the phone or the heat would go, or that meals would be a tiny bowl of pasta and thin sauce or too much Hamburger Helper with too little hamburger to help for a month or more. They'd been a proud family. They'd worn their repair tape inside their shoes, mended worn clothes and socks. Burgess had mowed lawns, raked leaves, babysat for grocery money.

Maybe that was what kept him on the street dealing with "people" issues, trumping any ambition to rise up the food chain. He knew firsthand about poverty and fear and drunks and violence. He knew what a driver desperation was. When other cops were scornful of the women who stayed with violent husbands, when they said in disbelief "why doesn't she just leave?" as though leaving were easy, he understood how deep a tie the sanctity of marriage vows could be—for better or for worse taken literally—and how much a woman would sacrifice or endure to keep her children warm and fed.

Children. Shoot. Tomorrow he'd wake up and his plate would still be full of them.

He stopped at a Dunkin' Donuts to get some cocoa and donuts and muffins, then pulled to the curb in front of Maura's building. Must be an early crowd. Most of the windows were dark. But there were lights in Maura's. He pressed the button and got buzzed in. Scary how easy it was. A house full of the vulnerable and they persisted in acting invulnerable.

Maura answered the door readily enough, but stepped back without a trace of recognition. Of him, anyway. She recognized the donut bags. "Oh, goody," she said. "You brought me something."

"Don't I always, Maura?" She'd aged a decade in a week, he thought, as she tipped back on her small feet and stared up at him. Those last hints of youth and beauty were gone. In their place was a frowzy old woman with unwashed hair and food-stained clothes. He wondered, without much hope, if her daughter had checked on her.

"Cocoa," he said, taking the cup out of the bag and putting it into her waiting hand. "I'm still working on what happened to Reggie, Maura. I have some questions you might be able to help me with." There was no recognition or response on her face. He hesitated. "Maura, do you remember me? Joe Burgess? I'm the detective? Reggie's friend?"

"Find Joe," she said, tipping her head sideways like a bright-eyed bird. "Reggie always said, you need help, Maura, you find Joe. He'll take care of it."

He was doing a piss-poor job of taking care of anything, but it wouldn't help her to hear that. "It's about Joey," he said. "I'm trying to find him. You got any ideas where he might go?"

Maura knotted her hands together, looking like an upright squirrel as she tipped her head to the left and to the right. She studied him like he was under a microscope. Then she nodded, as though he'd passed some invisible test. "You're Joe," she said.

"That's right, and I—"

"You're looking for Joey. I know. Joey's in trouble?"

Burgess nodded.

"He's run away, hasn't he?"

Burgess nodded again. Despite the lack of recognition, she was unusually lucid tonight.

"Claire wouldn't want you to know this"—Maura leaned forward, far into his personal space, bringing with her the too-familiar smell of unwashed skin and hair and careless bladder; if his life had a scent-track, it was unmistakably this—"but Joey will have gone to the cottage."

She moved away a little, so she could see his face. "Mind you, I said 'cottage' not 'camp.' This is Claire's place, so it is no camp. Long Lake. Harrison. Beautiful place. Better than most people's houses. Me and Reggie went up there once . . . not inside, you know. Reggie wasn't ever welcome . . . but we drove by hoping maybe we'd see Joey outside." She tapped a finger against her jaw. "Reggie, you know, he wanted to see how Joey was doing, and Claire, she wouldn't let him anywhere near, so Reggie had to sneak—"

She interrupted herself, her voice rising, angry and less controlled. "Ain't it just the biggest shame what that cold bitch put him through? Making him sneak around to see his own kid? Him renting a car when he didn't have no money, just for maybe a glimpse?"

Burgess was afraid he'd lose her before he got the information he needed, but before he could intervene, her face changed again, this time she looked dreamy. "He had a good job, you know, Reggie did. He bought me a present. You want to see?"

He wanted out of there. He wanted a linear explanation of

the visit to Claire's cottage and some details that would help him find it. He said, "Sure. I'd like to," and waited while she dug through the ratty tote bag again and pulled out the dirty white box. Dirtier and more worn than the last time he'd seen it. He imagined her opening the box and stroking the gloves, over and over, as she remembered Reggie.

"Gloves," she said proudly, thrusting the box toward him. "For the winter."

For form's sake, he opened the box again. The same nice, thick, sheepskin gloves with fleece linings she'd showed him at the station.

Maura started to cry. "He had a job," she said, "out at Mercer Metals, cleaning up the place, wiping down the equipment, odd jobs. Getting materials ready for the next day. Fixing things when they broke, which you know he was really good at. He was so proud. You know about that, doncha? How it mattered to Reggie to have a job and a paycheck and be normal?"

Since when had hearing the word "normal" caused so much pain? Now every one of the phrases that used "normal" seemed loaded. Normal life. Normal relationship. Normal family. He'd always thought there was a big distance between where he was and where Reggie was—had been. Now the gap didn't seem so big.

"You're sure it was Mercer Metals?"

She nodded, her face squinted and owlish. "I got this." She crossed the room to a dresser with a hundred candles on top. None of them were burning, but in the center, set up on a box above the candles, was Reggie's picture. One he'd never seen before. A fairly recent picture of Reggie smiling a big, pleased smile, his arm around Maura. They were dressed up, like they were going out to eat or something. "Our special day," she said.

It was an altar. A memorial. And man, he knew about that. He wanted to forget investigating and start lighting those candles. He wanted to get down on his knees with this half-crazy woman and pray for Reggie. To moan and scream as only the truly grieved can. He wanted to have the feelings Joe the cop had to hold at bay.

He jerked his wayward thoughts back to the job as she held out an envelope with a logo that looked familiar. The envelope was worn, with part of the logo missing. Still, he'd bet that if he took it back to 109 and compared it with the fragments from Kevin Duran's wastebasket and Joey's trash, the logos would match.

"He used to get his money in these," she said. "Every week. Reggie was making good money. He said when we'd saved up enough, we were going to take a trip."

"Where were you going to go, Maura?"

She looked over at Reggie's picture and smiled. "Cape Cod. We were going to stay in a place by the ocean and eat clams and lobsters and fried seafood plates and we were going to drink champagne and walk on the beach and watch the sunset. Just like a normal couple on a honeymoon."

Honeymoon? That was romantic. Burgess hated to interrupt her happy reverie but the clock was running. "Can you tell me where Claire's camp is?"

"Oh, sure," she said. She fished around in a drawer, sending a cascade of small pieces of paper tumbling to the floor. "I know it's in here somewhere." More paper fell as her search went from casual to frantic. It looked like a paper storm had occurred before she finally held up a small pink square. "Here you go." She gave it to Burgess with a little flourish.

On it, in Reggie's impeccable writing, was an address and a phone number.

"Thank you, Maura," he said. "I really needed this." He carefully wrote the information in his notebook and then held out the note. "Do you need this back or may I keep it?"

"Keep it," she said. "I don't need it anymore. I was just holding it for Reggie because . . . you know . . . he was always losing things." Her blue eyes fixed on him, suddenly both lucid and fierce. "Is Joey in trouble again?"

"I'm afraid so."

"If he didn't have those Libby eyes, I wouldn't believe he was Reggie's," she said. "There's none of his or Clay's decency in that boy. Although I don't guess I'm one to talk. Look at my daughter. If she had herself a shrine, she'd be lighting candles and praying for the day I'll be gone to bother her no more."

In the dim lamp light, he saw a tear glisten. "Seems like everyone has family trouble lately, Maura." He held up the donut bags. "Don't forget about these."

She gave him an indulgent smile. "Donuts are good, Joe. A clear mind and a stable family would just be better. That's what we both hoped for. What we tried to be for each other. I guess . . ." Her gaze, suddenly, went beyond clear, as though she was seeing right inside him. "I guess none of us are very lucky in that regard."

He knew this kind of sudden, piercing clarity was the flip side of half-crazy, but it still startled him. "Do you know if it was Joey who helped Reggie find that job?"

"I don't," she said. "I'm sorry. You'll have to ask him when you find him." Then, surprising him again, she said, "You know that that place has got a big circular driveway, so you'd better take two cars, block 'em both, be sure he doesn't get away. Next time, he might go somewhere I don't know about." She waggled a cautionary finger. "Maura knows a lot, but she doesn't know everything."

Before his eyes, her shoulders hunched and her eyes grew vague. The footsteps that had carried her with certainty and authority to the drawer to search and back to confront him slowed to an unsteady shuffle as she moved past him to the dresser and started lighting candles.

"You want to light a candle for Reggie?" she said.

It was crazy to encourage someone so unstable to light a single candle, let alone a hundred candles. "Sure," he said. "I'd like that."

He took a long look at Reggie's smiling face, lit a candle, and left.

He was opening his car door when his phone rang. "I think it's hit the fan," Kyle said. "Stan's not home and my cop gut's in a twist. Got any idea where he'd go?"

"Sadly, I do," Burgess said, and gave the address.

CHAPTER TWENTY-EIGHT

He had no time for this goddamned frolic. If he wasn't going to be home catching some z's, he wanted to go see Nick Goodall, then track down Joey and get some answers. The night had grown wilder. Wind and rain from the tail end of a late hurricane knocked down branches and hurled trash cans and debris into the street. Driving was like a big game of bumper cars, only it wasn't fun, and the going was maddeningly slow.

The knife-sharp pain in his gut was a persistent and painful reminder he shouldn't have let this happen. If he was the captain steering this investigative ship of fools, he was way off course. It was unacceptable at any level of SOP to postpone going after a major bad guy and a witness in a homicide to rescue a rogue officer. He didn't know many good police who wouldn't have done what he was doing. Cote wouldn't. But Cote was not a good police.

He and Kyle got to the house at exactly the same time, pulling in to the curb behind Perry's car. Kyle, grim-faced and dripping, got into the passenger seat. "Can this police officer be saved?" he said. His tone was light but his mouth was a tight line, the skin around it white.

"I'm still hoping. You wanna do a little Peeping Tom number, see if you can figure out what's going on in there?"

In the dim glow of a street light, Kyle's smile was grim. "You mean, if it's other than mad, hot sex?"

"Even if it's only mad, hot sex, he had a direct order to stay away from this place. At the least, we're gonna haul his ass out of there and whack him with a two-by-four. I'd be grateful if it were only mad, hot sex. My gut says otherwise."

"Just don't aim for his head," Kyle said. "Nothing there to register the blow." With a sigh, he got out of the truck and slogged away through the rain, his coat and hat glistening until he disappeared around the corner of the house. A minute later, he was on the radio. "It's bad, Joe. Got a Mexican standoff in the freakin' living room, two mad guys with guns, one of 'em Stan and the other big as freakin' Godzilla. They're both naked as jaybirds and there's a naked dame holding a phone, jumping up and down on the couch, hollering for them to stop."

Local cops hadn't held the husband very long, had they? What had they been thinking, that a long-distance truck driver wasn't a flight risk? He was that and every other kind of risk. He and his provocative little honey. Probably better if they'd locked up Stan. His little one-eyed guy must have a death wish to come back here and get in the middle of this. But Burgess knew. Both cop pride and young stud pride could make a man stupid and careless.

Bad as the situation was, Burgess hoped she hadn't called the cops. More bodies wouldn't make this easier, and would almost certainly mean Perry went to jail. And that all their jobs were fucked. This went south, Cote would laugh all the way to his termination hearing.

He got out his gun, checked the clip, and shoved it back in. You didn't go to a gunfight without a gun. "This could blow apart at any minute. That big guy in there, that's the husband, and he makes Stanley look sane. There's a slider around back, Stan says. You go that way, see if it's open. If you can't get in easily, break a window. I'll take the front." He hesitated. "I'm going to try to get Stan to put that gun down and get him out of there without getting any of us shot."

Kyle slipped away into the darkness, his wet coat a quick gleam of light as he disappeared around the side of the house.

Quietly, he let himself out of the truck and headed for the front of the house. The knob turned easily in his hand. He drew his gun and moved silently into the house, forcing himself to keep breathing as he wondered, was this going to be the time he'd finally have to shoot someone? You can't plan for this kind of situation, it's all read and respond. The mind tries to do it anyway. Then, as he moved into the dark hall, he felt the world slip away. His focus narrowed and tunnel vision took over.

From the lighted room ahead came a jumble of voices. ". . . away from my fuckin' wife. I already . . ."

"Your fuckin' wife called *me* and asked me over. Said she wanted to make amends."

"Didn't I tell you to stay the fuck away? Whatsa matter, you deaf or something? I'm gonna blow your effin' dick off, you slimy little . . ."

"The bitch said you were on the road, she . . ."

"You watch who you're calling a bitch, asshole. The woman's my . . ."

Burgess moved toward the light, listening. The voices told him the big man was closer and to his left, Stan to his right. He should have looked in the window, gotten a sense of the layout of the room. The wrangling continued. The two men warring for superiority, temper and testosterone straining their voices. Sounding like they were on the verge of explosion. He and Terry didn't have much time.

He slid along the wall until he could see part-way into the room. He saw the woman on the couch. She was waving her arms and urging them on . . . not urging them to stop, as Kyle had thought. Tickled pink at the idea of a shoot-out in her living room. A sick idea of a turn-on. To his left, he sensed more than saw the big man, standing close to the doorway. All he could see clearly were two huge hands and an unsteady Glock.

Across the room, a door was slowly moving, the dark opening growing almost imperceptibly larger as Kyle swung it in toward himself. As soon as Kyle was visible, Burgess moved, throwing himself into the room. He stuck his gun right in the face of the spitting gorilla. "Police," he yelled. "Both of you. Drop the guns and put up your hands or I'll blow your fucking heads off."

"No way! This fucker is gonna die." The huge man took aim right over his shoulder at Perry, his finger dangerously unsteady on the trigger.

"Put the gun down, goddammit!" Burgess yelled. "Put it down. Down. Right now!" The gun began to drop, but not fast enough. "Put it down." He repeated the order, getting in the man's face, commanding the man's attention. "This is not worth dying over." The big man's gun wavered slowly toward the floor.

"Good. Now keep it down. Terry . . ." Kyle's gun focused on the gorilla as Burgess crossed the room to Stan Perry, deliberately keeping himself in the big man's line of fire. As Perry stared in surprise, he said, "I said *both of you*. Drop your fucking gun, Stan. Drop it. Now!"

Perry's face was scarlet, his shaved head gleaming with sweat, his lips back in a snarl. Lost in his own tunnel vision, he was looking right through Burgess at the Gorilla. Not taking in Burgess's commands. He didn't drop his gun. "Drop it, Detective," Burgess repeated, blocking his view, forcing him to listen. "Drop it now. That's an order."

Comprehension swam slowly into his eyes, "Jesus, Joe," Perry said, "he's the freaking bad guy, not me." His jaw was stubborn, his arm rigid.

"An order, Detective," Burgess repeated, keeping his voice steady and calm, as if getting between two crazy-mad naked guys with guns happened every day. "A direct order from your sergeant. Like to get everyone out of here alive, Stan, if that's okay with you." He checked that Kyle still had the big guy covered. "Drop . . . the . . . gun."

"Like hell. I am not—" Burgess shoved his gun in his belt, delivered a full-bore right to his detective's jaw, then a left and right to the stomach, his fists carrying decades of experience with recalcitrant subjects, and the need to act first and argue later. Carrying all his anger and frustration with this investigation and with subordinates who think they're beyond the rules.

Stan, gaping with foolish astonishment, collapsed like a popped balloon, a dribble of blood starting at the corner of his mouth. Quickly, Burgess snatched Stan's gun, grabbed him by the arm, and walked him to the door. "You get out. Go sit in my car. And don't do another goddamned thing until I get there. Understand?"

Perry stood stupidly, rubbing his jaw and staring at Burgess with a betrayed look on his face. "I'm fucking naked," he said.

Stan's modesty was the least of his worries. "I said *go sit in the car.* You got that?"

Comprehension began to dawn. One hand rubbing his swelling jaw, Perry mumbled, "Yes, boss," and stumbled out.

Burgess turned back to the naked couple. "He's leaving, Mr. Barton," he said. The angry husband now looked like he wanted to kill Burgess for depriving him of the chance to shoot Stan. He also wore the look of a man just realizing that he's wearing nothing but a gun in a room where the other guys have guns *and* clothes.

The crazy wife, meanwhile, wore the crestfallen pout of a kid whose ice cream has fallen off the cone. She was, as Perry had said, hot, if you liked the pneumatic blow-up doll look and big hair. Kyle took the phone from her and replaced it on the cradle. "Appreciate it if you could point me toward Mr. Perry's clothes, ma'am," he said.

She gave Kyle an appraising look and licked her lips, like he was a snack brought out for her enjoyment. "What'll ya give me?"

Kyle pretended to consider. "Night in jail if you don't."

"Ah, hell," she said. "This way." She led Kyle through the door, closing it behind them.

Burgess tried to remember what Timmy Collins had said about the Gorilla. Something about priors, he was sure of that. He crossed to where the man stood puzzling out his next move, and took the gun from his hand. "You really shouldn't be waving this around, you know. Not with charges hanging over you and your prior record. It's probably not legal. And you really don't want to lose your job. Heaven only knows the trouble your wife could get into if you were locked up."

The Gorilla pondered that as he scratched his chest. "She do need to see me regular," he agreed. He jerked his chin toward the door through which Perry had gone. "You promise me that one won't be coming back?"

"He won't be coming back," Burgess said.

"You give him whatfor, dincha? And wasn't he some surprised. So . . . what . . . you're his boss?"

Burgess nodded. His heart rate still coming down, the room coming back into focus as the tunnel thing faded. Everything suddenly so bright the light felt loud. He didn't quite trust it had gone this easily. Was still waiting for the second level of all hell to break out. For death-wish chickie to bring the cops down on all of them. Stanley the stupid to rush back in and start things up again. Barton to lunge for his gun.

He half expected the little hottie to come out of the back claiming Kyle had put the moves on her. Instead, he heard the front door open and Kyle entered the room that way.

"Had to give Stanley his clothes," he said. "We done here?"

Burgess looked at the Gorilla. "We done?" The man nodded. "Okay," Burgess said. "That your truck out there?" Another nod. "Is it locked?"

The man shook his head. "Ain't got around to that yet. Just got out from the jail and I hadda come see Lorraine first." For the first time, Burgess noticed the pile of clothes on the floor. "I was gonna surprise her. 'Cept she had that guy here. Your guy." His little eyes narrowed in his big red face. "You sure he ain't comin' back? 'Cuz if he is, I'm gonna kill him. I'd hafta."

"He's not coming back," Burgess said. "Now, I'm leaving this gun in your truck. And I don't want to see you come charging out here after it, so you see that clock over there?" He pointed to the clock on the wall. "You give it ten minutes. Then you can come get it."

"Yeah. All right. Okay. Ten minutes and I can get my gun back." The Gorilla smiled like he liked the deal.

He and Kyle backed out the door. Not taking any chances. Outside, he ejected the clip from Barton's Glock, emptied it, and shoved it back in the gun. He wiped off his prints and left it on the floor of the truck. He hated like heck to give the guy back his gun. Stanley might be safe from getting shot, but sooner or later, this pair of idiots was going to bring some poor fool to grief.

Chapter Twenty-Nine

Perry's car was gone. Before Burgess could explode, Kyle said, "I told him to get the heck out of here, go home, and wait for us."

"He damned well better do it," Burgess said. "I lost years off my life just now, waiting for that big gorilla to shoot or for his demented honey to call the locals. Does he understand what happened in there?"

"I hope so."

"You and me both." He bent down, hands on his knees, suddenly shaking. "Jesus! I wish *I* did!"

He stayed there, grabbing air and letting the wind cool his sweat-soaked skin, until Kyle said, "Clock's running."

He straightened. Only a few minutes before the Gorilla reappeared. "Let's roll. We'll go by, explain things yet again to young Stanley. About getting everybody killed. Maybe suggest castration? Then, if you're up for it, I've got a line on Joey Libby. Maura says Claire has a cottage out on Long Lake. Joey's probably staying there. A rainy night seems like an excellent time for a visit."

"You don't want to see Goodall first?" Kyle said.

Burgess considered. He was hot to go after Joey before he moved again, but Goodall was a missing piece of the puzzle, one that might give them some answers. He nodded. "You're right. Goodall first. Give Stan some time to calm down." Give himself time to calm down, make it less likely he'd take Stan's head off. "Let's see what the drug guys found on his boat."

"I'll call Sage. He was going in with them. And let Michelle know I'll be late." Kyle got in his car and pulled away.

As he reached the corner, Burgess looked in the rearview and saw the Gorilla come out, still naked, his immense cock flopping like a donkey's tail. He trotted to the truck, got the gun, and pointed it toward the Explorer, grinning as he pulled the trigger.

Nick Goodall didn't look anything like the handsome rebel artist in his photographs. His long, greasy hair was gathered in clumps, like he'd been holding it in clenched fists. Dark circles underlined his eyes and a raw, red scrape scored one cheek like he'd been dragged over gravel. He glanced at their ID cards and walked to his couch, collapsing onto it with an air of utter defeat.

They followed him in. Took chairs facing him. It was a single, open room, loft-style, with high ceilings and exposed brick walls. A smoky fire burned in the large fireplace. The place was dusty, the counter piled with unopened mail, no sign of a muse looking after Goodall's creature comforts.

"Is there anyone else here?" Burgess asked.

"She left," Goodall said, shaking his head. "She just couldn't take Star anymore." He spoke as though they were aware of his domestic arrangements.

"I never meant for any of this to happen," he said. "Things just got completely out of control. Which, my crazy freak of an ex-wife Star being involved, I should have expected." His big scarred hands dangled between his knees, clasped like a penitent's. He had mad artist's eyes, a startling shade of peridot green rimmed with black, deep concentration lines fanning out at their corners, and a mobile, full-lipped mouth. A big, handsome rogue of a man come to grief. He wore black jeans and t-shirt, an unbuttoned black shirt and the unhealthy pallor of a man who's been drinking too much and eating too little.

Two empty Jameson's bottles on the coffee table flanking an open third, and the reek of sweated-out alcohol in the air suggested what his recent diet had been. Burgess wondered if the scrape was from a drunken fall or a fight. He thought Goodall would tell them soon enough.

"She said he needed to go in for treatment and wasn't cooperating. She said that we needed to help him, to force him to go because he wouldn't go on his own. She said that we were doing this for Reggie."

He said "she" the way you'd speak of something detestable and feared. "I'll get him to meet me for lunch, Nick, she says, and then you pick him up. You know Reggie will do anything I ask. And now—" His hand swept out and grabbed the bottle.

Burgess was instantly alert, Kyle beside him shifting to the edge of the chair. You had to watch the hands and the bottle. A bottle could be nasty.

Goodall poured a shot into his empty glass, drained it, and slammed it back down. He didn't offer them a drink. He wasn't their host. They weren't guests. As the penitential hands suggested, they were hearing confession. "Now he's dead and that cold bitch acts like nothing in the world is different."

He slumped back on the couch, head bowed. Abject. Defeated. "What the hell was I thinking?" A long pause. And exhalation of boozy breath. The hard-used hands knotted between his knees again. Wringing. Turning. "Shit. Christ. Oh my God, how in hell do I explain this? I did it because I liked him. I liked Reggie. And now he's freaking dead, man. Dead. Like forever dead." Goodall jumped up and started pacing, large feet in black motorcycle boots stomping along worn, wide-pine planks.

Before Goodall could speak again, Burgess did what he hated to have to do. He said the words that risked stopping the man in his tracks before he told them what they'd come to hear. The caution Constitutional law and tricky defense attorneys imposed on them. Technically, this was neither custody nor interrogation, but technically could get tied up in a million knots. If Goodall said something important here, he didn't want to lose it.

Decades of miserable experiences on the witness stand had taught him the questions that would be asked. You had a witness who told you what? And when? Had Mr. Goodall been drinking? Did Mr. Goodall seem upset? Intimidated by a late-night visit from two police detectives? Did Mr. Goodall understand the implications of what he was about to say?

Cautious as a man walking on eggs, he went through Miranda, and got the sheet signed and tucked away, Goodall as impatient as he to get this out of the way. Then Burgess pulled in a lungful of the boozy air and, trying to sound mild and unthreatening, said, "Are you confessing to Reggie's murder?"

Goodall whirled, fixing Burgess with crazy eyes in a ravaged face, looking like he was about to cry. "No. Yes. No. Hell, I might as well be. Jesus, Detective . . ." His voice rose to an anguished roar. "I don't know! I'd been drinking. I—" He kicked at a large, round stone sitting by the fireplace, sending it spinning across the wood floor to crash into the opposite wall. "I mean, I freaking set him up for it, didn't I? Me and my goddamned good-guy attempts to help him. I know her, dammit. I know her. How could I ever have believed her?"

"Can you tell us what happened?" Still in the low, gentle voice. A prompt to get Goodall going again.

"I was at the studio. Out behind our old house. It means I have to deal with her, but I still work there. It's cheap and it's a good space for the kind of work I do. So Star comes meandering out of the house as I'm parking. I'll tell you, Detective—"

He broke off. "You guys got names?"

"Joe Burgess," Burgess said, "and this is Terry Kyle."

"Joe," Goodall said. "Terry. You guys met my ex?"

"I have," Burgess said.

"Piece of work, isn't she." Goodall didn't wait for confirmation. "So Star comes out and she's all wide-eyed sweetness, which is how she gets when she wants something. If I don't say yes, it gets real easy to believe that she is a witch." He stopped, looked curiously at Burgess. "You didn't let her feed you anything, did you? Or give you coffee?"

"I did."

Goodall rolled his eyes. "There ought to be a warning sign. So she says to me, Nicky, you know my cousin Reggie . . . well, Reggie's not doing so good and he won't go and get himself some help. She says she's got things set up so Reggie can go to this clinic for help, only we've got to bring him there—"

Suddenly his fist slammed down on the coffee table, making the bottles jump. The empty glass rolled onto the floor and disappeared under the couch. "I'm such a goddamned wimp I make myself sick," he said. "But I was at the point where I would do anything to keep Star on an even keel. I wanted it to work out with me and Beverly. I wanted to be able to do my work without her hovering around. To sleep without her damned endless phone calls. To go somewhere with Bev without Star showing up and making a scene. After Star tried to poison her, Bev finally got a restraining order. Hell of a lot of good that did. Even the goddamned cops are scared of Star. Like she really could stick pins in a doll and work some voodoo on them."

His big hand knotted in his hair again, twisted, and then dropped to his knee. "Four freaking years we've been divorced and she still won't give up. She's just mean as a snake and evil to the core. She's waiting for me to come to my senses, she says."

He fished under the couch for the glass, refilled it, and drank.

"I came to my senses when I left Star. I'd have been a far sight better off if I'd also left my studio, but I couldn't afford to. Still can't because of the money it takes to support her." He scrabbled around on the coffee table, looking for something, didn't find it, and looked over at Burgess. "Ever meet anyone like that?"

"I've met *her*," Burgess said. "Can you tell us what happened on Friday?"

Goodall buried his head in his hands, speaking to them through the fence of his fingers. "Star said she was meeting Reggie for lunch and I was supposed to go down there with this guy she knew, Kevin something, and help them get Reggie in the truck. That was all. They were going to take him to some clinic she knew about." Goodall's shoulders heaved. "Just supposed to help get him in the truck."

"Where did you meet her?" Burgess prompted.

"Down on the waterfront. I was waiting in the truck with Kevin. When we saw them come out of the restaurant, we pulled up, stopped, and got out. I called to him. I said 'Reggie, it's okay. It's me. We just want to help you.' He sees me, and he's starting to smile when he sees the other guy. He turns and starts to run."

It didn't quite match up with Benjy's story, but there was plenty of overlap. Questions could wait until they had Goodall's version.

The sobs were steady now, deep, ugly sounds that wracked Goodall's chest and set his shoulders heaving. "I was trying to hold Reggie, trying to calm him down, and he looked at me, real lucid, and he said, 'Don't let them take me, Nick. Jesus, please don't let them.' I told him that they, that we, were all just trying to help. That was when the guy—Kevin—came over and said, real mean, for Reggie to shut the fuck up and get in the truck. I could see that Reggie was scared of him."

Goodall fingered the scrape on his face. "We were standing right by the door, and it was open. This Kevin guy shoved Reggie into the truck, Star was there by then, in the truck, helping to drag him in. So I said, 'Hey, wait a minute. Reggie's not comfortable' and this guy Kevin says to me, 'I'll show you comfortable.' He slams me in the jaw. I go face-down onto the sidewalk. By the time I'm back on my feet, Kevin's holding Reggie and Star's driving away."

He ran a shaky hand through his shaggy hair. "I won't ever forget that last look Reggie gave me. He's being shoved into the truck and I'm sprawled out on the ground, and he had this awful scared look on his face like he was going to his execution."

Goodall's voice dropped to a shaky whisper. "And he was, by God. He was!"

Burgess looked away, shifting his eyes around the room, trying to find something, anything, to fix on while he quelled the urge to throw this whimpering, self-pitying bastard through one of his own windows. He settled on the big stone, squeezing his own hands together until his knuckles were as white as Goodall's.

"So you never got in the truck?" Goodall shook his shaggy head. The sobbing continued. "You didn't go with them to this clinic? You let Star and Dugan do that?" Goodall didn't answer.

"Joe?" Kyle said.

He slid his eyes toward Kyle. Kyle was right on the edge of the chair, watching, trying to read his anger meter and judge how close he was to exploding. Kyle raised his eyebrows and Burgess shook his head. He only *wanted* to pound the guy; he wasn't going to. "Why didn't you come and talk to us?" he said.

"Because I'm a pathetic excuse for a human being."

Burgess couldn't have agreed more. "Okay," he said, "I've got some pictures I'd like you to look at, see if you recognize anyone. Then we'd like you to take us through it again so we're sure we've understood."

He held out his keys to Kyle. "Will you get my file with the pictures?"

Kyle took the keys, but he didn't move. "Maybe you should go, Joe. You know right where they are." As though Kyle didn't. He just didn't want to leave them alone together.

"In my briefcase behind the driver's seat. We'll be fine, Ter."

Kyle pulled on his coat, and headed for the door.

Goodall sat hunched and rocking, so wrapped up in self-pity he missed the interplay between them. If the victim had been a stranger, Burgess wondered, would he have been more sympathetic to this man's story? Probably not. He didn't have a lot of patience with self-pity or weeping drunks. With the cowards who witnessed or contributed to crimes and then refused to come forward. Goodall had probably been maintaining a fair level of intoxication since Kyle had said they'd be coming to see him, just so he could liberate his tongue and cushion their censure.

In a moment, Kyle was back with the folder. "Still raining like a bastard out there," he said. "Nasty."

As Kyle hung his dripping coat over the back of the chair, Burgess took out the picture of Kevin Dugan and showed it to Goodall. "Is this the guy?"

Goodall's eyes widened as he took the photo in a shaking hand and turned toward the light. After a moment, he handed it back. "Nope, sorry," he said, looking everywhere but at Burgess's face. "I've never seen this man before in my life."

CHAPTER THIRTY

Burgess reclaimed the photograph, letting the silence grow as Goodall squirmed on the couch, his eyes flickering around the room, looking at everything but the two detectives facing him.

The insistent ring of Kyle's phone broke the silence. He answered, barking a crisp, "Terry Kyle." He listened and opened his notebook on his knee, making a series of what looked like hieroglyphics on the page.

Goodall raised the bottle, but Burgess stopped him. "We're not finished," he whispered. "Like you to stay lucid 'til we're done, then you can drink all you want." The sculptor seemed on the cusp of argument, his face belligerent, and Burgess leaned forward, ready for what might come. Then Goodall's shoulders slumped. He burrowed deeper into the sofa, his hands back between his knees. Across the room, the fire snapped and hissed.

"Okay. Okay. That's great," Kyle said. "Thanks for letting me know." He snapped the phone shut and finished making his notes. "Well," he said finally, giving Goodall a friendly grin. "That was the drug guys. They've just finished searching your boat. You want to know what they found? Or maybe . . ."

Kyle's glance circled the room as though inventorying the pricey space, the artwork, the high-end leather furniture, and expensive rugs. "Maybe you already know?"

In a flash, penitent morphed into defensive. "I don't know what you're talking about."

"Your boat," Kyle said, "the one you're letting Joey Libby

use? We talked about it earlier on the phone. You said we could search it?" Kyle's cold eyes stayed on Goodall's face until the man nodded. "Drug team says your boat was like a pharmacy. Ecstasy, marijuana, OxyContin, Dilaudid, Rohypnol." He looked down at his notes. "Cocaine. You got an explanation for that?"

"That's not on me," Goodall said, shaking his head vehemently. "That's Joey. Little prick never did have any sense. Just does what he wants and fuck everybody. You can't think I—"

"So, maybe you could tell us about your relationship with Joey Libby?"

"I don't *have* a relationship with Joey Libby." The sculptor's hands had knotted up again and he was looking at the phone like there was someone he should call.

Burgess could have told him. Call your lawyer and don't say another word to us. But he'd already gone through the warning and wasn't about to repeat himself. Not with a signed waiver in his pocket. "He's been living on your boat."

Goodall exhaled a long, boozy breath. "*Renting* my boat," he said.

"What was the arrangement?" Burgess said.

"I just told you," Goodall said. "He was renting my boat."

"Since when?"

Goodall shrugged. "Since a couple months. He was going crazy living at home with Claire."

"What was the arrangement?" Burgess repeated.

"Claire gave me a check."

"So for two months or so, Joey's been living on the boat and Claire has been paying you rent? That right?" Burgess looked at Kyle. "What were the conditions of Joey's probation? Do we know?"

"Live at home. Keep a job. Stay out of bars, away from drugs, and out of trouble."

They knew Joey had taken Amanda Mercer to a bar. Burgess looked at Goodall. "Monthly checks? Weekly?"

"Monthly."

"How much?"

"No idea." Goodall shrugged. "The checks went to Star."

"Did you have the arrangement in writing?"

Goodall gave him a "you think I'm stupid?" look. "Like you said, Joey's supposed to be living at home."

Burgess didn't yet know if Goodall was stupid. Weak, yes. Self-indulgent and self-pitying. Irresponsible. Pussy-whipped. "But you know that the rent is being paid?"

"Otherwise I'd hear from Star, wouldn't I?"

"Okay, let's see if I've got this straight. Joey lives on your boat and Claire pays rent to your ex-wife, that's how it works?"

"Yup."

"It's a pretty valuable boat," Burgess said. "You keep an eye on it? Check up on Joey from time to time?"

Goodall scowled. "Claire said she'd take care of that."

"You know if she did?"

Goodall shrugged. "As long as the arrangement kept Star off my back, I didn't much care. I went down there once. The place was a mess. Kid wasn't even taking out the garbage. I called Claire and reminded her about our deal. I mean, I knew what Joey was like, didn't I? She said she'd get it cleaned up and keep a closer eye on Joey."

"You remember when that was? Last week? Last month?"

Goodall didn't. Maybe Tolliver could fill in some of the gaps in Goodall's selective memory.

"You keep insurance on the boat?"

Goodall gave him a suspicious look, then said, "Of course. It's a valuable boat."

"But you don't know if Claire was making sure Joey took care of the boat?"

"No. I do not. I don't know and I don't care. The bank cares. The loan on that boat pays for this place. Boat's been nothing but a headache. I've got nothing but headaches everywhere. Star. Claire. Joey. That damned boat. Goddamned kid was supposed to take care of that boat for me. And now this business with Reggie."

He rubbed his head. "I'm an artist, for Christ's sake, not a businessman. I'm just trying to do my work—I've got a big piece commissioned—and everybody's always at me, wanting something." He tangled his hands in his hair and bowed his head.

"Reggie's death gives you a headache? That's what this is to you?" Even through his anger, he'd noticed a change in the sculptor's behavior. As soon as the words, "supposed to take care of that boat for me" were uttered, the man had leaned forward, making a sucking sound as though he wanted to draw them back in. How was Joey supposed to take care of the boat? Not keep it neat or clean. Claire had that job. Was Goodall talking about a more permanent solution? One that would let him collect insurance?

Kyle cleared his throat. When Burgess looked at him, he nodded toward Burgess's hands, rolled up into tight, trembling fists.

"Walk us through last Friday again, if you would," Burgess said, forcing his fingers to uncurl. "When did you first hear from Star, asking for your help?"

Goodall reached for the bottle again and Burgess moved it out of his reach. "In good time," he said. "Now . . . when did you—"

"Jesus!" Goodall's chin jutted. "Since when can't a man have a quiet drink in his own home with some nosy parker cop telling him what to do?"

"Since Reginald Libby got killed."

Goodall folded his arms. "It wasn't my fault. I just got in too deep, is all, and then Dugan said—"

Not what he'd said a few minutes ago, was it? Back when he didn't know Dugan? Maybe the habit of confession was so ingrained he thought that all he had to do was admit what he'd done, act contrite, get absolution, and he could go back to communing with his bottle. "When did she get in touch with you about getting some help for Reggie?"

"Who?"

"Your ex-wife. Star Goodall."

"It wasn't Star that got in touch with me," Goodall said. "It was Claire."

There were flags all over the field. "Okay. When did Claire get in touch with you?"

"Let's see." Goodall fingered his chin, looking puzzled, as though he'd recently had a beard and someone had taken it while he wasn't looking. "Probably Thursday. That's when she dropped off the check." His hands scrabbled around the coffee table, organizing scattered magazines and mail into a neat stack.

Burgess looked at Kyle, who was taking notes. Kyle shook his head. "Claire was here on Thursday to drop off a check?"

Goodall reached for the bottle. Kyle moved it to the kitchen counter. "Hey!" Goodall half rose from the couch. "You bring that back here. That's mine."

"So Claire was here on Thursday to drop off a check?" Burgess said. "Tell us about that."

"Nothing to tell. She said that Reggie was in a bad way and she and Star were worried about him and wanted him to go to this clinic. She said they needed my help in convincing him. And she brought the check."

"She say where this clinic was?" Goodall shook his head. "Okay, so what did she want you to do?"

"I already told you, man. Star was going to meet Reggie for

lunch and then this guy Kevin and I were supposed to pick up Reggie, get him into the truck, and then they'd drive him to the clinic."

"Did you and Kevin meet near the restaurant or somewhere else?"

"I met him down by the waterfront. Had to. I'd need my truck to get home, wouldn't I?"

"So Kevin brought a truck?"

"That's what I said."

"Do you remember what kind of truck it was?"

"Big. Dark. Double cab. I can't tell you what make, if that's what you're asking. I don't pay attention to things like that."

"Truck have a logo?"

"Might have. I didn't notice."

Goodall fingered his chin again. "That scratch on your face," Burgess said. "Reggie give you that?"

"I told you. It was that guy. Kevin. Reggie hit him, though. Hit that Kevin guy. I betcha he's got bruises." Burgess hoped so. He ached to give Goodall some bruises on Reggie's behalf. Felt his fingers start to curl into fists again and forced them to relax. Business before pleasure. He needed the rest of the story.

"You ever met Kevin before?" Goodall shook his head. "Can you describe him, please."

"He was tall. Not as tall as me, but tall. A burly guy. Maybe in his forties. Dark hair."

"Eye color?" Burgess prompted. "Features? Anything about him that was distinctive? Any facial scars? What was he wearing?" He pulled out Kevin Dugan's picture again and slapped it down on the table in front of Goodall. "You're sure it wasn't this guy?"

"I don't remember."

"And you're sure that it was Star who helped push Reggie into the truck and drove away with him and Kevin? Sure that wasn't you?"

A look of sheer panic on his face, Goodall lurched to his feet, knocking hard into the coffee table and sending the empty bottles tumbling. "Gotta take a piss," he said. He crossed the room and disappeared through a door.

Kyle grabbed his coat. "I'll just take a look outside."

While he waited, Burgess examined the items on the coffee table. Along with the bottles and the glass, there was the neat stack of mail and papers Goodall had just arranged. Curious timing. Burgess looked through it. Some magazines, a couple unopened bills, and beneath them, a check from Claire Libby for $2000. No wonder Goodall had been willing to rent the boat to Joey, if this was what he was getting for rent. Joey could have rented a palace for that.

He brought the check up to the light so he could read the small print on the memo line. It didn't say rent, or Joey, or boat. It said, for services rendered. He wondered if the other checks were the same. Or if this check wasn't for rent at all.

There was a crash from outside, audible even over the wind and rain, and men's voices. He grabbed his coat and tried the door Goodall had gone through. Locked. He hurried out the front, following the noise around the side of the building. In the illumination from a security light on the building, two men struggled. Then one of them pushed free and started to run.

He didn't want to shoot Goodall before he got the rest of the story, so he took off after him, hearing the slap of Kyle's feet behind him. Goodall had reached a vehicle and was scrabbling for his keys when Burgess grabbed him and slammed him against it.

"Put your hands on your head," he yelled over the noise of the rain and wind. "Do it. Goddammit, do it now!"

Goodall, intoxicated, stubborn, now removed any doubt about his stupidity. He wrenched free, turned, and swung. His fist slid along Burgess's wet face, the impetus throwing him into Burgess's arms. Burgess shoved him away and moved in, delivering a small, punishing lesson from a lifelong professional to the man who thought that helping bring about someone's death was just another aggravating headache in a life that interfered with his creativity.

Take some aspirin. Swill some good Irish whiskey. And a lost life recedes into the annoying murmur along with corrupt tenants, a high-maintenance ex-wife, a bitch with a generous checkbook, and an unwanted powerboat.

CHAPTER THIRTY-ONE

They left a belligerent and unrepentant Nick Goodall at the Cumberland County Jail, wailing an unconvincing version of "what did I do?" at their departing backs. Rain was still coming down in sheets and the wind, twisting trees, showered the streets with branches and leaves. Burgess, hurting and wet after a day that had gone on too long, wished for Advil, a long hot shower, and bed. But the day was far from over. They still had to check on Stan, then pay their unannounced visit to Joey.

"We having fun yet?" Kyle asked, as they headed back to their cars.

Burgess fingered his bruised cheekbone. "There was a moment," he said.

"Yeah. You get to have all the fun."

"I do. Next time, I'm letting you fight the bad guys."

"Appreciate that," Kyle said. "I need to do something to earn my wings." They had to holler to be heard over the rain.

"Believe me, the last thing you want is wings," Burgess said. "It's a bitch to drive with wings. Driving's uncomfortable enough without that nonsense."

Stan Perry sat at his kitchen table, a glass of whiskey in front of him, holding an ice pack against his face. "You know how close we came to having everything go to hell back there?" Burgess said.

Perry shifted the ice pack.

"Christ on a cross, Stan, talk to me," Burgess said. "What the hell were you thinking? Terry and I hadn't come after you, you'd either be a dead man or in jail for homicide. You know that, don't you? Do you understand what we put on the line for you tonight?"

"I didn't ask you to."

Burgess wanted to hit him again. "Oh, to hell with it, Terry," he said. "Let's leave Stanley here to sulk and go find Joey Libby."

"I just had to . . . I needed to," Perry said. "It was important, okay. It was freakin' important, Joe." He rubbed his swollen jaw. "You didn't have to hit me so hard."

"More important than your job? Than the fact that someone's been killed and you're supposed to be finding out who did it? Than the fact *you* could have killed somebody . . . or had your fucking dick shot off?"

When Perry didn't respond, Burgess headed for the stairs, stopping at the door. "You coming, Ter? Like to get some sleep one of these days."

"You're getting soft, Joe," Kyle said. "You never used to need sleep." He turned to Perry. "Come along, Stanley. Get your gear. We've got to go catch bad guys."

"I'm not going anywhere," Perry said. "I'm on sick leave."

"Sick leave?" Kyle mimicked vomiting. "Sick leave is for wimpy patrol guys who freak out at a rash, not a hardass detective like yourself with a killer to catch. You keep this up, you're gonna be on permanent asshole leave, busted back to property crimes, if you're not out walking a beat. Now pull your head out of your ass and get your stuff. You can ride with me. I don't think Sergeant Burgess likes you very much right now."

"I don't like him," Burgess agreed. He pulled out his notebook, wrote the address of Claire's camp on a slip of paper, and gave it to Kyle. "I'll give the locals a heads up that we're coming. And we all wear vests. His MO may be picking on women, but I wouldn't trust that kid."

The long, slow ride out to Harrison would give him time to think through what they knew and devise a strategy for where to go next. There was an element, in any investigation, of responding to what was uncovered and going off in unplanned directions. Investigations were never linear—they were more like walking a maze—but this one had felt particularly unfocused. Now he felt like they were getting somewhere. That things were breaking. If he could keep his team together long enough to work that.

Reading Goodall's face and body, spotting the lies and listening for the answers behind the answers, he was sure that the man had gotten in that truck, gone along to keep Reggie under control. Been involved, somehow, at the end. When they were done with Joey, and rested, they'd have another run at Goodall, and get the whole story. He began making lists. Goodall's phone records. Claire's. Joey's. And Star's. Joey and Goodall felt like the weak links, the ones most likely to give up the others. Sooner or later, one of them would lead him to Kevin Dugan again. And it was Dugan he wanted the most.

Goodall's information, and the doors it opened, energized him, but not enough to counteract the postadrenaline letdown. He needed coffee and something sweet to get through the next few hours. They all needed energy and their wits about them to go after Joey, and to go at him once they found him. He called Kyle, suggested they stop for coffee. The amount of time and money he spent at Dunkin' Donuts, he ought to buy stock.

He was paying when his phone rang, Mary Libby's distraught voice exploding in his ear. "It's Clay, Joe. He's missing." She stumbled over that, grabbed some air, and tried to explain. "He went out . . . the dog was barking . . . something in the woods . . . and he hasn't—" Her voice dissolved into sobs.

Imagination put him right back in that farmhouse kitchen.

"Take a breath, Mary, and tell me what happened."

"Two hours ago," she gasped. "He went out two hours ago when the dog started barking. He told me to stay in the house and lock the doors. He even . . . hold on . . . please. Excuse me."

He waited impatiently as she got herself under control. "He loaded a shotgun, Joe, and put it on the kitchen table. Told me to use it on anyone who came through the door. When he didn't come back, I took the gun and went out looking for him. I called and called. He didn't answer. The dog didn't bark. Out behind the barn, out by the edge of the woods, I found Tucker, and oh my God, Joe, oh my God, someone had—"

He could hear her sobbing and retching, trying to hold the phone away from her face. Impatiently, he willed her back, even as chill seeped into his bones. He was at least forty minutes away. He needed to know what had happened, what she'd seen. Had she called the police or just called him? "Mary," he said loudly, drawing stares from the room as he tried to draw her back to the phone. "Mary!"

They'd all moved away from the counter and Kyle and Perry were watching him. "It's Mary Libby," he told them, covering the mouthpiece. "Clay is missing."

"I'm sorry, Joe," Mary said in his ear. "Tucker is dead. Someone cut his throat. I've called . . . called the state police and the sheriff's patrol, they say they're on the way. But can you come, Joe? Please? I need someone here that I can trust. Someone who knows what's going on."

"Forty minutes to an hour," he said. "Keep the doors locked and that gun handy."

He turned to Kyle and Perry. "Mary says Clay went out about two hours ago because he heard something outside. He left her with a loaded shotgun and told her to use it if anyone came through the door. When he didn't come back, she went out looking. Found their dog near the edge of the woods, its throat cut. I'm heading over there." He hesitated. "You don't have to come."

"Right," Perry said. "We should go home and get a good night's sleep, right, Dad?"

"I were your dad, you'd be grounded." He headed for the door, the others right behind him. Lot of detours tonight on his way to find Joey Libby. None that could be ignored.

The visibility was terrible, but spurred by concern for Mary and Clay, he drove fast. Too fast for the weather, for wet roads, and his own diminished capacity. He was bone tired. He'd gone into the day tired, ridden the roller coaster of emotions since. None of them had had time to recuperate from that standoff in Westbrook, never mind Nick Goodall's drama-queen performance. He knew Kyle and Perry felt it, too. And they were right on his tail.

A quarter mile before the turnoff to the farm, he rounded a bend in the twisty country road just as a huge branch from an old oak crashed down in front of him. He stood on the brakes, the ABS pulsing matching the pounding of his heart. Quickly, he pulled into a narrow dirt track that led off into the woods, grabbed his flashlight, and flagged down Kyle.

As the three of them wrestled the heavy, slippery branch off the road, Burgess thought this symbolized their whole investigation. Miserable. In the dark. Exhausting. With roadblocks everywhere.

As he got back in the car, his lights picked up something red a short way down the track. He switched on his flashlight and started walking, his feet squelching through muddy gravel, the seeping water a reminder to change into boots if they were going out looking for Clay. He still hoped they'd get there and find Mary and Clay having coffee in the kitchen.

The heavy rain hadn't completely obliterated what appeared

to be fairly fresh tracks. He pointed his light down the narrow road, moving it slowly from side to side, until the beam found that patch of bright red again. About fifty feet down, a red Audi was backed in under some overhanging pine branches. He didn't need to look at the plate to know whose Audi it was. His sense of urgency cranked up.

Good thing he hadn't followed his first instinct, and sent Kyle and Perry on to find Joey while he came here. It looked like they were going to kill two birds with this stone. Or maybe three. Fine with him, as long as the right birds got killed. He didn't have a good feeling about what was happening with Clay.

They were waiting back at his car, there for backup, even if he hadn't asked for it, getting wet because they wanted to be able to see and hear. "What?" Kyle said, shining a light on his face.

"Joey Libby's car."

"Man," Perry said. "This thing is so fucked up."

The track was narrow, with trees coming right to its edges, just barely room for a truck to pass, deep drainage ditches on either side where it met the main road. They didn't want Joey leaving before they got things sorted out. As a precaution, they used the fallen branch as a roadblock, then belt and suspendered it with Kyle's car. Joey, or whoever had parked this car, wasn't driving away.

They got in the Explorer and drove the last quarter mile to the farm. He stopped in front of the house behind a state police cruiser with its lights flashing, threw the truck into park, and hurried to the door. Mary answered, a hard-faced state trooper right beside her, and threw herself into his arms. "He was such a good dog," she murmured into his shirt.

He held her, letting her shed the tears she would have tried not to show in front of the trooper. She'd loved the dog, he was sure, but that wasn't what she was crying about. Over her shoulder, he caught the trooper's suspicious eye. "Detective Sergeant Joe Burgess, Portland police," he said. "We're investigating the death of Clay's brother, Reginald."

The trooper backed up a fraction of an inch, and gave up a name. Lovering. That was how the state police usually played it, sharing information grudgingly, if at all. But a freakin' name? Burgess wasn't pushing it. He was here for Mary and Clay, hopefully to avoid any more death, not to get into a pissing contest.

"Let's sit down and talk about this, Mary," he said. "I've got Terry and Stan with me. You have any coffee?"

"I could make some."

"That would be great, if you could."

She started bustling around her kitchen. "Bring them in, Joe. It's too rotten a night to leave them outside. I've got an apple cake, baked this afternoon, if you're hungry."

Not after a large coffee and two donuts, but feeding them would give her something to do, and that would help to hold her together. "I'll get them," he said. Lovering stood his ground by the door, showing Burgess who was in charge by barely giving him space to pass.

He got his boots from the back and followed Kyle and Perry inside. With four big wet men in dripping coats in the kitchen, the room felt small and crowded. Mary, in her wilted blouse and misbuttoned cardigan, looked weary and diminished. "What do we do now?" she asked, as she set out mugs and spoons and plates, poured milk into a pitcher, and found the sugar bowl.

Burgess looked at Lovering. "What's the plan?"

The trooper shrugged. "I'm not too far ahead of you," he said, grudgingly. "I was just interviewing Mrs. Libby about what happened."

Mary spooned coffee into the pot's filter, pushed the button, and the pot began to gurgle. She came and sat at the table with them, perching uneasily on the edge of her chair. She patted her hair and twitched at her collar, then, resting clasped her hands on the table, she lowered her head, repeating for everyone a more detailed version of what she'd told Burgess on the phone.

"It's been more than three hours. He wouldn't do that if he could get back here on his own. Not knowing how worried I'd be. Clay's not like that." Her eyes jumped back and forth between Burgess and the trooper, uncertain where to light. Who was supposed to be in charge.

"You have a topo map?" Burgess asked.

"It's here," she said, crossing the room and opening the cellar door. The map was pinned to the inside of the door. As they crowded around her, she indicated where they were, where the roads and the neighbors were, and where, according to her best guess, she'd found the dog. "All this here"—she indicated a swath of green—"is where the swamp and the beaver dam are. Beyond that is where the road turns and heads toward town. And this here"—she pointed again—"is where an old logging road goes back into the woods and climbs the hill."

"Does that come out back down the road about a quarter mile?" Burgess asked. She nodded. "Any buildings out there?"

"Here," she said, her finger stabbing a small black square along the logging road. "There's a half-finished hunting camp some guys from Massachusetts were building." She shrugged. "I think it was really a drinking camp. They never did get it finished. Just threw it up and then walked away. I hear the town's taking the land for unpaid taxes. Clay was looking into buying it. We like . . ." She shook her head, as though recognizing what she was about to say might no longer be true. "We like the privacy. The isolation."

"And that's the only structure?" She nodded. Burgess looked at Lovering. "How you want to do this?"

Lovering shrugged. "Guess we might as well check out that

dog, take a look around there, see if it tells us anything." He turned to Mary. "Does your husband carry a cell phone?" She shook her head. Without waiting for consultation, he turned and headed out into the storm, Kyle and Perry right behind him.

Perry paused, though, before going out the door, and took Mary's hands in his. "We'll find him, Mrs. Libby. Don't you worry. We'll find him."

Burgess slipped off his shoes, put on dry socks, and shoved his feet into his boots. They might need more bodies. They might need the wardens and their dogs. But there was no sense in calling in extra people until they had the lay of the land. Until they were sure Clay, or his body, wasn't somewhere close to where Mary had found their dog.

Mary was buttoning her coat. "You'd better stay here in case we need to call you, in case Clay comes back," he said. "And you need to wait for the sheriff's patrol."

"But I want—"

"We need you here, Mary. And keep that shotgun handy." Burgess finished lacing up his boots and headed out.

Chapter Thirty-Two

Things hadn't improved while they were inside. Wind howled like a banshee around the eaves of the old house, and where the new lights Clay had installed illuminated the night, rain poured obliquely in glowing golden needles. Once they were away from the house, Lovering stopped and tilted his hatbrim, staring at Burgess like the Portland detective was the pathfinder and he was a rube lost in the woods.

He leaned forward into Burgess's airspace, yelling to be heard over the wind. "I didn't want to say anything in front of Mrs. Libby. Looked like she was falling apart. So how are we doing this?"

Before Burgess could reply, a black figure emerged from the darkness. Four hands went to four guns before she stepped into the light and they recognized Mary. She looked at Burgess defiantly from under a yellow rain hat. "I'm not coming with you. I just want to show you where I found Tucker." Her shoulders were rigid and her chin was up, but the tremble in her voice told how little she wanted to see her poor, slaughtered dog again. Before her will failed her, she turned and headed away along the dirt road that hugged the side of the barn.

Lovering looked at Burgess and shook his head. Nothing to do but follow. They trudged through the noisy night following Mary's small, hunched figure, their meager beams sweeping the road and the roadsides, the loud night making conversation impossible. She moved fast—the gait of someone who has an unpleasant task she wants to get over with—but her short distance was actually closer to a quarter mile. The rain added misery to uncertainty, running off their coats, soaking pant-legs and sneaking in icy trails down their necks.

At last she halted, turning to face them. "He's over there," she said, using her flashlight beam to illuminate a huge tree, carefully avoiding the ground beneath it. "I'm going back. I don't want to see." As Burgess directed his light the way she'd pointed, she grabbed his arm and leaned into his face. "You find Clay, Joe. Find him. Oh, God, please find him." She wheeled and hurried past him, heading back the way they'd come.

Kyle's white face loomed out of the dark, leaning toward him. "I'm going to walk her back," he shouted. "I don't like her going back there alone. Like to see her safely inside with the door locked."

"Good idea. If sheriff's patrol is there, ask them to send someone to sit on Joey's car."

"Roger that," Kyle said. He disappeared down the track after her, invisible except for his bobbing light. Then it disappeared around a curve, leaving Burgess literally and figuratively in the dark. On a night like this, anything could happen. All the senses trained to keep them safe were blunted.

Before they crossed to the dog, they drew together into a small circle. It might only be a dead dog, but they were going into a crime scene. "In a line," Burgess said. "Eight feet apart. Check left, check right, check ahead. Everyone stays in line. Okay?"

Perry nodded. Lovering hesitated, then said, "Okay."

They spread out, paused to check their alignment, and started moving slowly forward. Burgess, in the center, got the road. Even over the storm, he could hear the two of them crashing through branches and leaves. Step, pause, search. Step, pause, search. When their beams were aimed forward, they could see the wet, crumpled form of the dog, its fur matted and flattened, reduced to the small heap that grew closer with every step. Death diminished everything.

TV liked to glamorize violence—the car crashes, explosions, dramatic gun fights. The reality was never glamorous. Nothing glamorous about cowardly teenage immigrants shooting a working man in the back, a possessive and violent boyfriend eviscerating his girlfriend, a frustrated boyfriend beating his girlfriend's tiny child to death. Nothing glamorous about a raped and strangled grandmother, her false teeth lying on the pillow next to sightless eyes.

Just a few days ago, that sturdy mutt had been vibrantly alive, placing itself defensively between Clay and himself, staking out its turf and letting him know who was boss. Had it done that again tonight? Gotten between Clay and whatever awaited him here in the dark? Dead because of its brave, loyal heart? He pictured Clay out on this road, calling his dog, following the barking to this place and finding—and finding what, he wondered? Joey? Joey and someone else? Did Joey really have it in him to hurt his own uncle?

The idiocy of the question slammed him like a punch. He ought to be long past the point of denial. Joey had it in him to hurt anything and anyone. Amanda had been a sweet, innocent girl. Reggie had been Joey's father. But what was at stake here that, in someone's mind, justified all this violence?

Step. Pause. Search. Like the Hollywood searchlights in the movies, their three beams moved together. Left. Center. Right. Center. Step. Slowly. Slowly. Slowly. Creeping over the branches and rocks and vegetation. Pausing at tufts of golden grass, hummocks of bright green moss, at the unexpected shine of wet rocks, the bone-white gleam of newly broken branches. Step. Search. Step.

Their slow march finally brought them to the base of the tree, their lights converging on the dead dog. They knelt around it as Perry reached out with gloved hands and lifted the head, revealing the ugly slash of red. "Something in its teeth," he said, laying the head gently down and reaching for it.

"Hold on," Lovering said. He pulled out a small camera, fumbled with the settings, and took a series of shots. "Okay." He put the camera away and fastened his coat.

Perry tugged until it came loose, then draped it across his palm and thrust it toward them. A small scrap of dark cloth with a placket and a button. Part of someone's shirt.

Lovering was giving him that pathfinder look again, though the next step was obvious. Search the area for any sign of Clay, evidence of a struggle, any tracks suggesting the direction whoever killed the dog might have gone. The question was: search together or each take a section. If they searched together, it would be more thorough. It would also take all night. He didn't think they had all night. He assigned sectors and they went to work.

He paused a moment as he passed the tree, considering the many strange places his career had taken him. Abandoned buildings and beaches, culverts and crypts. Boats, trailers, and freezers. A church steeple once. Out in all weather and at all hours. It was true, as the song went, that a policeman's lot was not a happy one. As he had so often through the years, he blessed the folks at L.L.Bean for making decent outdoor gear. His Gore-Tex jacket was good at keeping out the wind and the rain and holding in warmth. Except for a little water that had crept in over his socks, his feet were warm and dry. At some point, though, he'd slipped on some leaves and twisted his knee—the knee that high school football wrecked. Now it was torturing him. A policeman's lot.

"Look, Joseph. And listen." He switched off his flashlight and stood in the roaring darkness, hearing his mother's voice from forty years ago. The two of them sleepless while his father and sisters slept. "Look, Joseph. Listen." She'd taken his hand, there in the dark living room, and led him to the door, creeping together out onto the moonlit lawn. He'd silenced his breath with his sleeve and held himself still as a family of skunks formed a circle on the lawn and danced in the moonlight. Tonight there would be neither moonlight nor dancing. But her admonition to look and listen still served him well.

He could hear Perry and Lovering moving, the strange step, stop, step of a wedding march. Time to get to work himself. Yet something held him back, some sense that if he stayed still and listened, there was information waiting for him out there in the night. He took off his hat and held his breath, turning his head to listen. Lovering crunched more heavily. Stan moved more impatiently. And then, when both men had stopped, he heard it, a slight moaning, so faint it was almost lost in the wind. He listened hard, searching for a direction. He thought it came from somewhere ahead of him.

Ignoring their step, stop, step, he switched on his light and started walking. Twenty steps, swinging the beam from side to side, steady as a metronome. Stop. Take off hat and listen. Rain plastered his hair to his head. Listen. There it was again, so faint it might have been his imagination. He walked another twenty steps and stopped. This time it was clearer and closer. Five steps. He stopped and listened, leaning into the wind, turning his head slowly like a small human radar. The beam of light skipped over a messy forest floor. Fat trees with low-growing branches, a host of dropped branches, small hopeful pines and hemlocks, decaying trees. Glistening pieces of black ledge crusted with mosaics of lichen. No footprints. No tracks. No trail.

Forward five more steps. He was close now. He was sure of

it. Another moan that sounded like it came from beyond a large downed tree. He slid over the broad, slippery trunk, lifting his reluctant knee, and beamed his light around. Nothing. He pulled off his hat again, slowly turning his head, listening. Nothing but the roar of the wind.

"Clay?" he called. "Clay, can you hear me? It's Joe Burgess."

He thought he heard something but now he could get no sense of direction, just a muffled noise that wasn't the wind. He called for the others, two bobbing specks of light like fireflies in a field on a summer night. They couldn't hear him over the wind. He tried to call Perry's phone but the signal was too weak.

He was close. He was sure he was close. He shoved his hat down the front of his coat, ignoring the cold drip on his chest, and turned in a slow circle. The rain had matted the leaves and needles so that any tracks were obliterated, but about ten feet ahead, he spotted the muddy hole left by a disturbed rock. He headed that way. When he reached the rock, he did his slow turn again. Another ten feet away, a tree's thick lower branches swept the ground like a Victorian lady's skirt.

When he pulled the branches aside, his torch picked up something white. And red. Something that fluttered briefly and was still. To hell with wet hands and knees. He got down on all fours and crawled into the branchy cave. It smelled of leaf mould and fir and the unmistakable copper of blood. The body was curled around the trunk of the tree as though the man sought to make himself invisible. He'd very nearly succeeded, except for the bloody red and white flag of one exposed hand.

With the hat and dark, sodden clothes, he couldn't tell if this was Clay. Burgess grabbed one shoulder and eased the man onto his back. The body was warm. The man was breathing. His face was battered, bloody, almost unrecognizable. There was a shock of dark hair showing under the hat. And beneath the blood and the swelling, one distinct Libby eye. But this was not Clay.

As he stared down at Joey Libby's damaged face, Burgess felt like he'd just driven off the map into utterly uncharted territory.

CHAPTER THIRTY-THREE

Burgess was wet, muddy, and in a thoroughly vile mood by the time they got Joey out from under the tree. First, they had to wait until Lovering had taken his pictures. In Burgess's book, you took the time to take pictures when the victim was dead. Otherwise, preservation of life, even the preservation of a piece of crap like Joey, took precedence. And none of them had the background—or the X-ray vision—to determine whether Joey's stab wound was life-threatening. Getting stabbed in the gut was never nice.

Then Lovering, having found a victim who was clearly on his own patch, suddenly had to be in charge. Cooperation was one thing. They'd been doing that all along. Taking orders from a still-wet-behind-the-ears, puffed up tight-ass another. Lovering seemed to have forgotten that he was a trooper and Burgess was a sergeant. He'd also forgotten that the other two guys he was ordering around didn't work for him. That happened with the staties. Some of 'em had a bad case of "when we come in, we take over."

No doubt once they got someplace where there was phone reception, Lovering *would* bring in his own people to take over. Which was pretty much fine with Burgess, since he had places to go and people to see, but he'd promised to find Clay, so he tried to let it slide. Middle of the night in the pouring rain wasn't a good time for a pissing contest. Or was it?

The thought made him smile, and Kyle, catching it, grinned

back like he'd been reading Burgess's mind. Probably had.

Even with three of them carrying him, getting Joey out of the woods was a bitch. He was an easy 220 and limp as a noodle, and the footing and visibility were poor. They sent Stan Perry back down the track for Burgess's truck, where he would call an ambulance, while the rest of them carried the injured man out of the woods. It would have been nice to have Perry's youth and strength to help carry and take the pressure off the bad knee, but Perry was fast on his feet and Burgess wanted Kyle here with him.

As they struggled to get him out to the track, Joey moaned and cursed and muttered incoherently about "how he was going to kill that fucking Kevin if he ever got the chance."

Hopefully, Joey would never get that chance. He and Kevin Dugan would be locked up in separate facilities, with plenty of quiet years to calm down and reflect. His own knee was hurting so much he wanted to groan himself, but he wasn't wimping out in front of the pathetic excuse for a human being known as his godson, or the prissy, frowning Lovering. He wished he could have sent Lovering for the car, giving the three of them a little time alone with Joey, but he didn't have any authority over Lovering, and since they'd found Joey curled up around that tree trunk, the state cop had been acting like it was his find, his crime scene, and his victim.

In Burgess's eyes, Joey was no victim, except of the old adage, "Lie down with dogs, get up with fleas." Big surprise. You recruit some scum to help with your dirty work, then find that scum won't treat you any better than he's treated anyone else. He just wanted to extract anything that might help them find Clay, then read Joey his rights, and arrest the little prick for what he'd done to Amanda Mercer. Whatever grand plans he'd had to question Joey about his visits to his father, or whether Reggie had worked at Mercer Metals and if Joey had recruited him for that job, would have to wait. Possibly forever. Once Joey lawyered up, something Claire would see to as soon as she knew Joey was in custody, he wouldn't get another damned word.

As they waited by the track for Perry and the Explorer, Joey's eyes rested on him and recognition bloomed, followed by an awed, "Uncle Joe?" that brought a sharp stare from Lovering as Joey reached for his godfather's hand.

Burgess took it. "Help's on the way, Joey. You're going to be okay. We're going to get you to a hospital," he said. "We've called for an ambulance to meet us at the farm. Where's your uncle?"

"With Kevin, I guess." Joey grimaced and closed his eyes, keeping his scared little boy grip on Burgess's hand.

"What do you mean, you guess?" Burgess wasn't treating Joey like a victim, no matter how hurt he was. They'd come out here to find Clay, and finding Joey didn't end that.

"Uncle Clay's not stupid. Kevin had the knife, didn't he? And Clay's gun." Joey's shrug ended with a grimace and a groan.

"We need to find him, Joey."

Lovering was staring at him. Any second, he was going to interrupt and Burgess's chance to get information would be over. "You two come up here together in your car? He didn't bring a truck?"

"Yeah. Together," Joey said, squeezing Burgess's hand. "Oh, Jesus, Uncle Joe. It hurts!"

What really hurt was that this useless bastard had come out here with a bigger piece of crap than himself, planning to go after his uncle. It hurt that he had any relationship to this kid. That he and Reggie had tried, really tried so hard. It had worked when Joey was little, but since he hit puberty, they hadn't been able to make any headway against the tide of Claire's vengeance and venom.

"What the hell is this about, Burgess?" Lovering demanded.

Burgess ignored him. "If you two were working together, why'd Kevin stab you?"

"Because I . . ." Joey's attempt at a smile was horrible. "Had an attack of conscience. About Uncle Clay. About the dog." He closed his eye. The other one was swollen shut.

Burgess didn't know if he was conscious or unconscious, and Lovering was giving him a fierce stare that meant he was supposed to back off, but whether or not it was ultimately admissible, Burgess had one more question and he wasn't wasting these last moments on the Miranda. "I don't understand. If you're out of it, what does Kevin want from Clay, Joey?"

The eye that wasn't swollen shut flickered open. "The land. Claire wants that land and Clay won't play ball. He's working for them, not me. Kevin is. You know . . . nobody messes . . . with Claire."

Claire. Not Mom or my mother, but Claire. The monster in a girl suit. Lovering tried to elbow him out of the way, but Burgess stood his ground.

"This is all her idea?"

Another ghoulish smile on the battered face. "Every freaking bit of it."

"Why?"

"Financial independence for her little boy . . . she says . . ." Joey trailed off, grabbed a breath. "But really she couldn't stand it . . . that Reggie still had . . . anything. She . . . felt . . ." Burgess had to lean forward to catch the last word. ". . . owed."

God. Burgess could picture her saying it. Rage spread through him like poisoned blood. Kyle's hand dropped on his shoulder as he withdrew his hand from Joey's and took a step back. "Thanks, Terry," he said. "It's okay."

Then the words hit him. "Joey. You said 'them.' Who else is Kevin working for?"

"Claire . . . and—"

Before Joey could finish, Lovering shouldered Burgess aside. "Okay, that's enough, Burgess." And to Joey, "That's enough, son. You just rest easy now."

Fuck! He'd been so close to getting the story.

"Joey Libby," Burgess said, stepping up so he was shoulder-to-shoulder with Lovering and raising his voice, "you are under arrest for the assault and attempted rape of Amanda Mercer. You have the right . . ."

Lovering kept breathing down his neck, but at least he didn't interfere with this. When Burgess was done reading Joey his rights, he finished with the traditional question: "Do you understand?"

"Oh, fuck you, old man," his godson said. "You've . . . been chasing me . . . for that?" His twisted smile wasn't ugly just because his face was battered. It was ugly because his soul was twisted, too. Twisted enough so Burgess didn't put much faith in the attack-of-conscience story. "I didn't do a damned thing to that cock-teasing little bitch that she didn't want."

Burgess wanted to hit him so badly. Hit Joey, then pound the self-important crap out of Lovering, who had just fucked up a critical moment. He had no respect for cops who put power struggles ahead of doing the job. Solving crimes. He felt Kyle poised to intervene. He didn't even have to look. He and Kyle played cops the way Larry Bird–era Celtics played basketball.

He turned and walked away.

Lovering followed. "What's all that about? I thought you said you were investigating a murder?"

"Am. That piece of crap is the victim's son. He's got information we need and he's been avoiding us, aided by his doting mother, Claire." He watched Lovering process the name and nod. "And I was about to get a critical piece of information when you stuck your fucking nose in."

Lovering ignored that. "The arrest? What's that about?"

"While we were looking for him, we found a sixteen-year-old girl Libby had invited down to his boat. Joey's twenty-eight. Told her he was twenty. Once he got her there, he tried to drug her and rape her. When she resisted, he tore off her clothes and beat her up. Watchman down at the marina heard the commotion and pulled him off in time. And she's not the first. He's done time for assaulting his girlfriends before."

"He's your nephew?" Lovering persisted.

"Godson. Looks like I didn't do a very good job, did I?"

Lovering wasn't a total idiot. He backed off.

The truck came rocking down the track, headlights bouncing, and pulled to a stop. They loaded Joey into the back seat and tucked a blanket around him. Burgess and Lovering got the front, and Kyle folded himself into the back with Joey.

"Just like being in the Boy Scouts," Kyle said as they headed back to the farmhouse. "Maybe we should sing camp songs. You all know the words to 'Kumbaya'?"

"How about 'Down in the Valley'?" Burgess said.

"Oh, you old farts," Perry said. "Snoop Dog. 'Murder Was the Case.' That's the song."

Lovering offered no suggestions. Not even "I Shot the Sheriff." Burgess was trying to think of a suitable song to reflect the young cop's stupidity—something with moron or numbskull or blind asshole in the lyrics, when Lovering said, "You guys always like this?"

"Usually we're worse. We're on our best behavior, just for you," Kyle said. "Hope you appreciate it."

When they pulled up beside the house, Mary came running out. She flew right past Burgess, who'd gotten out to meet her, and jerked the back door open. Her frantic eyes scanned the figure on the seat, her face registering hope, then disappointment, then fury. She threw herself on her nephew, pounding at him with both fists, as she screamed, "Where is he, Joey? Where is Clay? What have you done to him?"

Burgess was tempted to let it go, but part of serve and protect was serving and protecting the rights of the scum as well as upright citizens. And there was always the law looking over his shoulder in the form of the defense attorney. It would look just grand in court if the scumbag's scumbag attorney said, "And isn't it true that you stood back and let Mrs. Libby attack my client while he was in an injured state? That you didn't intervene?"

Burgess leaned through the door and tried to pry her off her nephew, but though Mary was small, anger and desperation had given her terrible strength. It took all four them to get her out of the car. While three of them half-led, half-carried her back inside, Burgess leaned into the car. "You'd better start praying that your uncle is all right," he said.

"I am," Joey whispered. "Really. I tried. Listen . . ."

Burgess had to lean in to hear, a bunch of disjointed mumbling he'd need time to make sense of. Then Joey closed his eyes and drifted off. "That ambulance will be here soon. You'll be okay." Burgess tucked the blanket back around him and followed the others inside.

CHAPTER THIRTY-FOUR

Mary Libby stood in the center of her kitchen, a wild look in her eyes and a firm grip on her shotgun. "I'm going to kill him," she said. "Lord forgive me, Joe, but either he tells me where my husband is and what this mess is all about or I'll blow his smug little head right off."

"We can't let you do that, Mary," Burgess said, holding out his hand. "Please. Give me the gun."

"I'm not giving it to you, Joe. Not with Clay out there in who knows what state."

"You take justice into your own hands, Mary . . . you do something to hurt that boy . . . you become just as bad as they are."

Her eyes roved the kitchen. Four men between her and the door, all with their eyes on the gun. Three hands hovering near three guns. Only Burgess's did not. He stood quietly, his hand out. "Don't let them bring you down to this level. You're better than that, Mary. As soon as the ambulance takes Joey, we're right back out there. We're going to find him."

He extended his hand. "Please, Mary. Give me the gun."

He could tell she was wavering. "Stan," he said, "what's the ETA on that ambo?"

Perry consulted his watch, then went to the window. "Should be any time now. And Joey's car's still there. We've got sheriff's patrol sitting on it. Nobody going anywhere with that, so unless Libby was lying about Kevin Dugan coming with him—"

"My nephew doesn't know how to do anything *but* lie," Mary said. She turned her gaze back to Burgess, then bowed her head a moment, as though praying. No one moved and no one spoke. Without raising her eyes, she held out the gun. "Here. Take it."

Burgess took the gun, broke it, unloaded it. He put the shells in his pocket and set the gun on the table. Kyle and Perry lowered their hands, their faces and shoulders softening. Still watchful but not on high alert. Suddenly, it seemed like there was more oxygen in the room. Gun party over, Lovering stepped into a corner to use his phone.

"Claire's behind this, isn't she?" Mary said. Her normally serene and pleasant face looked aged and devastated. "Behind all of it, I mean. I don't know why I didn't realize that before. I've always known how she is. Who she is. The only part of Joey that thinks independently is his . . ." She didn't finish. There was no proper word for what she was thinking and even under awful stress, Mary Libby was proper.

"Two birds with one stone. Get rid of Reggie and get her hands on that land." She swept her straggling hair back behind her ears and looked at Burgess. "She never could leave poor Reggie alone. Throwing him out was never enough. She had to destroy him. I'm right, you know. I'm right. I wish I weren't."

She held up her hands protectively, as though she needed to hold them all at bay. "Excuse me. I can't stand this. I can't bear thinking about someone that evil. I'm going upstairs. Joe, promise me . . ." A shudder shook her small body. "Promise you'll find him." She waited for Burgess's nod. Then, shoulders squared and chin high, she walked out.

Out there in the woods, with the night, the storm, dealing with Joey's injuries and Lovering's arrogant interference, and the fact that Clay was still missing, Joey's words hadn't gone home. Now he saw with blinding clarity how simple all this was. The deadly combination of Claire's bedrock greed and vitriol toward Reggie and her willingness to do everything possible for her beloved son had brought them to this moment.

But what did "all this" encompass? And what had Joey meant by "they"? Was this just one long domino chain of violence or two separate crimes? The involvement of the man who called himself Kevin Dugan in both Reggie's abduction and tonight's events suggested it was all one, as did Mary's suspicions. The open question was how Reggie's employment at Mercer Metals and what Burgess suspected was a lethal exposure to a toxic chemical tied into all this? Was there something deliberate in that?

He needed to talk to Amanda Mercer's father. He needed to question Claire. And right here, right now, he needed to find Clay. He felt the explosive frustration of being unable to be in three places at once. Not that anyone at Mercer Metals would be available at this time of night to answer questions, and Claire refused to answer her door even at civilized hours, but the angry bull part of him would have sent Burgess pounding on the Mercers' door to get some answers, and jamming his unrelenting thumb on Claire's doorbell, despite the hour or Captain Cote's strictures about civility.

The possibility that Claire would have set Reggie up with a job that would destroy his liver and cause him horrible suffering and a horrific death gave the knife lodged in his gut a sharp twist. It must have showed on his face, because Kyle leaned forward. "Joe? You okay?"

"Going to be sick," he said. "Excuse me." As he left the room, he saw a look of derision on Lovering's face, like the little puppy thought he was the tough guy and Burgess had grown old and soft, easily upset by a little blood and violence.

He rinsed his mouth and splashed cold water on his face. The mirror gave him back a greenish, scarred face with dark, furious eyes. He came back into the kitchen just as the ambulance pulled in, and followed the others outside.

Two more state police cars had followed the ambulance up the drive, the whole yard alive with the psychedelic effect of red and blue strobes illuminating sprays of colored rain and bouncing off puddles. Two more troopers had joined Lovering, more assholes and attitude than Burgess could handle right now. Not that he had any choice.

Lovering introduced them. "Thomas will follow the ambulance and get a statement from Mr. Libby when he's able."

"Just so you all remember he's under arrest."

As they watched the EMTs loading Joey, Burgess scanned the crowded yard. His truck, Lovering's car, the ambo, two more police cars. And an empty space over by the barn. Clay Libby's truck was gone. It had been there when they came back with Joey. Masked by the noise of the wind and rain, no one had heard it leave.

How long had they been inside? Five minutes? Ten? Was it possible Kevin Dugan had come back with Clay's keys, so bold that he had taken the truck even with four cops nearby? Then another thought struck. One that seemed far more probable.

He rushed inside, pounded up the stairs, calling "Mary? Mary?" The upstairs hall was a row of closed white doors. He started with the nearest. It opened on a dark, empty bedroom. Same with the next. The third door was a bathroom. The fourth opened into the master bedroom. Two small lights burned on either side of a neatly made queen-sized bed. The room was empty, but a hastily discarded skirt and blouse lay on a chest at the foot of the bed, and in the wind from an open window, white curtains danced like ghosts.

He crossed to the window and stuck his head out. Below, a back porch roof, and a lattice for roses provided an easy ladder to the ground. Then he examined the room. A closet door was open, the light still on. On a shelf, an open box of .22 shells.

Not long ago, there had also been a rifle in the closet. A dent in the carpet still marked where the butt had rested.

Mary had taken the truck and he was pretty sure where she was going. He pulled the phone off his belt, called dispatch, and told them to send some people over to watch Claire Libby's house. He hated to do it. Mary was bound to get herself arrested. But he didn't want any more deaths in this case or on Mary's conscience.

Kyle and Perry came up the stairs. "Lovering sent us back inside. Didn't want us interfering with his investigation," Kyle said. His eyes were gleaming, like they did when someone roused his sense of irony. His eyes circled the room, noting the clothes, the window, and Burgess's face. "You think Lovering's noticed the truck is gone?"

"Notice? That arrogant bucket of snot," Perry said. "He'd be lucky to find his own ass. Never would have found Joey. Or the car. Or any other damned thing. Probably still won't, unless he calls in the wardens and the dogs."

"Bucket of snot." Kyle nodded approvingly. "Evocative. How long it'll be, you think, before our friend Bucket starts wondering what we're up to?"

"I'd say now," Perry said, as steps thundered on the stairs, Lovering and his colleague entering in a burst of rain and a rustle of coats.

"The truck's missing," Lovering said, glaring at them suspiciously.

"We didn't take it," Kyle said, folding his arms and glaring back.

Lovering's gaze shifted to Burgess. "The fuck's going on, Burgess?"

"*Sergeant* Burgess. Looks like Mrs. Libby's gone for a ride."

"Mrs. Libby?" Sawyer, the other trooper, said, stepping forward. "That the missing man's wife or the wounded man's mother? Or are they one and the same?"

"Clayton Libby is the man whose disappearance triggered the call," Burgess said. "Mary is his wife. This is their house. The injured man—the one we were on our way to arrest when we received Mary Libby's call—is their nephew, Joseph. Joey. Joey's mother is Claire. His father, Reggie is—"

He stopped. This was crazy. He didn't mind taking the time to fill these guys in, but Lovering was barely listening, and the other guy, Sawyer, already had his phone out. To heck with it. Lovering knew the story. He could share it with his colleague.

Then he remembered something his training sergeant had said to him, years ago. Burgess had asked the question that had been nagging at him—how do you deal with lowlifes and human degradation and all the ugliness and not be brought down to their level? Sarge had looked to see if he was serious, then said, "I try to act from who I am, not from who they are." It had stuck with him always.

They were all impatient. They all wanted to be in charge. What mattered here was a good result. For Clay and Mary. For Reggie. For justice.

"Reginald Libby is a homicide victim. We're investigating his death. We've been looking for Joey Libby and for Kevin Dugan, the guy who allegedly stabbed him tonight, in connection with that investigation."

Sawyer put this phone away, asked a few clarifying questions, and nodded. "So where do you think this guy Dugan is? Still out in the woods?"

"I have no idea. Joey said they came together. Dugan doesn't have a car. But Joey is a liar. So we don't know."

"You know where Joey's car is?"

"Quarter of a mile down the road. We've got sheriff's patrol sitting on it."

Sawyer nodded. "What does he want from Clay Libby?"

"Something about a piece of land that's in trust. Clay's the trustee," Burgess said.

He felt as impatient as Lovering looked. He wanted to get back to Portland and head Mary off before she got herself in serious trouble. He wanted to use the warrant they held to search Claire's cottage. He wanted to get back out there in the woods and find Clay before he had two dead Libby brothers on his hands. On his conscience. He knew Clay was only of value to Claire if he was alive and could transfer the land. But Dugan was a violent man with a short fuse. And Clay dead meant Claire could play some legal angles. He wondered who Clay had named as successor trustee?

A small, mean part of him wanted to be a fly on the wall watching Mary Libby and her gun confront Claire in her elegant living room. Until he remembered. Claire also had a gun.

CHAPTER THIRTY-FIVE

"I'm for walking that woods road," Burgess said. "Joey and Dugan knew about it. They parked the car there. And Mary said Clay thought there had been people around the place before. That's why he put up those lights. Maybe they'd parked there so they could scope things out."

He opened the cellar door and pointed to the topo map. "And there's this camp."

They were too tired for this. It had been a long, hard day. Though they were entitled to be there searching for their witnesses, this was state police territory, well beyond their jurisdiction. Sawyer and Lovering could call in the warden service and conduct a much more efficient search than the five of them ever could. He knew searching the woods in the dark for a missing man was like looking for a needle in a haystack, but he needed to give it one more shot before giving up. Perry had promised Mary they'd find Clay. It was Burgess she'd called for help. And they'd already found one needle tonight.

If he left, Clay's fate rested in the hands of two guys who had no idea what this was about and didn't share his sense of urgency. Clay wasn't just some lost guy, either. He was Reggie's brother and Burgess's partner in a decades-long effort to keep Reggie alive. He could almost hear Reggie's voice in the wind, feel his presence in the night. Goodness knew they'd spent plenty of wild, dark, dangerous nights together when they had no idea what was coming at them out of the darkness or what lurking dangers it held. He owed it to Reggie to try and see this through.

Kyle and Perry were waiting patiently for direction, Perry not even acting like a restless pain in the ass. Maybe tangling with an angry husband had had a sobering effect. If he wanted them to go, they'd go. And if Clay was injured, like Joey, and not dead, time might matter.

"If he's not there, it's probably time for search and rescue."

Lovering still wasn't hearing anything Burgess said, but Sawyer nodded. "Already called," he said, "but while we're waiting on them, that's as good a place to start as any."

They drove the quarter mile to where they'd left Kyle's car. A sheriff's patrol car idled on the verge. As they pulled up, the driver came to meet them. "All quiet here," he said.

They updated him, shifted their improvised roadblock, and headed down the road. At Joey's car, they stopped. Aside from fast food wrappers, empty coffee cups and soda cans, and crumpled napkins—the detritus of a slob—they saw nothing of interest until Burgess put on his search gloves and popped the trunk.

Coats and hats rustled as five heads leaned forward and five voices, like a grunting frog chorus, responded with surprise. Crammed into Joey's roomy trunk were two bales of hay and several plastic cans of gasoline.

"What the fuck?" Lovering said.

As the odd admixture of gassy fumes and hay rose toward them, Burgess remembered Dugan's file. "Kevin Dugan, or Leonard Josephson, which is apparently his real name, has a sheet which includes convictions for arson. He likes to burn buildings with people in them."

As far as he knew, Dugan was without a car. But he could easily remedy that. He seemed utterly without scruples. Was this meant for Clay and Mary's house or for their tenants, neatly solving the problem of the long-term lease? Had the rain kept someone from meeting a fiery death tonight? He closed the trunk and nodded at Lovering. "You'll want to get a warrant for that car."

They all climbed in the Explorer and headed down the track again, only to run into a bigger roadblock, piles of dirt and debris as well as fallen trees deliberately placed to block the road. Little was breaking in their favor tonight. Stolidly, they turned up their collars and switched on their lights. There was no longer anything of a Boy Scout outing about this. Just the grim trudge of weary cops.

It didn't take five people to do this. It was neither efficient nor effective, but he had no authority over Sawyer and Lovering. If he took Kyle, Perry would get aggrieved, and he didn't want to send either of them off alone, either to find Mary or search Claire's cottage. Too many people out there with bad intentions and guns. And *this* business needed to get finished. Then they could circle up and figure out what to do next.

A lot depended on what they found. His gut said they'd find Clay but not whether Clay would be dead or alive. The same gut that said they'd find Clay said they wouldn't find Dugan. But cop guts were both reliable and uncertain barometers. Right now, his gut ached. His gut. His knee. And his heart. He didn't want to find Clay dead, another stark, cold Libby face with the light gone out. He wanted something in this mess to end well, and finding Joey, despite the surprising remorse, didn't count.

Research shows that people walking in the woods in the dark always think they've gone much farther than they actually have. You could sure prove it by him. The track was rutted and muddy, full of rocks to stumble over and deep puddles to slog through. He thought they'd gone about thirty cold, miserable, knee-stabbing miles by the time they reached the clearing surrounding the cabin. It was probably less than two.

Like Mary had said, it was a ramshackle place, half-shingled, stickers still on the grimy windows. Gut or not, they had to assume Dugan was there and that he was armed. To an armed bad guy waiting in the dark, a flashlight beam was as good as a sign saying "Shoot me." They stopped well away from the cabin and switched off their lights.

"Okay," Sawyer said, as they circled up and leaned in, "what's the plan?"

"I've got the door," Lovering said. "Pete, you back me. The rest of you take the rear and the sides."

Burgess suppressed a "no way in hell," resisting the temptation to ask if Lovering was wearing his vest. It would sound too much like Mom wanting to know if her kid had mittens. Too much like jockeying for position. He'd rather have Pete Sawyer's cool head on the door. Or one of his guys. He knew they were ready. He was relieved when Sawyer said, "I've got the door."

Waiting in the noisy darkness felt like forever. The storm still hadn't blown itself out. Wind whipped branches overhead and periodically a tree creaked ominously or a heavy branch thudded. Behind him, the rustle of oak leaves was like a giant shaking a shower curtain. No one could hear them coming.

He barely heard the bang of the door as they crashed into the cabin, but through the windows he saw their stabbing lights and then, over the storm's roar, a shouted "all clear." He snapped on his light and approached.

There were gnaw marks on the door where porcupines had tried to chew their way in and the cold, dead air rushing at him stank of mildew and rodents. An eviscerated old sofa bled stuffing, and the two upholstered chairs were slick with blackish-green mildew. There was just one room. Primitive kitchen in the corner. A rusting woodstove. A cobweb-festooned oil lamp.

There was a thin trail of blood drops on the floor.

"Fuck!" Lovering said. "There's nobody here."

"Hold on." Burgess knelt and examined the blood, following the trail to the sofa. He studied the ruptured upholstery and the well-chewed bun feet, the telltale scrapes in the dust, the lighter area on the floor, and glanced at Kyle, who knelt by the other end. Kyle nodded. "Let's move this out."

"We shouldn't disturb . . ." Lovering began, but Kyle and Perry were already lifting the sofa into the center of the room. On the floor behind it, tucked into the space between sofa and wall was a dark bundle wrapped in a ragged carpet. A still and silent bundle.

Quickly and carefully, with an eye to preserving evidence if they couldn't preserve life, Kyle and Sawyer moved the bundle to the center of the room and unrolled the rug as the others provided light.

Clay Libby's head appeared, ashen skin a match for his gray hair, then his torso and his legs. His clothes were torn and bloody. Kyle put his ear on Libby's chest, holding his breath as he listened. The room was deadly silent, as though their collective will could breathe life into the too-still man on the floor. Kyle shifted his head and listened again, then lifted it and looked at them, eyes glittering, his face alight with "fuck the bad guys" triumph. "He's breathing."

CHAPTER THIRTY-SIX

It seemed years since they'd been eating Chris's roast chicken, since he'd opened the letter from Maggie and lit that candle for Reggie with Maura, the whole night a jumble of revelations about sex and family and violence grafted onto an already complex and troubling investigation. No time to process any of it. For hours, they'd been in response mode. Receive, respond, handle, move on. He had thirty years of that under his belt, enough to go on responding regardless of how tired he was, and to respond in a way that wouldn't ultimately screw things up.

Now, cold and wet, they crowded into the truck with another unconscious Libby and bumped back down the track. Miserable beyond description and, after carrying a second unconscious man through the stormy woods, sore, aching, and out at the far limits of exhaustion. Even Stan, their energizer bunny, was drooping, and Kyle, who grew fiercer and more wild-eyed the tireder he got, looked like a madman.

When the ambulance had rumbled off, red lights disappearing into darkness, they left Sawyer and Lovering to deal with the search for Kevin Dugan and to arrange for Joey's car to go to the crime lab, climbed into the Explorer, and cranked up the heat. Moisture from their clothes steamed the windows, sealing them into a small, opaque world that smelled of sweat and damp.

"Man," Perry said, "I am beyond fucking tired. Are we done yet?"

"What do you think?" Kyle said. "I'm betting Joe's still keen to search that cottage."

Perry slumped back against the seat, closing his eyes. "I got nothing left."

None of them did. They were reamed, gutted, depleted. Anyone with sense would go home and sleep. They'd come here to find Clay Libby and that mission was accomplished. No one could fault them for getting some rest.

On the other hand, if there was anything to be found at Claire's cottage, they had to get it now. As soon as she heard about Joey, she'd head to the hospital, but Claire wouldn't leave things to chance. She'd sweep that cottage. Clean it out or burn it. Do it herself or send someone. Maybe Dugan was already on the way. Joey might have lied about the car. Dugan might have stolen one.

He'd been surprised she hadn't cleared out the boat. Perhaps she'd still been in denial, or didn't understand the gravity of the assault on Amanda Mercer. Maybe the Mercers were complicit in Reggie's death, so she thought she had them buttoned up. Mama and Papa, at least, were, and she was arrogant enough to assume no one would suspect her. The phrase "depraved indifference toward human life" fit Claire Libby to a T.

The most compelling reason for searching the cottage was Kevin Dugan. Burgess thought Dugan had been staying at the cottage. Dugan worked for Claire. He'd left Reggie's building in Joey's car, in a hurry, and hadn't been seen since. Burgess wanted Dugan tied into this with physical evidence as well as Goodall's statement. He wanted anything that would tie Claire and Dugan. He wanted to check out that cottage now, never mind that they were all dead on their feet, because he didn't want to waste tonight's work; he wanted to build on it. He wasn't risking evidence being destroyed.

Reggie's loss was a hole too big to fill with an arrest and a prosecution, but bringing in those responsible would help. He wanted all the players—Claire, and Star and Nick Goodall, and his own loser godson Joey—all tied up in this, feeling the sense of loss and deprivation, the humiliation and defeat that came with getting caught, with body searches and incarceration. And he wanted Dugan so badly he could taste it.

There was still the risk that the criminal injustice system would screw up, hand out slaps on the wrist and a stern admonition to behave better next time. He'd seen the system's heart-wrenching failures, the injustice that came from having the money to hire good lawyers, from being socially or politically connected. Still, he kept his part of the bargain. His team brought in the bad guys, collected the evidence. They connected the dots, dotted the i's and crossed the t's. His team wrote clean warrants and did top-notch investigations. He'd served and protected his whole effing life. He wasn't stopping now just because he was miserable and exhausted and his knee felt like he'd been kicked by a mule.

"Earth to Joe, come in, please," Kyle said. The usual snap was missing from his voice.

"Marching orders, sir?"

"Sir? Terry, are you feeling all right?" Burgess said.

"Might ask you the same thing." Kyle's eyes were closed, his voice quiet in the dark car. "I am full of piss and vinegar. Ready to slay dragons. Rescue fair maidens. Find pots of gold at the end of the rainbow."

"Dementia," Perry's voice was a low growl from the back. "Detective Kyle is suffering from dementia, hunger, exhaustion, and the beginnings of sleep deprivation. I say we call this meeting over and go home to bed."

"Feel free," Burgess said. He was supposed to be supervising these guys. Not just managing the investigation, but managing his people. Part of managing was taking care. He was doing a poor job of it. "I know you guys are beat. You should go home, get some rest. As the lovely Scarlett O'Hara said, 'Tomorrow is another day.' "

"Notice you didn't include yourself," Kyle said. "You're sending us weary kids home to bed and you're going out carousing?" He smothered a yawn. "In case you hadn't noticed, it IS tomorrow, you pathetic old gimp."

That made the pathetic old gimp smile. "If searching Claire Libby's cottage is carousing, then that's what this pathetic old gimp is gonna be doing."

"You can't do that alone," Kyle said. "It's not safe, or sensible. I won't let you."

"And our sergeant is always safe and sensible. Why not just wait 'til morning?" Perry said, his voice barely audible. A few minutes more and Perry would be asleep.

"Because then the bad guys and evidence will have flown the coop. Bad guys think they're safe in the dark."

"We got a no-knock warrant?" Kyle said.

"No-knock. Nighttime. You name it. We've got an el primo warrant here. All the bells and whistles. Cars, trash, outbuildings. Boats and boat houses. Some really clever cop drafted this one and some really indulgent judge signed it."

"A policeman's dream," Kyle said.

"Stan? You wanna take Terry's car and go home?"

"Like hell. You guys are not leaving me behind. What's the matter? Don't trust me?"

"Oh, please," Kyle said in a high, fluting voice. "Don't let's start that."

"Start what?"

"You boys stop it. The both of you. If you want to come along, come along. Is either of you up to driving?"

"Oh, yeah," Perry said, "like you would be, old man, and we wouldn't?"

"Shut up, Stanley," Kyle said. "We're good, Joe. Be nice to find some coffee, though."

They grabbed coffee at an all-night gas station, then drove to the cottage. They left their cars tucked out of sight across the street and follow Burgess down a gravel drive. The rain had finally tailed off and the wind had dropped, leaving behind a chilly stillness that smelled of lake water, decaying leaves, and wood smoke.

The door to the attached garage was unlocked. Parked inside were Claire's silver Mercedes SUV and a dark, older-model American car. A hand on the hood showed the Mercedes engine was still faintly warm. Kyle noted the plate number on the American car and moved away down the drive to call it in, while Burgess and Perry checked the interior. There were dark smudges on the wheel that might be blood, and similar smudges on the seat. No way to know if it was the driver's blood or someone else's.

Kyle returned with a succinct report. "Belongs to one of the Libbys' neighbors. Likely stolen. Not yet reported. I called Lovering, gave him a heads up. Let's check the exits."

Before they explored the house, they checked their weapons. They'd tried to keep their guns dry, but safe was always better than sorry. Rain could make a gun stick in its holster. Make things slippery and unreliable.

Gun check done, they fanned out and circled the house. Along with the door from the garage into the house, there was a front door, and, in the back, a series of sliders opened onto a broad deck facing the lake. No lights were visible at the front of the house. When they met at the back, they found lights blazing through the windows, the big, high-ceilinged room lit like a stage set.

On that stage, a dramatic play was in progress. At one end of the room was Mary Libby, pointing the .22 in unsteady hands at Claire. Claire perched stiffly on a wood chair, her fingers curled like claws over the chair's sides. Her ever-perfect dark hair was mussed and she looked sullen and furious. On the floor between them, his back propped against the stone fireplace, was a large man in dark clothes, his wrists and ankles cocooned in duct tape.

All the stage props—overturned chair, broken vase, and scattered books and papers—suggested a struggle. A bloody wound on the man's head, a curled-up rug, and heel marks and a blood trail across the blond wood floor said Mary had surprised Kevin Dugan elsewhere, and dragged him in here. Not an impossible feat for a woman used to hefting sacks of grain and bales of hay.

The man was speaking, loud enough to be heard clearly through the open slider. He was angry, and his voice carried the shake of a bad-ass tough guy realizing he might be on the losing side. Bullies like Dugan were usually cowards. "Look, lady, I don't care what she's told you. I had nothing to do with what happened tonight. I'm just staying a few days with my friend Joey. That's all."

"Like you were *only* staying across the hall from my brother-in-law Reggie until he ended up dead?" Mary's normally gentle voice snapped. "Pardon my French, but that is bullshit, Mister Dugan, and you know it. For the last time, I'm asking you to explain what you were doing at our farm tonight." Her voice had the weary ring of finality as she raised the gun. "In detail. Including what she"—the barrel swung toward Claire, who flinched—"had to do with it."

"Let heaven and nature sing," Kyle whispered. "Go, Mary Libby."

"I'll settle for letting Dugan sing," Burgess said.

He'd expected Mary would go to Portland. Maybe Joey had said something in the car before they'd pulled her off. Maybe it was woman's intuition. She'd sensed that Claire, like a spider crouching at the edge of its web, waiting for victims, would be waiting here to receive a report of the night's work from Dugan. Wanting to know for sure that she could get her hands on Reggie's last asset. She wouldn't have wanted him coming to her house. He understood then what Joey had meant. Claire hadn't so much wanted the property *for* Joey as she'd wanted it *from* Reggie.

"Have you ever been shot in the foot?" Mary lowered the barrel until it pointed at Dugan's. "I've heard you have about seventy bones in your foot." Dugan flopped like a fish, trying to wiggle away. "All those little bones shattered? It's very painful."

"Look," Dugan's tremor had morphed into a whine. "It's not me you want. I'm just the hired man, okay? I just did what she told me to." He jerked his chin toward Claire.

"Shut up, you idiot!" Claire snapped. "Just shut up. You don't have to tell her anything. She's not really going to hurt you. She's just a sweet little farmer's wife. She hasn't got it in her to—" She shrieked as Mary put a bullet into the floorboard.

"My husband is missing, Claire. My dog is dead, and I know you're behind all this. Would you like to see just how sweet I can be?"

Burgess wanted to watch the characters play their parts and hear the plot revealed. To see Claire's entitled arrogance fade into understanding, her lies segue into confession. He wanted to watch Dugan spill his guts, as the lousy piece of shit was clearly preparing to do. But he was a cop. He wasn't supposed to let one person to shoot another, no matter how justified the shooter was or because he was overhearing good information. That was the freakin' job.

"Talk to me." Mary sent another bullet into the floor an inch from Dugan's foot, kicking up a shower of splintered wood.

"Hey! Jesus! Take it easy!" he yelled.

"We have to do something," Burgess whispered.

"In a minute," Kyle said. Beside them, Perry stepped back away from them, getting ready to move when Burgess said go.

"She said no one would think twice," Dugan said. "It was supposed to look like an accident. She said that old wino was just a waste of air and space who'd never done anything in his life except make her miserable. She never said the old fucker would be such a scrapper. He just wouldn't go easy. Took all I had to hold him down in that tub, me and that artist she hooked me up with. Not that he was much help. Asshole had to get pissed before he could do anything." Dugan hesitated and Mary got a look, like she was thinking of shooting again.

Burgess shifted and Kyle put a hand on his arm. "Not yet. Let him talk. Mary wants to hear this, too."

"Old man just gives me this look, ya know," Dugan continued, "and he says, 'You're doing all this for nothing, you know. You tell Claire she's doing all this for nothing. It's too late.' "

Dugan shook his head. "He knew what it was about." He jerked his chin toward Claire. "You want to shoot somebody, shoot that bitch. She said it was gonna be so easy. She gives me money. I get rid of the old guy. She gets the land. Mercer doesn't have to worry about a lawsuit. Everybody's happy. Only she stiffs me, doesn't she?"

The look he gave Claire was so venomous she scrabbled with her feet on the floor, moving her chair away. "Dugan," she said. "I'm warning you. Just shut up."

But Dugan wasn't shutting up. "If you're looking for people to shoot, why don't you shoot that artist, Goodall. He was the old guy's fucking friend, him and that crazy witch. Then she goes and sets him up, and her husband and me, we do the deed."

"Don't believe him, Mary. You can tell what sort of man he is. He'd say anything." Claire's voice was wheedling, shrill. "Come on, Mary, you know things between Reggie and me were over long ago."

Dugan shot a savage look at Claire. "Not so over you didn't want him dead. You still owe me twenty-five thousand dollars, lady. You or your friend Mercer."

"You were supposed to take care of him," Claire said, "*and* bring his brother around. Both. That's when you get paid."

"Take care of *him*. That was the deal. I won't even charge you extra for tonight's work. That didn't quite go as planned. Your kid, see, kinda got in the way."

But Burgess had focused on what had Reggie said. "You're doing this for nothing. It's too late." He flashed on something Maura had said about their trip to Cape Cod. Her dreamy smile when she said "a honeymoon. Just like a regular couple." He tried to remember the language of the trust documents. Was it just for Joey, or did it mention spouse and offspring? If Reggie had *married* Maura, would she acquire any rights?

Claire's scream recalled his attention. "You what? You hurt Joey?" She jumped up. "Oh my God! Is Joey all right?"

The gun rocked unsteadily in Mary's hands. "Sit down, Claire," she ordered. Her set face and taut body told him how badly she wanted to shoot.

"I'm going," Perry said, fading slowly into the dark.

"Your precious Joey turned into a whiny pain-in-the-ass just because I killed that dog," Dugan said. "He's like you, doesn't give a damn about what happens to people. Only tonight, he went soft on me. First he says I can't hurt his uncle, then gets all goofy over a freakin' dog. The fuck did he think we were there for? A tea party?"

"What did you do to my husband?" Mary said. She stepped closer, aiming the rifle at his crotch.

Dugan grinned like he was daring her to shoot. A maniac's grin. Crap like Dugan couldn't help bragging about their bad acts. Guy keeps his mouth shut and no matter how sure you are of what they've done, you can't lay a finger on 'em, but they have to talk about it. Like being a low life POS was a badge of honor and half the pleasure was watching decent people's horror at their acts.

"A little persuasion." Dugan grinned at Mary.

"You didn't kill him, did you?" Claire wailed. "I said convince, Kevin. Convince. He's useless to us if he's dead. You're such a moron, you—"

He had to break this up. Dugan was going to provoke her until Mary shot him. "Terry. We—"

"Mary won't shoot before he's finished. She wants to hear this," Kyle said, a firm hand on his arm.

Burgess was seeing a young Reggie, dazed and weeping, sitting in his apartment, face stark with pain. Reggie, never complaining or confessional, out at the end of his rope. "I'd do anything for her, Joe. Heck, I *have* done everything for her. Changed my major. Seen a shrink. Taking all these drugs, while she takes everything I give and just looks disappointed. When the drugs make me hurt, make me gain weight, make me sluggish and dull, she complains I'm not the man she married. We talk. We agree. She does whatever she wants. What the fuck am I supposed to do, Joe?"

Reggie, wanting so desperately to do right. To be normal, saying, "She doesn't want me. Just some idea of me. Now she's pregnant, when she swore she wouldn't. When she knows I'm not ready. She's like one of those insects that mates and then bites the male's head off."

Reggie had been right. It had just taken Claire a long time to finish biting.

He dragged himself back to the present, turning to tell Kyle to move, to get in there and arrest them before—to hell with Mary—he shot them himself, when sudden pain hit him, starting in his chest and running down his arm. Searing, breathtaking pain that filled his body with burning acid. He couldn't move. He couldn't breathe. The world gone black except for Claire Libby's twisted face.

Was this a heart attack? His career ending here in this soggy back yard, the investigation into Reggie's death unfinished, Maggie's letter unanswered, his unknown son ignored?

For what seemed like an eternity, he was stuck there, battling the gasping pain as he stared down that black tunnel at Claire, the heartless monster who had set all this in motion. Then Kyle's hand landed on his shoulder, gripping hard, Kyle's voice sharp and urgent in his ear. "Don't do it, Joe. Jesus. Joe. Don't!"

God, he hurt. He was on fire. Fuck his career. He should have done this a quarter of a century ago. If he had, Reggie would be alive. Maybe even healed. If he'd only acknowledged Claire's evil. He couldn't pull back.

Kyle's fingers dug in, shaking him. "Goddamit, Joe. Drop it."

Burgess saw the gun in his hands. Leveled. Steady. Aimed right at Claire. And wrenched himself back from the blackness. It took all his willpower to lower the gun, the effort feeling like he was breaking every bone in his arm, the pain of it starting tears in his eyes. He had always known she was a coldhearted bitch. He'd never comprehended the depths of her evil.

"What Dugan just said sounded like a confession to me," Kyle said. His hand stayed on Burgess's shoulder, fierce fingers biting right through the layers. "Come on. Goddamit! Put that gun away."

There isn't a cop alive who doesn't know how it feels to come close to shooting someone. A shooting that feels absolutely justified in the moment. Burgess closed his eyes, dizzy with emotion. Cops didn't get emotional. He should go sit in the car. Let them handle this. Get the hell out of here before he screwed this up for everyone.

"Oh, sweet Jesus, Terry. I almost . . . I didn't even—"

"That's okay. Come on now." Kyle's firm hands pulled him away from the window. Very slowly, they stepped back until they were out of the light. He bent over, hands braced on his knees, remembering how to get air in and out of his lungs, coming back into the moment. Back into being a cop who couldn't let civilians have a gun party without intervening.

"Wonder what's up with Stan?" Kyle said. "He should be in there by now."

Burgess was still trying to push Reggie's dead face out of his head, cap his rage, and quell the desire to do unspeakable things to Claire and Dugan. Long, slow breaths in and out. If you can breathe, you can think. You can respond. He was swimming up from some deep pool, Kyle's words barely comprehensible. "Stan's going in?" Kyle nodded. "We'd better go find him."

"I'll go," Kyle said. "Someone has to stay here, in case they run this way. Just please, don't shoot anyone unless you have to. Writing the reports for tonight is gonna be enough of a bitch without having to include discharging our firearms. I am in no mood to spend the next month driving a desk. You don't get overtime driving a desk."

"If Claire had a gun, she'd have shot Dugan by now."

"Saving the taxpayers all kinds of bucks and leaving the world a better place. The real coup would be if Claire and Dugan shot each other. That would be justice."

"If Mary wasn't in the middle."

Kyle slipped away into the night. Silent and quick as a cat. One second he was there, the next he'd disappeared.

When Burgess stepped back out to a place where he could watch the living room, a new character had come onstage. A medium tall man, sandy-haired, in a rich man's barn jacket— the waxed, weatherproof kind with leather trim—and creased dark slacks. The small, shiny handgun he was pointing at Mary looked a lot like the gun from Claire's front hall.

Something in the man's appearance was familiar. Something about the jawline and shape of the mouth. This was Amanda Mercer's father. The Mercer of Mercer Metals. The Mercer who wanted Reggie dead as protection against a lawsuit. But why would a respectable businessman have a gun? And what the fuck was he doing here in the middle of the night?

As he watched, Mercer moved toward Mary Libby. She raised the rifle. A .22 was not a close-range weapon. Not the weapon of choice for going to a gunfight. Where were Kyle and Perry? He didn't want to see any more Libbys hurt tonight.

Drawing his gun, he moved toward the window, half surprised that his arm still worked. As he came into the light, Claire yelled, "Norman. Outside. There's someone outside."

Mercer stepped through the slider and came toward Burgess as Kyle and Perry burst into the room, Kyle screaming, "Police. Drop the guns. Drop the guns." Ignoring them, he pointed the shiny little gun at Burgess's chest and uttered the ultimate movie cliché. "If you'd just stayed out of this, Detective Burgess, everything would have been okay."

"Put the gun down, Mr. Mercer." Burgess kept his voice low and easy. Over Mercer's shoulder, he saw Perry take the gun from Mary. Saw Kyle make a sudden dive at Claire and realized she had a gun out, pointed at Dugan. The gun exploded. Dugan began to scream.

"I don't think I will." Mercer's face was working, little eye movements and muscle twitches that gave lie to the calm. It was eerily quiet during those last seconds.

Two men with drawn guns, less than ten feet apart. Conversing like they were facing each other over a desk. Too close for a gun fight. Too late for anything else.

They fired almost in unison.

CHAPTER THIRTY-SEVEN

Burgess wasn't dead. That was why they wore vests—so they'd have bruises instead of holes in their bodies—but it was going to be a hell of a bruise. It felt like he'd been slammed in the chest with a two-by-four and it hurt like a bastard, bringing his body and soul into utter miserable, negative alignment.

It took several long minutes before he could drag himself over to check Mercer for life signs—knowing the futility even as he did so. Mercer hadn't been wearing a vest and Burgess's service weapon hadn't been a toy.

Then Burgess went inside to help deal with the living, pain surrounding him like a red cloud. He began with a call to Vince Melia while Mercer was still warm, barely able to hold his phone as he stabbed at the numbers. He snapped the lieutenant from sleep with the comment, "Knowing how you hate being left in the dark, I just wanted you to know we made some progress with the Reginald Libby case tonight. Got two stabbings and one gunshot wound hospitalized, two of those vics are bad guys. Nick Goodall and Claire Libby are in custody, and I got a suicide-by-cop victim here by my feet who didn't want to be the fifth arrest."

"Gimme a minute, Gina's sleeping," Melia said. Burgess heard him cross the room and a door opened and shut. "Okay, Joe. You wanna give me that again?" A few expletives later, Melia asked for directions and said he was on his way. "You call Cote about this?"

"I called you."

"Right. Of course you did."

"No worries," Burgess said. "He wouldn't touch this one with a barge pole. We've got a prominent businessman dead on the ground, one seriously wounded sociopathic hired killer, and a pillar of society in handcuffs, all in the service of some dead homeless guy. No photo ops here, unless he wants to poke at blood puddles with his shoe."

"Gotcha. I'm on my way."

"Bring coffee and some painkillers, would you? I'm a little bit shot."

Nobody talks about the aftermath—the paperwork, the interviews, the notifications, follow-up, mop-up. Those slick TV shows never show the thousands of hours cops spend at their desks doing paperwork. That's not exciting, it's exacting, and a case this messy and complicated tripled the load. Take any amount of normal report writing, add in actions outside the city in other agencies' jurisdictions, and you double it. Add in two attempted homicides, a prominent businessman's death in a shootout with a cop, a society matron arrested, and a career criminal wounded by said matron, combine it with three different crime scenes, and they'd be lucky if they got it done by Christmas.

Something else no one talks about—the endless hours finishing the crime scene, often while blood-soaked, filthy, and dead on their feet. Work that couldn't be put off to a better time, when they were fed, clean, and rested. When their feet didn't feel heavy as lead and their eyelids weren't lined with sandpaper.

They spent hours at the cottage, working with the state police and the ME's office, and having a fucking bloody territorial war over whether they could execute their search warrant or the state police now owned the scene. A three-way "discussion" between their chief, the AG's office, and the state police won them a partial victory. They collected Claire's cell phone, Dugan's cell phone, and Joey's, along with scores of other items that needed to be logged, tagged and bagged. Then Burgess spent more time on the phone with the prosecutors in the AG's office, a growling bear by that time, badly in need of rest, ice and oxy-something. More than half-past dead, though it was his phone that actually died.

Many hours in, the four of them grabbed food, so dazed they had no idea what they ate. A time-out between rounds that they all desperately needed. Kyle hunched over his plate, gaunt, hollow-eyed and cadaverous, his hand moving mechanically from plate to mouth. When he'd demolished an awe-inspiring pile of food, he raised his head and looked at Melia.

"Vince, can I get a transfer? I'm thinking meter maid, maybe. Kindergarten cop? I'm getting too old for this."

"Not a lot of overtime for meter maids," Melia said. "And everybody hates you. It's a pretty dangerous job."

"Oh, yeah. Not like this," Kyle said. "How many ladies you suppose jump out of their Suburbans, clutching their vintage eight-clip, pump-action twenty-twos, hide tiny guns in their bras, or try to commit suicide by cop 'cuz I'm giving 'em a ticket?"

"You'd hate it, Terry," Stan Perry said. "Such a waste of those cold eyes, fixing 'em on some young hotshot walking his pocket dog who failed to scoop the poop."

"Too old for this shit," Kyle muttered. "And I believe in scooping the poop. I'd be hell on wheels on the poop squad. I could be poop cop of the year."

"If you're too old," Melia said, "what about the fossil here?"

The fossil had just spotted a reddish smear on his shoe that was probably Mercer's blood and was working on it with a napkin with the arm and hand that still moved. He felt like someone had put a plastic bag over his head and tied it at the neck. Too dizzy and exhausted to think straight. No triumph in tonight's work.

"That's no fossil." Perry waggled a warning finger. "That's a superhero. Don't be fooled by the filthy clothes and grouchy demeanor. Guy can leap small buildings in a single bound and is more powerful than a speeding Smart Car. And bullets bounce right off him."

"I thank you for your kind remarks," Burgess said, giving up on the shoe and crumbling the napkin into a tight ball. His chest was a bright blaze of pain, and there was almost no part of him that didn't hurt, something that was true for all of them. They'd put in the night from hell and this was just intermission. They should all go home and shower and sleep, but hitting the suspects hard and fast now was important. They wanted to get the freshest, most unprepared versions of the stories that they could, and hours of valuable time had already passed.

He set down his fork, surprised by his empty plate. He didn't remember eating. "Let's go talk to some bad guys and find someone who can think straight to write us warrants. I want Star Goodall, search and arrest. I want to search Claire Libby's house and Nick Goodall's apartment. I want that Mercer Metals truck."

"I'll put Sage on it," Melia said. "And I'll do the note to Mercer's family. No sense even talking to Cote until that's done properly."

"If Sage goes to arrest that freakin' witch," Perry said, "tell him take an army and be careful."

"Roger that," Melia said. "Army. Careful. Usually I tell my people to be careless—more exciting that way, but today I'll make an exception."

"Oh, life is always exciting around our superhero," Kyle said. "We go out to execute a search warrant and what do we get? We get gun parties. We get stabbings. We get shootings. We get exploding windows. We get good gals shooting at bad guys and bad gals really shooting bad guys. The pleasant company of poker-assed staties who cling to our coattails, step on our coattails, and then steal our coats. We get sick, twisted shit in the name of mother love, which, by the way, I know something about."

The carbs were clicking in. His eyes were brighter and he was grinning. "We got stone-cold sociopaths and we got stone-cold mamas and we got monumental sacrifice to greed. Man, we get so used to everyday ugly we forget what serious ugly looks like, 'til it rears its head like it did last night and we remember how crazy this business can get." He stood. "Let's go get 'em."

Burgess half-expected Kyle to stick his hand out for a team handshake before they dropped some bills on the table and filed out of the restaurant. He was glad it hadn't happened. He could barely lift one arm and the other felt heavy as lead.

It was an enormous job to do all the interviews—trying to get admissions documenting the multiple offenses committed by all the defendants. Even unproductive interviews with snarling, uncooperative witnesses like Claire and her pitbull lawyer took time. But she'd shot Dugan in front of two cops, so she wasn't wiggling off any hooks no matter what stunts her lawyer pulled.

He was just sorry he didn't get to go at Kevin Dugan, but Dugan was in the ICU and the docs said it was iffy. He'd get much of that story from Joey—the little shit would give up plenty to explain away the incendiary materials in his trunk, and from Nick Goodall, the man who said he wasn't there.

Goodall, shaking with the DTs and looking hellishly sick, was ready for confession, and Burgess, feeling pretty shaky himself, was there to hear it. The details of how Reggie had died, even though he'd gotten much of it listening outside Claire's cottage, jerked the knife around in his gut until his insides felt like confetti. He sat sweating, trying not to jerk when the pains stabbed him, here as Reggie's witness, not about his personal pain. To speak for the dead and strive for justice.

The effort to control his anger made him dizzy as Goodall described getting Reggie into that room to meet with someone Star had found who'd developed a new treatment for PTSD. It had taken two of them, two big men, to get Reggie into that bathroom and force his head into the water. Teamwork, Dugan had called it. He'd put his knee into Reggie's back, forcing him up against the edge of the tub, while Goodall forced Reggie's head under water and held it there as Reggie thrashed and fought.

As Goodall spoke, Burgess saw that still, wet figure lying on the dock. Saw Dr. Lee's fingers reach out and sweep back the mat of graying hair. Saw Reggie's face. Cold. White. Dead. He shouldn't be in here. Someone else, someone objective, should be listening. He couldn't breathe past his anger. Couldn't summon his objectivity. He flexed his hands, trying to still their urge to wrap around Goodall's neck and squeeze.

The second Goodall concluded with "until he was finally dead," the door opened. Kyle, who'd been observing, saying, calm as anything, "A minute, Joe?" Nothing on his face that said he was there to prevent another death. To keep a superhero from crashing and burning.

Burgess, famous in the department for exploding when someone interrupted an interview, went meek as a lamb. Soon as the door closed behind him, he was down on his knees, retching. Melia wanted to call an ambulance. When he could speak, Burgess refused. He wasn't missing a single, painful word. He was here as Reggie's witness, and the story wasn't done.

They switched places, Kyle finishing the interview, while Burgess watched on the monitor in Melia's office.

When they'd sent Goodall back to the jail, Melia said,

"Almost lost it back there."

"It was unprofessional. I'm sorry."

"Working the case was unprofessional."

Burgess shrugged. "We brought in the bad guys."

"What if you'd lost it in there? Gotten your hands on him? What would that have done for our case?"

Thinking about what he'd wanted to do, Burgess said, "Given us one less suspect to prosecute? Saved the state time and money?"

"How about given the state one *more* person to prosecute—you. And cost me one senior detective. How would that have served your friend?"

Burgess's shoulders felt like he was carrying boulders. "Everybody fucks up."

Melia just gave him a look. "I've got a department to run, Joe. A city to protect. So I'm giving you two choices: go on leave immediately and go see a shrink, or hand the rest of these interviews off to Terry and Stan."

Melia and an army couldn't have put him on leave. Shrinks worked at the pace of snails and always wanted him to talk about how he felt. Right now, that could be answered in a sentence: He felt like killing people. Which left option two.

"I can still watch?"

"Can you control yourself?"

Burgess stared down at his clenched hands. Tried to breathe with a chest that didn't want to expand. "Sure," he lied.

Star Goodall was predictably impossible, changing her story more often than starlets change their outfits. She tried to pin the blame on everyone, including Reggie, claiming she wasn't in her right mind because of her childhood molestation by Reggie and Clay. Despite having admitted that she'd had lunch with Reggie, and the evidence that it was a trick to lure him there so that her ex-husband and Dugan could force him into the truck, she claimed to have been unaware of their intentions. She wouldn't agree to a polygraph. At least, interviewing her here, they were safe from her potions. Still, Burgess, observing, felt a chill when she narrowed her eyes and said they'd be sorry, and pain, as though her long, white fingers had deliberately shifted that knife in his gut.

At one point, Kyle, waking from a between-interviews catnap on the floor of the conference room, snarled that it was like something from Agatha Christie. That brought Perry out of his own personal funk—he'd been skulking behind his screen, hiding his bruised face—long enough to ask who Agatha Christie was, and whether she'd been charged yet.

Burgess was hunched over his keyboard, typing one-handed and trying to hold a pounding headache at bay until he finished his initial reports, when he received the predictable visit from Cote. The captain pursed his duck's-ass mouth and quacked like a goddamned duck about how much he resented being kept in the dark, where were their reports, and why had it taken three men and so much overtime to catch the suspected killers of one homeless man. Cote avoided the fact that he'd told them not to investigate at all and to stay away from the Mercers, and for once didn't raise the subject of kid gloves. These, Burgess supposed, were small mercies.

They eventually put together all the details of Mercer's involvement in what had become such a total, pathetic, hideous cluster fuck. Some of it from Joey. More from a surprise visitor.

Burgess was at his desk, trying to ease the ache in his head and the one in his chest, and feeling as miserably grouchy as he ever had in his life, when one of the secretaries approached him warily. She was followed by someone he took for a child until she slipped past her guide and held out a hand. "Dana Lyndeman, Detective. I hope I haven't come at a bad time?"

"Up to my ass . . . I mean . . . we're pretty busy. What can I do for you?"

"Looks like I can do something for you," she countered, taking some white pills and a bottle of water from a capacious purse. "And then I'd like to talk to you about Mercer Metals."

Burgess took the offered medicine, found her a chair, and waited.

Responding to his puzzled look, she said, "I went back through my files . . . found that friend of Reggie's. I treated him back in the spring. And it was in my notes that he'd worked at Mercer Metals." She shook her head ruefully. "So I went out there. Saying Mercer wasn't happy to see me was an understatement. He was sure you'd sent me. Then he started to lecture me. Told me I didn't understand the challenges a businessman faced. The necessity to make hard choices. Like those men's deaths didn't matter at all."

She shook her head angrily, a lot of fierce energy in a compact package. "When I told him I was going to report him, he got right up in my face and said if I did, I'd ruin him and put a lot of good people out of work. In his words, before I was done, I'd have the EPA, public health, OSHA, and a dozen other alphabet acronym agencies on his back and he'd be filing for bankruptcy. He said poorly paid public servants like you only understand black and white, while so much of business is in the gray areas. And that I'm a naïve crusader who ought to stay behind her desk minding her own business where she can't do any harm."

She popped up out of the chair, hands on her hips. "He told me it wasn't easy to run a profitable business. It took hard choices. A man had to be ruthless. Like practicing medicine and treating terribly sick people is just a walk in the park."

"Balancing your books on the backs of disposable men," Burgess said. He could taste the bitterness in his voice.

"It gets worse," she said, a woman who'd seen so much, yet could still be amazed. "Mercer said he was doing those men a favor. They'd been abusing their livers for years. They would have died anyway. He was just substituting a fast death for a slower, more painful one, so why did I care?"

"Practically a saint," Burgess said. In the land of the hateful, Mercer had been king.

"I shouldn't say this, but I'm not sorry that he's dead. He was so evil he scared me, and I feel like I wrestle with the devil pretty often."

She started to explain the science of the chemicals Mercer had exposed the men to, and how they were used in the business, but it was beyond him at the best of times, and he was far from his best. Burgess held up a hand. "Can you write it out for me? For the files. For the lawyers. I know you're very busy, but would you?"

"Glad to. I know you're busy, too," she said, lasering him with her eyes like she was reading all the aches and pains in his body and his heart. For a moment, her small, cool hand rested on his forehead like a blessing. "Take care of yourself, Detective, please. We need some people on the good guys' side."

They kept at it as long as they could, catching catnaps, brief nights of sleep, and meals on the fly, until they'd done all they could do—warrants, searches, interviews, more interviews, and processing all the evidence. Then, utterly exhausted, they went home to sleep.

CHAPTER THIRTY-EIGHT

By the time they picked their heads up, it was almost Halloween. Fall's warmth had given way to chilly gray. Kyle was looking forward to an evening with his girls—one fairy princess and one growing-up-too-fast Miley Cyrus. Perry looked forward to a night of overtime in the Old Port, keeping drunk teens and drunk bikers from getting into too much trouble. Maybe breaking a few heads. Burgess was planning to sleep, get groceries, do laundry, and spend a mindless evening answering the door, handing out treats, trying not to think about Reggie. Or—worse—about Chris.

He wouldn't expect to find Chris home during the day, yet knowing she was gone gave the place an empty feeling. Warm afternoon sun touched the gleaming floors. The pot of orange and yellow chrysanthemums still bloomed on the bookcase. Her clothes were still in the closet, her scent on the adjacent pillow. He wondered when she'd realize that he was nothing but an ugly, irredeemable bundle of black anger, give up on him, and come back for her clothes. How long it would take for her scent to fade?

He'd warned her getting involved with a cop was a risky business. No one had warned him that opening his heart would be equally risky. He stripped off his clothes in the bathroom and showered. His body felt beaten and tender, red in a dozen places where his clothes had chafed, one side of his chest a huge pulpy bloom of purple. His knee was swollen. His eyes were red, the lids at half-mast. He stumbled naked into the bedroom, fumbled in the drawer for underwear, and finally had to face his side of the bed. The bourbon. And the letter. Again.

He folded the letter, put it back in the envelope, and carried it, and the bottle, into the kitchen.

The soft mattress and fresh sheets were like a goddess's embrace. He was asleep before his eyes had finished closing. He didn't move. He didn't dream. It was dark when the phone woke him, an insistent shrilling that years on the job had left him unable to ignore.

He stuck a hand out from beneath the warm covers, grabbed the receiver, and grunted a rough, "Burgess."

"If you don't want *us,* I can understand that," a small voice said, very slowly and distinctly, "me and Neddy are used to that. But Chris loves you and you are breaking her heart. She won't stop crying. You've got to do something."

"Nina?"

He got a shaky and uncertain "yes," the expectation that he would yell at her carried in that single word. He marveled at the courage it had taken for her to make this call. Yes, she knew him, and yes, they'd spent a lot of time together. She was a gutsy kid and one with a strong sense of virtue. She was also a bit afraid of him, and had to be intimidated by the idea that while Chris was eager to adopt Nina and her brother, Ned, Burgess was not. He wished half the adults he knew had her courage.

"Where are you?"

"We're with Chris. Me and Neddy. At Doro's house."

Doro was Dorothy, Chris's mother.

"And Chris is crying?"

"It's pretty terrible, Joe. Hold on. Doro wants to talk to you."

"Nina . . . wait." But Nina had given the phone to Dorothy.

"That poor little girl," Dorothy said. "I told her to leave you alone. We've all been reading the paper and watching the news. I told her that you needed to sleep. But Nina's got that stubborn sense of right and wrong. When she sees that something needs fixing, there's no stopping her. You were asleep, weren't you?"

"I was."

"Go back to sleep, Joe. This thing can wait. If you and my daughter are supposed to be together, another day won't matter."

"Doro . . ." His voice was feeble, an old man's voice. "I just don't . . . did Chris tell you what's going on?"

"With your personal life, you mean? About the letter? About your son?"

"Yes."

"I'm in no position to advise you, Joe. I've got to be on my daughter's side. I want Chrissy happy this time. You make her happy, and . . ."

There was a silence. "Understand me, I'm not saying this to put any pressure on you. But I think she makes you happy, too. I think you two have got that thing that makes relationships worth having. Together you're more than you are apart."

"But Doro . . . me and kids . . . I'm just not . . . I'm not nice enough. I don't have the patience." How many times in the past week had he longed to do violence?

"Listen, don't think I blame you for your hesitation about that. Chrissy has had a rescue complex since before she was Nina's age. She's always rescued things. Birds, chipmunks, stray cats. Once she married a doctor without a soul, hoping to find him one. This time it just happens to be you, and Nina and Neddy. Excuse me."

She coughed to clear her throat and buy some time. "Chrissy has always wanted to be a mother. It's a huge tragedy that she can't have children. I thought she'd come to terms with it, but wanting to adopt isn't unreasonable. If she has to choose between you and them, Joe, she's got to go for them. They're helpless. Vulnerable. Without any family. And she can give them those things. Not that you don't need her, too. But you've had a mother, and a childhood."

Another pause. He put on the light but didn't get out of bed. He was still hoping for more sleep. "And now, out of the sky," she said, "out of the blue, you're getting the one thing she wants. A child. A child of your own. And you?" She said it both sadly and matter-of-factly. "You don't want it. So you can't blame her for leaving. She needs some time to think this over."

They both did.

For days now, he hadn't had a moment to think. He'd just been responding. Responding and being a cop. No time to think about Maggie's letter or the child she said was his son. Too much sad, ugly time to think about other parents and children and how the whole thing could get so twisted up. Parents like Claire, who loved so much, and in so many wrong ways, that she created a monster. Parents like Mercer, whose life was so filled with the gray murk of making money that he had no space for the simple black and white of parent and child. Parents loved their children. That was their job. Their calling. It was supposed to be one of the major considerations that influenced their choices and decisions.

Burgess knew far too much about parents who put themselves first. His father had been a prime example. A tyrant who beat his wife and his children, drank up the grocery money, whose footsteps inspired terror in the house. He knew the need to protect others weaker than himself, like his mother and sister, influenced his decision to become a cop. While Mercer's choice for his daughter, Amanda? To ignore her needs completely. And tell her she needed to toughen up.

What crap! And the wife was no better. When Melia delivered

the news of her husband's death—Burgess wasn't showing up on her doorstep with her husband's blood on his shoe—she went into a screaming frenzy. She claimed that Melia was lying, that her husband didn't own a gun, couldn't have shot at a cop, and was an innocent victim of a police shooting. That they would be hearing from her lawyers. Then, according to Melia, she had smoothed her hair, straightened her jacket, and walked away without a word to her daughter, who had been right beside her, leaving Amanda standing in the hall in tears.

A policeman's lot is not a happy one.

Now he lay in bed, flattened by the case, exhausted by playing through the pain, listening to Doro and not knowing how to respond. "Look . . . tell Nina . . ." But there was nothing to tell.

"Take some time to think, Joe. You sound much too tired for that now."

Like her daughter, Dorothy was kind and caring, and had the same knack for going straight to the heart of things. Dully, he said he would, and put down the phone. He shut off the light and lay back down, but sleep had become elusive. Several times, he brought himself right to the edge, but he couldn't crawl over.

If he couldn't sleep, he might as well work. He made it as far as the kitchen, and got tripped up by Maggie's letter. He opened it and took out the photograph. No way this child wasn't his. "Congratulations, Detective. It's a boy."

What the fuck did he know about raising a kid? He knew a heck of a lot more about arresting a kid that age. He was limping toward the door when the phone rang again. Irritated, he snatched it and snapped, "Burgess."

"It's Judge . . . uh . . . Maggie's husband, Detective Burgess. Is this a good time?"

There would never be a good time. There would never be a better time. "It's fine."

"You got the letter?"

"I did."

"I'm sorry to be pushy. I guess . . . I know . . . you need more time with this. It's only that Dylan keeps asking have I heard from you yet . . . and I don't . . ." There was a long silence. Burgess pictured a man overwhelmed by children and death. "I don't know what to tell him."

Another silence. The man wasn't making this easy. And Burgess had no idea what to say. He hadn't had a second to think about this since he'd opened the letter.

"What should I tell him? Do you think you'd like to meet him? Are you still thinking about it?" The Judge had recovered himself and was doing the judicial thing. Pressing for a result. "If you don't want to . . . if you already know that, I'd just like to go ahead and tell him."

The words might be brief, but the subtext was volumes. How odd to be talking to Maggie's husband as images of their times together skittered through his brain. So many years, so much life, other women. So much sadness and loss and emptiness and regret. He could smell the herbal scent of her hair, feel the slender strength of her body. Remembered talking in bed, the intimacy of voices in the dark.

"I'd like to meet him," he said. Before the words were out, he'd had no idea he was going to say them.

"Veteran's Day weekend?" The man spoke in a rush, as though he feared Burgess might change his mind. "That would give you a few days."

It seemed too soon, but otherwise, he could put it off forever. "I could do that."

"I'll make arrangements and let you know. Is this the best number?"

"Let me give you my cell." He dictated, heard the man writing it down.

"He might like to call you . . . between now and then . . .

would that—?"

"It would be fine. Just so he understands, I'm really busy right now. We're wrapping up a big case. If I can't talk, it's not about him."

"Okay. So I'll make the arrangements and I'll call you. I . . ." Whatever he was going to say, he reconsidered. "I'll be in touch."

Burgess put down the phone and reread what Maggie had written. He spent a long while staring at his son. Then he picked up the phone again.

"Doro? It's Joe. Is Chris there?"

Chris came on before he knew what he was going to say. He really didn't have anything to say. He just wanted to hear her voice. "Joe," she said. "You called."

It did what it always did. Hit something inside him. Something erotic and something grounded. "You taking the kids out trick-or-treating tomorrow?"

"You bet I am."

"Like some company?"

"I would. We all would." He thought he heard a smile in her voice. "Can you come around five? We were going to go out early."

"It's a date," he said.

He put the photo away, grabbed his coat and keys, and headed out. As he drove, he checked his messages. Melia had left a long one, bringing him up to date. Reggie's brother was doing okay. So was Joey Libby, and Joey was singing like a canary. He was sorry to miss it. Reminded himself that there were plenty of other competent cops around who could take statements, do interviews, write reports.

He thought about Joey, in the dark car, clutching his hand. "Am I going to die, Uncle Joe?" His reassurance that Joey would be okay. And then Joey's surprising sob. "I hope so. I don't want to die like this. Like the worthless piece of shit I've been.

When I saw what Dugan was doing to Uncle Clay, it hit me what a fucked-up mess this all was. What a fucked-up mess I am. I tried to stop him. That's how I got stabbed." Joey's hand, tightening in his, Joey sobbing in the dark. "Oh, God. I hope he's okay."

Burgess stopped at the grocery store, bought a bottle of champagne, a bakery cake, a dozen of those candles that come in glass jars, and a bouquet of flowers. Then he parked outside Maura's apartment and rang the bell.

Once again, she let him in without question. He could have been a bad guy. A drunk or a druggie. Someone with a jones for one of the other residents. Her vulnerability terrified him, but worse was the knowledge he couldn't change it, couldn't fix it, couldn't do anything but try to keep tabs and check in, like he'd done for Reggie. He climbed the stairs, his knee reminding him he should have worn his brace and taken painkillers, and knocked on her door. Waiting, he heard the slow shuffle of her feet and the clumsy rattle of chains.

She smiled at the flowers. "Kind of you, Joe," she said. "But it's not my birthday." She was having a lucid day.

"We're holding a private memorial service for your husband," he said. "Just the two of us."

"I'm taking my meds," she said, acknowledging his unspoken question. "For Reggie." She stepped back so he could enter. "Did he tell you? He said he was going to. I liked having it be our secret, but he thought someone ought to know, just in case."

"He didn't need to tell me," he said. "I'm a detective, remember?"

She nodded. "Let me find something for those flowers."

As she shuffled toward the kitchen, she turned. "Claire and Joey had been pressuring him about the land, you know, and they wouldn't let up. They were even threatening to put pressure on Clay and he felt that he'd already asked enough of Clay.

One day he says to me, 'Maura, I've given up everything and I've been as patient as a man can be, but all of this has got to stop.' And then he says, 'If we're married, Clay can be *your* trustee. I guess that lawyer who wrote the thing, the one who insisted I put in provisions for my spouse and other children, understood better than I did.' "

Maura smiled. She looked better today. Her hair and clothes were clean and the apartment was neat. "That was my Reggie, wasn't it? My husband Reggie." She gave the word "husband," all the gravity and love and importance the word could command.

Burgess felt tears starting.

She opened a cabinet and struggled to reach something on a high shelf. "Can you get this down for me?"

He reached past her and brought down a nice cut-glass vase. "Thanks," she said. "Reggie always used to do stuff like that for me. I don't know how I'm going to . . ." She faltered, then flung herself against his chest.

Still holding the vase, he closed his arms around her. "He couldn't stop thinking about other people, could he?"

"Not our Reggie," she said.

Maura put the flowers in the vase and set it on table. As the air filled with the scent of lilies, they put the candles he'd brought—those safer candles in their glass jars—around the wedding picture and lit them all. Then they opened the champagne and cut the cake.

From his circle of light, Reggie's purely happy, goofy smile beamed out at them. "He said he felt so normal that day." Maura smiled back and hummed. "Thanks for doing this, Joe," she said. "I can almost feel him in the room."

Burgess could, too, and something inside him started to unknot. Across the years came Reggie's voice, a little scared and shaky. They were nineteen. In the jungle and in the dark, and the world was full of danger. "You'll be here for me, Joe, and I'll be here for you."

The ends of the knot, Burgess's big, dark knot of hate and anger, unwound, lifting weight from his chest. He felt Kyle's steady hand on his shoulder and heard him whisper, "Breathe, Joe. Breathe."

He took a deep breath, drawing in lilies and hot wax, champagne bubbles and chocolate. He looked at the picture and thought of Reggie, however briefly, achieving the normal he'd been striving for. It was that image, not the brutal scene in a bathroom Dugan had described or the still, cold body on the dock, that he wanted to hold.

Reggie had shrugged off Claire and Joey's hold. Kept a secret. Tried to protect the ones he loved. Burgess thought Reggie the Can Man, who had spent so many years of his life going to the redemption center, had finally been redeemed. Now his spirit was reaching back.

"I'll be here for you, Joe."

And Burgess, who wore a large, ugly, plum-purple bruise on his chest as a reminder that he was not dead, was going to go on living. Striving, as he and Reggie had for so long, for some kind of "normal."

ABOUT THE AUTHOR

Kate Flora's eleven books include seven Thea Kozak mysteries, two gritty Joe Burgess police procedurals, a suspense thriller and a true crime. *Finding Amy* was a 2007 Edgar nominee, has been filmed for TV, and is being considered for a movie. Projects under way include *Death Dealer,* a new true crime involving a Canadian serial killer, a romance, and a screenplay. Flora's short stories have appeared in numerous anthologies, including the Sara Paretsky edited collection, *Sisters on the Case.* Flora teaches writing for Grub Street in Boston. This eighth-generation Mainer currently divides her time between Massachusetts and the coast of Maine, where she battles slugs, deer, and her husband's lawn mower, trying to make the world safe for perennials.